Killer Moves

TABLE OF CONTENT

Killer Moves

By Varsha Dixit

Chapter 1

It was a deathly storm—a storm that could kill, a storm that did.

The night was like the depths of the Mariana Trench—wet, stygian, and dangerous. The winds howled like a lusty pack of wolves, and the raindrops pelted down with such force that they stung the rare person or animal that had not yet taken shelter. Thick treetops bent down, skimming their roots like old arthritic men tying shoelaces. Electric wires snapped like twigs all over the city. The entire town plunged into darkness.

The storm did not differentiate between the rich and the poor. It showed the same vengeance to tin roofs as it did to the pride of the state—Sirsa palace, a magnificent 150,000-square-foot sandstone creation on twenty acres of land!

"Kriti! Kriti! Answer me, Kriti!" The fifteen-year-old lanky boy with a narrow face and floppy hair walked around in the darkness, his hands outstretched in front. The boy was Prince Kabir—heir to the Sirsa royal lineage—and the girl he sought was his twin sister, Princess Kritika. For the last two days, the children were the acting adults to a bevy of servants and staff. Their parents and grandparents were out of town for the inauguration ceremony of a rehabilitation center for abused women in Bhopal.

Those who knew Princess Kritika also knew that the svelte and soft-spoken teenager did not blanche in the face of bungee jumps, sky dives, and the usual household crawlies. However darkness was her nemesis—a nemesis she was yet to defeat, unlike her brother.

Chitra Rana, Kabir and Kritika's grandmother, felt that the fear of the darkness had been planted in her granddaughter at the time of her birth. Kabir's delivery had been fast and easy, his eagerness to move on to the next thing evident even as an infant. Kritika, however, had struggled in her mother's womb for excruciating minutes when the umbilical cord had wrapped itself around her delicate neck. She had emerged from the womb, her skin as blue as faded ink and mottled with ugly webs of bumpy red veins. But Kritika had survived. The doctors called her a miracle baby. It was an actual miracle that her grandfather, King Bhoopendra Rana, had not fired the doctors.

"Kriti! Kriti!"

All the outside noises were amplified in the quiet and large house, drowning Kabir's voice.

The glass door next to him shook as the wind slammed it from the outside.

A pale flickering light appeared in the room. "Prince! Prince!"

Kabir saw his nanny, Simi Miss, accompanied by two guards in the blue and white staff uniform embossed with the Rana's royal family insignia at the pocket—a red maple leaf inside a golden sphere.

"There is a city-wide power failure because of the storm," Simi Miss said as she sheltered the candle in her hand to protect the flame from the cold draft that permeated the room.

"What about the generators, Balbir?" Kabir asked one of the guards.

"Prince, no one can go to the outhouse because of the fierce winds," came the prompt reply.

"The wind should die in some time." Simi Miss said, her focus on protecting the wavering flame.

"Whatever! I will find Kriti myself."

The Prince sauntered to them, his gait one of arrogance rather than teenage awkwardness. He was being groomed in princely ways since he was in diapers, thus molding his incorrigible defiance into incorrigible superiority. "The path to success is lonely because it is narrow—there isn't any room for more than one," is how he often explained his uppity behavior to those who cared enough to inquire.

"Princess Kritika is not with you?" asked the nanny.

"Do you see her?" Kabir clucked his tongue impatiently. "But I know where she is."

Because I sent her there!

"Princess fears the dark. We have to find her." Simi Miss gestured at the staff.

Kabir halted near her, his smirk loathsome. "If we leave her alone in the dark long enough, Kriti might be cured of this stupid fear. She might finally see the light!"

Sarcasm came easy to Kabir yet Kriti never grew weary of him. The twin bond was something Kabir could not shake off, even if he tried. Kriti was a few minutes younger than Kabir, but she had a better read on him than he had on her. He might forget her in his pursuit of torturing the world, but she never stopped looking out for him.

"You *think* you like to be alone, but you are most miserable when you are, big brother!" she would mock him with the roll of her eyes.

Kabir grabbed the candle and jogged out of the room, uncaring that he had left the nanny and the guards in darkness. He trotted in the corridor that led to the living room. Rounding a corner, he slipped on the white and black marble floor but caught himself just in time.

A loud bang spooked Kabir as a gust of wind sprayed water on him, extinguishing the candle. "Brilliant!"

One of the many glass doors between the porch and the living room swung open. The wind rushed inside, causing many expensive porcelain and glass curios to slip off their perches and shatter on the floor.

Nice! Kabir grinned manically. The fury of nature made him feel alive. He tossed the candelabra, uncaring, letting it roll away.

Reaching for the door, Kabir grasped the damp, slippery knob of the door flattened against the slick stonewall. He jostled with the wind but somehow managed to pull the door shut and reached above his head to latch the bolt.

The Prince froze.

What the hell!

A slim ghostly figure was staggering in the sleeting wind and rain on the terrace garden that jutted out from the first floor above the porch steps.

Kabir felt his heart knock against his ribs. "Kriti!" he whispered hoarsely.

Kritika's white summer frock stuck to her like a second skin. Her thin body was bowed from the waist as she fought the whipping winds pushing her closer and closer to the edge of the terrace with its dangerously low balustrade.

She does not realize how close she is to it!

"Stop, Kriti. No!" Kabir screamed.

She did not hear him from such a distance. She had her back to the balustrade and Kabir.

Kabir spun around, running in the direction of the curved marble staircase that led to the terrace. The blood pounded in his temples. He slipped on the steps and his chin crashed on marble. Adrenaline caused Kabir to feel no pain, and he was back on his feet, taking the steps two at a time.

Lightning struck somewhere on the grounds and lit up the palace in ghostly blue light just as Kabir hurtled onto the terrace. Rain pellets hit his face, leaving him with limited vision.

He heard the soft thud through the forceful gale and beating rain.

Something had hit the ground.

A bolt of excruciating pain ripped his chest and his legs gave way under him. Kabir fell on his knees, his face misshapen as his insides experienced bone-crushing pain. The rain and wind beat him down further into the marble floor splattered with broken clay pots.

"Kriti! Kriti!" Kabir called, his face bowed against the fury of nature as he crawled toward the spot he had last seen his sister. Reaching the metal railing, Kabir caught it and somehow pulled himself up. And then he saw her.

"Kritika!" A scream ripped out from his throat, the raging storm drowned it.

The Princess lay on the ground nearly thirty feet below, unmoving, her body broken and splayed awkwardly like a wooden puppet with joints bent at odd angles. Her mouth was twisted in shock. Her eyes were open and stared right back at him. Lifeless and dead! The wind and rain slapped and shook her body like an excited dog tussling with its favorite toy.

"Kriti! Kriti!"

Prince Kabir nearly went over the rail after his sister but a hand grabbed him, pulling him back to safety.

"Kabir, stop." The hand and voice belonged to Shreya Kulhar, his sister's best friend from the boarding school. She was here to spend Holi with them. "What are you doing?"

Shreya was soaked from head to foot and her long hair stuck to her scalp and neck.

Kabir sobbed. "Kriti! Kriti!"

Shreya leaned over his shoulder and saw Kriti's body. Her eyes widened and then she swung her gaze back to him.

Letting go of Kabir's shoulder, she hastily backed away from him. "You killed her!"

"What? No!" Kabir moaned, his voice guttural, his tears mixing with the rain water. "I would never!" A sob escaped his mouth—the first of many.

"I was in her room when you told her that you had left her Walkman on the terrace. You planned this!" Shreya cried, clutching her sides like they were hurting.

"It was a joke. I was just messing with Kriti." Kabir choked. "I would never . . . no! She fell over. I was downstairs."

"You are bleeding." Shreya pointed at his chest.

Blood trickled from his chin.

Kabir remembered his fall at the stairs. Deprived of speech and rationale, he curled on the floor, mindless of the storm.

No! No! Kriti can't be dead. He had lost the only person he loved. The rain beat down on him, harder than a leather strap.

Shreya dropped to her knees and pulled at his hands that covered his face. "You didn't kill her? You promise? Answer me!"

Kabir continued to weep.

"Answer me, Kabir, answer me!" she moved closer to his pinched face.

Kabir was not sure what Shreya saw, but one moment she was pushing him away and the other she was trying to make him sit up.

"C'mon! We have to go." She shook his shoulders. Her eyes overflowed like his, and her voice quivered. "Not everyone will believe you."

Kabir snapped his eyes open and jerked. He caught Shreya by the neck "I would never hurt Kriti! She is my sister. Why do you keep saying I hurt her?"

Shreya made strange gurgling sounds and yanked his squeezing hands away from her throat. "You are choking me!" She took deep breaths. "You fought with her in the afternoon in front of everyone. What did you threaten to do when Kriti would not give you the remote?" Shreya wiped her nose with the back of her hand.

I will bloody throw you off the terrace!

A new kind of fear gripped the young boy's heart.

"C'mon, Kabir! C'mon! I'm only helping you because Kriti loved you and she was my best friend." Shreya pulled on his shoulders as she got to her feet.

Shocked into silence, Kabir lurched to his feet. Both teenagers somehow made it to the door. The storm was winding down.

Screams and loud calls from the foyer pierced the night. Princess Kritika had been discovered.

Fresh tears trailed down Kabir's cheeks upon remembering the image of Kriti's twisted body that was now imprinted on his mind—her lifeless eyes boring into his, her elbows and knees broken like a mangled doll.

Kriti's death would always live in him.

Chapter 2

11:05 pm, February 2017

An Apartment in Mumbai

A bulb with a dirty oval cover lit a square room with minimal furniture. The chipped green wall turned an ugly yellow under the harsh light. The only sound was the constant knocking of the chair legs on the cracked mosaic floor. The single occupant in the room stared at the wall in front of him, his mouth agape.

"Now you all are truly revealed," he murmured, wetting his lips with his tongue. His eyes glittered in a feral manner. "My beauties!"

Jumping up, the man walked to the wall and ran his fingers lovingly over the glossy pictures, tracing the faces of the girls, their bodies. He placed his cheek against the pictures and then turning kissed the pictures longingly.

He walked back and retook the chair. Unzipping himself, he released the growing bulge in his pants. Within seconds, he was running his hands over himself all the while staring at the pictures. The chair started knocking again, back and forth, back and forth, rising in crescendo. His eyes stayed fixed on the photographs while his mouth loosened, and his eyes dilated. The man climaxed in minutes.

A sigh tumbled from his mouth that creased in a content smile. His head fell back as he relaxed in the warm afterglow of an orgasm. He stared at his shrine on the wall.

"Thank you for letting me be a part of your life . . . and your death." He murmured gratefully to the pictures of the women he had killed over the years. He rubbed his soft belly. "Time for new pictures. March is coming ladies."

He yawned and fell into a deep sleep; a peaceful smile on his thick dark lips.

#

3:43 am, February 2017

An Apartment in Kolkata

The simple wooden platform bed with the green mosquito net rattled intermittently.

A quiet moan burst forth from the man asleep on the cotton sheet printed with big red hydrangea blossoms. Streetlight filtered through the open slats of the plantation-style windows, throwing some light in the cluttered, dark room that smelled of old spice and even older newspapers.

Tkkkktkk! Tkkktkk!

The bed shook as the man twisted and shot up, his usually piercing gaze dilated with fear. Cold sweat poured down his face and back. It hurt to breathe. He took some calming breaths and reached under his pillow.

He yanked out a chain with the *rudraksha* ¹beads. His fingers rushed over the corrugated beads as he chanted softly. A few minutes later the man's breathing mellowed and some color trickled back on his gaunt cheeks.

The man turned to the empty side of the bed and stroked the bare pillow next to him. "I will lay my life for them, La. But if Aisha does not listen . . . This time Aisha must understand the urgency, La. She has to listen and open herself up to those who seek her." The man's voice was deep and raspy like a chain smoker, even though he had never smoked. His eyes were hooded, his nose sharp, and his face gaunt and long.

Suvabrata Ghosh was a brilliant mathematician and professor as well as a powerful psychic and tantric extraordinaire.

Suvabrata became quiet and began to nod as if he were listening to someone, someone who mattered. But there was no one else in the room.

1 Rudraksha is a seed traditionally used as prayer beads in Hinduism.

Chapter 3

7:30 am, March 2017

Morarji Desai Park, Mumbai

"Staying alive, *staying alive! Aah aah! Staying alive."* The woman gritted her teeth as the remix version of Bees Gees classic song pounded in her ears through the minuscule headphones. Her worn gray and blue sneakers struck the cement, crunching light gravel as she swerved to the side to avoid the slow walkers who were slow enough to freeze their fat rather than burn it.

Sweat trickled down the side of her face and her T-shirt—wet with perspiration—clung to her skin. A humid breeze from the ocean sailed through the Crepe Myrtle trees that ran next to the jogging path. Aisha Khatri, petite in size, was an everyday sight in the park.

Four minutes later Aisha slowed down, coming to a stop near a chipped green bench rife with engravings by lovelorn couples with sharp blades. Sinking on the bench, Aisha grabbed a thick wad of tissues from her track pants and used them to reach under and pull out a fanny pack. Ninety-nine percent of people not wanting to touch anything undesirable used gloves; Aisha used her tissues. Those who observed her would probably label her a "germaphobe" and Aisha would not correct them. Only she knew that it wasn't the bacteria, a living organism, that she was avoiding. She was avoiding something far worse and rather dead.

Taking out a small water bottle, she drank the few ounces in a long swallow. Sitting back, Aisha caught her breath and watched the other runners, comparing their style and form with her own. After nearly two decades of jogging, she could distinguish the experienced runners from those who were merely trying to break their new shoes.

"Morning, Aisha!" A buxom older lady with short salt and pepper hair, a broad smile, and broader hips, sank on the bench nearby.

Inwardly Aisha groaned. "Morning, Roberts aunty!"

"So, done your fifty kilometers?"

Aisha smiled at the standard joke between them. "Nope, did a hundred today!"

"Why don't you—"

"Just run to Lonavla instead?" Aisha finished for her.

Ms. Roberts harrumphed. "So, tell me, what happens to that girl who was hit by the car on Friday?"

Aisha tossed her a sly smile. "You know I'm not going to reveal the suspense of my show."

Mrs. Roberts harrumphed again.

"Aisha, I have a senior citizen kitty at my place tomorrow. Please ask your father to join us. I have asked him so many times." Mrs. Roberts' fair and flabby face crinkled in a most unbecoming way. Aisha was reminded of a pug.

"You know how he is!"

Fifty-something, Diana Roberts nursed a crush on Aisha's father, sixty-six-year-old retired Supreme Court Judge Rakesh Shankar Khatri, who could give men a decade younger an inferiority complex with his straight back, fit appearance, and brilliant wit. After Aisha's mother's untimely demise sixteen years ago, her father had never remarried. Aisha knew in her way—like the woman of the house does—that her father liked the company of the fairer sex and vice versa. However, he had never brought anyone home or remarried.

Aisha flexed her foot as she glanced at her watch. "I'll see you la—"

Diana Roberts wasn't finished. "I saw Kiara's latest picture in *Vogue*. Very nice but very exposing. Almost her private—"

"I thought she looked great!" Aisha snapped, her eyes narrowing. The older woman took the hint and stayed quiet.

Aisha had raised her twenty-year-old niece Kiara Khatri, aka Kia, as a mother. Kiara's parents had died when she was an infant and her paternal grandparents had adopted her. Kiara's mother's side of the family was not the kind you wanted to raise a child in. That is why even Kiara's mother had run away from home when she was sixteen.

Four years after her brother and sister-in-law's demise, Aisha's mother too had died after a short but painful struggle with pancreatic cancer. That was the day Aisha had changed. Literally. Aisha had been fifteen then.

Aisha realized that Ms. Roberts was staring at her, expecting her to say something. "Gotta go! I'll ask Papa one more time."

Grabbing her fanny pack, Aisha briskly headed outside the park, nodding to the regular folks but not stopping to talk to anyone. Once inside her building complex—Villa Bell Towers, Aisha waited for the elevator, her mood introspective.

Tactless old bat!

Diana Roberts, with her judgmental comment about Kiara, had crushed whatever happy endorphins had been swimming in Aisha's blood stream.

Aisha and Kiara were always thick as thieves, compadres in crime, mother and daughter, sisters and best friends! But not since the past year. To be exact, not since Kiara had decided to follow her late mother Zara Kaur's footsteps and became a model.

Aisha frowned while punching the elevator buttons, the thick wad of tissues between her fingertips and the elevator button.

Kiara with her five-feet-eleven slim build and sharp looks was an instant success in the modeling world. Agencies opened their doors for her like a mother embracing her child. Aisha had fought with Kiara to continue in academics for she was a brilliant student, but Kiara had chosen to pursue both.

Eventually, Kiara had modeled more and studied less. Aisha's father—Kiara's grandfather—had declared himself as a 'no fire zone.' Aisha was fighting a lonely and losing war.

All I'm trying to do is save Kia from becoming a disaster like her mother!

Chapter 4

Aisha took the elevator to the seventh floor and used her keys to open a dark double-paneled wooden door that had a festive gold and red *toran*² hanging above.

Her father was sitting across from the window in the living room and glanced up as she came inside. As always, he had an autobiography in his hand. Today it was Steve Jobs.' "There you are. The driver is here. You are getting late for work."

"Yes, Papa. Going for a shower." Aisha turned to the young girl sitting at the dining table, wearing a bright frock of yellow and pink flowers and oiled hair neatly tied in two braids. She had a fifth-class English book open in front of her. "Pinky is breakfast ready?"

The maid pushed the chair back. "Yes, Didi."

"No, no, you study. I'll serve myself after the shower. Is Kia up?"

Pinky burrowed herself in her book.

A quick shower later, Aisha donned one of her many cotton skirts and a short-sleeved peasant blouse. She tied her waist-length dark hair in a sloppy bun on her nape, lined her eyes with eyeliner and then took some time in choosing her favorite accessories—*jhumkis*³. Shoving her phone and charger in her colorful cloth bag, Aisha cast a last glance at her neat room and walked out. Pinky was no longer on the dining table.

The door of Kiara's room was shut.

I'll say a quick bye if she is not sleeping.

Aisha knew the door would be open; Kiara never remembered to lock doors, be it her room or the house. The room was empty and moderately untidy.

Where has she gone so early in the morning? A cold sensation crept up her spine. Aisha shivered. This is not good.

Aisha quickly moved away from the door. "Papa, Kia is not in her room."

Her father continued to read his book. Pinky came out of the kitchen, a cup of coffee and a plate of toast in her hand. "Pinky, where's Kia?"

Darting quick glances at Aisha's dad, Pinky offloaded the food on the table. "Didi . . . breakfast." She fled to the safety of the kitchen.

"Okay stop! What is going on? Where is Kiara?"

Her father shut the book with a snapping sound. "Aisha, come and sit here," He used his 'judge voice,' the one that silenced hardened criminals and seasoned lawyers alike.

Aisha sank in the chair across from him. Her nerves danced and tingled as if a spider was crawling on her skin.

"How old are you?"

"Seriously?" Aisha muttered.

"Speak up and don't mumble."

"Thirty-two this April. Also, I'm getting late for work. As you said, the driver is waiting."

"And how old is Kiara?"

"Twenty, but she acts twelve." Aisha puckered her heart-shaped mouth, irritated.

"So, you are not prehistoric, and Kiara is not a baby. Let her breathe and you go live a life. You have done enough for her and me."

"Papa, I *have* a life and a career."

"Your career of writing dialogs and concept notes for TV shows is the only thing that is fake about you, Aisha. I know you don't like your job." His father's sharp eyes bore into her.

"Papa, it has paid our bills along with your pension. That is what has helped us live a certain lifestyle, so I'm very appreciative of it." Aisha played with the ring on her finger.

"Yes, it has, and you are right. But now you can take it easy. Kiara makes more money than you and I did in the last decade."

Aisha snorted. "Money is not the only criteria. She has to enjoy what she does."

"She enjoys it, Aisha. You are not seeing it because you don't want to."

"Papa, the industry she works in is shallow and superfluous. Vain . . . exploitative. I could keep going."

"You are confusing Kiara with Zara."

"No, I'm not. I'm not calling Kia a druggie or a sl—" Aisha felt her chest tighten.

The retired judge adjusted the glasses on his nose. "Kiara has an excellent upbringing. She is strong, confident, has a good head on her shoulders, and is smart enough to judge people and situations aptly. Thanks to *you*."

Aisha could only stare at her father. Emotional words were as rare to him as Halley's Comet.

"It's true. I was selfish like most men are. We had barely got over your brother's death when your mother passed away." His eyes turned down. "I let you, a child herself, become that person who held this family together. You helped Kiara and me to breathe and function normally. You helped us rise above the tragedy. It was my job, but I let you do it because it was the easier option."

Aisha leaned over and squeezed her father's knee. "It's okay! I loved being that person. It's an honor to be that person."

Her father patted her hand rather quickly. He wasn't big on physical gestures. A pat was an equivalent of a hug, and he had patted her hand twice already. "Kiara is your life and you are hers. Don't dig in your heels, Aisha. Don't force Kiara away. Otherwise, she might start hanging out with the wrong set of people. Also, you should now start doing things women your age do."

Aisha raised an eyebrow. "And what do women my age do?"

"They have a family, a husband, a few kids."

"I have a kid."

"Kiara is your niece, not your child. You need to realize that. Someday, she will find out about what really happened to her parents. She will need you most then."

Aisha blinked. "Why would she find out? Did she say something to you? Did you say something to her?"

Her father shook his head. "You coerced our relatives and me to lie about how her parents died. And now, in hindsight, I don't think it was a good idea. I'm just saying it is better she hears from us than from some stranger. She is meeting many people now. The truth is bound to come out."

"How do I tell Kiara that her mother was dealing drugs to socialites or getting high and sleeping with half of the fashion industry? Or that her mother was the reason Kiara's honest-to-god cop father—my brother and your son—was shot multiple times? Kiara was a foot away from him in her crib." Aisha's chest heaved and there were red spots on her cheeks. "Somewhere, I have made peace with the cancer that took mummy away from us, but I can't forgive my brother's murder because of the bi . . . witch of his wife."

"Zara was murdered too."

"She brought it on herself." Aisha sucked in her cheeks.

"They burned her alive, Aisha. Nobody deserves that."

Aisha rubbed her eyes. She could feel a headache developing behind her eyes. That was not good. "So, where is Kiara, Papa?"

"Handle it like an adult, Aisha. Kiara said yes to the whiskey calendar shoot and has gone to Goa for a week. She will be back on Sunday."

The chills found her again. The sun dimmed, plunging the bright room in unexpected darkness.

Aisha shot from her chair. The darkness disappeared. The room became bright again as it was a few seconds ago.

Spooked, Aisha rubbed her forearms trying to flatten the goosebumps on her skin.

What is going on? What the heck just happened?

"Aisha! Are you okay?"

"I am. I am." Aisha caught the concern on her father's face. Taking a few deep breaths, she sat back in her chair. "Can't say the same for your granddaughter. I should have spanked her when she was younger. How can she go off like this? And to Goa? For a beer calendar?"

"It's whiskey! Aisha, you can't watch over Kiara every minute. Tell her about her parents so she can understand why you are so neurotic about her going out of town. Everyone should know the truth about themselves. Kiara is your niece and one day you will realize that you need and deserve more. In your shows, you get your women characters married five times even though they represent the most regressive kind of thinking. Yet, you can't find one man for yourself."

"We do that just for the ratings," Aisha grumbled.

Retired Justice Rakesh Shankar Khatri shook his head and went back to his book. "Stop bothering me and go to work."

Aisha turned on her heel and went to her room. "I'm going for sure but not to work!" With a frown playing on her forehead, she started throwing some clothes in a bag.

Where are all these cold sensations coming to me from and why? This hasn't happened before. Is Kiara in danger?

---

2 Torans are used to decorate the main entrance of the home.

3 Jhumkis are hanging earrings.

Chapter 5

Kabir Rana rested his elbow on the leather console, adjusting his dark shades as he steered the wheel with his other hand. Kabir had dropped the "Prince" tag from his name more than a decade ago. Now he was simply Kabir Rana, an Ad Maker and fashion photographer. His cell rang. He took the call on the SUV's Bluetooth.

"Hi! Heading to Goa?" A familiar voice flooded the car's interior.

"Hello to you too, Shreya! Yeah, for the annual week-long calendar shoot. Young beautiful women, aged whiskey, and beaches! What more could a man ask for?" Despite his answer, Kabir's expression was not that of a man looking forward to the things he had just described, but rather that of someone angry at the thought of what he would have to endure.

"Try and enjoy, Kabir. Do mingle, socialize, and date, for goodness sake. It has been six years since the incident." Shreya's tone was gentle.

Kabir was silent. They both knew what Shreya—his best friend of so many years and a psychiatrist—was alluding to. Six years ago, Kabir's beautiful young wife Lavina Salve had committed suicide by jumping from their twelfth-floor apartment. She was only twenty-seven. Many in the media and police considered Kabir the murderer—the one who got away. After all, Lavina had jumped off while he had been sleeping in the next room.

Suspicious. Damning.

Kabir's knuckles on the wheel tightened to the point they whitened.

"Hey, you there?"

"Sorry, was just reading a text." Kabir lied, pressing his foot on the pedal.

The scenery whizzed past him. In his rearview mirror, he saw the vehicles following him that carried the models, his ad team, and the personal staff reduced to specks.

"Why don't you talk about it? I won't even charge you!" Shreya teased.

A side of Kabir's mouth lifted in a smirk. "I will pay you to stay out of my head."

Shreya chuckled. Kabir could imagine her shake her short bob as her small eyes crinkled at the corners. He reduced the speed of the car.

"Fine, have it your way. Now, give me the details. Who is the best-looking model?"

"Since when did you start batting for the other side?" Kabir quipped.

"Ha ha! I wish. Just want to know my competition . . . in case I ever decide to become a model." Shreya retorted.

"I would make you a model for sure . . . but twenty years—" Kabir ended his thoughtless utterance. That was the time he had suffered a loss that had scarred him forever. It hadn't left Shreya unscathed either.

"Give me a name, Kabir."

Shifting in the soft leather seat, Kabir played along. "Kiara Khatri."

"Kiara! Hmmm. Describe her?"

Kabir smiled. "She's five-eleven with doe-shaped dark eyes, classical Mehr Jessica cheekbones, a full mouth, deep brown thick hair, and legs that don't end."

"You already sound half in love with her."

"That was my professional opinion as her boss."

"I'm sure her personality is rocking too!" Shreya insisted.

"Kiara has been with my agency for years now, but this is her first shoot with me."

"Kabir, you have to take her out for at least one date." Shreya egged him on.

"I'm her boss, Shreya."

"Then fire her and ask her out on a date." Shreya laughed.

Kabir smiled at the sound. Shreya's happiness was fundamental to Kabir. He knew that she knew that, but she also knew that Kabir would never say it.

Kabir changed the topic. "So, when do you get back?"

"In a month and a half. What, are you missing me already?"

"Always!" Kabir replied with no hesitation.

Shreya was his only family even though she wasn't related to him. His life was a cracked mirror in an empty house—it could reflect light but owned no light of its own.

"May I remind you, I'm just a seventeen-hour flight away?"

Shreya was in Boston, USA, for a couple of months, pursuing essential certifications related to her profession.

"We'll grab dinner when you get back."

"And a movie?"

"Yes, and a movie as long as I get to choose."

"Fine, deal! Hold on; I'm getting a text." Shreya paused. "Darn it. This is important. Don't forget to ask that Kiara out. Gotta go. Bye, bud!" She disconnected the call.

"Bye!" Kabir murmured to an empty car.

Shreya was a whirlwind of energy, hard to pin down. Here a moment and gone another. She always blamed her lousy organizing skills, but Kabir knew better. Having lost her mother at an early age, then her father when she was eighteen, and after one short-lived and unhappy marriage, Shreya—just like him—was focused on work.

We both are worn down by tragedies.

An unexpected surge of loneliness crept up on him.

His sister's death twenty-one years ago had torn his family apart. None of them had recovered from it. Kabir had been packed off to a boarding school and he saw his parents only a few times after that. His dad was the first to stop visiting him and then so did his mother. They didn't even show up at his graduation ceremony. It affirmed what Kabir always knew in his heart. *The wrong child had died that wild night.*

After college, Kabir had dropped the 'Prince' tag and removed all traces of his royal lineage from his identity. He had studied, worked, traveled, and then opened his ad agency.

Kabir's work was considered legendary, groundbreaking, and he had won multiple awards but he never graced award ceremonies for one was expected to give speeches there.

Whom will I thank?

Chapter 6

"**That Kabir** killed his wife? Lavina Salve? Shit!" Aisha's voice kept rising just like her hand did—from her mouth to her forehead. "Then why isn't he in jail?" she hollered in her cell at her assistant, Rustom Unawala.

"Because there was no proof. Remember the police, Boss?" Rustom quipped.

"This is the guy whom Kia is working with? What else did you find out about this murderer Kabir?" Aisha scratched her brow. Panic was twisting her heart into a rope.

My baby is with a killer! Is that why I got those chills? Shit!

"Are you seriously going to Goa?" Rustom digressed. "What about the shoot?"

Aisha shook her head. "Don't worry! I have all the scenes written for the next two weeks. A few dialogs here and there and that's it. What are we shooting this week, reincarnation or re-marriage?"

"Both!"

"No worries, it is easy, Rusty. Also, I'm not abandoning Veena and you. I will be available 24/7 by phone and text. I have already spoken to Sarita and told her it's a family emergency. She understands." Sarita Tanwar was the director of the sitcom Aisha was the lead story and dialog writer of. Veena Gupta and Rustom made up Aisha's writing team. "I have been doing this for the last seven years. So, don't panic. This is your time to shine. Show that you are a 'can-do' kind of a guy."

Rustom grunted.

"And keep digging for whatever you can find on this creep Kabir Rana."

"He is successful. Has won many awards."

"Probably bought all of them. And again, murder trumps all that!" Aisha's nostrils flared. "Where is he from?"

"Hold on."

Aisha waited. She could hear Rustom clicking keys on the keyboard.

"Everything goes back ten to twelve years. Nothing about this guy before that."

Aisha sat back against the seat of the taxi. "What does he look like?"

"Hmm." Some more keys were clicked "Surprisingly few pictures of a guy who takes pictures for a living. Some grainy pictures of this Kabir are all I can find on the net. He is tall for sure. Shit!"

"What?"

"You are not going to like this."

"Just tell me!" Aisha narrowed her eyes, expecting the worst news and Rustom did not disappoint her.

"This dude is pretty wild." Rustom sounded impressed. "He dates models. And he likes them young."

Crap! "Keep digging, Rusty, please. Anything you find on this creep—big or small—call me, okay?" Aisha hated the pleading tone in her voice.

"Of course, Boss."

"TTYL." Aisha hung up, her black eyes as gloomy as the overcast sky passing above the cab.

Her phone rang, and Aisha recognized the caller. She groaned.

Of course, he would know!

It was her late grandmother Pramila Chowdhury's neighbor and boyfriend, Suvabrata Ghosh. Suvabrata was the most-disliked person on Aisha's side of the family. His intimate friendship with Pramila—a woman nearly two decades older than him—had caused much strife between Pramila's family and Suvabrata. Aisha was the only one in her family who was in touch with him.

Aisha answered the call but kept her tone firm. "Hey, Suva! This is really not a good time."

"I know. That's why I'm calling." Suvabrata said, his voice unusually deep and dry.

Aisha stayed quiet.

"I dreamed about you last night, Aisha. Don't go to Goa. You are walking into something very sinister."

Who uses words like 'sinister'? Aisha thought, not bothering to ask how Suvabrata, residing in Calcutta a thousand miles away from her, knew of her plans even before they were formulated.

For Aisha knew precisely how. Her grandmother Pramila, she and Suva were kindred spirits. If it was any other time and Aisha wasn't this worried, she might have rolled her eyes at the word 'spirits.'

"Kia is there." Aisha offered in a stilted voice.

"You have never experienced such darkness." Suvabrata said, his voice low.

Aisha bit down on her rising panic. "Let me repeat. Kiara is there. I don't want to be rude to you—"

"Why not? Everyone else in your family is."

Aisha kept her silence.

"I had to call you. La would not forgive me if I didn't." Suvabrata used Aisha's grandmother's nickname. "She only asked one thing from me—to watch over you and Kiara. Moreover, she doesn't let me forget that."

"Nani died six years ago." Aisha's voice was curt.

"Aisha, you can't run from what you are."

"If I am running at all, it's from what I'm *not*. She accepted my wish to stay away from this mumbo jumbo. So should you." Her lips thinned into a line.

Suvabrata exhaled. "You use so much energy in curbing, controlling your powers. Your abilities are unique. Not many people can—"

"Look, I'm busy right now." Aisha cut him off.

"I can help you, Aisha. I can help you control them. You can decide who can reach—"

"Bye!" Aisha ended the call abruptly and switched off her phone. Her hands were trembling. She stared out of the window, her usually smooth forehead marred by deep lines.

Darkness in the world of telepaths, psychics, and clairvoyants means only one thing—death.

Aisha wiped her clammy hands on her skirt. "Dammit, Kia, why don't you listen?"

Chapter 7

Kabir watched the road, his mind somewhere else.

The conversation with Shreya had him thinking. On a whim, he called up his PA of few years, Vikas Mishra, who was traveling in the staff car behind.

Vikas answered on one ring. "Yes, Kabir?"

"Vikas, inform all the drivers that we will be stopping at the next *dhaba*[4]."

Vikas answered in the affirmative and Kabir hung up. He understood the surprise in his portly assistant's voice. However, Vikas did what made him get along best with Kabir—blindly follow Kabir's instructions.

A few kilometers later, Kabir spotted several parked trucks near a single-story structure. Nothing screamed dhaba as did green and blue walls adorned with scrawling red letters and a cluster of small shops and ratty music stores. Slowing down, Kabir gave the indicator and pulled his black SUV to the side. His entourage parked appropriately around.

A cloud of dust arose around them. Kabir waited a few seconds and then walked to the staff car.

Vikas was already out, stretching his back and flexing his arms. Kabir wanted to tell him someday that a man who had a belly like Vikas should not wear a tight T-shirt and even tighter jeans. "Let's take a fifteen-minute break. Can you order some tea and some food for everyone?"

"The models will not eat or drink from here." Vikas grinned, his chubby face wreathed in a smile.

"Kabir?" The high-pitched voice belonged to Ameena Afreen, his shoot coordinator. Touching sixty, Ameena's hair was dramatically cut with silver and blue side locks—long and sleek on one side and a dark undercut on the other. Today she wore a loose orange kurta that nearly reached her ankles and broad white pants. Tons of silver jewelry graced her ear, neck, and wrists. Ameena aka Amee hobnobbed with the who's who of the fashion industry and was the tough ringmaster that kept the models in line. "Why the stop?"

"I got hungry. The models can get off and stretch a bit. Do you think they might want a bite?"

Ameena raised a perfectly penciled eyebrow at him. "None of them will even step a foot in these tacky surroundings." She cast a disdainful look around.

Kabir waved a dismissive hand. "I'll ask them." *I'll ask Kiara.*

His strides were long and quick. Kabir knew that his tall frame in black jeans and black shirt and his austere face cut an authoritative figure. He was in the business of looks and unconscious mind manipulation. He believed in first impressions and rarely gave second chances.

He reached the van the models were traveling in. The door was already open.

Kabir stepped inside.

"Hi, Kabir!" Striking people between the ages of nineteen to twenty-four chorused.

Kabir did a quick headcount. "Someone's missing?" He retorted even though he knew very well who it was—the one he was looking for.

"Oh, Kiara stepped out. Can you believe she actually stepped out *here*?" A girl with short hair, pouty lips, and smoky eyes simpered. She bent forward, causing the round collar of her blouse to reveal more than Kabir wanted to see. She was the nineteen-year-old.

Sit properly! Kabir bit the avuncular retort back and stepped right out of the van.

He immediately spotted the tall girl in a simple T-shirt, form-fitting jeans, and flat Greek sandals. *Kiara.* He went and stood next to her as she paid a young boy who handed her a glass of tea.

"Dhaba chai?" Kabir let her know of her presence.

Kiara glanced at him, turning her swan-like neck. Her face dominated by a pair of coffee colored and doe-shaped eyes was striking. Except there was nothing doe-like in her glance; it was arrogant.

She is not in awe of me. Good!

"Do you want one?"

"Sure." Kabir reached in his back pocket.

"I got this one. Next time you can pay." Kiara's voice was naturally husky.

Kabir noticed Kiara glance at her cell.

"Next time?"

"What, I'm not shooting for the calendar next year?" Kiara gave him a cheeky look as she sipped her tea.

"We'll see!" Kabir took the tea from the boy. They stood next to each other in silence, sipping the hot, sweet beverage.

"How long are we stopping for?" Kiara asked.

"How long do you want to stop for?"

"Long enough to eat a grease-dripping onion omelet and bread!"

Finally, a model who eats. "You like dhaba food?"

"My family—my grandfather—loves to travel by car. Boo and I always wait for those trips."

"Boo?" Kabir was already bored.

"Bua. My aunt."

"And your parents?"

"Died in a road accident when I was a baby."

And you still like to travel by road? Kabir couldn't help his questioning glance.

"I know what you are thinking. However, my granddad refuses to let any of us be scared by anything. He is a retired Supreme Court Judge."

Kabir finished his tea and nodded at Vikas who walked past them. "That is the third time you have glanced at your cell in the past minute? Possessive boyfriend?"

"Worse. Possessive aunt. Boo."

"Single old women can be a tad cranky!" Kabir did not understand Kiara's chuckle following his words.

"How did you know she is single and old?"

Kabir shrugged. "You just mentioned her and your grandfather making road trips, which implies no husband or kids. She probably raised you so she's old. If she is old and single, she is cranky!"

"Who is old and cranky?" It was Amee accompanied by a few models.

"She too is old and single." Kiara murmured in her tea.

Kabir ignored that. "We'll eat something and then leave."

The models voiced their vehement displeasure.

"Those who don't want to are welcome to go back to the van." He pointed at Kiara. "You come with me!"

"You don't know my name?"

Kabir paused mid-stride. Kiara nearly came up to his height and her gaze was bold. Kabir heard the sudden silence around him.

Amee jumped in. "Listen you—"

"Kiara is right. My apologies! Kiara, would you do the honor of joining me for some grease-dripping eggs and bread?"

"My pleasure!" Kiara sashayed past him.

Kabir followed her. "You know you just put yourself on Amee's hit list? She hates a model who talks back."

"Can't help it. I was raised strong."

"Single old ladies are more ferocious than wolves?" Kabir took the charpoy across from Kia.

Kiara laughed. "You should meet the single old lady someday."

"I'd rather not. I don't think she and I will gel well." Kabir shot back, waving a waiter down.

<u>4</u> Roadside Eatery. A Popular stop for all those travelling on highways. Known for greasy but delicious food.

Chapter 8

Several Hours Later

Donna Paula, Panaji, Goa

"It should be here somewhere." Aisha used the light from her cell phone to study the ragged hand-drawn map on a torn piece of paper. The evening light was fading quick.

"You are no Picasso for sure!" she grumbled, thinking of the dubious concierge who had drawn the map to Kriti Villa—the bungalow where Kabir was housing all the models.

He is probably choosing his prey right now while I'm stumbling around like an inebriated baboon.

Aisha planned to furtively check out the place Kiara was staying in and the people she was staying with and then, of course, to casually bump into her.

Kia must be shown that when it comes to her safety, she can't outrun me. Her Boo's got her back, whether she likes it or not.

Aisha halted to take stock of where she was. The rectangular bungalows, some with actual turrets, were huge and lit with soft lights and were eerily quiet. The street in front of the home was secluded and illuminated by dim sconces.

Straight out of an old black and white movie.

The air smelled thickly of salt and water. The Arabian Ocean lay behind the grands mansions.

Aisha scratched the back of her head. "2978A, where are you?"

Sudden headlights and a rumbling sound from behind caused Aisha to jump to the side of the road. A black truck lumbered past her. Aisha was able to catch the words 'catering.' It stopped at the bungalow at the end of the road.

Catering! That must be it. Food for everyone at the villa.

Aisha ran up to the driveway where the truck had parked. She glanced at the illuminated black house number plate. 2978A.

Aisha took tentative steps into the driveway. The bungalow was all modern architecture—whitewashed exterior with several cantilevered floor and corner windows.

The smell of *rajnigandha*[5] and roses mingled with the salty smell of the ocean, ripening an evening that still held the warmth of a sun that had set some time ago. The garden that ran alongside the driveway was lush with landscape lights under hedges and marble statues.

Sounds of moving feet pushed Aisha out of her stupor. She turned to see a few men in black shirts and trousers pull out large trays of food and carry them inside the wooden doors of the bungalow into a bright foyer. Thinking quick, Aisha took out some tissues stuffed in her pockets. Using them, she grabbed a clipboard with some invoices that lay on the floor of the truck.

Her hands were not the steadiest as Aisha stepped inside and went past the foyer. A chandelier of small uneven lights hanging from thin silver-colored pipes spanned nearly half of the ceiling. Masculine furniture—mostly browns and grays with patches of red—created a striking contrast.

"What is this place?" All Aisha saw were people in uniforms. She took the hallway on her right and went past a few rooms that were beautifully adorned yet empty. *Where is everyone?* Aisha came back to the carved staircase near the foyer.

"Who are you?" A male voice startled her.

Aisha turned and saw a young man in a tight T-shirt and jeans.

Muffin top! The thought made her realize that she had missed her lunch and it was close to dinner time.

"You don't speak English?" The man asked, hitching his jeans up on the side.

"I'm with the catering. I heard that models . . ."

Shit! Why did I say models?

Aisha was sure the man would grab her by the neck and throw her out.

The man's mouth twisted unpleasantly. "Models, eh? Everyone wants to see the models. But if I show you the models, what will you show me?"

Aisha was too jaded by her years of work in the media. She had fielded several indecent proposals with the same ease that she put down flies with rolled-up newspaper. "What would you like to see?" she fought a yawn.

The sound of soft footfalls made them turn. Aisha saw a tall man dressed in all black come down the stairs. He was lean, and his face was grim. Aisha could only stare. His presence caused a sea of change in the demeanor of the young pervert next to her.

"Do you need something, Kabir?"

Kabir, the killer?

Aisha took a few steps away, her eyes enormous. *This is him?*

Aisha was expecting a man in his fifties with a flabby gut, balding scalp, beady eyes, and bad body odor. In Aisha's imaginary Dummy Killer 101, killers had terrible body odor. However, Kabir was nothing like she had imagined.

Kabir Rana was tall—easily topped six feet. His body was lean with broad shoulders and slim hips. He walked with casual grace, and when he stopped at the bottom of the stairs, he crowned Aisha by nearly a foot. His hair was dark and gleamed under the light with flecks of gray at the sides. His forehead was wide, his nose straight. He had chiseled cheekbones and a thin but bow-shaped mouth.

Kabir ignored her and addressed the pervert. "Why aren't you at the back? The models are hungry. Amee just texted me. Where is the food?"

"I'll get on it right away!" The man scurried away.

Kabir turned and saw Aisha who was still staring at him. "Who are you?"

"No one!" Aisha bit her lower lip. "I mean catering. I'm from catering."

"If you are done then leave. Don't loiter." With a sharp turn, he disappeared in the hallway—the one with empty, unoccupied rooms.

Douchebag!

Uncaring of the instructions, Aisha trotted behind the 'muffin top' who had gone into the arched doorway in front of her. She passed a man cave with pool tables, a video game console, plush recliner chairs, a card table and several other paraphernalia men could forgo sex for.

Next, she passed a dining room replete with black and white art on the wall and a table to feed a dozen. At the other end of the dining table was a glass door leading to a backyard bathed yellow with hidden lighting. Glancing to make sure no one was following her, Aisha quietly opened the door and stepped outside.

An impeccably landscaped backyard with a pool greeted her. Aisha could hear the ocean behind the gray stone boundary wall at the end of the lawns. She saw female forms lounging on the chaise across the pool.

The models! Kia!

Aisha had barely taken a few steps when a voice stopped her.

"Where do you think you are going?" It was the pervert. He stepped in front of her. Aisha stepped back.

"Don't try this funny business with me. I will take you down in seconds." Aisha threatened, turning all her five-feet-four-inches of fury on him. She threateningly closed in on him.

Briefly, his eyes glittered as if he was ready for the fight but then he backed off. "Get out or I will cancel your company's order."

Shit! Aisha rued. She would hate to cost anyone their jobs. "Fine." She spun around and hurried back in the house. *It's too busy right now. I'll come back here later in the night. The backyard wall is easy to scale.*

Aisha hurried out of the front doors. Her eyes fell on the seal on the floor at the entrance. It was a bright red maple inside a golden sphere. *I have seen this before! Where?*

Back in the hotel, Aisha spoke with Rustom and Veena, responded to a few emails, and chatted with her Dad who reiterated his advice about giving Kiara space. Around 10:30 pm, Aisha once again stepped out of her room.

As she waited in the valet area outside the hotel lobby, a familiar face chanced upon her—the concierge who had drawn her the map to the villa.

"You are heading out at this time, Madam? And alone?" He inquired, his tone nasal. "Where to?"

Aisha pursed her mouth. None of your damn business!

"Be careful, Madam. Panaji is not safe at this time of the year. Too much crime, murders . . . of girls!" The concierge lowered his voice for effect. "Especially the ones who go about alone."

"Too much talking also!" Aisha snapped, trying to ignore his garlic-rich breath that skimmed her face.

The concierge ducked his head and muttered. "Hope that the murderer who kills women doesn't see you!"

"Whatever." Aisha quelled her unease and glanced away.

In minutes, the cab she had ordered came. Using the tissues, Aisha opened the cab door and got in. She spotted the concierge leaning on the valet stand. His eyes were fixed on Aisha.

His stare gave her the goosebumps.

5 Tuberose.

Chapter 9

The taxi took Aisha to the Donna Paula area but this time she had herself dropped off at the beach that ran behind the villas.

She paid the driver—an old man who had taken his own sweet time to bring her here—pit stops at a petrol pump, a restaurant to pick up dinner, and finally to drop off the food at his house! He had not charged Aisha extra and as she had time to spare, she had okayed all the stops.

I got to see more of Panaji than the typical tourist spots.

"Half an hour and I'll be back." Aisha handed him some extra cash.

"Be careful, Madam. The beach might not be safe at this time."

"Yeah, I'll be fine." Aisha murmured, getting off.

Gosh, why is everyone out to scare me?

Taking out a slim torch from her bag, Aisha switched it on. The moon slipped in and out behind the clouds. Sweet smells of seaweed and coconut were crisp on the deserted beach. Aisha went down the wide concrete steps to the sand. Her sneakers sank in it and some warm sand trickled in from the side of the canvas shoes. It was warm and grainy yet soft against her skin.

Aisha swept the area around her with the torch.

A few empty stalls stood locked and covered with tarp that was held down by rocks. The chirping of crickets was loud and contrasted with the sounds of the waves crashing on the beach a few meters away from her.

Several tiny flies and bugs started hovering around her torch. "Ugh!" Shaking her hand, Aisha switched it off. She blinked, adjusting her eyes to the dark. The moon was a perfect crescent in a sky covered with twinkling stars.

"Wow!" Craning her neck back, Aisha drank in the sky studded with stars. The smog of Mumbai never allowed for such fabulous views.

Sighing, Aisha treaded in the direction of Kriti Villa. She kept glancing around, making sure there were no unpleasant surprises. Life had given enough of those to her and family. The police had never found the killer of her brother and sister-in-law, but they had unearthed a lot about Kiara's mother, supermodel Zara Kaur.

A junkie and a drug dealer!

Zara had hidden her side business well from her husband of a year, ACP Vishesh Khatri.

After his son's death, Rakesh Khatri had relocated his family from Cochin to Delhi. The Judge's career had flourished, and they had been happy for a while but when Aisha was merely fifteen and Kiara four, Aisha's mother Vidya Khatri had been diagnosed with pancreatic cancer in the advanced stages.

In less than a year, Vidya Khatri had passed away. Aisha and her family were devastated. They had just stopped functioning.

Then Aisha had seen the bigger picture—her mother had shown it to her in a dream one night. All her family required was a sacrifice, so Aisha made it. The hardest wasn't a fifteen-year-old raising a four-year-old or bringing a grown-up man out of crippling depression or running a house with zero experience. The hardest was giving up on her dream and ambition—to join the force and become a cop.

It still hurts! Aisha scrubbed her hand over her face.

Something protruding from the ground caused Aisha to stumble. She switched on the light.

It was a shoe—a woman's shoe, plum in color with silver flowers on the sides.

"Stop littering the beach, people." Sighing, Aisha bent down, gingerly picking the shoe by its heel. She forgot to use the tissues.

A sharp piercing pain laced Aisha's head. She went inert and winced, still bent over. Her head felt like it was being pricked on every side by needles simultaneously. Her heart seemed to stop and then take off with such force that Aisha feared it would rip out of her chest. A familiar and awful metallic taste oozed into her mouth that made her want to vomit.

Aisha dropped the shoe.

Stooped, she waited, her eyes tightly clenched. This was not the first time she had experienced such misery and Aisha knew it would not be her last. Side effects of being a strong touch telepath. A strong touch-dead-only telepath!

Aisha took a few deep breaths as the pain slowly ebbed away, leaving her dazed and unsteady. She knew her skin would be ice cold to touch even on a raging hot and humid night like tonight.

Slowly straightening, Aisha gazed at the solitary shoe and her head tilted sympathetically.

I'm so sorry!

Aisha remembered the pinpricks on her brain. They all sounded like the screams of a young female in deep grips of agony. The owner of the footwear had not died a painless death.

What could have happened to her? Aisha closed her eyes. No, no. I can't go there. I must stop right now.

Immediately, Aisha started recalling the newspaper headlines from today morning, the address of the hotel she was staying at, the number of streets she had crossed from the hotel to here and other mundane things that she had done today. This was her years old and tested mechanism to stop herself from tapping deeper into the feelings of the dead.

It's just not a good place to go.

Aisha's telepathic ability had been dormant until she had touched a dead person—her mother. She had dropped to the floor like a bag of potatoes and stayed there for some time. Aisha had been fifteen at the time. Her father told her later that the doctor had been unable to feel her heartbeats or find a pulse for a few minutes but fortunately, they were able to revive her.

Aisha had woken up to face two facts: she wasn't normal, and she had just got her periods for the first time, lying on the floor, surrounded by her father and a bunch of doctors.

In those few minutes where the doctors had thought her dead, Aisha had gone so deep in her mother's dying thoughts that her soul seemed to have deserted her body. She had experienced her mother's frustration over dying early, her deep-seated anguish and worry over the fate of the family she was leaving behind, and her bone-gnawing yearning to see Kiara grow.

Those few moments gave Aisha clarity—she would do whatever it took to give her mother peace. *Kia was the key to that!*

A sharp call by a night bird brought Aisha back to the present. Pulling out a mini pack of tissues tucked into her jeans pocket, she picked up the shoe again, this time making sure to keep the tissues between her fingers and the leather. She found a trash bin a few feet away and headed in that direction.

Fortunately, Aisha's Nani had moved in with them after her mother's death and she had understood why Aisha's eyes were haunted and her sudden aversion to touch anything or anyone. Pramila and Aisha were cogeneric souls. Except Pramila was the complete ESP buffet—touch telepath whether dead or alive, psychic, *and* clairvoyant.

Pramila became instrumental in helping Aisha understand her ability. She had called it Aisha's *gift*. The dead could reach her. And like a car door, Aisha's telepathic senses only opened one way—toward the dead and vice versa.

However, Aisha hated her uniqueness, and after several attempts at trying to convince Aisha to embrace her exceptionality, Pramila had given up. Resigned, she had helped Aisha master abilities to shut down her telepathic tendencies.

Blocked and 'request denied,' Aisha's telepathic abilities only crept up on her on the days she was stressed or tired. However, after so many years of practice, Aisha immediately knew how to shut down her spidery senses.

Reciting as many countries as she could remember under her breath, Aisha dropped the sole shoe inside a foul-smelling bin.

"Very thoughtful of you!" A masculine voice came from the darkness ahead.

Startled, Aisha swung her light in the face of the person and then quickly shut it off. *Shit! Kabir, the killer!*

Kabir was a dark silhouette framed against the twinkling stars and the silver-tipped clouds. "I'm sorry, I did not mean to startle you. I thought you were . . ." He broke off. "Anyhow, have a good night." He turned around and went in the direction of his villa.

Chewing her lips, Aisha watched him walk away.

With him out and about, I can't sneak in the villa. Dammit! Aisha's eyes narrowed thoughtfully. Why the hell is he out at this time? What is he planning? I should find out.

She saw Kabir head to the wooden pier that extended over the sea. He treaded with slow, confident strides, seeming to be familiar with the area, his hands tucked in his front pockets.

A wise or a bad idea, only time will tell. Aisha made enough sounds to let Kabir know that she was approaching.

Kabir tossed her a glance over his shoulder. "There is no litter here."

There is. You.

Aisha gave a contrived laugh. "I was coming to the pier. Do you live here?"

"No." Kabir moved to the other end of the pier, rebuffing conversation.

Aisha pursued him. "I'm a tourist."

Kabir's only response was a grunt that could either mean sod off or sod off.

Aisha stayed quiet. *Now what?*

She took a deep breath, squared her shoulders. *In for a penny, in for a pound.* "I'm in Panaji only for a couple of days. I came here in the morning. Because of the models and the hype around the calendar shoot, the beach was very crowded. So, I thought I'll come now and at least see the famous Donna Paula beach before I leave."

Silence.

Kabir continued to look out to the sea. The breeze was strong closer to the ocean and it ruffled his hair and the collar of his T-shirt.

Aisha watched him; his stillness was eerie.

"You are a tourist too?" Aisha prodded.

"I'm here for work." He replied after a few seconds.

"Oh! What do you do?" Aisha moved closer.

"Lie."

Aisha paused. Now, that's honest.

"I make people look beautiful and then others use that contrived beauty to sell things. So, as I said, I lie!"

Aisha faked some enthusiasm even though his bluntness surprised her. "You have something to do with the calendar?"

"You are a genius." Kabir replied, staring at the ocean.

Aisha felt herself color. It did not sound like a compliment. "So, the models are not pretty? All that beauty is a lie?"

"The beautiful can be vain, supercilious, selfish, and narcissist. So, it wouldn't be wrong to say that beauty can be ugly too."

Aisha was glad that the night hid her confused face. *Is he high?*

They both fell quiet, observing a lonesome seagull treading the waves, slowly searching for food.

"Fish and chips and beer would be nice!" Aisha thought out aloud. There was something about being outdoors. It always made her ravenous.

"I wouldn't mind a beer. How old are you?" Kabir's voice warmed a bit.

"Old enough."

"Stay here." Kabir turned around and jogged past her.

Aisha pressed into the wooden metal railings behind her as he went past her. She got a whiff of his perfume. *Citrus mixed with aqua.* Aisha watched Kabir's lean form disappear into the villa through the gate.

Thoughtful, she raised her face to the sky with clouds that seemed white like the tips of swan's wings. The silver moon coupled with the restless ocean waves evoked a similar restlessness in her.

Kabir came back in a few minutes, holding two beer bottles in his hands. "I have something for you in my shirt pocket. Can you grab it?" He leaned closer to Aisha.

Even though his sudden proximity flustered her, Aisha did not forget to pull out tissues as she took the bottle, freeing his one hand.

Her action made Kabir pause as he watched her. "The bottle isn't *that* cold."

Aisha's laugh was stunted. "I'm a germaphobe, sorry."

"Did you use tissues when you grabbed the litter?"

Dang, he is observant! "Pretty sure I did." Aisha fiddled with the cap of the bottle in her hand.

Kabir pulled out a shiny wrapper from his pocket. "Chocolate. There were no fish or chips."

"Thank you!" Aisha swallowed and took the chocolate, avoiding his fingers.

Aisha clinked her bottle with his and took a swig. "This is nice!"

"Local beer." Kabir said sipping his drink.

"Your house is beautiful."

Kabir kept drinking his beer in silence.

Aisha could not see his expression, but she could feel his gaze on her face. She felt a need to fill the silence.

"So, who is the most beautiful model in this shoot?"

Kabir stilled. "You are the second person to ask me that today. Kiara Khatri."

Crapshoot!

A massive wave crashed near the pier, spraying them with a fine mist. Aisha moved to the side, bumping into Kabir. He put a hand on her back to straighten her. His hand was warm, yet Aisha shivered. Aisha shrugged off his touch; Kabir took his leisurely time in moving his hand from her back.

"You probably want to know what she looks like?" His voice came from somewhere above her head.

Ugh, no! Aisha took a quick sip of the beer.

Kabir started describing Kiara in detail from her hair to her face to her body.

Aisha's anger grew. Abruptly, she turned to move away.

Kabir clamped his fingers around her wrist. "Where are you going?"

"I'm getting late." Aisha snapped. His fingers quickly heated the skin of her wrist. She tugged, trying to free her hand but he did not let go.

"Are you married?"

"What? No!"

Kabir tugged Aisha close, his grip firm. "Are you jealous of the girl I just described."

"Never!" Aisha said with conviction.

Kabir lowered his head to bring it closer to her face. Aisha looked up. In the darkness, Kabir loomed over her like some magnetic hero from a historical romance dribble—dark, aloof, and brooding.

With a suddenness Aisha did not anticipate, Kabir brushed his lips against hers. His lips were softer than she could ever imagine lips to be.

Aisha felt her lips quiver even as her heart raced. Rooted to the spot, all she could do was stare at him.

"To strangers!" Kabir whispered, his hot breath grazing her face.

Aisha and Kabir were so close that they could see in each other eyes. Their eyes locked and stayed that way, neither of them blinking. Aisha's eyes dropped to his lips that were hovering near her mouth and her lips unconsciously parted, glistening and inviting.

Chapter 10

Kabir growled low in his throat. The woman whose features he could barely make out was rousing him intensely. A sane part of him acknowledged that it was the mysterious dark night, the deserted beach, and the sounds of rushing waves that were weaving the magic around them.

Like she and I are the only ones in this world. And her scent. Vanilla and honey.

Kabir's nostrils flared to take a deeper whiff of her perfume. She too was aroused; he could feel it in the way her pulse raced under his fingers and how her lips parted for him. It was sheer madness, but right at this moment, he wanted nothing more than to taste her.

Kabir dipped his head, brushing lips again with Aisha. He felt her gasp on his lips. Intense anticipation tightened his muscles. She was all woman—soft and sweet.

As Kabir went to deepen the kiss, she backed away.

"Stop! What are you doing?" She kept retreating from him.

Kabir studied her eyes, wide in panic, and her heaving chest.

Did I read the signs wrong?

"I have to go." She ran past him. Kabir did not stop her.

Aisha ran in the direction of the waiting taxi. She lurched in her rush to get away.

What the hell is wrong with me? How could I let the man touch me? We kissed. I'm certifiably insane!

"Wait! Hold up!" Aisha heard Kabir call out.

She did not stop.

A hand wrapped itself around her elbow.

Aisha turned, surprised. Kabir was quick.

"Come for the shoot tomorrow. I'll give you the personal tour." He insisted, his other hand lightly trailing over her chin.

"You won't even recognize me." Aisha scoffed, hating the way his light touch was making her sound breathless.

"I will remember your voice. I don't forget things even if I want to. My mind is mapped that way." Kabir was now a dark silhouette, thanks to the moon and clouds playing peekaboo.

Shoot!

Aisha tossed her head to the side, making Kabir drop his hand. "Maybe. Goodnight! Thanks for the beer."

"I'll take that." Kabir took the beer bottle from her limp hand.

"Oh!" Aisha had forgotten all about it. "Thank you. I have to go now!"

Getting in the cab, Aisha directed the driver to take her back to the hotel. She saw Kabir watching her—an enigmatic shadow in the darkness.

#

"Strange woman." Kabir murmured as a thoughtful smile curved his mouth. A part of him wanted to see her face and another did not. What if they both disappointed each other in the unforgiving light of the day?

The darkness is an apt cover for hiding, and no one knows how to hide better than me.

On his way back to the villa, Kabir tossed the beer bottle into the trashcan Aisha had thrown the shoe.

The beer landed on top of the soft litter inside and rolled to the side. The single plum shoe with the silver flowers was gone.

Chapter 11

Next morning around 11:00 am, Aisha approached Kriti Villa again from the beach.

Her stomach knotted worse than necklace chains dumped carelessly in a drawer. It had all to do with her weird encounter with Kabir.

Just thinking of him, Aisha felt her stomach flutter. His spicy scent, the feel of his soft lips and rough hands made her legs tremble.

Playing mom, the lady of the house, completing her own education and writing courses, pursuing a secret obsession and long hours at work did not leave Aisha with much time for love. She could barely squeeze in some time for friends.

Aisha smoothed her hair touching her earrings—today blue and green infused with glass work that matched the green of her long skirt and contrasted with her fuchsia top.

"What the heck!" She groaned, noticing the crowd of bystanders. A few policemen and private security staff held them off.

"Excuse me! Move! Excuse me!" Using her elbows, Aisha pushed and got pushed back but somehow, she managed to reach the front. She spotted Kiara easily—standing tall against the pier railings, her head flung back, a sheer white see-through knee-length shift under which she wore a shimmering gold one-piece. Her hair was styled in a stiff afro, and her face was made up in shades of silver and gold.

Oh my! Aisha gawked at her niece.

Aisha had never visited Kiara at work. She had seen her pictures in magazines and billboards but seeing Kiara all professional in person was something else.

A few other stunning models sat, stretched, and posed around.

No one comes close to my Kia!

Aisha felt pride tug at her heart. Kiara was the centerpiece of that composition.

"Kiara, move a bit forward, slightly to the left." A woman behind a camera shouted through a megaphone.

Kabir stood next to the woman, tall and focused, studying the image on a monitor placed in front of him. Aisha tried not to stare, but she couldn't draw her gaze away from his mop of dark hair.

I'm still nursing a hangover from last night . . . on him. Damn!

Metallic clinking noises broke out on the pier.

The models screamed and stepped back hurriedly.

Aisha saw Kiara's startled expression and heard her surprised shout. Kiara tottered and then disappeared from view.

In a blink, she was gone.

Aisha felt her heart explode in fear.

"Kiara!" Aisha pushed the cop in front of her. She ran as fast as her legs could propel her.

Please, let her be okay! Please, please!

Kabir and some production people were ahead of Aisha. Everyone headed for under the pier.

Aisha sprinted around the scratched and weathered damp pillars that supported the wooden walkway. Her feet kept sinking in the wet sand, but she kept moving.

She spotted the small group of gathered people. "Please move, please move!" Aisha saw Kiara sitting half up, wincing in pain. Aisha dropped to her knees next to her. "Oh my God, are you okay?"

Aisha ran her hands over her niece's body.

"Boo! What the heck are you doing here?" Kiara stared at Aisha like she had seen a ghost.

Aisha ignored her questions, relieved to see no blood or bones popping out of place. Her eyes clashed with Kabir's who was helping Kiara sit up. His dark eyes were fixed on Aisha, a thoughtful frown on his forehead.

Shit! Did he recognize my voice? Aisha moved her eyes away.

"Seriously, Boo! What are you doing here?"

"Are you okay, Kia?" Aisha cupped Kiara's face, her voice husky much like the night before.

"Boo? This is your aunt!" Kabir scowled, tilting his head in surprise.

"Yes, this is my aunt." Kiara voiced, her mouth lifting a little.

Why are they talking about me? Why is he surprised? Aisha touched Kiara's foot.

"Ouch!"

"Sorry!" Aisha murmured.

"You said she was old." Kabir voiced, irritated.

"I did not say that. You assumed it." Kiara retorted even as she shifted on her bum.

Oh, for goodness' sake! Aisha got to her feet.

The few people gathered around them gave her room. She gestured for Kiara to stand up.

"What?" Kiara glanced at her.

Aisha gestured her again, keenly avoiding a biting pair of eyes that were staring at her.

"Why aren't you talking, Boo? What's wrong with your voice?"

"Yes, please tell. What's wrong?" Kabir shifted, his elbow on his knee as he glared up at Aisha. "Last night you were talking just fine." he accused, not a sliver of doubt in his voice.

Shoot! Aisha clamped her mouth and color flared on her cheeks. She winged him a brief guilt-ridden glance.

Kiara jerked her head back. "Yesterday? What are you talking about, Kabir?"

Aisha exhaled and went into the damage control mode. "Nothing, Kia. Last night I came looking for you. I bumped into him and that's it. I went back; it was late."

Aisha refused to look at Kabir.

"Kiara, do you think you can stand with support?" Kabir ignored Aisha.

Kiara nodded, doubtful.

Kabir lifted Kiara's arm and put it around his shoulder. "I got you. Try to get up."

Kiara put her hand on the ground and tried to get up. "Ow! My foot, I think it is twisted. Look at it. It's all red and swollen around the ankle."

"Let's get you to a doctor first and out of these stupid clothes." Aisha snapped.

Someone in the crowd handed Aisha a long terry robe. "Thanks!" Aisha helped Kiara put it on, her expression brisk but her touch gentle.

Kabir took Kiara's weight and helped her stand up in a fluid motion.

"Let me look at you fully!" Aisha murmured. Lowering her head, she walked around Kiara ignoring her niece's eye roll.

"It's just her ankle!" Kabir barked at her.

"You are a doctor?" Aisha mocked. Her guilt at duping him was minuscule when compared to her concern for Kia.

"Stay still, Kiara!" Kabir bent and swooped Kiara in his arms.

Aisha felt something curdle inside her. Kabir and Kiara walked out from under the pier.

"Boo!" Kiara called, forcing Aisha out of her inertness.

Chapter 12

Kabir took long loping strides to the villa. Anger fueled his body to move faster despite the tall human he was carrying. A muscle ticked in the side of his cheek. The scent that came from behind him only added insult to his bruised ego.

Yesterday night's five-minute encounter had lingered in his mind most of the night and today morning.

Kabir was the kind to roll out of bed the second his eyes opened, whether he was alone or not. But today morning he had stayed a few minutes in bed, shifting his dark head in the soft goose down pillow, watching the pale golden sunrise over a gray ocean. The white curtains at the side of the open window fluttered like a woman's veil.

In that breeze, he had imagined the face of the mysterious woman he had met last night on the beach. The features he had given her had been delicate, sweet, and kind, matching her lilting, graceful voice.

But now, that image had shattered like a crystal flung on the floor.

She is a fraud and a liar. And a germaphobe. Crazy woman!

Kabir's lip curled and his eyes narrowed.

"Sir, here! Here!"

One of the production guys pulled forward a chaise. Another had an ice pack in his hand.

Kabir lowered Kiara carefully on the chaise. "Are the others all right?" He asked Amee, detesting how aware he was of the dark-haired woman pouring herself over Kiara, all the while speaking soothingly in her gentle voice.

"Yes, everyone is fine. I sent the models back to the house." Amee replied.

"It is so surprising. The railing seemed fine in the morning. I leaned on the spot myself." Vikas mumbled, smacking his head.

"Last night, I too—' Kabir paused.

From the side of his eyes, he noticed Kiara's aunt still for a second. He knew she too was thinking about their meeting.

"Let's go and see it." He began walking toward the pier, trailed by Amee and a few others from production.

"What about a doctor for Kiara?" Kiara's aunt's voice stopped him.

Kabir turned to look at her and felt some satisfaction when the woman wouldn't meet his eyes. Her gaze was skittish. *Good! You should feel guilty.* "Vikas, call Christin!"

"I already did, Boss. Dr. Christin is on his way."

"Anything else?" Kabir asked the aunt tersely.

She snorted but did not say anything, and just went back to pressing the ice pack against her niece's ankle.

"Sorry, forget to do the introductions." Kiara said. "Kabir, this is my aunt, Aisha Khatri and Boo, this—'

Kabir spun around and walked away, not waiting for Kiara to finish.

"He's like that only." He heard Kiara say. He did not hear the aunt's response.

So, the liar has a name. Aisha! Nothing unique about it, just like her.

Kabir reached the spot where the railing had come apart. Getting down to his knees, he studied it. A sharp acidic smell lingered there.

"She is lucky to not have broken her neck," Amee said over his shoulder.

Kabir paled as he stood back up. The mere thought of another dead woman caused him to feel an excruciating tightness in his chest. Panic flooded his bloodstream and his nostrils flared as he breathed from his mouth, feeling a lack of oxygen.

Kabir treaded quickly to the edge of the pier to hide his sickly expression and racing breath. His hands were sweating. He discreetly wiped them on his jeans and wrapped his shaky fingers around a wooden post, staring out at the ocean.

Kabir took deep calming breaths.

"The railing was cut purposely!"

Kabir kept his back to the woman who, until a few minutes ago, he knew only by voice.

"I said, the railing was purposely sawed off. Did you not hear me?"

Kabir exhaled sharply and turned around. "What?"

Aisha's eyes were the same as Kiara's. Right now, they were accusatory. "I said the rail—"

"I heard you the first time." Kabir retorted and walked back to his team.

He heard her footsteps trotting behind. "Look at the metallic dust and wood shavings under the railings. The wind did not blow it all off. Also, the remaining ends smell of cheap glue."

So that is what the acidic smell was!

Kabir stopped abruptly. "What are you? A cop?" He snapped at the woman whose head reached no further than his shoulders. He noticed a strange expression flit across her face.

"No, I'm observant." She paused and added after a thought. "And concerned. Very concerned."

With that, she pivoted and walked away toward Kiara.

Kabir watched her stiff back, and then he glanced at the broken railing. Going closer, he squatted down, studied the spot, and sniffed the edges. Vikas squatted next to him.

"Fuck. She is right." Kabir exclaimed.

Chapter 13

Aisha joined Kiara who was sitting on the chaise. A young crewmember held an umbrella over her and another pressed the ice pack to her ankle.

"Are you going to tell me what is happening, Boo? What are you doing here?"

Grumpily, Aisha took the ice pack from the man. "I'll do it. Thank you." She pressed it lightly against Kiara's ankle. "Why do you think I came here? You can't just take off like this! Dad and I were so worried."

"Dada is fine with this. He trusts me to make my own decisions."

"If this is such a great decision and you are so confident about it, then why the hell didn't you tell me?" Aisha shifted the ice pack, which was now slippery.

"Because I knew you would overreact. And look how wrong I was!" Kiara jeered.

"Do you even know who this guy is? This Kabir? He is a k—"

"Did someone order a doctor?" A cheerful voice interrupted them.

Getting to her feet, Aisha turned in the direction of the voice. A man in his thirties, wearing a bright floral print shirt and jeans and holding a weathered leather bag, stood there.

"Finally!" Aisha waved at him.

"Dr. Christin or Chris, at your service. Who am I treating, the model or the younger sister?" The doctor asked, staring at Aisha

Aisha could not help a surprised laugh. "The model. And I'm the aunt."

"And I'm fine. It's not a fracture, just a sprain. There is no deformity around the ankle or numbness." Kiara protested. "Compress and painkillers, and I'll be fine!"

"Are you a doctor who is faking to be a model?" Dr. Christin crouched next to Kiara.

"No, she is the family quack." Aisha smiled. There was something open and charming about the Doc, unlike the other men she was recently meeting.

Dr. Chris examined Kiara's foot, prodding it with quick fingers. "She's right. It's a sprain. You fall from that height and you come out with just a sprain? You are a lucky girl!"

Aisha sent a thankful glance to the sky.

"Keep icing the foot, take painkillers every four to six hours. Give some rest to this foot. You should heal just fine in a few days." Dr. Chris said.

"So, we can travel?" Aisha asked.

"Travel? Where am I going?" Kiara scowled.

"Back home to Mumbai. Where else? You can't work now."

"Why can't she work now?" A curt voice interrupted.

"Exactly!" Kiara matched Kabir's attitude.

Aisha glared at Kabir, but she addressed her niece. "Did you not hear Dr. Chris? Your ankle is broken."

"Sprained!" Dr. Chris interjected, still squatting next to Kiara.

Aisha shrugged. "Working on that foot will only make your ankle worse. You could get disabled for life or get a permanent limp."

Kiara covered her eyes. "And she wonders why I ran away!"

"You ran away?" Dr. Chris smiled. "From her? I wouldn't!"

"Can I talk to you?" Kabir barked from somewhere behind.

What a rude man! Talking to a nice doctor in that tone! Aisha gave Dr. Chris a sympathetic smile.

The doctor's expression was amused as he clarified to Aisha. "He wants to talk to you."

"Oh!" Aisha colored even as she scowled at the ad maker. "What?" She matched his curtness.

An arrogant nod was all Kabir gave her and then walked away sharply, expecting to be followed.

"Walk of a tyrant!" Aisha muttered.

Dr. Chris egged her. "Tell that to his face."

"Oh, I will." Aisha started in Kabir's direction.

"Boo!" Kiara called out, warningly.

Aisha joined Kabir who had stopped ahead, closer to the gate of the Villa's backyard.

Kabir stopped on the higher edge of the sandy slope, ripe with boulders and stunted pale roots of plants that never grew. Aisha halted next to him, but she perched her flats on the tip of a boulder, giving herself a few inches, even if they were on-the-edge kind of inches.

"You might need a safety harness at that height." Kabir raised an eyebrow for sarcastic emphasis.

Aisha ignored the taunt. "Listen, about Kia—"

"Kiara is contractually bound to finish the shoot. Her injury isn't dire. All precautions will be taken. I'll ask Chris to hang around the sets."

Aisha's hand fisted at her sides. She was done being told off. "Kiara is young enough to be your daughter."

That got his attention. Kabir stared at her, his face tight. A muscle moved in his cheek.

"What did you just say?"

"You heard me." Aisha ignored all the alarm bells going off in her head. "You might be a God in this industry, but I could care two hoots. You stay away from my niece."

Aisha felt some satisfaction as Kabir's face turned a darker shade of red.

"If Kiara walks away from this shoot, I'll make sure she will not get another modeling job." He bit out. "And then, I will sue you for everything you have."

Aisha wanted to stomp her foot and shout out obscenities. What made her spitting mad was that every word of his threat could become a reality and the law would side with him. "Glad I didn't kiss you last night."

Kabir did not bat a lid. "Thank you for sparing me. I hate tasting fake stuff."

Aisha blinked, taken back at the blister his words caused. Last night, she had come close to being kissed for the first time in a long time, and today morning when she woke up, she sincerely regretted it hadn't happened.

Kabir's words had just trashed that memory. It was hard for her heart not to bleed some more.

"Are you going to say something?" Kabir asked, continuing to stare at her.

Aisha felt no rejoinder coming. "I will. Eventually."

She hopped off the boulder and went toward Kiara who was being helped to her feet. Sometimes her intense emotions for Kiara, for her brother's killers, her unfulfilled dreams crushed her.

"And I'm *not* old enough to be her father." Kabir taunting words stopped her.

Crossing her arms, Aisha tilted her head back and looked at him over her nose. "Thank you, Doofus. You just convinced me to stick to Kiara closer than her shadow. Congratulations!"

Chapter 14

Police Headquarters

Panaji, Goa

A police Gypsy pulled outside the square two-story building colored in bright colors. The parking lot was busy on a sunny afternoon. Roaring vehicles and bleating horns driving in and out of the lot displaced grainy dust.

"This is the police head office?" asked the man on the passenger side, with prep haircut and dark Ray-Bans. A pencil mustache crested above his full mouth.

"This is Goa! Everything is colorful. Even police." Replied the Inspector in the driver seat.

Returning the salute of the constable who opened his door, the man alit from the Gypsy and slipped into the jacket he had been holding in his lap.

"So, why is the CBI coming to Panaji, Sir?" The inspector asked, still in the driver's side.

"Because criminals are."

The man grabbed his laptop bag from under the seat and went inside the building. There was an inspector already waiting for him at the wooden reception desk. Exchanging salutes and handshakes, the man was taken to the second floor and the largest door in the corridor with the sign—Police Commissioner, DGP Meisha Rego.

"Come in!" was the curt answer to his knock.

The man opened the door and walked in, followed by two inspectors. He walked to the woman in the khaki uniform, several epaulets adorning her shoulders.

The man gave her a sharp salute and then extended his hand to her. "Good afternoon, ma'am! SSP Parth Mangal. CBI."

The commissioner shook Parth's hand and then offered him a seat. "Hope you had a good flight."

"I did, thank you." Parth said, hooking an arm around the empty chair next to him.

"So, what brings you here? Before you answer, remember - no bullshit." The commissioner said, a burly woman with a heavy jawline and wide set eyes.

Parth shrugged. "I don't Ma'am. In the past year, there have been two unsolved murders of young women. Same modus operandi—raped and strangled. One of them is related to the LG, Delhi. This news might become national soon. At then it will look good for you, the Commissioner of Police, that you had already involved the CBI."

"So, CBI is here to make Panaji police look good?" The Commissioner gave a snarky smile. The two inspectors grinned mockingly at Parth.

Parth scratched the collar of his starched white shirt. "You are right, Ma'am. It will be good even for us that CBI was a part of this investigation. You will get credit for any arrests made. Just mention to the press that CBI was involved."

"Did your bosses approve of this? You guys are known to go back on your word."

Parth took out a white sealed envelope from the inner pocket of his jacket and placed it in front of the commissioner. "It's on paper. Approved and signed by the bosses."

The commissioner opened the envelope and read it. She tried to hide the surprise on her face. "This is official?" She asked, sitting back.

"Commissioner, I'm just here to go through some files, visit the murder scenes, log in some interviews. I'll be here for a week or two and then I'll head back to Delhi." Parth lowered his voice. "Also, sightseeing is on the list, unofficially of course."

"So, you are not here to tell us how to do our job?"

"I'm just here to show that CBI does other things besides wiping the ass of corrupt politicians."

That made the commissioner laugh. She put her elbows on the table. "I have heard of Vishwanath Mangal, your father. We all are very proud of him."

"Thank you. Our family is very proud of him too. Now, Dad is retired, enjoying life with my mother in Nainital."

"It is hard to believe that such a driven RAW director is living a retired mundane life."

Parth showed his teeth in a quick flash. "He is still living dangerously. He is living with my mom."

The Commissioner smiled and snuck the envelope in the top drawer. "I have been doing some digging of my own. It is hard to believe, Mangal, that with your case closure rate, you are so relaxed about this thing. Sightseeing as you said it."

Parth grinned. "I have gone on my mother's side, which is why I'm so relaxed. As for the high closure rates, off the record, those cases weren't hard. And we all know having family connections in the department helps." He adjusted his jacket. "Off the record, of course."

Commissioner studied his face and then said. "Okay, so what do you need from Panaji police?"

"A car with a driver who knows the city. And accommodations." Parth got to his feet and extended his hand out to shake.

Commissioner took his hand and held it, her grasp firm. "I don't like surprises."

"Yes, Ma'am."

The commissioner got to her feet. She turned to one of the inspectors. "Send Inspector Arvind inside and make sure Jacob is available to SSP Mangal." She turned to Parth. "What are you packing, Mangal?"

Parth touched the left side of his jacket. "The usual. Department issued Smith and Wesson."

"Good. I don't like Rambo's in my city either." The Commissioner walked out of the door with Parth following her.

Chapter 15

Parth fiddled with the car stereo and settled back once he found a local station playing instrumental Konkani music. The sun was hot but not searing. The traffic was lighter here unlike his hometown, Delhi. The Gypsy went past colorful buildings. Blue, green, and red colours dominated the stucco exteriors on the sides of the narrow straight road.

He turned to the driver, a swarthy middle-aged man with round dark eyes, wavy gray hair, pock marks on his cheek and a bulbous nose. "Jacob, let's go to the first murder site."

"Sir, not to the guest house? You must be tired."

"I'm a single man, Jacob. Even if I sleep for an hour, I sleep very peacefully. And on the plane, I slept for three hours." Parth chuckled. "Are you married?"

The driver's fleshy cheeks tinged red. "Third marriage, Sir."

Parth gave a low whistle. "Third? Jacob ji, now you will sleep in your afterlife only."

The constable laughed and made a cross sign. His ample gut touched the steering wheel.

"So, no suspect for any of these murders?"

"All this nonsense is done by tourists, Sir. So many people going in and out of the city at all times. And girls are not careful nowadays. It's so easy to get girls from beaches and parties." Jacob honked at the person in front blocking his way.

"So, these two girls were both tourists?" Parth turned the AC duct toward himself. When it threw some coarse dust, he moved it back to its former position.

"Yes, Sir. One from Delhi, the LG's niece, and one from Mumbai, a college student. Both very beautiful!" Jacob said, signaling for a right turn.

"Oh, what a pity. Beauty should never be wasted!" Parth fiddled with his belt. He sat back. "So, what are the good places to try some local food near the guesthouse, Jacob?"

The driver duly provided Parth with names of good local restaurants and then the conversation moved to the touristy things. By the time they reached the destination, the town had been left behind.

The Gypsy crawled up a narrow path lined up by small bushes. Jacob parked next to a scratched yellow sign that read Lopez Point. "We are here, Sir."

Parth unbuckled his belt and got off. He rubbed his stomach. "Plane food sits heavy!" He pointed at the board that shuddered in the wind hitting it from the ocean. "Who is this Lopez chap?"

"He was a rich fisherman who built the biggest church in the village."

Parth walked on the red soil and stared out at the calm ocean that shone golden and bluish gray in the sun. Several hundred feet below was an isolated rocky beach.

"What a view! But no crowds here."

The air was ripe with the smell of salt, palm trees and whatever the house nearest to this place was cooking.

"Sir, this place is away from the city so fewer tourists here." Jacob shared.

Parth pulled up his dark jeans lightly and sat on a protruding gray boulder. He took out a cigarette from his shirt pocket and rolled it between his fingers. Jacob appeared on his side, bending forward, a lighter in his hand.

Parth waved him off. "I quit. It's been seven months. But it still helps me think. When I'm holding this, don't disturb me. Wait near the car."

Jacob backed away. His creased brow indicated that he could not quite get a read on the CBI officer.

After few minutes of listening to sharp shrieks of an odd bird or two, sounds of lumbering traffic and the waves much below him, Parth got to his feet and walked to a spot near the sign. He scuffed the ground with his shoe. "This is where they found her?" He put the cigarette back in his pocket and smiled affably.

"Yes, Sir! Some local boys who used to come here to play found the body."

Parth opened the side of the car door. "Let's go, Jacob."

"Where to, Sir?" Jacob quickly hustled behind the wheel. "To the guest house?"

"No, where the was second body was found." Parth said, putting his head back.

Chapter 16

Kriti Villa.

In the Night.

The dining table that sat up to twenty people was entirely loaded with various kinds of food.

Some models took their plates and parked themselves in front of an enormous TV in the adjoining informal living room. Other models and the crew were seated at the table itself.

Aisha sat across from Kiara at the table.

Kabir was at the head of the table, away from them.

Aisha made sure to keep her body leaning in a manner that she could stay hidden from Kabir behind the model sitting next to her. She kept shooting glances at Kiara who refused to look her way. Kiara had been giving her the silent treatment after earlier informing Aisha, "I'm not going anywhere. It is unprofessional. Kabir needs me."

'What Kabir needs is a noose!' Aisha would have retorted, had he not been standing right there.

"Can you pass the cucumbers?" asked the model sitting next to Aisha.

"Sure." Aisha passed her the oval plate, full of glistening cucumber slices.

The model took it with a brittle smile. "Thank you, Aunty ji."

Aisha smiled evenly. "You are welcome." She wasn't offended. In her mind, she was as old as Gandhiji's stamp on the rupee note.

Aisha did notice Kiara's mouth tighten, even though her niece focused on her dinner.

"So, are you her mummy?" came the snide comment from another model a few chairs away.

"No, I'm her Bua—aunt." Aisha took another spoonful of her quinoa.

She noticed Kabir glance in their direction, listening to their conversation. His look wasn't kind; it was more like a shark watching a school of clown fishes.

The model who had asked for cucumbers earlier gave a sharp crack of a laugh. "Aunty ji, I heard you were trying to sneak in the villa last night and Kabir caught you and threw you out."

Aisha glanced at the man who had allegedly thwarted her imagined break-in last night. Kabir met her stare, his dark eyes gleaming with unholy light under the chandelier hanging over the dining table. He smirked at her.

Aisha's own gaze narrowed in challenge. Her smile was harder than chipped ice and did not quite reach her eyes. "Oh, he caught me all right!" She cooed and was satisfied to see the mockery on his face replaced by irritation.

"How could you, Boo?" Kiara spoke, her voice heated.

"Oh, so now you are talking to me?" Aisha blurted.

The snarky model interjected. "Aunty ji—"

"Shut up already." Kiara grabbed her glass of water and upturned it in the model's lap. "Cool off, bitch!"

"Kiara!" Aisha gasped, covering her mouth.

Everyone else was shocked into silence.

Kiara pushed her chair back and grabbed the crutches kept on the side of her chair. The model was on her feet, yelling louder than an emergency vehicle as she waved her fists.

"Kia, apologize to her." Aisha called out, but her niece was already limping away in the direction of her assigned room.

"I'm so sorry!" Grabbing a napkin, Aisha went over to the screaming model and tried dabbing her wet clothes.

"Don't touch me!" The model yanked the napkin from Aisha's hand and threw it on her face. "You both are fucking mad."

"Calm down, Preet. It's just water."

Aisha's eyes widened as she heard who had come to her rescue.

"But Kabir, you saw how vicious Kiara is. You should throw her and aunty ji out."

Aisha exhaled, blowing a curl off her face and addressed the model. Even though she was acutely aware of Kabir standing next to her, Aisha did not glance at him. "I apologize for Kiara. Please excuse her behavior; it has been an exhausting day for Kia."

Aisha left the dining room and followed Kiara.

Chapter 17

Aisha found her niece in a room painted in beautiful gray tones.

Rich and colorful Thanjavur paintings in golden frames adorned the walls. Kiara sat on the bed of white sheets piled high with maroon and gold cushions. Her legs dangled down as she stared at the walls, her expression blank.

Aisha got on her knees and slipped her palm under Kiara's foot, the one she had twisted. "You should elevate—"

Kiara pulled her foot away. "Stop it." She grimaced in pain. "What is wrong with you? Why are you doing all this?"

Aisha stayed down on her knees looking up at Kiara, her expression even. "You should apologize to that girl. I have raised you better, Kia."

"You are not my mom; stop acting like it." Kiara snapped.

"You may not think of me as your mom. However, for me, you are my daughter."

"Enough, Bua." Kiara raised her hand and shifted back into the bed. "Your so-called love is suffocating me. Why are you hell-bent on killing my dreams?"

Aisha's mouth parted, and she jerked to her feet. "I'm killing your dreams? Me?" She beat her chest for emphasis.

Aisha fought hard to control her anger, but Kiara's accusations had ripped a big one in her heart. "I have raised you since you were four. I gave up everything just to be there for you, Kiara. My dreams, aspirations, my normal everyday life. I was just a teenager myself. I gave up everything just for you, and you are saying, I'm suffocating you?"

"Well, maybe you shouldn't have made all those sacrifices. No one asked you to." Kiara flared. "You could have had your own career and family."

"I have a career and you and dad are my family." Aisha cried out, her voice thickening.

"Oh, now are you going to cry? Seriously, Bua?" Kiara blew a raspberry. She shook her head, resigned. "Wow! Not fair. Fight with words, not saline water."

"Keep quiet!" Aisha sniffed and flopped on the bed. She sat facing away from Kiara. They both sat quietly for a few minutes.

"Dada says you are scared of losing me, like you lost granny and my parents."

"Tact was never your strong point."

"I lost them too, you know. Dadi and my parents." Kiara's voice cracked. Neither of them looked at each other.

"Now what happened to fighting fair?" Aisha reached out and took Kiara's limp hand. Kiara did not resist. "Yes, I fear losing you. And for the past few months, I feel I have already lost you."

Kiara shifted closer to Aisha. "I love you, Boo, and you are right. You are my mom. But you can't live in constant fear for me. If something has to happen–"

Aisha placed a hand on Kiara's knee. "Shush. Don't. Come back with me. You are stunning and talented. You will find something else."

Kiara sat back against the soft pillows. "I'm not going anywhere. And you must accept that. This opportunity is huge. This is my big break. Why won't you understand?" She pursed her mouth, frustrated.

"Kia listen to me. Your boss, that Kabir is a murderer. That's why I'm here, that's—"

Kiara jerked up. "Boo—"

Aisha leaned in, her voice urgent. "He killed his wife. God knows how many women he has killed."

"Bua!" Kiara simply took her chin and turned Aisha's face gently toward the door.

Aisha's eyes widened as she saw who stood at the door. The one she had just accused of murder.

Kabir!

He stood there tall and angry, his furious dark eyes focused on her.

Aisha slithered off the bed. "I . . . was . . ." she stuttered.

"Get out of my house." Kabir's frame seemed to shake with rage, and he took a step forward, his cheeks clenched, his expression twisted and ugly. Abruptly, he turned sharply and left the room.

Kiara and Aisha exchanged worried glances. "I'll apologize to that model, you go and apologize to him." Kiara's voice was concerned.

"Let's switch?" Aisha grimaced.

"He will fire me, Boo!"

"He will kill me, Kia." Aisha whispered, her hands twisting her skirt.

"Kabir was a suspect but the police found no evidence of him being involved in anyway. He was wholeheartedly cleared. His wife Lavina was an ex-alcoholic and had a history of mental breakdowns. All this came out after her death. Kabir had no idea. Boo, she was sitting drunk on a balcony railing. It was an accident."

"How do you know all this?"

"I'm your niece; I do my research too. Except, I do it myself and not have my gossipy assistant do it."

"Rustom doesn't gossip." Aisha scratched her brow.

"That's all he does."

Aisha sat down, her expression miserable.

"So, you are going to apologize to Kabir, right?" Kiara jutted her lower lip out.

"You really want this assignment that bad? Are you sure? Because if you are not, we can just slip out of this place. No one will notice." Aisha beseeched.

Kiara watched her silently. Her firm look was her answer.

"Fine! But I have a condition too. I'm staying in Panaji. Till you are here, I'm here. I won't interfere with your work. Deal?"

Kiara stayed quiet.

"Deal, Kia?"

Her niece gave in. "Fine! Deal."

Aisha pressed a quick kiss to Kiara's cheek. "Do take the painkiller and keep your foot elevated."

Kiara nodded and squeezed Aisha's hand. "I will. But how will you get to the hotel?"

"I'll manage, Kia." Aisha went to the door.

"Hold on!" Kiara grabbed her cell from the nightstand and pressed a few buttons. "I'll just order a cab for you."

Aisha gave her a flying kiss. "Order a coffin too! And please lock your door."

Chapter 18

Standing at the back porch, Kabir stared at the inky black ocean with crashing waves. His insides burned. His temples hurt because of the fierce clenching of his jaw. By now he should have been used to the allegations, but he wasn't. They still seared him.

After calming Preet, Kabir had followed Kiara and her aunt. He had been irritated, all set to rant at them about professionalism, make them squirm a bit, especially the aunt, and then let them off the hook. But hearing Aisha's sweet voice, he had paused outside the door, eavesdropping on their conversation.

It may not be right, but it seemed fair for the aunt had tricked him on the previous night.

The nervousness on Aisha's face under the pier had confirmed that last night she knew precisely who Kabir was.

Hearing her talk to her niece, Kabir had felt a grudging respect for Aisha. She had raised her niece, loved her to a fault, and like every parent, she was scared to let go of Kiara in the big bad world. He had felt a softening in him.

Maybe I had swarmed her last night? Perhaps she had wanted to come clean to me but was nervous? Was she as taken by the magic of the night as I was?

Kabir could not stay outside anymore. He had stepped into the room. And then he had heard Aisha confess the actual reason she wanted to whisk Kiara away.

Kabir felt his body quiver with rage—fury at the unfairness of his life. The women he loved never lasted for long in his life and not by his choice. Kriti, the twin sister he adored, had plummeted to her death. His mother never got over the death of her favorite child and moved out of the country and away from him.

After several meaningless flings, he had met Lavina at one of Shreya's party. They had hit it off instantly as if a connection existed between them. Kabir felt like he had found his soulmate. He could not wait to get married to Lavina, overlooking her reluctance or nerves. Even Shreya had suggested to slow things down but Kabir had never listened.

I was in love! His mouth twisted.

For a year, everything was great and then Lavina went back to her old ways—drinking. Kabir begged her to stop; they had arguments that led to separate bedrooms and separate lives. Kabir took solace in his work, cutting Lavina and the pain she caused out of his life.

He did not hate Lavina for drinking or breaking their marriage, but he did hate her for dying.

The day Lavina died, all hope for a normal life perished. Hope was repugnant to Kabir, love blasphemous. His work was the only thing he had, the only thing that made him feel alive.

Soft footsteps stopped behind Kabir. The tinkling noise of light jewelry and a familiar scent brought him out his bottom-of-the-barrel thoughts and reignited his rage fueled by pain. He spun around.

Aisha stood there, the light of the moon falling on her face, enhancing her skittish eyes.

"I'm sorry." she said softly.

"Sorry for what?" Kabir challenged.

"Sorry that you heard what—"

Kabir lunged and grabbed Aisha by her arms and pulled her close. A startled squeak escaped her mouth even as she tried to free herself.

"Why the surprise? Isn't this how murderers behave?" Kabir snarled in her face.

"Let me go. Right *now*." Aisha stopped struggling and met his eyes squarely, her mouth clamped into a thin line.

Kabir studied her face. He saw no fear, only contempt. He tightened his grip on Aisha's shoulders, digging into her soft flesh. Still no fear, only pain!

Her pain brought some sense to his turbulent mind.

Kabir pushed her away. He turned away. "Leave and never come back."

Behind him, she cleared her throat. "Till Kiara is here I will stay. But I won't come in your way."

"You will not enter my house."

"Okay."

Kabir pivoted around and said slowly, for emphasis. "I will woo Kiara. Saying yes or no is her prerogative, not her aunt's."

Aisha's eyes ignited like the tip of a sparkler. "Over my dead body!"

"I'm used to dead bodies, right?"

Aisha stared at him, speechless.

Kabir veered and walked away from her.

#

The jerk! I will kill him myself." Muttering repeatedly, Aisha tugged the cloth satchel that hung across her body.

The cheek of that man! Kia will listen to me. I will forbid her from going anywhere near him. Aisha paused. The more I prohibit Kia, the more she will freaking do it! She has too much of her dad in her.

A sound from the side distracted her.

White circular pillars lined up on either side of the back porch. Aisha thought she saw a dark shape behind the pillar on the far left.

"Hello?" Aisha called out, narrowing her eyes in that direction.

The moon had gone behind the clouds. There was hardly any light on the porch. Aisha took a few steps in that direction. She thought the shape moved.

"Hello?" Aisha increased her pace. She turned around the pillar in anticipation. "Got you."

The corner was dark but empty.

"What? I was sure I saw someone." Aisha took a few steps further and saw the side of the garden that wrapped around the house. *Whoever was behind the pillar could have escaped through the garden on the side.*

Aisha smacked her head. *What am I thinking?*

Aisha walked out of Kriti Villa. There was a spring to her step. Kiara and her relation seemed to be on the mend. Aisha walked down the front steps. Just as the humid wind hit her face and neck so did a realization. Kiara was all grown up.

And she knows how to research people.

Aisha's stomach fell like it had been dropped from a tremendous height.

#

A pair of glittering eyes, hiding behind a parked car across the street, watched Aisha steadily as she walked away, totally oblivious to his presence.

"I see you . . . You are a liar, too." He whispered and licked his thick dark lips.

Some spittle landed on the side of his mouth. His voice took on a dream-like quality as he saw himself naked, leaning over Aisha. He shivered with delight imagining how the soft skin of her neck would feel between his hands as he slowly choked the last breath out of her body.

He felt himself getting painfully hard and resisted the urge to touch himself. *Not on the street!* He giggled as excitement rose in him.

He wanted to shout out loud in sheer ecstasy, but he knew better than to attract attention. If she knew about him, she would become careful. Harder to kill! And, he *had* to kill her every time.

He saw Aisha get in a cab and drive away. His mouth twisted in genuine pleasure as he quietly sung his favorite childhood rhyme.

"There was an old woman who lived in a shoe.

She had so many children, she didn't know what to do;

She gave them some broth without any bread;

Then whipped them all soundly and put them to bed."

Just like Suvabrata had warned her, darkness had found Aisha.

Chapter 19

"The CBI officer I'm driving around, Mary, is an idiot." Jacob said to his third wife. She ignored him like she usually did at this time of the night.

"Mary, are you listening?"

A cushion hit him on the face. "Shut up, Jacob! I'm watching TV."

Jacob threw the cushion back, but he made sure he threw it at her feet. He was scared of his wife. She was twice his size and perpetually angry. The third marriage also wasn't working. Compared to Mary, his former two wives seemed like Angels who played harps.

A sudden knock roused Jacob from his bout of self-pity.

"Answer the door, Jacob," Mary ordered.

"Yes, Mary." Scratching the side of his neck, Jacob walked to the door. Adjusting his white vest that sat snug over his rotund belly, Jacob opened the door.

"Hi, Jacob." Parth waved at him.

"Sir, you?" Jacob saluted and then became self-conscious for he was more undressed than dressed. He hid behind a panel of the door, shielding his body. "Sir . . . do you need something?"

"I want to see some famous Panaji nightlife. So, go and change. I'll wait outside."

Jacob just stood there, his mouth open.

"C'mon, Jacob, you are not getting any younger. Let's go!"

"Nice shirt, Sir!" Jacob muttered, staring at the bright yellow and blue shirt Parth wore over a khaki Bermuda. Then he went inside to change.

Fifteen minutes later, Jacob and Parth headed to a swanky pub on the beach. Traffic was light currently. Local people and tourists were out on foot in significant numbers, enjoying the nightlife. Strains of Goan music peppered the air. The night breeze was refreshing.

As they stopped at a red light, Parth saw two young women dressed in skimpy clothes walking on the side. They were pretty with lithe sun-touched limbs, loose hair that fluttered in the breeze and smiles that brightened rooms.

Parth leaned out of the car and called out. "Hola, girls! Can I give you a ride somewhere?" He beat the side of his Gypsy. "Police!"

The taller girl turned around and smiled. "Hola? You are in the wrong continent dude." She poked her tongue at him and laughed, not slowing down.

"Wanna ride?" Parth persisted, leaning out of the window.

"Buzz off, Amigo." Still laughing, the tall girl flipped him off. Her friend gestured at her to keep walking.

"Damn." Grinning, Parth sat back. He caught Jacob's disapproving look. "A bachelor can have some fun!"

Jacob shook his head but went back to focusing on the road. Parth killed time by asking Jacob about his family and his job.

A few kilometers later, Jacob pulled into a parking lot of a shack-like structure on the beach. The bright flashing green and pink neon sign on the shack read Beber.

"Beber in Portuguese means drink." Jacob said, parking the vehicle.

"Then let's go and get some Beber." Parth got out.

"You want me to come with you, Sir?" Jacob was surprised.

"Of course, I'm not partying without my wingman."

Jacob joined Parth, the former's dark, swarthy face shining in anticipation.

The bar was packed with people—a mix of foreigners and Indians. Music was loud and the lights low. Nearly everyone inside was dancing, drinking, or making out. The atmosphere was vibrant and smelled of sweat mixed with perfumes.

Parth picked up beers for Jacob and himself and then motioned Jacob to the door at the back. Going through it, they ended on a wooden deck on the beach. The ocean was frisky, making big waves.

Several pubs like Beber stippled the beach on either side. Colorful paper lanterns hanging from poles swung in the breeze. Couples and small groups of people peppered the sand. Some bonfires on the beach added to the vibrant atmosphere.

Parth pointed at the closest group. "Jacob, I will pay you five hundred rupees if you have that pretty girl in the white dress agree to go on a date with me."

"Sir, I don't do all this!" Jacob hid his face behind the bottle he was sipping from.

"Okay, then you pay me if I get her to agree to go on a date with me. Deal?" Parth extended his bottle to him.

Jacob grimaced. *Bloody CBI idiot. The things I do for this job.* Reluctantly, he walked down the wooden stairs to the girl his boss had pointed out.

"Oh, tell her I'm a cop. It might impress her."

Parth smirked as he saw Jacob bungle around the group. The girl laughed openly at him. She glanced at Parth, slowly lifted her hand, and showed him the middle finger.

Jacob lumbered back. "Sorry, Sir! I lost five hundred."

Parth gave a crack of a laugh. "You give up easy. This place is full of possibilities." He winked at the driver. "Now I'll try."

So, for the next few hours, Parth chatted with a few women hanging on the beach. He only went for the attractive ones.

Chapter 20

Left alone, Jacob propped his elbow, under his head and hummed at the stars. The cell tucked in his shirt pocket rang. He pulled out his cell phone and saw the name of the person calling him. Jacob sat up. "Good night, madam! Sorry, sorry, I meant good—"

Commissioner Meisha interrupted him. "Did I wake you?"

"No, no Madam. I'm out with the CBI officer."

"He is still with you? At this time? What is he doing?"

"Umm . . . Madam, we are at Vaingunium beach in the Beber pub."

"What are you doing there?"

"Um . . . eh!" Jacob scratched the side of his head. "Sir is getting company for the night." He blurted out.

There was silence for a few seconds then the Commissioner asked. "What did he do all day?"

"Nothing much, madam. He went to the murder sites, took some selfies. Then I dropped him at the guest house. Sometime back he asked me to show him Goa nightlife."

"Keep a close watch on him. I don't want the CBI outsmarting us. Got it, Jacob?"

"Yes, Madam," Jacob nodded vigorously.

The Commissioner hung up.

Jacob swiveled his neck, trying to spot the man he was supposed to be watching. He saw Parth at some distance, trying to charm some other woman.

"Desperate this man is. Idiot!" Jacob slipped the cell back in his pocket and went back to his earlier repose position—elbow under the head.

Sometime later, a nudge on his foot woke Jacob. He opened his watery eyes and had trouble focusing on the man looming over him.

It was Parth.

"Yes, Sir!" Jacob sat up, rubbing the sleep and drool off his face.

"Jacob, you go home. I have found some company."

The driver got up like a sloth. "Okay, Sir." He saw the woman in shorts and a tank top standing behind Parth. A line of glowing bracelets covered her left arm from wrist to elbow and a flower headband decorated her head.

"Sir, can I drop you somewhere?"

Parth grinned a boyish smile. "Why, so you can tell Commissioner where I went?"

"No . . . no, Sir!" Jacob stammered.

"See, you should not have told me earlier that the Commissioner was a distant relative of yours while trying to impress me. And among all the thousand Panaji policemen, I get *you* to drive me around the town."

Jacob stared at Parth. Shock had rendered him quiet.

Parth tossed a look to the girl waiting for him. "What's your name, darling?"

"Sunny . . . Sunny Leone." The girl giggled.

"All right then!" Parth put a five hundred rupee note in Jacob's pocket. "Tell the Commissioner that you left me with Sunny Leone."

"Sir! Sir!" Jacob called out as Parth walked off with the girl.

Parth waved over his shoulder. "Go back to Mary. I will find you when I want to find you. Tomorrow morning or afternoon, Jacob."

Chapter 21

Next day, Aisha alighted from her cab and paid the cab driver a generous tip. She was in a generous mood. She had slept for nearly ten hours, eaten a sumptuous breakfast, submitted herself to a hot stone massage followed by a pedicure.

On supremely hard, long days, Aisha had reconciled herself with the thought that when Kiara grew up, Aisha would get her life back. But now that Kiara had grown up, all Aisha was left with was a hollow feeling of emptiness.

Aisha was no procrastinator, so she had jumped right into thinking and planning. And the first thing to do was?

Take a vacation! And what do you know, I'm already in the right place.

Aisha had promptly texted her dad, her boss, and Rustom.

Her father had directed her not to bother Kia and bring back a bottle of Fenny. Her boss had grudgingly given her the time off and requested a few bottles of Fenni. Her assistant had merely requested that Aisha get a crate of Fenni for the guests at his funeral.

Aisha walked on the beach, holding her sandals. Today it was teeming with tourists, locals, and food carts. Restaurants were open alongside the beach. Sounds of traffic, live music, and human chatter appeared grotesque in comparison to the vast and mysterious ocean. Hurtling jets skis and a few speedboats created commotion there too.

Aisha noticed the crowd ahead of her. "Offo, for goodness' sake. Enough with the gawking!" Hitching up her white cotton skirt with blue leaf life pattern on the border, Aisha went around the crowd that meant walking ankle deep in water. "What the...?" She saw the two bodies nearly half-kilometer out in the ocean.

A person was flailing in the water, and a man was swimming toward her.

Shit! Kia!

Aisha panicked and ran into the water.

"Boo, wait! I'm here."

Aisha turned to Kiara's voice. Her niece stood near the pier, waving at her.

The security let Aisha pass through. "What's going on?"

Kiara slyly pointed at an older, bird-faced woman standing in the water calf deep, her hand covering her mouth, her eyes fixed on the figures in the water. "That is Ameena Afreen, the model coordinator. Her daughter, Nagma, went for a swim in the ocean and I'm guessing the current pulled her away from the shore."

"And who is rescuing her?"

"Kabir. He went right after her."

"He did?" Aisha could not keep the surprise out of her voice as she focused on Kabir and the girl as they swam closer to the beach. "This place is jinxed. Something or the other keeps happening here."

Some men from the crew and Amee ran deeper into the water to help Kabir and Nagma. The latter was struggling to catch her breath but other than that she appeared all right.

"She's fine, Amee. She's okay." Kabir said, breathing hard, his face clenched because of the exertion. He carefully handed Nagma over to the crew members.

"Thank you!" Amee hugged him and then quickly went to her daughter.

Kabir walked past the pier. Someone handed him a towel and he used it to wipe down his face and hair. He came toward Kiara, his expression pleased. And then he noticed Aisha. His smile disappeared, and he changed directions.

Kiara winged her an apologetic glance.

Aisha waved her hand. "Don't bother! How is your ankle?"

"Better. Much better. I took my painkillers, gave the ankle hot and cold compress. As you can see, I have a crepe bandage on."

"I'm impressed!" Aisha smiled. "But where are the crutches?"

"C'mon!"

Aisha chuckled. "I'm messing with you Kia. You did good."

"Hey Kiara, we are taking a break for some time. Kabir and costume are deciding on the wardrobe for the evening shoot." One of the crew members called out.

"Evening shoot! He is making you work in the night, too?"

Kiara gave Aisha a pointed look. "No big deal! It should be fun. We are going to some place called Lopez Point. It is Kabir's favorite, favorite spot. I have been told it has a view to die for."

"Just be care—" Aisha stopped herself. "Great." She gave the 'thumbs up' sign. "You have fun! Text me when you get back."

Kiara whistled. "You are really backing off, Boo. I'm so proud of you."

Aisha snorted. "Smartass. Let me know when you have time tomorrow and we'll go for a coffee." She turned to walk away, her heart heavy.

Dammit, it is hard to let go of your child!

"Boo come join me for lunch. They have a buffet laid out inside."

Pausing, Aisha glanced at the villa. "No, it's okay! You go in. I have plans."

"You have plans? What plans?"

"To go and seek the man of my dreams?"

"You are on a roll." Kiara snickered. "Just don't get yourself pregnant, okay?"

"Kia, keep your voice down!" Aisha looked around to see if anyone had heard. There was no one around them.

Kiara winked at Aisha and then began to hobble slowly. Aisha lent her an arm. "Boo, you do know how babies are made, right? Let me tell you a big secret: it's not the stork."

Aisha laughed. "Oh stop!"

#

Kabir came to the wide window of his sea-facing bedroom. He looked outward as he pulled the dry black tee over his head. He saw the pair—Kiara and her aunt. They were laughing and chattering while coming upon the villa, but they halted at the gate.

Kiara appeared to be inviting her in, but Aisha shook her head. She blew Kiara a kiss and urged her to go in. Kabir knew why she wasn't coming in. Because of him!

Good!

He saw Aisha turn, pause, and then tilt her head up. She was staring directly at him. Kabir stilled and could not help but stare back.

Chapter 22

Aisha did not understand what made her look up, but she hated whatever that feeling was. Her gaze locked straight with Kabir's and she could not look away. She felt he was staring right into her mind, reading her thoughts. The intensity of Kabir's gaze even at such distance and through the glass surprised her.

"Afternoon!"

A cheery call jolted Aisha. She blinked and pivoted away from the man in the window.

"Morning, Doc! The girl who was rescued, is she okay?"

Dr. Christin stopped next to her. "Yes, she's fine. Just swallowed some water and in a bit of a shock."

"Good you were here."

"I live in that smallest villa at the beginning of the road. Kabir is a friend of mine. So, when he shoots his calendar he has me hang around. Some models tend to ... you know what." He made a sign as if tipping something in his mouth. "So, this whole week, I'm the doctor on set."

"The girl was lucky someone spotted her!" Aisha and Christin fell into easy steps, walking next to each other.

"Kabir saw her. The number of people he has saved around here!"

Aisha blinked. "Really? More than one?"

"Yup! There is no lack of idiots who decide to go swimming in the ocean without understanding the ocean currents or knowing how to swim."

Christin observed Aisha's face. "Stupid me! I just impressed you about another man, didn't I?"

Aisha laughed consciously. *Did I look impressed?*

He put a hand over his chest, looking crushed. "Give me a chance to make amends. May I take you out for coffee?"

Aisha paused. *This is unexpected!* She had not dated in a long time. *Maybe it's time to change that fact.* "Why coffee? Isn't it time for lunch?" Her look was bold and confident.

Christin's features lit up. "Absolutely!"

"But only if we go Dutch, please!"

"I do not know any Dutch restaurants here."

"I insist, please. I will pay my half of the bill." Aisha crinkled her nose. "Please?"

"Fine! This time we'll do it your way. Give me a few minutes. I'll be right back."

"Sure," Aisha grinned.

Christin jogged away to his house.

Aisha clamped her lips, feeling a rush of nervousness and excitement rushing to her stomach.

What am I doing? The first day of freedom and I literally asked a man out.

Reaching in her satchel, Aisha pulled out a lip gloss and coated her lips thickly with the pink cotton candy gloss. A shadow passed over her. Aisha looked up, her eyes widened briefly.

It was Kabir. He was going in the direction of his crew that was gathering the props and lights near the pier.

Taking a deep breath, Aisha jogged behind him. "Excuse me! Excuse me!"

Ignoring Aisha, Kabir kept treading away from her.

"Hold on, please!" Aisha stumbled, the sand made it harder to run fast.

Flexing his shoulders, Kabir finally stopped.

Aisha came up on his side. "I just want—"

"I told you to stay away from me!" Kabir did not even deign to glance at her.

"Yes, you did. But—"

Kabir commenced walking, leaving her mid-sentence. Aisha reached out and grabbed his arm. His muscles were firm and sinewy under her fingers. Her fingers curled around his arm, the sensation surprisingly thrilling. Aisha stared at her hand over his skin lost in the fuzzy feeling that enveloped her. It was like holding your favorite old T-shirt.

Chapter 23

Kabir stopped watching Aisha's face. Her touch was soft on his arm like cotton. Her lashes resting against her cheeks were long. Her nose short, thin and her heart-shaped mouth appeared pouty because of the gloss. The rapt way she studied her hand on his arm was endearing. Her hands were soft and petite.

At that moment, Kabir could not bring himself to brush off her touch. So, he quietly cleared his throat; it suddenly felt clogged.

Aisha raised her eyes at the sound and dropped his hand as if she were holding something on fire. "Sorry!" She too cleared her throat. "I just wanted to apologize for calling you a mur . . . I was wrong. You couldn't have killed . . . hurt anyone."

"Why?" Kabir's voice was terse, and he switched his gaze from her face to the horizon.

"Because someone who risks his life to save others is not capable of taking it. He knows the value of a life. It is—"

"Invaluable." Kabir finished.

"Yes!"

Kabir flicked his gaze back to Aisha. "Still, 'stay away from me' clause stands." He watched her closely and saw the flash of irritation cross her eyes.

"Fine!"

"But you are free to hang with Kiara in or out of the house."

A smile started at the end of her mouth, traveled to her eyes, and stayed there. Her cheeks were round and her mouth small and fleshy. She would always appear younger than her age. Her nutmeg eyes were expressive as if feelings were a free commodity. What Aisha felt was reflected in her eyes.

The signs of an optimistic soul. A complete opposite to me.

#

Aisha wasn't easily fazed yet the scrutiny of Kabir's dark hooded gaze made her fidget and she felt warm as if the equator had suddenly shifted closer to her.

"Hello!" Christin's voice interrupted them. "Hi, Kabir." Then he glanced at Aisha. "Ready?"

"Yes," Aisha nodded.

"Ready for what?" Kabir asked.

"We are going for lunch and you are not invited." Christin quipped.

"I wouldn't dream of interrupting," Kabir said, a sting to his voice.

Dr. Christin's cell rang, and he looked at it.

"Just give me a minute." He walked away for privacy.

Aisha moved to follow him when she was stopped by a gentle yet firm touch—Kabir's hand on her arm.

Aisha tipped her head back, trying not get distracted by the warmth of his touch that had traveled right from her arm to her toes.

Kabir leaned closer, looking straight into Aisha's eyes, his expression unreadable. "I will be asking Kiara to go out tonight."

He dropped Aisha's arm and walked to his crew, leaving Aisha staring at after him.

Lout! Jerk! How can he? Aisha felt like kicking something or someone. But the 'someone' had walked away.

"Are you planning to have lunch with me or are you going to make me the lunch?" Christin came back.

"What?" Aisha's look was sharp, but she immediately tempered her irritation. "Sorry, I just . . . He's just..." She pointed at the tall man standing some distance away, giving instructions to his team.

"I know, he's harsh. And aloof. But Kabir is one of the good guys."

Sure, and I'm Mother Teresa!

"So, where are we going for lunch?" As a test, Aisha placed her hand on the doctor's arm lightly.

She wasn't happy with the results. She felt nothing on touching the doctor. No sparks, no tingles and definitely no proximity to the equator.

Damn!

Chapter 24

On D. B Marg, near the overhead water tank, sat a gray building on a quiet triangular plot enclosed by a rusty chain-link fence broken in several places. The windows on all floors were shut. The parking lot housed a few old model cars and an odd motorbike and a few scooters. The area was devoid of any human sounds. The place seemed to belong to some grainy film reel rather than the present day.

Jacob parked the Gypsy in a spot farthest from the entrance. Once he shut off the engine, he quickly made a cross sign.

"Was that for the dead or the ones alive?" Parth asked, taking off the seat belt.

"Sir, please don't joke about the dead! Their spirits might hear you." Jacob replied somberly.

Parth took off his Aviators and cleaned them before putting them in his shirt pocket. "Jacob, if you were a spirit and you were free to go anywhere in the entire world, would you spend your time hanging around this dump, just so you can curse the asshole with a sense of humor?"

Jacob clucked his tongue. "Sir, can I wait outside. I . . . don't like the smell inside."

"Me neither." Reaching inside the Gypsy, Parth pulled something out of the bag tucked under his seat. Opening the indigo plastic bottle, he took out some viscous gel and applied it liberally around his nostrils. "Put this on; the smell won't bother you much."

Jacob took the bottle. "Vicks! Doesn't this help you smell better?"

Parth paused and gave him a clear-eyed glance. "Don't be the next asshole with the sense of humor. Remember the spirits?"

He smirked when he saw Jacob hurriedly reach down and kiss the small golden cross that hung around his thick neck.

The two men walked inside the building with a sign painted in white and blue on its front, A.S. Mortuary. The interiors were dank, and the smell of mildew was strong.

Parth went to the man at the reception. "I'm here to see the Chief Examiner." He flashed his credentials. "Parth Mangal, CBI."

"Please go to the basement. Use that lift." The receptionist pointed to the side.

The stench was what hit Parth first as he got off the elevator. It was like he had walked into a room full of rotten eggs. One could taste the foul smell, which was thick enough to cut through. The sound of the metal door closing behind him made Parth spin around.

Jacob was gagging. He frantically kept pressing the elevator call button. "I can't. . ." He took the elevator and went up.

Parth pressed Vicks further into his nostrils and took tentative steps in the corridor, which was chilly.

"Here!" A woman popped her head out of a room, some distance away and waved at him.

Parth went through the wooden door. There were some faded brown stains on the floor and empty portable steel stretchers lay around in no particular order.

Parth avoided stepping on the stains; he knew what old dried blood that had seeped through porous floors looked like.

He focused on the chubby-cheeked and middle-aged woman in green scrubs, sitting at a desk overflowing with paperwork. The woman was heavy set, fair skinned with dark frizzy hair that was more gray than black. Her small eyes behind rectangular glasses studied Parth back.

"Like what you see?" Her tone was as wry as the expression in her eyes.

"Sorry! SSP Parth Mangal, CBI." He put his hand out. She didn't take it so Parth dropped it, feeling like he was facing his fourth-grade teacher.

The teacher who made him stand in the trash bin that would be full of pencil shavings, crumpled paper and a few sticky things that did nothing to tame a rebellious nine-year-old. He still called her occasionally.

"Dr. Madhuri Lorso." she said, waving her hand as she slapped a paper that was about to slip off the desk. "So, why is the CBI here?" She took off her glasses.

"Because of the murders of the girls I mentioned on the phone. Dr. Lorso, did you conduct an autopsy on any of them?"

Dr. Lorso rubbed the bridge of her nose. "You are here for the files?"

"The files too, yes. But can you tell me something about the condition of the bodies?" Parth leaned on a bookcase behind him.

"It's all there in the files. I have them in my office. You can make copies and take them." Madhuri Lorso got to her feet and grabbed her glasses.

"This is not your office?"

"No, I just finished an autopsy. A sixty-year-old organ doctor found dead under suspicious conditions." Her dark eyes held amusement.

Parth did not understand the joke.

"He had only one kidney."

"Oh!"

Parth followed Dr. Lorso to her office on the first floor. It was clean, organized, and spotless, and smelled lightly of antiseptic.

"So, whose desk was that in the basement?"

"Whoever is working the night shift on that day."

Parth felt like he had just passed a hazing test. He sank in the comfortable chair with the upholstered back.

Dr. Lorso walked to the file cabinet behind her chair and unlocked the top drawer. She pulled out two thick manila folders. Pressing the intercom button on her table phone, she called the peon in.

"Make copies of these for Sir. ASAP."

Parth waited for the peon to leave. "Dr. Lorso, please tell me what you think of the bodies?"

"It's all in the files."

Parth leaned forward. "It's *never* all in the files."

Dr. Lorso sat back and studied his face for a few minutes. "What do you want to know?"

"Your interpretations based on your experience."

"You really want *my* opinion?"

Parth nodded, surprised that the woman who had so many plaques and awards from reputable organizations framed on the wall behind her required this level of reassurance.

Lorso exhaled. "Okay. The killer is skilled and knows the importance of DNA and evidence. While raping the women, he wears condoms and pours bleach over the women's mouth, hands, and genitals after."

"So, he does rape them?"

"Violently. There is considerable vaginal tearing. And deep bruises on their arms and legs where he holds them down."

"And why the pouring of bleach on those body parts?"

"Because he touched those parts and wants to make sure he leaves no DNA or prints for us to find."

Parth linked his hands together and rested his chin on them. "So, he might be in the system? We might have his fingerprints."

Lorso's eyes widened. "I never thought of that!"

"Anything under the nails?"

"Generic dark fibers that could belong to any garment. No skin or hair. Like I just said, he knows about forensics."

"Did you test the blood of the girls for traces of any drugs?" Parth asked.

"Yes. High quantity of diazepam was found in their blood. I would not recommend that dosage to a horse. And these were women between 50 to 60 kilos."

"Diazepam as in Valium?"

Lorso gave him her first smile, revealing front teeth that overlapped. "I'm impressed."

Parth shrugged. "So, these women probably never knew what was happening to them because of the drugs."

"Not a chance. Hallucinations would have been strong. They would see colors and images. They would be unable to distinguish between reality and hallucinations. Also, since it is a muscle relaxant, it would have rendered them incapable of fighting back."

Parth scratched his chin. "But how would such high dosage be given?"

"They were not junkies; no needle marks on their bodies and their organs were healthy. These were fit women, women who looked after themselves. Valium was probably crushed in food or mixed in the drinks."

"So, a waiter?" Parth tapped his chin.

"Now you are asking me to do your job!"

They were both quiet for some time.

"Anything else, Dr. Lorso?"

"Yes. Catch this monster. He does not possess even an ounce of humanity."

"With a bullet or cuffs?" Parth jested, getting to his feet. He reached out to shake hands.

Lorso shook his hand and gripped it. "Make it a bullet. In the head."

Parth let go of her hand. "Thank you for all your help." He walked to the door when Dr. Lorso stopped him.

"One advice. Keep my name out of the investigation. I have been the acting Chief Medical Officer for the last four years. Never promoted to Chief. No one likes me around here, neither my staff nor the police."

Parth wasn't surprised. It was common for deserving women to be often overlooked because of their gender. "Because you are hard-working, intelligent but lack a penis?"

Lorso took her glasses off. She folded them meticulously and placed them on the table. "No, because I'm officially single and unofficially gay."

Parth stared at her for a few seconds and then spoke, his expression shuttered. "Officially *and* unofficially, I don't care."

Chapter 25

Early in The Evening

Lopez Point, Goa

Aisha made her way up the steep climb. She often stopped to catch her breath and admire the view. The sea was calm and a stunning aquamarine. The sun was close to setting and painted the sky in beautiful colors of red, gold and pink. The breeze over the ocean was cool.

"I could live here forever," she sighed, staring at the sea.

Aisha resumed her hike, a small backpack on her back and a misshapen thick branch in her hand. She had picked it on the way and was using it as a walking staff.

Today, Aisha had ditched tissues for a pair of gloves—uncomfortable ones she had saved from hair color kits. The gloves kept riding up and her hands were beginning to sweat.

Lunch with Christin had been perfect. Light, friendly and delicious.

After lunch, Aisha had gone to the famous Church Square and hung around there, catching up on Goa's history. Kiara had texted to meet her at Lopez Point where she was currently shooting close to six.

Seeing that text had set off butterflies in Aisha's stomach. She wanted to meet Kiara but not her niece's boss. Aisha paused and brushed her sweaty locks aside.

That man really rubs me the wrong way. What the heck do I do? Run away because he confuses the crap out of me or stand in between Kiara and him? Don't think he is Kiara's type but Kia is young; she could be easily brainwashed.

Aisha glanced up. The end of the hike was near. She could hear sounds carried down by the wind—sounds of humans nearby. Probably the ones she was heading to meet.

Aisha noticed that she was on a sandy ledge that jutted out, providing a perfect place to sit. Heliconia brush with pointed flaming red buds, pale green Sisal, and lush plants with circular plastic-like leaves taller than her grew on that side of the mountain.

Sitting down cross-legged, Aisha decided to enjoy the view for a bit longer. She shaded her eyes against the setting sun's light that turned the surface of the water iridescent.

"Oh my!" Aisha's mouth eased in pleasure as she trained her eyes on a particular spot far away in the ocean—the spot where a school of dolphins was splashing and diving in and out of the water!

Aisha reached in her backpack. One of her gloves got caught in the zip and ripped. "Screw this!" Taking off her gloves she bundled them in the backpack.

Aisha was quick to pull out her DSLR with eighteen pixels and mega zoom. She had a great camera but was a sloppy photographer.

Aisha's philosophy was simple. I will take a thousand bad pictures if that is what it takes to get one good shot! Much like how I tackle life.

With excited fingers, Aisha uncapped the lens. The cover slipped between her fingers and rolled away to the nearby underbrush.

Aisha shrugged. She aimed her lens on the dolphins. For the next several minutes she leaned back and forward, went from squatting on her bums to sitting on her knees to lying flat on her stomach, all the while her fingers pressing the button on her camera that made sounds like the buzzing wings of a hummingbird.

After nearly ten minutes, Aisha held her camera aside and finally rested. She had maxed out on taking pictures even going by her 1:1000 ratio. The front of Aisha's jeans and her shirt were grubby and dusty as if she had just been in a sandstorm, but she didn't care. She just sat there watching the dolphins until they were gone. Aisha turned to put her camera back.

"Sheesh! The cover."

Aisha remembered the cap that had rolled away from her. Hoisting her backpack, she went in the direction it had rolled in. Aisha moved the brushes aside and stepped in the foliage searching for it. She moved the low-lying leaves with her stick to spot the black circular cover.

After some more prodding, she finally saw it a few feet ahead from her. "You little piece of shit, you are quick!" Grinning, Aisha picked it up and capped the lens and slid it back in her backpack.

As she turned around to go back, she saw something that made her pause—a certain shade of green color that seemed incongruous among the natural green. A narcotic-sniffing dog could not be as curious as Aisha Khatri.

A few sweeps of brushes and overhanging branches, and Aisha saw it and she stood there transfixed.

"What the hell?" Aisha moved closer to her discovery.

A minivan painted in olive army green was covered with leaves and dust yet was in good condition. The exterior held dust but no proof of neglect like rust or dents.

"Did you parachute yourself here?" Aisha said as she walked around the van. "Aha!"

She saw the narrow path ahead of the van. She walked down on it. Aisha was gazing at a small and steep dirt road that went down to the beach and then disappeared in trees and came up again on the other side connecting with the fisherman village. However, the road going down was tricky with a sheer drop on either side.

One must be a damn good driver to go down this route!

Aisha went back to the van and glanced inside through the driver's side window. She saw nothing but the reflection of her head. The glass was heavily tinted on both the driver and the passenger's side. A weird smell had her attention.

Aisha crinkled her nose and moved around the van, sniffing. It was strongest at the rear near the double back door. Aisha sniffed some more.

"Bleach! So much bleach." Aisha waved her hand in front of her nose. Casting furtive glances, Aisha grasped the handle of the van, forgetting her hands were bare.

Chapter 26

Aisha howled. Millions of needles attacked her head like a herd of predators ripping the skin off bones. The blood throbbed in her temples fiercely and the electric pressure behind her eyes increased with every passing second. Aisha was sure her skull was about to explode.

Cleaving pain washed Aisha's body causing her to fall to her knees. Her teeth bit hard into her lower lip, drawing blood, and her eyes clenched tightly, fighting the horror those screams ricocheting between her ears continued to invoke.

Aisha pressed both against her hands against her temples. "Stop!" She pleaded.

All breath seemed to desert her body. She bent over gagging and repeating, "Stop, please stop! Go away!" The pressure into her head forced some bile into her mouth. Her body rocked.

"Go on! Leave me alone. . ."

Eyeless faces, mouths with sharp pointed teeth open in agonized screams flew down at Aisha, surrounding her from all sides, cutting off all light.

Aisha clawed the air in front of her and somehow managed to stagger to her feet. She ran blindly into the foliage and burst out on the other side.

She stumbled around unseeing and finally stopped. She opened her eyes. The faces were gone. Aisha saw herself standing on the ledge, inches away from a fatal drop.

"Shit!" Aisha backed away, her breathing harsh. The faces were gone, but their pain continued to wash over her. Pale and cold, her eyes haunted, Aisha wrapped her arms around her torso and waited.

Soon Aisha started muttering. Things she had eaten today, the places she had visited in Goa, the names of all books she had ever read.

Kabir's face popped in her head and stayed. Aisha felt drawn to his dark gaze. The pressure in Aisha's head receded. Her insides stopped heaving. Some color came back in her face and her mouth tasted less acidic. Aisha pulled a few deep breaths. The screams became silent, her mind calm.

Taking out her water bottle, Aisha guzzled water and upturned the remaining drops on her face.

Aisha wiped her face, her hands still shaking. What the heck? The voices were so loud. It's never been like this. It was as if all those girls were standing next to me.

Aisha stilled and then started pacing. "Girls...did I think girls? More than one?" She blinked her eyes.

Unbidden, the hotel concierge's words came to her mind. Panaji is not safe at this time of the year. Too much crime, murders . . . of women!

A twig snapped behind her.

Aisha spun around. A fat squirrel ran past her legs.

A thought clicked in Aisha's head. *A morgue van! It must have been a morgue van or an ambulance.* She bent over, resting her hands on her knees. Her expression relieved. "Yes, that's it. It has happened before. The explanation is simple." Her laugh was shaky.

Aisha recalled an earlier incident when she was eighteen. A doctor—a family friend—had visited them in his nursing home ambulance. When the doctor was leaving Aisha had accidentally placed her hand on the van's back door. Her world had exploded similiarly.

But there had been no faces, no screams.

Aisha straightened. *Rubbish! I'm overthinking. It's definitely an ambulance, thus the overpowering smell of bleach.* Aisha put her hand on her chest. "That's it, an ambulance!" Her smile was relieved even as her eyes didn't lose the anxious expression.

Something pushed Aisha to retrace her steps to the abandoned van. Stopping at some distance, Aisha clicked a picture or two with her phone and then made her way back to the ledge. She noticed that the van did not have any number plates.

Chapter 27

Kabir stood with his digital technician of three years, Uzaafar Khan. "Uzi, frame this shot more like the model reclining on the horizon with the sun positioned under her back. The sun kind of seeps out of the hollow of her back."

"We can, but we will have to hurry. The sun is almost gone. Or we come back tomorrow." Uzi pulled his starfish cap lower over his ears.

Uzi was fond of his caps. He had one of every kind, even if bizarre. The only time Uzi's hat had been confiscated on the set was when he came wearing a cap with a pair of boobs fixed on either side.

"No. Tomorrow and the day after is reserved mostly for the look book and some cover shots near the villa. Then I pack the models off."

"Okay, get them ready." Uzi went to speak to his assistant.

Kabir addressed the models resting under a canopy nearby. "Kiara, we will have you lie on that table. I want Moira, Charlie, and Porschi in a triangular formation around the table." Then he turned to Vikas. "Have Kiara helped up there and we are draping the pink and golden fabric over her. Put a rush on it."

"Boss." Vikas left to do as ordered.

Kabir walked to the models. Along with a crewmember, he helped Kiara get comfortable on the table. "Better?"

"Yes, thanks! Is my make-up okay? Not too dark, right?" Kiara gracefully moved her legs to the table.

"It's perfect. It complements the potpourri collection." Kabir tried not to stare at her face. It reminded him of Aisha; she had a tendency of slipping in his thoughts at the most unusual times. "You all are looking drop-dead gorgeous." Kabir gave one of his usual grim smiles to all of them.

"Charlie and Moira, you give me sides poses. Porschi, please angle yourself over Kiara's torso, just hovering. Kiara, you give me a smooth bodyline, left knee bent and a melancholic look. Porschi your look is angry. Kiara, hold your hands up in an intertwined pose, look up at the sky, wondrous. Charlie, throw your head back and then look at the camera, raw and intense. Questions?"

The models were seasoned; they understood what Kabir wanted. He walked back to Uzi. "Are we ready?"

"Yup! Take a look."

Kabir looked at models through the powerful 200-megapixel camera positioned on the tripod. "The composition looks good.

Just make sure to drop the frame half an inch. Dada move that last reflector in." He clapped his hand to get everyone's attention. "We are shooting in fifteen seconds."

The make-up team hurried the final touch-up on the models. The prop teams moved back.

"Models, positions. Shooting in five!" Uzi's assistant yelled on the megaphone. "Five, four, three, two, one."

"Hold!" Uzi, grinning, slapped the side of his cap. He turned to Kabir. "We have a new model. Look."

"What?" Kabir peered at the monitor. "You have got to be fucking kidding me." He stomped closer to the models. Kabir was gritting his teeth. "Kiara, your aunt!"

Puzzled, Kiara got up and turned to glance behind her. "Boo?"

Aisha waved tentatively. "Hi! We . . . had plans?" She chewed her lower lip.

"Get out of my shot!" Kabir bit out.

Aisha felt her cheeks redden. Everyone glared at her except Kiara.

"It's okay. I'll just go back." Aisha spun around.

"Where are you going?"

Aisha's look was stony as she pointed her chin up at the man who was staring down at her.

"Getting out of your shot, as you so politely requested." Aisha retorted.

"Boo!" Kia's tone was cautionary.

"Instead of going down five kilometers to the beach, you could simply take a few steps this way and stand with the others here." Kabir was holding to his patience by a thin line, a very thin and fragile line.

Aisha stared back at him, her eyes narrowed in defiance.

"Boo!" Kiara's voice was pleading.

"Fine, whatever." Aisha took a step forward. The short climb from where Aisha stood to the flatland was steep. Kabir bent down and offered his hand to her.

"Yeah, right!" Aisha sneered. Using her stick, she took a few quick steps and climbed the steep side.

Kabir's eyes glinted as he straightened, dropping his hand.

"Oh my God, what happened to your clothes?" Kiara murmured. "Did you fight with a bear?"

"I'm about to. Watch me." Aisha griped loudly enough for a certain someone to hear. "Looking good, Kia!" Aisha haughtily walked to join the others near the canopy.

"Do you have anyone else coming to meet you, Kiara?" Kabir could not resist that jibe, watching the haughty woman stalking away.

"Only a bear." Aisha called back.

Kabir felt his mouth twitch at her impudent response, but he bit down on the soft lining of his inner cheek and walked back. He got to his former position. "Ready, Uzi?"

Uzi gave the thumbs up sign.

One of the nearby crew members got a bout of sneezes. "Get him something, someone, please!" Kabir hollered, turning his head and then he saw what was making the man sneeze.

Aisha was standing in front of the man and brushing the dust off her clothes.

"Do you mind?"

Aisha glanced up and saw everyone staring at her.

"Your dusting is making the poor man sneeze his life out. Is it too much to ask you to stop?" Kabir's words, spoken with exaggerated slowness, had the desired effect. Aisha stopped, and her cheeks turned red as if touched by the scarlet hue of the sun.

"Sorry!" she said gruffly to the man who was stuffing his nose in his T-shirt and putting some distance between her and him.

Kabir went back to doing his job. A sudden thought came to him. The way she had come up was one of his favorite hikes and he had done it innumerable times. It was also very tricky and treacherous. "Did you fall down there?"

"No." Aisha's retorted. Her expression was like 'you wish!'

"Then the dust on—"

"We are losing the light, Kabir!" Uzi interrupted.

Kabir snapped his attention back to his work. "Models, ready?"

They gave him the thumbs up. "Shoot!" Kabir ordered, focusing on work instead.

Chapter 28

Aisha, who had been glaring at Kabir's back, looked down at the ground, her eyes narrowed.

The light around her dimmed unexpectedly. Out of the darkness, letters came rushing at her. They arranged and rearranged themselves.

Thoi.

Julie.

Nafeesa.

Aisha jerked, and the darkness fell away. *What is going on? What are these names?* Aisha raised her head, disoriented. Her heartbeat was racing. *This place is driving me nuts. Why am I so cold?* She rubbed her forearms.

Sounds of clapping distracted her. Everyone around her was applauding something or someone.

"What is going on?" Aisha asked the woman standing next to her.

"Uzi," she pointed at the short man next to Kabir, "when he takes off his cap, it's a sign that the shoot is over. Pack up!"

"Oh!" Aisha's glance clashed with Kabir's. He was watching her.

Aisha steered her eyes away from him. It had been hard not to look at the man dressed in all black, running the show. Kabir knew his work and he did it well. Few words from him were all it took to steering a crew of fifty or more, including the diva models.

Aisha's gaze somehow found its way back to Kabir who was studying something on the laptop.

Uzi, Vikas, Amee and two more people were gathered around him even as he stood a head taller in the crowd. All of them huddled around the laptop, studying the pictures taken.

Aisha ran her eyes over Kabir's head full of dark hair with slight gray on the sides. A smooth wide forehead, dark lashes that covered eyes that could laser a person, a long sharp nose, a pronounced jawline that served as a red flag to his mercurial temper and a mouth, perpetually clamped in a line.

Abruptly, Kabir looked up straight into her eyes. Aisha felt jolted. Something passed between them. Her mouth felt dry.

A man carrying a reflector passed between them.

Aisha felt unshackled. Blindly, she headed for Kiara who was coming toward her.

"So, Boo, what did you think?"

Aisha helped Kiara sit in a chair under the canopy. She dropped her backpack near Kiara.

"You were fabulous. Very poised. I didn't know you were such a pro, Kia!" Kiara could not hide her flush. "I'm sorry, I have been a bitch about your modeling. You are a natural," Aisha exhaled. This was hard for her too. "Just like your mom."

Kiara gazed at her, surprised. She blinked her eyes to hide the sudden sheen in them. "Boo, you do pick your moments."

Aisha's expression was wry. "I know. I have a knack for timing. Remember that snot-faced, zit-popping machine Roy?"

"How can I forget Roy?" Kiara covered her eyes. "You interrupted my first kiss."

Aisha laughed. "You can thank me."

"Thank you." Kiara did a mock bow.

"Noted. Now, let's get you into some proper clothes." Aisha glanced around. She waved to the lady who was chaperoning Kiara. "Kia's clothes, please."

"So, what happened to *your* clothes?"

"Oh this?" Aisha glanced at her jeans and shirt that still held some streaks of dust. "Nothing!"

"You were clicking photographs again, weren't you?"

Aisha blew a raspberry. "What? No—"

"Photographs?" A smooth voice purred. Kabir's voice!

Chapter 29

Aisha's innards cringed.

"Oh, hey Kabir, join us." Kiara's smile was mischievous as she sucked in her cheeks. "Boo loves to take pictures. Don't you, Boo?"

Aisha made a strangled sound in her throat. She refused to look at the man standing next to them.

Unfortunately, Aisha had not raised her niece to be a quitter. "Kabir, you should see Boo's pictures." She ignored Aisha's sharp intake of breath. "Like right now, while you wait for the team to load up and for us to change."

"Sure!" Kabir drawled.

"No! No!" Aisha shot warning glances at Kiara. "Please, I'm sure you have something else to do." She did not raise her eyes higher than the topmost button of Kabir's shirt.

"Actually, no! I'm free." Kabir reached out and grabbed a plastic chair and kept it behind Aisha. "Sit."

Aisha gave him a tightlipped, narrow look from the side of her eyes.

Kabir's eyes glinted. "Please!"

"Here is her camera." Kiara had unzipped Aisha's backpack and held out the camera to Kabir.

"Kia!" Aisha tried to grab it but Kabir pulled it away from her reach.

"I'll be back." Kiara got up slowly from her chair and hobbled away to change her clothes, giving a wink to Aisha.

What the hell?

Kabir had taken the seat Kiara had vacated. He turned the camera on. "They can't be that bad."

Aisha sat down with a thump. She lunged, hoping to get the camera by surprise but Kabir pulled it away. Again!

"Like I just said, they can't be that bad." He pressed the play button.

"They are perfect." Aisha sat back, primly placing her hands on her knees. Her gloves were back on.

Kabir pointedly glanced at her hands, even as he fiddled with the camera.

"Germs. I have issues with germs remember?"

"Hmm, is that the only thing you have issues with?" Kabir glanced up, his look teasing.

Aisha felt warm. She clamped down on a smile. Kabir went back to studying her photography.

Aisha kept glancing at Kabir's bent head as he studied her pictures. He seemed riveted. Aisha tried not to flash a smug grin.

After a few minutes, Kabir glanced at her, part incredulous part amused. "These are so bad! Seriously crap."

Aisha's mouth formed a surprised 'O.' She managed to snatch her camera back. "No, they are not. Not all of them."

"Yes, *all* of them," Kabir grinned.

The smile of the Devil! "You know, shooting models who are beautiful is easy, but shooting nature—"

Kabir grabbed her camera back and got up.

"What are you doing?" Aisha muttered, jerking to her feet.

Aiming it at sea, Kabir put his eye to the viewfinder.

"Idiot." Aisha hissed with annoyance.

Others on the set were stopping to watch them.

Kabir kept clicking, adjusting the lens, switching it from horizontal to vertical. Then he thrust it in front of her face. "Have a look." Saying that, he stalked off.

Aisha snorted at his back. "Whatever! Jackass."

Out of curiosity, she ducked her head and started viewing the pictures Kabir had taken. They were beautiful.

It appeared like the land was extending straight into the ocean. The brown of the earth and the dark blue of the water blended seamlessly and the drooping palm tree with its variegated yellow and green leaves added a dash of striking color.

What the! How did he get all that? Aisha resumed her seat and turned to look up at the scene Kabir had framed.

"And?"

Aisha schooled her expression, realizing Kabir had circled back to her. "And whatever! You are just doing your job, I guess." She did not raise her head.

Kabir dropped back in the chair and leaned toward her. Aisha raised her eyes. Their faces were close.

"I will give you lessons for free. If you..." Kabir paused.

Aisha felt a frisson of awareness toward him. Her eyes widened and Kabir's grew hooded.

"If?" Aisha wet her suddenly dry lips.

Kabir's hooded gaze followed the movement of her tongue. "If you..." His eyes stayed locked on her lips.

Confusion and anticipation widened Aisha's eyes. She dipped her face toward Kabir, for it was a strain to hold it up. "Convince Kiara to go for dinner with me?"

Aisha froze momentarily and then she sat back with a thump. *So, this is what an ice bucket challenge must feel like.* She swallowed thickly.

Kabir sat back.

Aisha could feel Kabir's eyes on her face, but she refused to acknowledge his glance.

"So, I'm guessing your silence means yes."

"Kabir, the buses are loaded." Vikas interrupted them.

Wordlessly, Aisha got up. She grabbed her backpack and pushed her camera in it and closed the bag with a snap.

Kabir too rose.

Aisha left them and moved to the side, waiting for Kiara. She did not have to wait for long.

"You ride with me in van, Boo," Kiara said, limping using a crutch.

"Sure, let me get that." Aisha relieved Kiara of her bag.

Aisha took Kiara's oversized tote. She slugged a bag and Kiara's tote on her back. They kept slipping.

"Give it to me," Kabir appeared from behind. His hand extended forward.

Aisha recoiled. "No!"

Kiara raised an eyebrow at her tone. "So, did you see my aunt's pictures?"

"They were stunning." Kabir murmured, an edge to his voice.

Aisha walked next to them, silently.

"So, Kiara, how about you and I go out for dinner tonight?"

Aisha stiffened. He wasn't kidding!

"Sorry, Kabir. Boo and I had dinner plans. Rain check?" Kiara flashed an apologetic smile.

Vikas, who was waiting near the van, held the door open for Kiara.

"Well, she can tag along!" Kabir purred smoothly.

Aisha bristled. "Because we already have plans and you want to join us, you will be the one tagging along," Her smile was taunting.

Kabir smoothly turned to Kiara. "So, dinner around eight." He waved at the models in the van. "See you all at the villa. Excellent work, everyone." Kabir and his assistant headed to the black SUV parked ahead.

Kiara and Aisha climbed in and Aisha took a window seat behind her niece, not really in the mood to talk. She did not understand the melancholy knocking on her mind. Aisha watched the outside, her glance stony. Then she saw him.

A man in dark blue jeans, a white shirt and a gray sports jacket was standing at some distance. He sported a thin pencil mustache and his eyes were hidden by a dark pair of Ray-Bans. Aisha stared at him, wondering what about the man had caught her eye.

It's the way he stands—back straight, legs slightly apart, chin up. His arms relaxed at his side, but he seems wired, like he could break into a run any second.

Aisha saw the man take off his glasses. His eyes honed on Kiara sitting ahead of her. As he was about to glance away, his eyes snagged with Aisha's.

His eyes narrowed when he realized she had been watching him. He put his shades back on and walked past their van.

Chapter 30

Kriti Villa

That Evening

"What are you writing? Your face looks weird."

Aisha lurched her head up. "What?"

"Your face looked weird, Boo. What are you writing?"

Aisha glanced down at the pad in her hand—the pad she had picked up from the side table.

The hair on Aisha's nape stood up and her skin started cooling. She read what she had written.

Thoi.

Julie.

Nafeesa.

Sandhya.

Four names now? What the heck, man! Aisha tried to keep her expression casual for Kiara was in the room. Technically, she was in Kiara's room, getting ready for dinner.

"Just doodling. What was my expression like?" Aisha strove to keep her voice casual as she ripped out the page from the pad.

Looking in the mirror, Kiara plucked her eyebrows. "I don't know. Very intense, like you were angry. Chillax Boo, it's all rad." Kiara went back to her eyebrows.

"Chillax? Rad? Are these even words or just sounds your generation makes?" Aisha mumbled, staring at the page in her hand. She slowly crumpled it and tossed it in the trash can.

Who are these girls? Why am I obsessing over them? Should I talk to Suvabrata about this?

Aisha rubbed her arms.

"Found it!" Kiara held up a blue V-neck high-waist ball flare dress.

"It's rather short, Kia."

"Nope, its perfect." Kiara put the dress on her bed and then started taking things out of her vanity and putting them into a smaller bag.

"Do you like him? That Kabir?" Aisha chewed her thumbnail.

Kiara took her time answering the question. "He is successful and handsome."

Aisha inhaled sharply. She wasn't relishing her niece's tone or her wishful expression.

"Okay, he is a tad older than me, but you always say I am older than my age. So, he and I should work by that logic." Kiara zipped up the smaller bag.

"Kia, he is even older than me."

"So what? You are merely eleven years older than me."

"Kiara Khatri!"

Kiara looked up to reveal a smile. "Gotcha!"

"Shit! Don't scare me like that ever." Aisha stretched. She sniffed at her armpits. "I need a shower."

"You are such a lady. But seriously though, no promises regarding Kabir. We will see how the evening pans out, okay?"

Over my dead body! "Sure," Aisha nodded.

This grown-up Kiara is going to give me ulcers, stones, and hemorrhoids and all in one night.

Getting up, Aisha walked to the window in the room. *I need some air.*

She parted the sheer curtains fluttering in the breeze. The window was wide open.

"Gosh, Kia!" Aisha turned to pull the sliding part of the window to close it. She froze.

Chapter 31

A dark form darted and disappeared around the side of the house.

This time Aisha was sure she had seen a man's back disappearing. She noticed some models walking back into the house from the beach.

Was it someone passing by or someone lurking outside the window?

Aisha shut and locked the window. "Kiara, can you please keep your windows and door locked? Don't be so careless." She pulled the sheer curtains firmly over them and the thicker dark ones too.

"Sure," Kiara grabbed a fresh pair of undergarments from her suitcase.

"Boo, can you use the shower upstairs? There are spare bedrooms that are not being used. Go up the stairs and to your left."

"Are you mad? I'm not bathing anywhere but in this bathroom." Aisha's voice was firm.

"It is 7:40 already. Both of us can't get ready by eight. Kabir is my boss and he is very punctual. Please, please." Kiara put her arms around Aisha. "I can't climb the stairs. Please, Boo! Please, please."

Aisha started laughing. "Behave, Kia. You are not five that I will fall in—"

Kiara tightened her arms. "Please, please."

Aisha laughed and pulled back. "Okay, fine, just stop squeezing the life out of me."

"You can use any bathroom. This house is just a big fat hostel right now. People walking in and out of rooms all the time."

That is why it is so easy for people to walk in and out of this place unnoticed. Horrible security! Aisha's eyes wandered back to the window.

"Okay, so you are wearing this and I'm wearing this!"

"What?" Aisha glanced at the clothes Kiara was pointing at. "You got that blue thing for me?" Her frown was dark.

"You are not going for dinner in your shabby clothes." Kiara pouted.

"Just give a ratty T-shirt of yours."

"Oh, c'mon. When was the last time you took time off, Boo? When was the last time you did anything for yourself? Your life is me, Dada and work all the time, every day. You need a break. We are in Goa and in a fancy, swanky villa. Let's dress up. Let's have some fun. Let's party?"

Aisha rubbed her face. "Kia, why?"

"Please, please, please," Kiara came to her, arms extended.

"Okay, stop right there! Fine, I'll do it."

"There's a make-up kit with the dress." Kiara clasped her hands and turned away. "I want some pictures of you and me."

"Can I be the one taking pictures?" Aisha teased and then sobered, remembering the most recent critic of her photography. *Jerk!*

"Not a fat chance." Kiara handed Aisha her clothes. "Now, go. Remember, up the stairs and then a left. And your time starts now."

"Haha!" Aisha let Kia push her to the door. "Lock this behind me."

"Yeah, yeah, go!" Kiara gently pushed Aisha out of the room and shut the door and locked it with a resounding click. "There, it's locked."

"Of course, you would lock me out." Grumbling, Aisha took slow steps in the hall.

Katy Perry was loudly 'Roar'ing somewhere from above, but no one she knew was in the living room or dining room behind her. Just some household help moved around.

Aisha went up the wide, curved marble steps. She hugged her things tightly. At the landing, Aisha came upon a glass wall that overlooked the garden. "Wow!" The view of the lush landscaped garden was stunning. A circular gray seal with a design embedded in the center of the garden caught her eye.

Aisha crinkled her brow. *I have seen it somewhere.* She followed Kiara's instructions and ended up in front of a shut white door.

Tentatively, Aisha opened it and went inside. It was quiet in this part of the house. Aisha's eyes skated over the elegant living room with silk gray and brown furniture with splashes of indigo blue in artistically placed cushions and thick curtains. Her feet sank in the thick and soft gray carpet.

"Damn!"

Aisha saw that her shoes had left a brown stain on the carpet. She hastily stepped off the carpet and bent down, her hand outstretched to brush off the dusty mark. Her fingers lost their grip and the make-up bag slipped out of her hands and hit the floor.

"Who's there?"

"No one!" Aisha replied and then winced.

Going by his voice, Kabir sounded close.

Chapter 32

Soft footfalls later, Kabir appeared at the door of the room that faced the living room. "What are you doing here?" His dark eyes were narrowed, and his mouth was clamped in irritation.

Aisha could only stare. It wasn't Kabir's irritation that had her tongue-tied. It was the fact that he was bare-chested, showing off his muscled ripped torso with dark nipples, flat stomach with a thin line of black hair disappearing in the front of his jeans. His jaw was covered in white foam.

Aisha blushed from head to toe. She focused on picking up her things.

"Asking again, what are you doing here?"

"Kiara." Aisha cleared her throat. "She sent me up here to shower."

Kabir walked over to her and stopped right in front of her.

Dammit, he even has perfect feet!

"Shower, with me?" Kabir drawled from somewhere above her head.

Asshole! Aisha cussed on hearing the amusement in his voice. She took a whole thirty seconds gathering her things and composure.

Trying to keep her expression neutral, Aisha got to her feet with as much dignity as she could muster. She could do nothing about the color running riot over her cheeks or her racing pulse. *I will be super aloof!* "She sent me to one of the spare rooms upstairs. She is getting ready downstairs."

Kabir put his hands on the side of his lean hips. "For our date?" His tone, like his words, was purposely goading.

Aisha tried not to let her eyes wander anywhere below his neck and above his nostrils.

Very limited options. Forgot the mouth. "I don't know this place. I'll just go back the way I came." *Aloof. Super chilled.* She turned around.

"Stop."

Aisha kept walking to the door.

A hand appeared on her elbow. "Did you not hear me?" Kabir's voice was soft but clipped.

Aisha swung her head, her glance patronizing. "I don't respond to threats."

Kabir moved into her personal space. Aisha was forced to look up at him. He was close enough, so she could smell the masculine salt of his skin mixed with the spiced cologne. "What do you respond to?" He stared into Aisha's eyes, his voice smooth like melted butter.

For a second, Aisha forgot to breathe and then a chuckle escaped her mouth and her shoulders twitched. Another chuckle. Within seconds, Aisha was laughing. Hold-your-side kind of laughing!

In response, Kabir mouth moved side to side and his eyes crinkled at the corner. "What's so funny?" His dark eyes reflected some of Aisha's amusement.

"You." Aisha wiped her eyes sobering. "Standing in shaving foam, acting all seductive."

"Seductive? Is that what you thought I was doing . . . with you?" Kabir tilted his head to the side and fixed his amused eyes on her.

Aisha lost some of her humor but not all. "Uh!" Her answer was a quick short nod.

Kabir reached out and held Aisha's arms, holding her in place. Bending down slowly, keeping his eyes locked with hers, he rubbed his cheek slowly against hers. The foam was soft and his stubble prickly.

Aisha was not prepared for the intimate feel of his skin on hers. She inhaled sharply, and her lips trembled. She felt like she had dived into a pool of warm water that smelled heavenly.

"Stop!" Aisha moved back. Her voice was husky.

Kabir straightened. Aisha averted her face from the broad expanse of his smooth light brown skin and dark hair that peppered over his chest. He was so close, Aisha's hands itched to touch that smooth skin. "I have to go." Mumbling, she turned blindly for the door.

"Are you a virgin?"

"None of your damn business!" Aisha bit out.

Dropping his hands down, Kabir literally took a step back. "Oh!"

For a few seconds they just stood there, still.

Aisha was the first to speak in a strangled voice. "What is that 'Oh' supposed to mean?"

Kabir treaded in the direction of the room he had emerged from. "Nothing. You should get going. There is a spare room with a shower right down the hall. The last door on the right." he called, disappearing in his room.

#

"**She is** a virgin! She's a virgin?" Kabir slid the razor down the sides of his cheek. He stopped and propped his wrist on the porcelain sink. "A virgin at her age?"

He resumed his shaving. As a principle, and in effort to never let things get complicated with the fairer sex, he only sought the company of experienced women who were looking for a 'no strings attached' kind of relationship.

Aisha's laugh had taken room in his ears. Her laugh was the kind that made one want to join in.

I nearly kissed her! Kabir's mouth hungered at the memory of how close Aisha's fleshy lips had been to his. He had been trying to tease Aisha as she was mocking him but then he had not bargained for how soft her skin felt under his calloused fingers, how entrancing her eyes were up close, how her smell made his mouth water for a taste of her and how Aisha's closeness affected him. He had not wanted to let her go. His arousal strained against his jeans.

Kabir wasn't remotely interested in Kiara. But Aisha was a different story. Attraction, anger, humor, even tenderness!

In two days she has made me feel more than I have in years.

Kabir's hand stilled. His past broke into the present. His eyes hardened, and his mouth clenched into a thin line. *Aisha must go. She has to.*

Mindlessly, he pressed the blade deeper in his cheek. A drop of blood emerged, coloring the white foam red. Kabir did not flinch. He was used to blood, but usually it wasn't his.

Chapter 33

Rushing inside the spare room, Aisha locked the door behind her. She touched her cheek and then brought her fingers down. She saw the white foam on her fingertips. Shuddering, she closed her eyes.

What is happening? Why do I react to him like that? I work with good looking men; so many actors, directors. All powerful men but why does that Kabir affect me so much?

Flinging her things on the bed, she went in the bathroom.

Ten minutes later, Aisha rushed out in a towel, her hair dripping water down her bare back. "Late! Late!" She dried and stuffed herself into the dress.

With one hand she blow-dried her hair and with the other she applied mascara, nearly coating her cornea instead of the lashes. She folded her used clothes in a neat bundle and stuffed them in the empty drawer of the nightstand. Aisha grabbed the bracelet from the make-up bag. *Kiara is so thoughtful.*

"To a fun evening!" Aisha muttered and tugged the door handle. The door wouldn't open. "What the hell?" She checked the bolt to make sure it was unlatched. Aisha fiddled with the handle and pulled it with all her strength. The door quivered but stayed shut. *Someone has locked me in the room!*

"HELLO! HELLOOO!"

Aisha banged with her fists, but she already knew that no one would hear her because of the loud infernal music in the hall outside.

"Dammit!" Aisha thumped her fist one last time and then flopped back on the bed. "Why would anyone lock me in here?" Then her eyes widened and then narrowed. "Oh, that horrible man!" Aisha paced the room. "Kabir must have done this so he can seduce Kiara. I will kill him!" Her steps quick like her thoughts.

Aisha paused, and her gaze shifted to the wide windows.

She ran and unlatched them. They easily swung out. Aisha looked down at the grassy area underneath the windows. *I'm only on the second floor.* A plan began shaping in her head. Aisha ran back to bed and tugged the duvet to the floor. She pulled the sheets off the bed and twisted them into a rope like form. "The end justifies the means, Kabir Rana!" Running back to the window, she threw the twisted sheets down. The ends dangled a few feet away from the grass.

Aisha tied the other end around the curtain rod above the window. She gave the sheet a hard tug. The rod did not move much. "Good, you shall do long enough for me to slide to the ground."

Aisha picked up her wedges and tossed them one by one out of the window. She heard them fall in a soft thud.

"Kia, I'm coming!"

Chapter 34

Whistling a song by the Scorpions, his favorite band at one time, Kabir walked back into the house. The slight ocean breeze tossed his front hair and brushed his face. Quite a few parties were going on in the adjoining beach and multiple bonfires bestowed an orange glow on the sky, drowning the silvery points of twinkling stars. On such nights, Kabir would usually hole up in his room, put on Elgar's Cello Concerto and read a memoir.

But not today! Today he had fallen in a trap of his own planning. His feelings for tonight's dinner were ambivalent.

A part of him wanted to bait Aisha and woo Kiara with words and wine, and another part of him wanted to yell 'to hell with everything' and bed the first woman he could find.

Aisha! Kabir gritted his teeth and smacked a low brush he passed.

Nervous energy was building in him and he did not like that. It was always a sign of a storm on the horizon. And he hated storms since that fateful night twenty-one years ago.

Kabir followed the path around the pool.

After Kriti's death, what had kept him sane was Shreya's advice: Don't let yourself feel too much. And he had followed that advice every single minute of his life. But somehow, Lavina had slipped past his defenses and made him happy. But the love, the happiness had been fleeting. Post Lavina's suicide, Kabir had reached a point of no return and had nearly taken his life but Shreya had saved him . . . again.

Kabir was jerked out of his thoughts as something soft fell on his face. "What the hell?"

He looked up and saw the twisted sheet fluttering out of the window. Kabir took a few steps back to get a better look. Good thinking! A women's footwear came sailing out of the window and landed close to him, then came the other.

Kabir continued to look up and in seconds he saw a slim fair leg hook itself over the windowsill followed by the other. Once the feet were planted securely on the window ledge the woman appeared out on the window. Kabir instantly recognized the blue dress.

Aisha! He had seen the blue dress in her hands earlier. She had back crossed the dress between the legs and tucked it in the front.

She is going to jump off the ledge! Kabir felt fear and anger swell in him. His stomach lurched. He ate his shout for he did not want to startle Aisha into falling. The consequence was too fearful to imagine.

Images of Kriti and Lavina lying dead on the ground, their bodies bent grotesquely, flashed in front of his eyes. "What the hell are you doing?" He growled softly.

A sharp intake of breath. Aisha glanced down even as she held the window edge tightly. "What are you doing here?"

"Get the fuck back inside!" Kabir's hands curled inward and sweat emerged above his lips.

Aisha narrowed her eyes down at him. "Don't talk-" She slipped. A startled shriek escaped her mouth as she hurtled down to the ground.

Kabir had less than a second to react. He stepped forward, legs wide, his arms outstretched, hoping to catch her. Her legs slammed in his chest as she slipped further onto him. Kabir staggered even as his arms went around Aisha's body reflexively. They both fell back, she on him. Kabir's body cushioned Aisha from hitting the ground.

"Oh my God!" Aisha yelped and turned in his arms. She pushed him back on the ground. Her body pressed into his from breast to knee. "You saved me!"

Kabir grabbed her by the shoulders and pulled her into him. Their faces were inches apart. "What the hell were you doing? You could have fallen—"

"I did fall." Aisha poked him in the chest, still sprawled on top of him, her legs straddling his. "And it is all your fault!" She sounded amused.

Kabir let his head fall back on the grass, her body was making him very aware that Aisha had curves that were all too arousing. "Get off me."

"What?" Aisha wrinkled her brow and then she felt his male body under her. "Oh! Oh!" She slithered to the side and then got to her feet. Self-consciously, she tugged her dress out from the front and glanced around for her shoes.

"You are such an idiot." Kabir ground out, getting to his feet. The bitter taste of fear he had experienced minutes ago came back to him.

"Why are you overreacting? I'm not that heavy and it was just one floor," Aisha replied, sliding her feet in her wedges. "Someone locked me in the room and the music was so loud outside. I kept banging but no one opened the door."

"No one locked you. That latch is faulty. You couldn't call anyone?"

"My cell phone is in Kiara's room." Aisha grumbled.

"Come for the bloody dinner." Kabir bit out and pivoted.

"You are scared of heights?" Aisha taunted. She was still mad at him for the 'virgin' comment.

Kabir paused and slowly turned around to face her. "What did you say?"

"Oh, you poor thing! What if I had been a story above and another story above?" Aisha mocked, raising her hand slowly above her head. "And another story, and another story. High up there and then phhbt!" She teased, throwing her hands downwards and tilting her neck to the side and sticking her tongue out, imitating a death-like pose.

Kabir could not control his rage and he grabbed Aisha, his fingers biting her skin.

A surprised squeak escaped her mouth.

"You fool! You think it is funny plummeting off a building?" He shook her.

Aisha's surprised expression was covered by loose hair that fell on her face.

"You think death is funny?" He continued to shake her, his fingers tighter than bands around her arms.

"Stop it!" Aisha struggled in his hold. "You are hurting me!"

Kabir could not calm the fury permeating his body and mind. "Should I drag to you to top of a building and push you down? You want to fly?" All he saw was Kriti and Lavina's body.

Aisha gasped and then before Kabir could understand what happened, Aisha hooked her leg behind his calf and pulled him down, tripping him. Stunned, he lay on his back and stared up at her.

Aisha hastily retreated from him. "Asshole!" Rubbing her arms, she ran away.

Chapter 35

"**He assaulted** me. I'm calling the police on that mad man!" Walking blindly, Aisha massaged her arms still hurting from the Kabir's biting grip. *He has given me darn bruises. Jerk!*

"Boo!"

Aisha swiveled toward the sound. She saw Kiara standing at the back gate, leaning on a crutch. Aisha stomped in her direction.

"You look mad. What happened?"

"I could seriously kill that man!" Aisha stopped near her niece.

"What happened to your dress? And why do you have grass stuck in your hair?"

"I got locked in the room, had to jump off the second story and if that wasn't enough, your dick of a boss nearly killed me." Aisha brushed her hair with quick impatient strokes.

"What? You jumped off a floor?" Kiara ran concerned eyes over Aisha.

"Excuse me, Kiara!"

Aisha and Kiara turned at the interruption.

It was one of the assistants. "Kabir sends you his apologies. He won't be joining you. But he said you should go ahead and eat. The cabana has been set on the beach."

"Thanks, Mohini!" Kiara nodded at her. Then she raised her eyebrow at Aisha. "Shall we eat?"

"Whatever!" Aisha's tone was snippy.

She helped her niece to the white collapsible cabana that had been set up on the beach.

"Sexy!" Kiara breathed as Aisha helped her sit on one of the silk ottomans.

Aisha grunted, not the least bit taken by the beautiful interior of the cabana. The floor was a wooden deck laid on the sand. A thick shaggy beige carpet covered most of the deck. Several silk red colored ottomans were grouped around it and on one end was a cream divan with red cushions stacked on each side. Small decorative lights went around the top of structure and the side. In front of them was the opaque dark sea with small white waves foaming and crashing a few feet away.

"I'm famished, Boo," Kiara removed the covers off the bronze dishes already placed on the table. "Oh my God, look at this spread."

Usually a glutton, Aisha gave a dull smile to the Chicken cafreal, rava fried fish, hummus and pita chips, tomato and rice pilaf, lamb kabobs and bebinca.

"Okay, I will eat, and you tell me exactly what happened. You rarely get angry but when you do, you have a tough time letting it go. So, tell me what happened between you and Kabir?"

Exhaling, Aisha began.

When Aisha finished, Kiara sighed. "Boo!"

Aisha frowned. "You are feeling sorry for that cad?"

Kiara put down her plate. "His wife committed suicide by jumping from their apartment on the twelfth floor. Broke her neck and shattered her skull."

"Oh!" Aisha bit the inside of her cheek. She cringed remembering the way she had mimicked a dead person.

"It gets worse." Kiara swallowed. "His sister fell off the terrace and died nearly two decades ago."

Robbed of words, Aisha could only stare. Finally, she asked. "You are not conning me?"

"Most of the people that work with Kabir have been with him for ages. Some of us know about the sister because one of the models, she is not here for this shoot, but her family knows

Kabir's family for generations. He is from a royal lineage. The Ranas. He's a freaking Prince."

Kiara's words jogged Aisha's memory. "Rana. That name sounded familiar. Wait, Sirsa!" Aisha gasped. "That's why that emblem in the front garden seemed familiar. Last to last year, while hunting for a palace location for a shooting, we discovered the Sirsa palace. We wanted to shoot our serial there, but we were denied permission."

Aunt and niece became silent for a few minutes. Aisha clutched her stomach. "Shit, Kiara! I gave him an effing LIVE demo of death by jumping."

Kiara choked a laugh. "Yes, you did."

Two servers came carrying more trays with food. Aisha kept fiddling with her food even as Kiara indulged her appetite.

"Shucks, Kia! Now, I'm feeling bad." Aisha closed her eyes. *I know what death of loved ones can do to a person!*

"It's okay, Boo. He will get over it."

"Don't we all?" Aisha sighed. "Gosh, all I wanted was a simple vacation."

After dinner, they walked back to the villa.

Kiara paused and pointed at the beach. "Why don't you go and take some pictures. Photography always makes you feel better."

"Correction, please! Bad photography always makes me feel better."

Kiara laughed.

"Today, I will just call it a night. Anyways, my cell and backpack are in your room. I'll pick it up and head to the hotel."

Kiara pushed her cell in Aisha's hand. "Here, take my cell. It has a good camera. Look at the beach with all those beautiful bonfires. Great setting. Go!"

"But—"

"I insist!"

Aisha opened her mouth.

"I'll use your cell to call you if I need anything. Go, woman!"

Aisha pulled Kiara's cheek. "Later, gator!"

Aisha turned in the direction of the beach.

"Hey, Boo! Take my picture."

"Sure," Aisha turned around with the phone's camera ready to take a shot. A startled laugh escaped her mouth.

Kiara was imitating the 'broken neck dead woman' pose.

"Oh, you are the devil itself."

"Toodles!" Kiara blew her a kiss and went in.

Shaking her head, Aisha waited until Kiara went inside the house. She trooped in the direction of the populated beach.

On a whim, Aisha took off her wedges and let her sole sink in the gravelly sand that had been warmed by the heat of the day. It trickled through her toes and hugged her feet.

Unlike the light sand playing around her feet, Aisha's head felt heavy. She stopped near the pier gazing at it. It had been cordoned off and was under repairs since the accident.

Aisha shuddered and moved on. She stopped at some distance from the first group gathered around the bonfire. They were a mix of Indians and foreigners. One of them held a guitar, strumming it lightly.

A girl in the group was singing softly, her voice low and soulful. The light from the bonfire lit her face in a warm and luminous orange glow. Her eyes were closed, and her head swayed slowly, and in that moment the girl's face held a sea of content.

Aisha sank to her knees and raised the phone. She opened and clicked some pictures of the bonfire.

An odd sensation pricked her neck as if someone was watching her. Her hand holding the cell wavered.

Aisha swung her head sideways and saw that 'someone.'

Chapter 36

Kabir was sitting few feet away from her, all by himself. Aisha and Kabir's eyes met and held.

Aisha felt some heat in her cheeks that had nothing to with the nearby bonfire. She dropped her gaze and self-consciously tucked her hair behind her ear.

Aisha got to her feet, her eyes wandering back to the lonesome figure dressed in black.

Meeting Aisha's gaze steadfastly over the beer bottle pressed against his lips, there wasn't a flicker of emotion on Kabir's chiseled face. The orange fire gave a warm glow to his features but there was no softening in his expression.

As Aisha was about to pivot away, she saw Kabir reach out and pull something from behind him. It was another beer bottle. He planted it in the sand near him and went back to his solitary drinking.

Aisha's eyes flickered between Kabir and the bottle. Standing still, she chewed her bottom lip, her eyes slanted, confused. Still unsure, Aisha stood where she was. Something akin to exasperation flashed in his eyes. Reaching in the pocket of his shirt, Kabir pulled out something shiny and threw it near the bottle in the sand.

A bottle opener.

Aisha wrinkled her nose. I am being invited to my wake.

Taking small steps and ignoring the flutters in her stomach, Aisha went near Kabir. He continued to sip his beer and stare ahead of him.

Aisha sank in the sand a foot away and a few inches behind him. Sounds of intermittent applause made her glance in the direction of the bonfire. The girl had finished her song. Aisha saw the girl whip her head and glance at Kabir, her mouth creased in an inviting smile. Kabir raised his bottle to her and the side of his cheek hitched up as he gave her a smile.

Aisha's brow crumpled.

The girl noticed Aisha. Her eyes narrowed and then she shrugged and turned back to her friends.

In a fluid movement, Kabir leaned over grabbed the bottle from the sand and opened it. He glanced at Aisha briefly as he held it out to her.

Sounds of waves and nearby conversations of other people were the only sounds between Aisha and Kabir.

Grudgingly, Aisha took the bottle and their fingers brushed. She was quick to move her hand and the bottle even as the fleeting warmth from Kabir's fingers lingered on her skin.

They sipped in silence.

Just like the night on the pier. Aisha studied the back of Kabir's head. His dark hair was neatly cut above his shirt collar, his back was straight and there was a strange stillness about him. Aisha opened her mouth to say something as he turned to flick a gaze at her over his shoulders. Their eyes connected briefly and then Aisha blinked and stared at the hemline of her dress. When she glanced up, Kabir was back to staring at the ocean.

"I did not know about your wife and sister." Aisha spoke haltingly.

Kabir's hand, which was raised to take another sip, stilled. "And now you know. How?"

Aisha cleared her throat.

"Kiara?" he asked.

"But the others told her." Aisha was quick to defend.

Again silence.

"I have seen a lot of death too," Aisha said in a muffled voice.

That earned her a hooded glance.

Kabir took some time but then he asked. "Who?"

"My mother. And my brother and his wife—Kiara's parents."

More silence followed where each sipped their beers.

"Yet you can laugh?"

Aisha drew circles in the sand, taking her time answering. "To me, nothing emphasizes the importance of life like death does." She paused.

"How old were you when your mother passed away?"

"Fifteen," Aisha went back to her art.

"And when your brother and sister-in-law passed away?"

"Eleven," Aisha's finger stilled. She glanced at him. His gaze was fixed on her. "And you?"

"Fifteen, just like you, when my sister passed away and thirty when my wife did."

"I'm sorry!" She was talking to his back.

"I'm sorry too . . . for your losses."

Aisha nodded and swallowed.

"You made sacrifices for Kiara, for your family. You found a cause to live."

Aisha tasted her beer. "And you..." It wasn't a question. Kabir stayed quiet. "Your family? Your parents?"

"Dad passed away two years after Kriti died. I was shipped to a reforming school and my mother left the country."

Despite herself, Aisha felt her heart go out to the young boy he must have been. *I always had Dad, my rock. Nani and a bunch of empathetic aunts, uncles, and cousins!* "Why didn't your mum stay?"

Kabir's voice was flat. "Because her prefect daughter had died but her awful son lived. After Dad, there was nothing for her here."

Chapter 37

Aisha bit her lips to control her emotions. "She should have stayed."

Kabir glanced at her. Aisha wasn't quick enough to hide the sheen in her eyes. "Drink your beer." His lips creased in a humorless smile.

Aisha took a shaky breath.

Kabir reaching into his trouser pocket pulled out a folded handkerchief. He handed it to her.

"Thanks." Aisha dabbed her eyes.

"Sorry for tackling you back there." This time Kabir met her eyes and did not look away.

Aisha nodded. "It's okay! I should not have teased you. I did not know. You are so smug all the time and when I saw you terrified I could not resist. I . . ." she trailed off at the gleam that came in his eyes.

"I'm *not* smug all the time."

Aisha turned her eyes away.

"Why do you always look away? Something wrong with my face?"

"What? No!" Aisha felt herself color.

"Then look at me and don't look away." Kabir's voice sounded thicker than usual.

Aisha felt a heat pulse in her body at his words and the way he spoke. "A staring competition?" she murmured, picking some sand, and letting it trickle down slowly from her palm.

"Hi there?"

Aisha and Kabir turned at the voice. It was the girl who had been crooning earlier. Her eyes were on Kabir. "Got more beer?"

"Sorry, none. She took the last one." Kabir tossed Aisha a look.

Aisha opened her mouth but then shut it.

"Well, that shack there," the girl pointed at the nearby Tiki, "they serve beer. If you want to buy me one."

"I was just," Aisha moved, "leaving."

Kabir reached out and wrapped his hand around Aisha's wrist. "No, you are not." He tugged Aisha down. Still holding her wrist, he turned to the girl hovering near them. "I have cash if you want to buy a beer for yourself."

"Okay!" The girl in the white and blue caftan extended her hand. Kabir took out some money from his pocket and dropped it in her outstretched palm. "I will be there for some time. You can join me when you are done here!" She gave Kabir a coquettish glance under her lashes.

Kabir flashed her a smile. "Cheers!"

Aisha tugged her hand free and Kabir let go. The girl walked away.

"Don't judge her. It's Friday night in Goa."

"I'm not judging her or anyone else. I work in the television industry; nothing surprises me."

"What do you do in TV?"

Aisha scratched her temple. "I write sitcom stories and dialogs."

"Really? For those over-the-top dramatic serials?"

Aisha's mouth creased at the corners. "What was that about not judging?"

"Touché!" Kabir raised her a toast and took a sip. "Get up."

"What?" Aisha titled her head to the side.

"Get up!" Kabir stood tall over her.

"You are used to giving orders, aren't you?" Aisha said, not moving an inch. She raised her bottle very slowly and took a sip. Her look was defiant.

Kabir grinned, boyish.

Aisha tried to ignore how handsome he looked.

"I apologize. Will you please rise so I may show you something?" Kabir started brushing the sand off his clothes, putting most of it dangerously close to her dress.

"Oh God! You are worse than Kia when it comes to bullying me!" Aisha muttered, getting to her feet. She straightened her dress and grabbed Kiara's cell. She left her sandals in the sand.

Kabir walked some distance down the sandy slope. "Come and stand here." He paused, his glance cheeky. "Sorry! Please come and stand here."

Aisha rolled her eyes but did as asked. She ended up standing in front of him. "Now what?"

"Today, you will learn some basics of photography. Please open the camera on your phone."

"You don't have to!"

"I want to. Will you kindly do me the honors?" Kabir drawled above her head.

Snorting, Aisha opened the cell and held it in front of her.

Kabir ignored the rude sound. His mouth creased in an unrepentant grin. "Kindly look through it and please compose a good frame for me."

"Ugh!" Aisha moved the cell scanning the beach.

\#

Kabir crossed his arms and studied the woman in front of him. He found Aisha wholly intriguing. *Tragedy is common to both of us, yet she overcame all that.*

Kabir's eyes strayed over her, his look more intimate. Her hair, usually in a ponytail, hung loose today, falling below her shoulder. Her skin was smooth, and her heart-shaped mouth highlighted by her fuchsia lipstick. Her cheeks were round and her chin pointy, giving her face a pixie-like appearance.

She is so easy to talk to. No judgments, just kindness. Everything around her seems simple.

Kabir let his eyes trail over Aisha's body. She was focused on finding something she could take a picture of. Her shoulders were straight, her breasts voluptuous, her waist curvy and her backside firm and round. Kabir groaned mentally. He wanted Aisha badly but her inexperience with men, her innocence, was as visible as a beacon atop a lighthouse.

The models leave the day after and then I will never meet Aisha. It will be good for her and for me.

Kabir's eyes had a look of longing as he watched Aisha. I don't want Aisha to lose her inner joy or peace. I could not bear that. Once I get back to Mumbai, I will refer Kiara to another agency.

Chapter 38

"**Okay, this** one is damn good. Look." Aisha beckoned Kabir. Her eyes shone, and her smile was wide. She held the phone like she was holding a newborn.

Kabir leaned down to her shoulder to see the frame she had composed. "What are you taking a picture of?"

"What?" Aisha narrowed her eyes. "You can't see it?"

Kabir shook his head and clamped his mouth. His eyes glinted at her indignant expression. "No, I can't. All I see is a blob of orange."

"A blob? Excuse me!" Aisha brought her hands holding the cell down. "I don't think you know what photo. . ." she trailed off realizing how asinine she sounded, saying that to a man took pictures for a living.

Straightening, Kabir crossed his arms over his chest, pulling his black shirt tighter over his chest as he cocked his head to the side, his expression amused. "Go on, you were saying?"

"Whatever," Aisha pressed the home button to close the camera.

"Don't. Open the camera and hold it up." Kabir prodded her forearm. "Go on, take a picture."

"So, you can make more fun of my photography?"

"Photography, really?" Kabir murmured.

"What did you say?"

"Nothing. C'mon, make your frame."

Aisha rolled her eyes but did as told.

Kabir put his face next to her, trying to see what Aisha saw on her phone. His chin lightly grazed the bare skin of her shoulder. The sensation seared Aisha to her toes. Tingles sparked on her skin.

Aisha shifted, trying to focus on the phone in her hands and not on the man next to her. The breeze did more damage. It bathed her with his spicy smell. Every breath of hers smelled of him. *Dammit!*

"Okay, now zoom out." Reaching over, Kabir's fingers splayed over Aisha's. She swallowed, trying to act unaffected.

"Zoom out so you can add nuances, show background; something that makes your subject more interesting."

Every time Kabir spoke, he slightly turned his mouth to her and his hot breath touched her nape like soft pricks. Aisha quivered.

"Are you cold?"

"No." Aisha shook her head. Her loose hair brushed Kabir's face.

Chapter 39

Kabir tried not to inhale the citrus smell of Aisha's hair. He failed. Seeing her shiver, he moved closer, trying to warm Aisha. Kabir wasn't prepared for how good she felt against him. Fitting perfectly under his chin, the rest of her body went up against the rest of him. He felt himself harden painfully. *I have been without a woman for too long,* Kabir cursed.

Aisha was a poster child for all inexperienced with men. This should turn him off but in Aisha's case, he was insanely attracted and strangely possessive. Today afternoon it was his call to Christin that had ended Christin and Aisha's lunch date, but Kabir had simply been unable to focus on the shoot, constantly thinking of what Aisha and Christin might be doing.

Kabir exhaled.

Aisha turned her head at that sound. "Are you okay?"

Kabir's face was mere inches away from hers. They stared at each other. His gaze dropped to her lips very slowly.

Aisha's lips parted, showing the tip of her teeth. Her pink tongue moved tantalizingly within the cavern of her mouth. Kabir in that minute wanted nothing more than to a take a deep taste of her warm mouth and lock lips with her for an eternity.

Kabir's eye flickered back to Aisha's. Seeing the unchecked and answering desire in Aisha's coffee colored eyes, Kabir's body tightened, the sensation soulfully stirring. Aisha did not know how to hide her feelings. Her eyes were truly mirrors to her mind and heart.

Groaning softly, Kabir dipped his head and Aisha's eyes closed, her lips parting in anticipation.

Aisha felt herself melt. She wanted this kiss so badly. It was like an insane craving. She wanted to be physically connected to Kabir.

Sudden loud laughter filled the air.

Kabir stilled, his mouth nearly brushing Aisha's. Desire was pierced by common sense. *Fuck!* Kabir frowned at Aisha's upturned face. Her lashes were long against her smooth skin. Her lips soft and parted invitingly.

Kabir briefly closed his eyes as his insides ached. All he wanted was to pull her into him and mingle her breath with his. *She is not in my league; she is a hundred leagues above me.* Kabir opened his eyes, his mouth twisted harshly.

Feeling nothing but air on her lips, Aisha opened her eyes. Kabir was close, but his face had lost all tenderness, all desire. She blinked at the scowl that rode his forehead.

"What happened?" Her voice was a soft murmur.

"Nothing," Kabir snapped and moved away from her. "I suggest you focus on taking pictures, but of course if you want to get laid. Ask me nicely," His voice was icy. "I might indulge. There are not too many women your age I fuck."

Aisha could only stare at him for a second and then anger and hurt flashed in her eyes. She felt like he had thrust a hot knife in her heart. "You are such a jerk!" The closeness she had just felt with Kabir robbed her of words. She angrily moved to go around him.

"What, no pictures either?"

"Sure, I could take your picture if you would oblige me by dying!" Aisha snapped and then she averted her face. Aisha took quick angry steps to grab her wedges.

A couple strolled directly in her line of vision. She noticed the man. His shirt hung un-tucked and his jeans were rolled up to the calf. The young woman on his side wore a strapless printed maxi.

The man appeared familiar to Aisha. She studied his face with the smooth forehead, deep set eyes, thin mustache, and the pronounced jawline. And then it came back to her. He had been at the shoot earlier today.

At that moment, the man noticed Aisha too. He stopped and stared at her.

A sudden acute pain cudgeled her body. Aisha stumbled, and she clutched her chest, her face folding in pain.

A low, painful moan erupted from her throat.

Sweat gushed from every pore and her body trembled violently. Her heart felt lacerated like someone was squeezing every ounce of blood from it.

All the oxygen seemed to desert her.

Aisha could sense each cell in her body shrinking. Her blood seemed to turn to ice, her arms felt weighed down by lead, even as shooting pain pricked her all over and strong nausea threatened to buckle her legs.

Aisha's breath became shallower by the second. Like a shroud being pulled slowly over a corpse, Aisha felt death overcome her bit by bit.

She had a moment of clarity. *Someone I love is dying!*

Kabir, who had come to her side, noticed Aisha's pale face and trembling body. Bending, he touched her shoulder. "Aisha, what happened? Bloody hell, you are cold as ice."

Unknowingly, Kabir's touch jolted life back into her. Aisha shrieked. Turning blindly, she ran for the villa.

The panic wasn't new. She had experienced this exactly thrice before—once when her brother had been murdered in his house twenty kilometers away; the second time the very minute her mother had breathed her last in the hospital; And lastly when her father had been in a deadly collision but fortunately survived.

This time Aisha's panic had another name. The name of the one she loved the most—Kiara.

Chapter 40

Aisha did not feel the small stones prick her feet or the undulation of the sand. Her head pounded, and she pushed herself to run faster. Aisha saw the villa's back gate in front of her. She flew over the steps, dashed around the patio, hurtling inside the house through the back door.

She careened the corner and managed to keep running. She reached Kiara's bedroom door and shoved it hard. It was locked. Aisha pounded the door with her fists. "Kia, open the door, open it!"

"Aisha!" Kabir reached her and grabbed her forearm. "What are you doing? You are waking everyone up." He dropped her sandals next to her.

Aisha swung to him, her eyes wild, her mouth bent. "Kiara *never* locks doors. Can you open this?" She rattled the knob loudly even as she kicked the door.

Kabir grabbed Aisha and pulled her to him. "Stop it!"

Aisha struggled in his grip. "You don't understand! Let me go." She twisted her head.

"Calm down, Aisha." Kabir shook her lightly. Some of the models and Amee appeared in the corridor.

"Didn't you hear me! She never locks her door!" Aisha kicked Kabir on his shin.

"Ooof!" He reflexively dropped his arms, releasing her. Aisha threw her body on the door.

"Stop her, Kabir! Stop this infernal racket!" Amee gestured.

"Aisha, Kiara is sleeping—"

"She is sleeping through all this noise at her door?" Aisha spoke hoarsely.

"Do you have the key?" A new male voice interrupted.

Aisha turned. It was the man from the Lopez Point and the beach.

A loud crash came from behind the door. Something heavy fell inside and glass shattered.

"Kiara!" Aisha screamed. The stranger dashed between her and Kabir and crashed through the door. The door quivered but stayed.

"C'mon! Together!" Kabir gestured at the man and they both fell on the thick door. It splintered in the middle. Kabir stumbled through and Aisha was quick to follow. The stranger trailed her.

The room was dark, but the broken glass of an open window was noticeable to all in the room. Aisha stumbled in the dark.

Kabir found the light switch on the wall and flicked it. They all saw Kiara.

"Kia!" Aisha ran to her niece struggling on the floor, her fingers around her throat. Kiara's face was white, her chest heaved as she drew big gulps of air.

"Boo . . . Boo!" She kept pointing at the window behind her. "Someone tried to kill me!"

Aisha sucked her breath in and hugged Kiara to her chest. "You are safe, baby. You are safe."

Kiara was shaking like a lone paper under a fan. Aisha hugged her niece tight, her eyes fighting tears even as they studied the state of the room. The bedside lamp lay on the floor, the window behind the bed open with one side of the glass broken and scattered on the floor.

Kabir crouched next to Aisha and Kiara. "I have called for the doctor. Let's help Kiara on the bed."

"No, not on the bed." the man who had followed them from the beach said, even as he strained his head out of the window looked around. "He's gone. Move back!" He gestured to Amee and the models crowding the room.

Aisha shifted protectively, blocking her niece from their curious gazes.

"Who the hell are you?" Kabir jumped to his feet. His body was tightly wound like he was about to swing a punch.

"Parth Mangal, CBI." He held out his badge to Kabir. "Everyone, please step outside. There is evidence in the room that should not be contaminated. I'm calling my team."

"You are not calling anyone. I will call the commissioner. This is my house." Kabir stepped up to the CBI officer.

"Well, then you should have been here protecting your guests rather than flirting on the beach. Their security is your responsibility." Parth provoked Kabir, taking a step in his direction.

"Please, just shut the fuck up, you two. I need to get Kiara to the living room." Aisha's voice was forceful.

Chapter 41

"Thanks!" Aisha took the offered glass of water.

"Sure. Let me know if you or Kiara need anything else. Anything, okay?" Amee said and left the living room.

Aisha helped Kiara drink some water. Kiara winced as she swallowed.

Aisha felt a new tidal wave of rage, the kind one could surf on, when her eyes were again drawn to the thick and ugly red welts around Kiara's neck. Whoever had come in her room had come to kill her.

"When will your team arrive?" Aisha asked Parth who was hovering close. "I want to apply something on the bruises."

"They should be here anytime." Parth flexed his shoulders, standing at the corner of the room. It allowed him to keep an eye on the room Kiara had been attacked in.

Two people from the production team had been woken hurriedly and were guarding the room from outside the house. The broken window was another point of entry now.

"When does the police ever arrive on time?" Kabir made the acerbic comment from his seat.

Aisha glared at Kabir; he just made an irritated sound and got to his feet.

"The medicine should kick in soon." Aisha had given Kiara some painkillers. "You are so brave." Aisha wiped Kiara's glistening forehead. "Did you see who it was, Kiara?"

Kiara shook her curls. "No. It was dark. I was sleeping and then . . . I woke up to him sitting on my chest . . . crushing my throat." She struggled to speak.

"Can you describe that person? Height, weight? Did he say anything to you?" Parth added.

"He was heavy and strong. . ." She trailed off observing Aisha's stricken expression. "I couldn't get anything else. Sorry!" Her eyes filled with fresh tears.

"You did nothing wrong." Aisha flared. Kiara's pain made her want to lash out and she did. "How the hell can someone get in the house so easily? Zero security in this place with so many girls here! So bloody irresponsible." Aisha's cheeks were red with anger and her eyes leveled with Kabir's, accusing.

Kabir did not say anything. His expression was that of guilt.

"Kiara and I are leaving for Mumbai first thing tomorrow morning." Aisha's voice, like her expression, was unyielding.

"Boo, please." Kiara pleaded, still struggling with her speech.

"No, your aunt is right." Kabir interjected. "You are no longer contractually bound, Kiara. You can leave."

Kiara began to protest and then, as if it took too much effort, she lay back on the sofa. "Fine, whatever you all think is right."

Aisha grabbed another stole and wrapped it around Kiara's shoulders.

"Don't disturb that area. We will be taking pictures of the marks on her neck and dust for fingerprints." Parth requested.

"You won't find any prints; he wore gloves and a mask." Kiara replied, her eyes still closed.

"Did you fight back?" Aisha asked. She had made sure Kiara knew self-defense like herself.

"I hit him in the ribs. And once I was able to sock him on his cheek. That's when you started banging on the door. He was surprised, and his grip loosened. That's when I shoved him off me and he fell against the lamp. That is all the damage I could do. He was strong, and I was surprised."

Aisha squeezed Kiara's hand. "You did good."

"You have long nails. Did you scratch him?" Parth dropped down on his haunches. "There might be DNA under your nails."

"No, he was fully clothed. Tight dark clothes from head to toe."

Parth stilled and then nodded, studying the floor.

"The asshole came prepared." Aisha spoke bitterly.

Parth got to his feet. "He's not getting away. We'll get him."

There were sounds of a car pulling up in the driveway. "I'm posting policemen in the front and back of the house." Parth walked outside.

Kabir, who had been quietly listening to them, grabbed his cell phone and dialed. A phone rang upstairs. "Come down immediately."

A door opened somewhere on the first floor and Vikas came down in his pajama and T-shirt. He looked disheveled. He stopped for a second upon seeing everyone gathered and then hurried down straight to Kabir.

"What happened, Boss?"

Kabir took him to the side and started speaking, his tone low. In a few minutes, Kabir came back to them. Aisha did not acknowledge him. "After the cops are done, Kiara and you will be shifted upstairs in the empty room in my suite. I have ordered additional security; they should be here soon."

"Thanks!" Kiara nodded.

"The security is top notch." Kabir said, looking at Aisha but she kept her face turned away. He pivoted and walked away from them, sitting closer to the front door.

"Boo?"

"Do you need anything, Kia? Something to eat?" Aisha knew Kiara was about to defend Kabir. But that is Kiara, always rising to defend others. But today there had been no one to defend Kiara.

She noticed Kiara's eyes droop. Aisha grabbed a small round cushion and placed it behind her head. "Take a nap. When the police want to talk to you, I'll wake you."

"Thanks. You will be here, Boo?"

Aisha swallowed. Between Kiara and her, her niece was the brave one. "Right here. Next to you. My chops ready." Reaching out, she planted a kiss on Kiara's forehead. Aisha gently stroked Kia's hair. Kiara's eyes closed as she held on to Aisha.

Aisha watched her for a few seconds then sighing, she turned her head. Her gaze clashed with Kabir. For a few seconds neither of them glanced away. Then Aisha sharply swiveled her head. She felt him come over to them. Aisha realized that except for a sleeping Kiara, Kabir and she were by themselves.

"It's all your fault!" She hissed.

Kabir rubbed his forehead. "I was with you when this happened."

"Exactly. You were out. The back door was open. You have so many models living here and deplorable security arrangements."

Kabir exhaled. "I'm sorry. You are right, it is my fault. In my defense, something like this has never happened before."

"News flash: there is always a first time for everything. If you had security at the house, that maniac would have never got in. Kia would have never . . . Do you realize she nearly died?" Aisha's voice broke and she stuffed a fist in her mouth.

Kabir was beside her in a flash. He clasped her shoulder. "I'm sorry."

"Don't!" Aisha pushed his hand away from her shoulder. "Just don't!"

Kabir's face closed. "Is this because of what I said to you earlier?" They both were speaking in hushed tones so as to not wake Kiara up.

Aisha's eyes were incredulous. "Oh, don't flatter yourself. You don't even come close to what I feel for Kia. You are inconsequential; she isn't." Aisha snapped, switching her gaze to Kiara.

Wordlessly, Kabir got to his feet and went back to his former position near the front door.

Aisha swallowed, her eyes crowding with tears.

Chapter 42

After few minutes, Parth walked in. He came straight to Aisha. A middle-aged woman trailed him, leather bag in hand. "This is Dr. Madhuri Lorso."

Kiara's eyes flew open.

"You weren't asleep?" Aisha asked.

"No, just listening." Kiara's gaze moved to Kabir who kept his distance, watching them silently.

"Is there an empty room we can go to?" Dr. Lorso looked at Parth.

"Yes, there is one at the end of the corridor." Kabir led them.

Dr. Lorso and a lady constable helped Kiara to the room. Aisha walked up to Parth. "Just letting you know that this is not the first attempt to hurt Kiara."

"It isn't?" Parth's glance held surprise. "So why did you not inform the police?"

"My fault. I should have made more noise."

"So, what happened?"

"Two days ago, Kiara was posing on the pier and she fell down. That's why the twisted ankle. Anyhow, she fell because the railing had been tampered with. There were obvious signs. Neat cuts on both ends, smell of glue at the joints."

"Are you a PI?"

"A Private investigator? No!" Aisha shook her head. "Why?"

Parth smoothed an end of his mustache. "Because things that are obvious to you are not so obvious to most. Just now when you described the clues pointing to the tampering of the railing, that's not something a civilian would notice."

Aisha kept glancing at the room Kiara had gone into.

"How did you know that Kiara was in trouble? I saw you running. Did she call you?"

Think! Think! Think! Aisha shook her head. "Ugh no! I did not know what was going on here. I had a big argument with Kabir and I was very upset. He said horrible things to me, so I just ran to get away from him."

Parth studied Aisha's face, his gaze piercing. He seemed to believe her. "So, does Kiara have any angry boyfriends, present or ex?" Parth probed.

"No, she is very focused on her career."

"You are her...?"

"Bua."

"Shouldn't you inform her parents?"

"They are dead." Aisha left it at that. "I'm taking her back tomorrow."

"Good luck with that. There is a massive storm expected to make land tomorrow afternoon. A deep depression in the Arabian Sea. Everything is going to be closed after ten in the morning. Airports and roads included."

"How come no one mentioned that?" Aisha glanced around. Kabir was parked at the other end of the living room with Vikas. She stalked over to him.

"So now I know why you said yes to letting Kiara go tomorrow." Aisha accused.

Kabir turned to her his face weary. "What did I do now?"

"Oh, don't use that tone with me." Aisha wagged her forefinger. "Everything is closed tomorrow. We are trapped in this bloody house of horrors because of the damned storm."

A muscle worked in Kabir's cheek even though he went still. "What storm?"

Vikas twitched his shoulders. "It changed direction last minute, Boss. It was supposed to head toward Kerala but now it's going to hit here tomorrow afternoon."

Kabir started pacing the room. Aisha lobbed a glance at him. His expression was dark just like his clothes. He caught Aisha staring at him. "I'll check on the security that was to come." He bit out, leaving the room abruptly. His assistant followed him.

"Odd chap!" Parth remarked, joining her.

Aisha could not contain herself. "The concierge at my hotel said women are getting attacked and killed in this city. Are they?"

"This is police business. So, no comments." Parth's tone was dismissive.

Aisha put out a pleading hand. "But at least please tell me if this attack on Kiara is random or if she fits some obscene pattern of some idiotic deranged sociopathic killer."

"She is random."

Aisha nodded, relieved.

"What do you know of patterns?"

"Nothing," Aisha was quick to reply.

"I'll repeat, what do you know of patterns?" Parth crossed his arms over his chest.

"Nothing!"

"Your words were 'pattern of a deranged sociopathic killer.' I know behavioral analysis terms when I hear them." Parth's gaze was hard.

Aisha exhaled. "All my life, I wanted to be a cop, the investigative kind. My brother was a cop."

The sound of an opening door made them turn.

Chapter 43

The lonesome figure paced the empty street near the villas. The light in the area was dim. He glanced at his watch. It was close to 3:00 am. The wind was picking up and spinning dust. One or two other people on the road ducked and kept their head lowered to protect their eyes from the prickly grains swilling around.

But not this man. His face was bent but to hide the feral, wild look in his eyes. His hands were curled into fists. "That bloody bitch. I failed again. Her silly fuck of an aunt interrupted!" Spit pooled at the side of his mouth, like a rabid animal. *I'll strangle them both.*

"Frustration will make you commit blunders. Calm down. Or we will never be able to kill her." He was talking to himself. "Calm down, idiot!" Two voices, one person.

"I will calm down, but I need to kill! I need to see the light go from her eyes. I need, need, need, need it." His voice was high pitched.

"Shut up, shut up! Keep your voice down. Find some random girl and kill her. Get rid of your itch."

The figure halted, jerked his head up and glanced around.

A woman was walking ahead of him. By her wrinkled and dirty jeans, faded top and simple footwear, she appeared poor. "This one is not perfect. This one is fat. You know how she looks. She is always beautiful. '

"This one is a compromise, you eunuch. If you don't get your itch out, you will make mistakes. Go take her, kill her, and throw her in the ocean. The storm will take her far away. Her body will never be found. Go!" he assured himself.

"But where will I make love to her? The van is not here." The man followed the woman on the deserted street, darting quick glances about him to make sure they were alone.

"Love?" A chortle escaped his throat. "What you do to them is *not* love. Knock her out, take her to the beach, and then do what you want to do to her. Because of the storm, the beach will be deserted. Hurry before someone else comes!" He ordered himself. A chuckle escaped his throat.

The sound caused the woman to stop and cast a look over her shoulder. Their eyes met, and her eyes widened. She saw the madness in his eyes.

"I think we've been made."

The man smiled at her.

The woman broke into a run.

"Ha ha!" He gave chase. He loved hunting! A leopard hunting a fleeing deer. His stubby legs outran the girl. Before she could scream, he lunged and jumped on top of her, bringing her down. A sickening crack and the deer lay still.

"Oh shit! Shit!" He turned the girl around. Blood streamed from her forehead that had cracked open like shell, the brain oozing out like a yolk. He jumped back from her and bending in the bushes, he threw up. He staggered and fell on the ground. The wind was blowing harder, rousing more than dust.

"You, stupid dog! Drag her to the beach." Words burst from his mouth.

"But! But!" The man scuttled on his bum.

"Before anyone else comes."

"No, no!" The man whimpered.

"Shhh!" He soothed himself. "Just don't look at her face. Her body is all woman. You can still do what you like to do to her. '

"I can?" The man now got on his fours and started crawling toward the body of the still woman.

"Of course! Just don't look at her face. She is still breathing." There was the wild laugh again.

The man shot to his feet and grabbed the nearly dead woman by her legs, avoiding glancing at her face. He dragged her to the pavement and then keeping an eye out for any witness, carried

her all the way the beach.

Chapter 44

Salty water coursed over Aisha's head. She sank in deeper and deeper. Her lungs felt like they were being crushed.

Aisha felt herself choke.

She tried to move her hands and legs, but they lay paralyzed on her sides. Her head throbbed with such pain that Aisha was sure it had cleaved in two. Suddenly, an odd shape came up.

Rocks under water!

Aisha could only stare with horror as the frothy water rushed her body toward them.

"HELP!"

Aisha bolted upright. Her heart thundered and sweat trickled down the sides of her face.

Shit!

Aisha wiped her face.

A nightmare? And I had a starring role in it? Breathing heavily, she closed her eyes and the rock formation loomed back at her instantly.

Familiar black and white stills crossed behind her closed lids.

Thoi.

Julie.

Nafeesa.

Sandhya.

Ann.

"Stop it!" Aisha opened her eyes and jumped off the bed. *The list is growing! Now five!*

Aisha swung her face sideways. Then, she breathed easy. Kiara slept peacefully at her side.

Last night, Christin, who had been roused out of his bed, had given Kiara painkillers and a sleeping pill.

I must speak to Suva. Who are all these people? What is happening to me? Aisha rubbed her forearms to get some warmth in her body.

Rattling sounds from outside distracted Aisha. She pulled the sheet off that still clung to her legs and padded to the window. She parted the silk curtains and saw the outside.

"Damn!"

The storm was on the horizon. The sky was the color of night in the day. The waves were rising as high as skyscrapers and crashing with enough force to make the wooden and weathered pier shudder. The sea nearly covered the pier. The gale was wreaking havoc on the beach, making tiny sandstorms all over.

Aisha put her hand on the thick glass. It vibrated against her palm because of the bullish wind hitting it from the outside. The dark angry cloud rumbled, and Aisha saw lighting fall in a zigzag bolt and hit the water at some distance. She forgot the nightmare in the raging madness of nature. "Spectacular."

Aisha cast one more look at Kiara in deep sleep, softly snoring, and then went in the adjoining bathroom.

Sometime later, she took some clothes out of her bags.

Kabir had organized them to be moved from her hotel. Kabir had organized a lot of overnight security for the place, barricading the Villa off in preparation of the storm but all from the phone. No one knew where he was. He had holed up somewhere. Aisha wasn't even sure he was in the house anymore. She had not seen him after their last conversation.

Where is he?

Aisha stepped out of the room and nearly jumped out of her skin. "Oh excuse me!" She apologized to the security guards at the bedroom door. One of them was a burly woman with arched eyebrows and a masculine jawline. She was dressed in black shirt and trousers with a yellow company logo on her shirt. "Kiara is still sleeping. I'm just going down for a bit."

"Yes, Ma'am." She replied. "We won't be moving from here."

"Thank you!" Aisha smiled and was about to walk past the door Kabir had emerged from yesterday, bare-chested with shaving foam. She paused and titled her head to the door. There was no sound from the other side. *Where are you?*

Sighing, Aisha went downstairs. Most of the models were gathered in the informal living room that overlooked the back yard. Front seats to the storm! Aisha went to the dining table that was stacked with food as always. She grabbed a plate and went straight to where the fruit was kept.

"Excuse me!"

Aisha shifted. She saw Kabir's assistant, Vikas, standing behind her. Aisha's eyes cooled considerably. She had not forgotten how he had behaved with her the first time she had met him.

"How is Kiara?" Vikas asked hesitatingly.

"Sleeping," Aisha's voice was terse.

"If you need anything please let me know. We have security guards posted all over the house. Kiara will be safe now."

Aisha nodded briskly.

His face color tinged a darker shade. "If you need anything from Kabir, I'm in touch with him."

"Where is he?"

"Around here."

Aisha's eyes slipped to the stormy scene outside. *Just hope he is not loitering around out there.*

Vikas turned to go and then halted. "I am sorry about . . . that day." He swallowed and continued. "It was a joke."

Aisha waited, her expression far from pleasant.

"Please don't say anything to Boss." He swallowed heavily. "I need this job. My mother . . . she has . . . cancer."

"Oh! I'm sorry."

Vikas gave her a grateful smile. "Thank you. It's a painful disease."

Aisha remembered her own mother's pain. "It is. Hope she gets well soon."

Vikas lowered his eyes and replied. "She won't. There is no hope. But, thank you." He turned to go.

Aisha stopped him. "I will pray for her. But promise me, no more crap like that."

"Never. Promise. I just got carried away. I'm not the brightest bulb in the pack." Vikas's smile was wry.

"You are fine the way you are." Aisha gave him a wide reassuring smile.

"Thank you so much. Let me know if you or Kiara need anything. Anything at all."

"Will do. Thanks!"

Taking some food, Aisha moved toward the formal living room.

"Hi, Boo!"

Aisha looked up; Kiara stood at the stairs.

"Hi, baby!" Aisha went immediately to her niece.

Aisha noticed the scarf Kiara had draped around her neck. "How are you feeling?"

Kiara came down. "It's hurting but bearable. I'm ravenous!"

"There is lots of food there." Aisha shepherded Kiara to the dining room. The models and Amee welcomed Kiara amidst them.

It became dark rather quickly and that is when the electricity went out. The wind sounded like the loud howls of wild beasts. The walls of the house shook with the force of the gale. Invertors came on when it got darker.

By 4:00 pm it seemed like the middle of the night outside. That was the time the rain started, accompanied by hail. Thunder boomed and crashed like a giant machine gun let loose. Bolts of electricity hit the ground outside, washing the backyard in eerie blue light.

There was no conversation inside the room as everyone was freaked by the wrath of nature. Some were chanting prayers.

Fear overcome by faith.

Aisha stood up and stretched. Kiara glanced at her.

"I have to go the loo!" Aisha went in the direction of the stairs. Amee stopped her.

"Aisha, there are several bathrooms downstairs."

"I know. I just. . ." *I need some me time!*

"Take the candle or a torch. Just in case you need one." Vikas suggested.

"Sure," Aisha picked up a thick lavender candle and a box of matches kept on the table.

The security woman started to move with Aisha.

"Please, I'm just going to the bathroom. You stay here." Aisha went up the stairs and entered the suite. It was dark. Aisha lit the candle in her hand.

Another loud thunderclap rolled over the house. She jumped.

A self-depreciating chuckle slipped from Aisha's mouth. "Idiot!" She took careful steps toward the room Kiara and she were sharing.

A muffled sound made Aisha pause. She immediately halted, all her senses alert.

That wasn't the storm. Someone else is here.

Chapter 45

The sound came again—a low moan from just behind Kabir's door. Aisha put her ear to the door. More lightning fell outside. This time the painful moan was louder.

What the—?

Aisha pushed the door open and stopped at the threshold. She took a few minutes to adjust to the darkness for the room was pitch black. The curtains were shut. Only a sliver of light passed through the crack between the curtains.

The room appeared empty. Aisha took hesitant steps in the room.

Loud thunder boomed again.

This time the painful whimper was clear and close. Aisha glanced down. It came from the bed she was standing next to. There was a rolling shape on it covered by the sheet.

Lightning crashed again. The shape shuddered violently.

Aisha kept the candle on the nightstand and gently raised the sheet.

"Kabir!" She cried in surprise.

Kabir lay on his stomach on the bed. His head was buried in the pillows, his fingers fisting in the pillowcase tightly. The shoulders were taut, and goosebumps covered his arms.

"Hi!" Aisha called out, her voice hushed.

Kabir was shivering uncontrollably. She tentatively touched his shoulder. "Oh God!"

His T-shirt was soaked with sweat. Panic seized Aisha. All she knew was that she had to help. Aisha got on the bed. "Kabir! Talk to me. What happened? Please turn around. Please!" She gently touched his hair; it was soft and springy to touch. His fingers continued to twist in the sheets. More thunder boomed over them and lightning crashed outside.

"No!" Kabir turned and before Aisha could react, he hugged her around her waist, burying his face in her stomach.

"Oh!" Aisha squeaked, surprised. She fell back on the bed, her knees bent under her.

She glanced down shocked. His shoulders were trembling. The lightning clapped outside again. His hold around her stomach tightened.

He is scared of the lightning.

Aisha's inhibitions collapsed on seeing the strong commanding man, who could silence most simply with his eyes, so crippled by fear.

She bent over Kabir's icy body and spoke close to his ear. "It's okay! Nothing to be scared of. Lightning is just a natural electric discharge and lasts for only seconds."

Kabir's arms stayed clamped around her. Aisha maintained her even tone, frantically remembering all that she had learned in school about storms and read over the years. "Water and ice whiz inside the cloud and the warm air forces them to go up and the gravity, of course, tugs them down." She stroked Kabir's head and back, her fingers enjoyed the feel of his muscles and contours. "Everything happens in a cloud that is compressed tight like a box. So, all that push and pull far away from us, very far from us, creates static and thus electricity so it's a natural phenomenon, nothing to be scared off."

Aisha heard Kabir murmur something even as he moved restlessly against her abdomen.

"What?" she asked in a hushed voice.

Tilting his head, Kabir turned his face to her. His eyes were clamped tightly, and his pale mouth twisted like he was in mortal pain. "What . . . is thunder?" His voice was hoarse like he had been screaming for hours.

"Oh! I know this one," Aisha tried to maintain a casual demeanor. She bent over him, her voice in his ears, all the time stroking his back and hair. "All that electricity I mentioned earlier? Do you remember that? Do you?" She forced him to respond.

Kabir nodded in her lap. Restlessly, he moved up to her waist.

"Well, all that electricity needs to get out." Aisha winced. *I'm really winging it here.* "So, like a high energy child . . . umm . . . it rushes through the air causing all those particles to bump or vibrate." Aisha paused and smiled to herself.

Kabir's skin did not feel as icy anymore and his shivering had mellowed. He moved up and without warning.

Aisha gasped and toppled back on the large bed. Kabir stirred; his body her pinning Aisha down. He snuck his face between her neck and collarbone.

The warmth of his body and the feel of Kabir so close to her rendered Aisha speechless. *Oh my!*

"Don't stop . . . please?" Kabir said in her ear, his tone pleading.

"Yes, yes!" Aisha replied breathlessly. "The electric current . . ." She struggled not to react to the feel of Kabir's hard body moving over her. Mindlessly, Kabir crushed Aisha's breasts with his muscled chest. His strong arms bound her to him. His chiseled face rubbed continuously against the soft skin of her neck. A strange lethargy filled Aisha. "Is super-hot so it heats up all the . . ." She closed her eyes and her body arched against Kabir as he continued to rub his body against her. "Particles it touches."

Aisha's hand, which had been stroking his back reassuringly, now touched him exploring, caressing, and fondling.

Much like the cloud discharging electricity, the air between them shimmered, heavy and charged.

Aisha's head fell back on the bed. Kabir, still half delirious, spoke urgently against her skin, pressing his mouth against her chin. "Go on. You were saying?"

"Hmm?" Aisha licked her dry lips, shocked by the desire that was swirling in her, much like the storm outside. *I will die because of longing.*

"The electricity . . . umm," she inhaled the clean smell of his hair against her face. "When the electric bolt passes through the air, its hotness, in turn, heats the air." Kabir tightened his arms around her waist, pulling Aisha close into him.

Chapter 46

Aisha closed her eyes even as delicious sensations overwhelmed her body and mind. "When the air heats up, it expands quickly, forcefully creating more," Aisha paused as her one hand urgently twisted in Kabir's hair, pulling him closer and her body shamelessly melted against his angles. "vibrations. Those vibrations are what we hear as thunder."

In a flash, Kabir grabbed Aisha's arm and gently pinned them over her head. He now hovered above her, his mouth twisted, yet his eyes were dark and lucid in the flickering candle light. "And what is this fear that I suffer from? This fear I have suffered for decades, Aisha?"

Aisha took her time in answering. She ran her eyes over Kabir's face. His lashes were wet and stuck to each other. She saw deep anguish in his eyes. Aisha freed one hand and cupped his cheek. Kabir turned his face in her hand and held it against his lips. "Fear is nothing but the past spoiling your present. Nothing else."

Kabir's anguished eyes turned tender. His lean fingers touched the side of her eyes. "Why are you crying?"

Aisha had not realized her eyes had overflowed.

The old authoritative Kabir who was good at demanding things was coming back. "Answer me. Why are you crying, Aisha?"

"Because you are."

Kabir bent his head and kissed her forehead. He placed lingering kisses against her round cheek. "I can't resist you!" His voice was tortured.

Aisha closed her eyes, relishing a sense of power and desire. "I can't stand the sight of blood."

Kabir, again, tucked his face in her neck. Aisha thought she would swoon because of the pleasure as she shifted her neck to give him more room to burrow against her. "Why are you scared of blood?" He asked against her skin.

Thunder rumbled over them. Aisha felt him shiver again. Instinctively, she stroked his shoulders.

The lightning hit the garden outside. Kabir jolted like it had fallen on him. He rolled on his back but dragged Aisha on top of him. Aisha raised her head.

"Kabir, look at me!"

"Go on." He kept his eyes tightly shut. Kabir's voice was hoarse, and his skin took on a sickly pallor. Aisha could sense he was fighting his fear.

Aisha moved closer as it seemed to comfort him "I discovered the bodies of my brother and sister-in-law. They were murdered brutally. There was so much blood. Everywhere! I was eleven." Kabir gripped her hand tighter. Aisha glanced up; eyes open Kabir was really listening to her. "Kiara was a newborn; her face was smeared with her father's blood. I wiped it off her . . . off Kiara's face . . . since then I can't . . ." Aisha's throat choked up.

"It's okay!" Kabir whispered, wrapping his strong arms around her. Aisha burrowed her face in his chest. "Thank you for sharing that with me."

Aisha simply nodded.

"We really have to find better things to bond on." He murmured ruefully in her hair.

Suddenly, it hit Aisha—the intimacy of their bodies on the bed. Aisha moved back. Seeing the awkwardness, Kabir dropped his arms.

Aisha sat up and shifted away. "Are you okay now?" She smoothened her hair.

Kabir nodded and sat up. They both glanced at each other self-consciously.

"No more lightning." Aisha glanced at the curtains.

Kabir nodded, watching Aisha in the pale flickering light of the candle.

Aisha slithered off the bed and went to the door, a bit dazed.

"Do you need the candle?"

Aisha turned.

Kabir stood near the rumpled bed, tall and dark in track pants and a college tee. He was far removed from the austere man he usually appeared to be.

"You can keep it." She paused. "Will you be okay?"

Kabir nodded and wiped his face. "It's just rain now. I think the worst of the storm has passed."

"May I ask, why are you so traumatized by lightning."

Kabir hesitated. "My sister Kriti, she fell off the terrace . . . during a storm. A storm like this . There was a flash of lightning . . . I was the first one to see her." He rubbed his eyes.

Aisha nodded. She felt close to tears at the pain in his face. "You are right. We do have very weird commonalities."

Aisha and Kabir glanced at each other. Tentative smiles glimmered on their faces.

"It is comforting to know I'm not alone." Kabir said softly.

Aisha could only nod. Her hands were craving to hold him, yet she left the room, closing the door behind her.

Kabir stared at the door and then slowly sat back on the bed. A deep regret burned in him. A gut-wrenching physical longing.

Pulling up the bedsheet, he wore it like a blanket over his shoulders and wrapped it around him. He walked to the thick curtains and peeked outside. The rain was heavy. In some distance, he saw the lightning flash in the clouds. The thunder was so low that he could barely hear it and yet his muscles tensed, and he shivered.

Kabir focused his dark gaze on the rising waves rather than the thunder. He felt tired yet light, like a massive weight had been pushed off his chest. He remembered the words, he had just voiced.

It is comforting to know I'm not alone.

Kabir smiled and tucked his nose in the sheet around him and inhaled. It still held Aisha's scent. Vanilla and Honey.

Another deep yearning stirred inside him.

Chapter 47

"**Are you** coming down or not, Boo? We leave in two hours. Everybody is hanging near the pool." Kiara's irate voice sounded in the room.

"I was thinking of going for a run. I have packed all our things." Aisha had the call on speaker as she slid her feet in her running shoes.

"Don't go for a run. Come down and socialize."

Aisha could hear the sulk in Kiara's voice. "Just a short run, I promise. It clears my head. I'll be back before you know." She ended the call and bent down to tighten her laces.

Who am I kidding? I'm running from him.

Aisha, for the hundredth time, remembered the feel of Kabir's arms around her, the warmth of his embrace, the feel of his skin under her fingers. Every line, every groove of Kabir's face seemed to be etched on her mind.

Just then her cell rang again. Aisha glanced at the name. Suvabrata!

"Hello!"

"How is Kiara?"

After her granny's death, it was always like this. If Aisha was depressed, Suva would call; if Aisha or Kiara fell ill, Suva would call; if Aisha was craving anything, say a mango mousse cake, it would be delivered to her magically.

"She is okay," Aisha answered and asked, "Suva, do you know who it was?"

She had understood a long time ago that there was something seriously off about people like her grandmother, Suvabrata, and herself. What it was and why it existed, Aisha had been resolute not to find out till now.

But the fear—that something could happen to Kiara—and the feeling that she had to do everything to protect Kiara had created some chinks in Aisha's determination.

"No, I do not, Aisha. This evil is old has been alive for long. Stay close to her, will you?" Suvabrata warned.

Aisha shot up. "Why? Is she going to be attacked again? Is she in danger?" She ran to the door.

"Calm down, Aisha. It's precautionary. In all this, did you realize that when Kiara was so close to death, she was able to reach you? Maybe that means that not only the dead but even the dying, are able to connect with you. I did not know that about you. Did you?"

Aisha froze, her hand on the door's knob. "I'm just glad that Kiara was able to reach me. Do you know how she did it while the bastard was strangling her?" she blurted.

"Your love for Kiara is that of a mother. And a mother loves her child unconditionally. You are more open to Kiara than you will be to anyone else. Your psychic connection with her is the strongest. She must have thought of you when she was being attacked. Thus, you heard her. That might have opened a new channel or frequency in your mind. Has anything else happened?"

Aisha remembered the names hounding her and the dream where she felt like she was drowning. "No. Nothing else."

Suvabrata was quiet for a few seconds and then spoke. "How often does a car come out of the blue and hits a pedestrian fatally? Doesn't that make you wonder, why did the person choose that very second to cross the road? Why not a few seconds earlier or later? Why did the driver drive that car in that stretch of the road at that very instance? Why didn't the driver drive a few seconds slower or a few seconds sooner? A difference of a few seconds, a few minutes could have saved a life or taken it."

"Don't talk in riddles." Aisha hated the pleading tone in her voice.

"Our conscious and subconscious actions set off a chain of events. Your choices will decide what happens next. Open yourself to the spirits, Aisha. They will guide you. Embrace your uniqueness."

"I don't understand this mumbo jumbo. Nor do I really want to." Aisha muttered quietly.

Suvabrata exhaled loudly in her ear. "Stubbornness is in your blood. Go for a run, Aisha, go for a run. But don't forget, there is no running from who you are. Embrace it! Don't fear the road less traveled."

"What does that even me—" Aisha became quiet when she realized that Suva had hung up on her. She tiptoed out of her room and made her way out of the house, completely avoiding the pool area.

Chapter 48

Slipping on her headphones, Aisha started a slow warm up jog.

The sky was overcast in various shades of gray; the wind held the chill of the last night's rains. The path was strewn with artifacts, manmade and natural—cans, broken pots, junk food wrappers, leaves, small stones, and uprooted plants.

The vibrations of running feet on the ground behind her caused Aisha to turn her head sharply. "Whoa!" She lost her balance.

Kabir grabbed and righted her. "You okay?"

Aisha pulled her earphones out. "Yeah! Umm, what are you doing here?" Self-consciously, she avoided looking at Kabir. Aisha wasn't a huge fan of make-up but right now she would have given an arm or leg for some.

"Going for a run, just like you!" Kabir smiled down at her, a sunny smile framed by a gloomy sky. She ran her eyes over his face.

Never seen him so relaxed!

"You like what you see?" Kabir drawled.

Aisha laughed and flushed at the same time. His words left her tongue-tied. "See ya!" She turned around and sprinted.

"Hey, let's run together." Kabir followed. He kept pace and they ran wordlessly until the end of the road.

Aisha felt oddly buoyant and free with him next to her. They slowed at a fork in the road.

"Where?" Aisha asked, the exercise putting back the shine in her eyes and the color in her face.

Kabir was breathing harder than her. "You run fast, and your breathing is so even. Did you run track in school?"

"I did. Track, swimming, archery. I was getting ready for something."

They started walking. Aisha and Kabir's languid steps took them in the direction of the beach.

"For what?"

The words slipped out of her. "I wanted to be a cop."

That stopped Kabir short. "Really?"

"Just like my late brother."

"Then why didn't you become one?"

"Mom passed away when Kia was just four. She and my father needed me."

"And you were what, fifteen?" Kabir's smile was one of empathy.

He reached out, gently put a warm hand around Aisha's nape and pulled her into his chest. Aisha rested her face against his chest, her eyes bemused yet happy.

This doesn't seem weird.

"You just love to help, don't you?" Kabir spoke in her hair.

Aisha swallowed a few times like an olive was stuck in her throat.

"Thank you for last night." Kabir said above her head, still holding Aisha close.

"We all have bad days."

"Aisha," Kabir paused.

Aisha looked up at him. He met her eyes and his gaze was arrested. Aisha's insides tightened in anticipation.

"I think, I'm . . ." Kabir's voice was thick as he stared deep into her eyes. "Not think. I'm sure that I'm—"

Matshe aikta! Pale!" A shrill voice rang out.

Chapter 49

Aisha and Kabir turned at the interruption. A couple of men in hospital uniforms stood with an empty stretcher, a constable behind them.

"Local dialect. They said excuse us."

Even as Aisha moved back, Kabir stayed there, conversing with them in Konkani—the local language.

"What are they saying?" Aisha asked, observing the scowl on Kabir's face.

"They found someone on the beach. Come," Kabir took Aisha's hand and followed the trio down the beach.

Aisha went along, her hand in Kabir's. *I could get used to this!* Her impish smile flickered between his broad back and their clasped hands.

"Is that the cop who came to our house for Kiara?"

Aisha squinted at the crowd of mostly policemen at some distance from them.

"Parth?" She let go of Kabir's hand. Kabir continued to hold hers lightly.

"He's a weird guy. I should ask the Commissioner for someone else."

"Parth is better. He is CBI. These things take time."

Kabir gave Aisha a lazy smile and held her gaze. "If you say so!"

Aisha blushed.

Parth noticed them and broke away from the group.

Aisha tugged her hand and finally, Kabir let go.

"What's going on? What happened?" Aisha asked.

"A body was found on the beach." Parth's mouth was somber, his eyes hidden behind his Ray-Bans.

"A body?" Kabir asked.

Aisha swiveled and peered at the crowd, especially closer to their feet. "Oh!" She covered her mouth and turned around. She had just seen a part of the figure and it was naked.

"Let's go Aisha!" Kabir put a hand on her back.

Aisha took a deep breath and shook her head. "Just a minute, please! Was this done by the same person who attacked Kiara?"

"No. There is nothing similar between this and Kiara's attack. Can I talk to you, Ms. Aisha?" Parth gave Kabir a pointed glance. "Alone?"

"I'll wait for you." Kabir said to Aisha. Giving Parth a cold glance he walked away.

Parth waited until Kabir walked away. "Your boyfriend doesn't like me." He took off his glasses

"He's not my boyfriend." Aisha ignored the thrill that shot in her at Parth's slip.

"Doesn't really give off brotherly vibes!"

"You wanted to talk to me about something?"

"I did some looking up. You are Judge Khatri's daughter and Kiara is his granddaughter?"

"Yes."

"I spoke to my father. He is very well acquainted with the retired Judge."

"Okay." Aisha's nod was brisk. Because of her father's profession and no-nonsense temperament, he made more enemies than friends. She wasn't sure on which side Parth and his father stood.

"Your father saved my Dad's hide a few times. Quoting my father here."

Aisha smiled, relieved. "Who is your father?"

"Retired RAW head. Vishwanath Mangal."

"Oh. I will ask Dad about him."

"Sure." Parth shrugged.

"So, Kiara will continue to get police protection in Mumbai too, right?"

Parth negated by a sharp shake of his head. "Here, yes. Mumbai, no. The attack on Kiara is being considered the work of some fan who got too close."

"A fan?" Aisha repeated. "I think that bastard was there to kill her. Also, do you know about my brother?"

"I do. My condolences."

"Kiara does not know how her parents died." Aisha confided.

"That's a big secret to carry and hide. You should tell her."

Aisha snorted. "Sorry, haven't really found an appropriate time to tell her. 'Hey Kia, guess what? Your parents were butchered in their beds. So, what do you want for dinner tonight?'" She jeered.

Parth put his glasses back on.

Aisha exhaled. "Did your doctor find any DNA from Kia?"

"No, Dr. Lorso did not get anything."

"So, no luck of finding the creep in the NCRB database?"

Parth cocked his head to the side. "You know about NCRB?"

"National Crime Records Bureau?" Aisha nodded. "Yeah, I know it exists. Is it updated regularly?"

Parth smirked. "It is. But not as often as it should be."

Aisha nodded. "I guess, see you later then. You promise to keep looking for Kia's attacker?"

"The Panaji police will."

"Thank you!" Aisha joined Kabir who was talking to a boy in a hospital uniform.

Kabir bid the boy goodbye as he saw Aisha approaching. "That was the son of my gardener. He is the ambulance driver. Was telling me about the girl they just found on the beach."

Aisha shuddered. "Let's go for that run." Then she paused. "Did he tell you how the girl died?"

"She was strangled."

Chapter 50

"You had the nerve to lie to my face?"

Parth spun at the angry voice. Aisha stood in front of him, her face mottled in anger.

Parth stared at her and then turned to the attendants who had shifted the body to the stretcher. "You all leave now. And disperse all the onlookers." He ordered to his constables. Finally, he turned to Aisha. "Follow me." He led Aisha and Kabir away from his team.

Aisha stopped, her mouth pursed in anger.

Parth did not take off his shades. "Personal courtesy aside, don't ever raise your voice at me." His pitch was mild, but his words were clipped.

"You said there was nothing in common between this incident here and Kiara's attack." Aisha did the quote and unquote gesture. "A lie, a big fat lie! Day before yesterday, Kiara was attacked, and the creep tried to strangle her. Today you find a body a little distance away from the villa and this poor girl was strangled to death. No similarity?"

Parth took off his shades and took some time in folding them. Then he crossed his arms over his chest; his nostrils flared, and his upper lip curled. "I'll tell you what is not similar, Miss Aisha. Your niece is alive, safe, and probably being pampered—wrapped in a blanket enjoying some goddamn herbal tea. Protected by you, the policeman and the security guards your boyfriend has provided. Whereas this girl, merely seventeen or eighteen years old, is dead. Beaten, raped, strangled, and tossed in the water like a piece of trash. The family, the mother and the father will never see her or hear her voice. She is not going to fulfill any of her dreams, big or small. And you know what? That is what she was probably thinking when she was dying. This girl died here alone—scared and tortured. So yeah, in my mind there is nothing common between her and Kiara. And truth be told, I'm going to focus on finding *her* killer." His voice was a quiet snarl.

"Okay, that's enough!" Kabir stepped between Parth and Aisha.

Parth glared at him. "You both should leave. This is a crime scene. Police only."

"Skkksh!" The whipping sound of the tarp made Aisha turn reflexively. All the air left her lungs. She gagged and sharply glanced away.

"What happened?" Kabir asked, bending down his face wreathed in concern. Aisha violently shook her head.

"She saw the body or what is left of the face." Parth voiced casually.

Kabir put an arm around Aisha's shoulders and led her away. "You are shaking. If it is any consolation, the fish did that. Long after her death. I'm sure she felt nothing of that." Kabir tried consoling Aisha in the only way he knew.

By stating the facts.

#

"**Did you** inform Dr. Lorso that she is getting the body and she has to do the autopsy on this one?" Parth said, heading toward the Gypsy.

"Yes, Sir." Jacob nodded, trotting dutifully.

"Officer Mangal! Officer!"

Parth glanced up. Aisha was walking toward them.

Jacob chortled. "If it was her niece it would have been better. The model."

"Should I call Mary, Jacob?"

"Sir!" Jacob made a resigned sound and walked past Parth just as Aisha reached them.

Chapter 51

"Yes Ms. Khatri. Back to yell at me again?"

"No . . . no!" Aisha stopped taking a few breaths. She had been running hard to reach the beach before Parth left. "I want to apologize," she swallowed, "and I want to help."

"Where's the boyfriend?"

"I sent him to be with Kiara in case she finds out about this. . ." Aisha cleared her throat.

"What do you want to help with?" Parth asked, clasping his hands behind his back.

"With this case. Here, look at this." Aisha pulled out an ID card from a slim wallet tucked in her running clothes.

Taking the ID card, Parth studied it. "BCBA? What is this?"

"I'm a Board-Certified Behavior Analyst. I have my Master's degree in Applied Behavior Analysis. I can profile this creep for you. I can help you find him."

"Or you can have me fired from the force. No, thanks." Parth handed the ID back.

"Please hear me—"

"Are you in the police?" Parth asked, taking off his glasses.

Aisha stayed quiet, chewing her lower lip.

"Or CBI or a consultant hired by the CBI or the Panaji police?" Parth asked, rubbing his glasses over his shirt.

"You can hire me and that will make me a CBI consultant. Don't pay me, just hire me." Aisha pleaded. "I can help. You asked me earlier why I knew about the pattern of a deranged sociopathic killer. I'm qualified." She waved her identification.

"What other cases have you worked upon?" Parth shot.

Aisha's answer was silence.

"Have a nice day, Ms. Khatri."

"Hold on!" Aisha grabbed his arm. "Okay fine, I haven't worked on any case, but I do have vested interest here."

"That means you are already biased, and therefore, your conclusions and deductions might be tainted." Parth removed Aisha's hand from his arm. "Also, if I need a profiler, CBI has several experienced ones."

"Parth, please. I have an instinct for these things. What is the harm in trying me? My dad is a retired judge, my brother was a policeman. I promise there will be no breach of ethics. I respect the law. Also, a department profiler will be working on several cases and not just this one. I know how bureaucracy works; tiers of permissions and red tapes even for those in the department. By the time they create a profile, who knows how many more women would have lost their lives?" Aisha dropped her voice. "Please, let me make a profile. If it makes any sense to you, fine. If not, kick me out of this investigation."

"I am not a fan of dynastic anything. Politics or police!" Parth's voice, like his expression, was unyielding. "Let me do my job and you do whatever you do."

"Dammit, Officer!" Aisha stepped closer, putting her hands on her hips, aggression seeping from her body. "I have the right to protect my family. Kiara is like my daughter. Do you have any idea what it feels like to have to your family attacked? I could not catch my brother's murderer but I'm not going to let his daughter become a victim. You can put me in jail but I'm going to go after this guy. And you know what? I have a gun and I know how to use it. I'm going hunt this animal down, with or without your help."

Parth studied Aisha's feisty expression for a few seconds. "Jail is not a bed of roses!"

"It is better than the ugly truth that I did not help those I loved. Family matters!"

Parth took out an unlit cigarette from his pocket and rolled it between his fingers.

Chapter 52

Aisha watched Parth, perplexed.

Parth shifted his gaze. "Jacob! Jacob!"

His florid-faced driver ran toward him. He appeared like a whale discovering it had legs.

Aisha cringed. "Look, that jail part was more of an analogy. I haven't broken any laws yet. We were just talking!"

"Yes, Sir?" The driver was breathless.

"Jacob, you need to get in better shape, man. You need to run more."

Jacob's face tinged a dark red. "Sir . . . it's . . . the sand . . . that stopped . . ."

Parth waved a dismissive hand and put the smoke back in his pocket. "So, all the case files are in the back of the Gypsy, right?"

"Yes Sir, in the leather accordion briefcase. You wanted everything in one place because of the storm, right?" Jacob breathed hard, clutching his side. "I also got the files from Dr. Lorso's office."

"Good job, Jacob! Now you and I are going for a ten-minute run."

"What Sir? No Sir!" Jacob visibly shrank away from Parth.

"Yes, we are. C'mon. I will give you a head start. we will run in the direction opposite from all the houses." Parth bent down and rolled up his jeans and then slipped his jacket off, hooking it over his shoulders.

"But . . . but Sir!" Jacob gaped.

"Yes, you need to decrease your butt. C'mon! I'm doing this for Mary, your wife."

Jacob muttered something under his breath.

Aisha clamped her mouth and stared at her shoes.

Sheer embarrassment made Jacob flee in the direction Parth had pointed out.

Parth gave Aisha a hard look. "In all that you said, only one thing made sense to me—family matters. Three ground rules. You talk only to me. The second I say you are gone, you are gone. And if you break any of the first two rules, I will not hesitate for a second in destroying you, Ms. Aisha. Clear?"

"I get that." Aisha tried not to let distaste for Parth show on her face.

Parth put his shades back on. "You have ten minutes."

"Thank you! Thank—" She was talking to his back.

⧣

Aisha glanced at her watch. "Ten minutes!" She ran to the Gypsy. The ambulance and the other two police jeeps had left.

"Shit!" Aisha noticed one lonesome constable near the vehicle. "Parth Sir called you. I think he found something."

The constable took off after Parth.

"And your time starts now!" Aisha heaved inside the jeep and scrambled to the back. The leather accordion bag was shoved under a seat. Grabbing it, Aisha swiftly opened it.

She flipped the first file open and scanned it. She read the name and nearly fainted. Sweat appeared on her face.

Nafeesa Khan!

Aisha scanned the next file and her eyes went straight to the name of the deceased. Thoi Elviz!

The file slipped from her hands. Gasping, Aisha covered her mouth.

How did I see these names? Why did I see these names? What is happening to me?

Aisha also realized that she was running out of time.

"Oh man, this is not good." Aisha picked up the files even as her hands shook violently, and nausea swarmed her. She avoided looking at the pictures of the bodies and focused on the text instead. *This will take too much time.* She took out all the multiple files and flipped them open to the relevant pages and clicked several pictures.

Once done, Aisha stuffed the files back and peeped out of the driver-side window. She saw Parth and the other two policemen walking toward the car.

Aisha scurried to the back door of the jeep. Nimbly, she jumped off into the nearby bushes and waited till the police jeep drove off.

Standing up, she brushed off leaves and twigs and headed in the direction of the villa. Head bent, Aisha studied the pictures she had taken. A partial of a body. "Ugh!" She grimaced. Aisha was about to swipe to the next when her fingers stilled. She enlarged the picture.

Her heartbeat raced, and her body went cold as she stared at what was visible of the murdered woman from thigh down. The unfortunate woman wore only one shoe.

Aisha's fingers traced the shoe—plum in color with silver flowers on the side.

Aisha's stomach twisted painfully. She had seen this shoe earlier.

It was the shoe I found on the beach. The night I had plans to sneak inside Kriti Villa. The night Kabir caught me. Or did I catch him?

Chapter 53

The door opened to the conference room and Commissioner Rego walked in. The few policemen in the room got to their feet and saluted her.

"At ease!" The Commissioner waved at them and took the front row seat. The policemen sat behind her. "So, where is the CBI boy?"

The door opened again.

Jacob came in, rolling a white board behind him. Parth came in holding the other end.

"Morning, Commissioner!" Parth called out, wearing his usual attire—white shirt and ironed jeans with a tweed sports jacket.

"Another few minutes and you would be late, CBI!" One of the cops drawled out, his tone snarky.

"Another few minutes, Sir ji, and you would be early." Parth said with his trademark smirk.

"Huh?"

Parth went to the drawing board. "Just matching nonsense with nonsense."

There were a few chuckles.

"Morning, everybody!" Parth tipped his head. "And thank you for gracing us with your presence."

He flipped the white board to the other side. There were two pictures on it—one was a map and the other part was covered with a white chart taped over whatever was written. "At this time, I would like to bring another team member of mine." Parth opened the door and ushered Dr. Lorso in.

"Lesbo!" A policeman sitting in the back row said loudly to his colleague.

Dr. Lorso hesitated.

Parth pushed aside some chairs and grabbed the collar of the surprised policeman who had voiced the insult. "Your disrespectful shit has no place in this room. You will respect her, or you are off this case."

"Officer Mangal, let go of him right now." The Commissioner was on her feet just like everyone else in the room.

Parth continued to hold the Inspector who struggled in his restraint. His face turned red and Parth let him go abruptly.

The man tottered as he rubbed his throat.

"Show some respect!" Parth straightened his clothes. "Sorry, Commissioner. I was just keeping my presentation lively."

The heavyset Commissioner eyeballed Parth's bland face for a few seconds, then sat down, her expression disgruntled. Her officers mimicked her movements.

Jacob gave a sly smile noticing everyone's surprised face. He was used to Parth's shenanigans by now.

Parth walked back to Dr. Lorso. "Sorry you had to hear that."

"Finish your show so we can get back to some real police work." The Commissioner ordered, her face lined with angry lines.

"Yes, Ma'am." Parth turned to the board. "Komal Das and Aditi Kavuri, Ages twenty-one and twenty-three. Bodies found on March 24th, 2016 and December 29th, 2016."

"We know all this!" One grim faced policeman reminded.

Parth stuck a picture on the board. "Victim number seven. Ann Jacob found two days ago on Donna Paula beach. Raped and strangled. Ann had turned eighteen last month."

There was silence for a few minutes as everyone stared at Ann's picture.

"Victim number seven? CBI is weak in math also? If it is the same killer, that would make Ann number three not seven." A cop pointed out.

"Good point. And an obvious one." Commissioner Rego agreed with her Inspector. Her look to Parth was condescending.

Parth reached out and removed the white paper that covered one side of the board.

There were four more pictures on the board. "Meet victim number three, four, five, and six! Thoi Elviz, Julie Fernando, Nafeesa Khan and Sandhya Arora. Ages twenty-two, twenty-one, twenty, and twenty-three respectively. Bodies found on March 30th, 2014; December 26th, 2014; March 20th, 2015; and December 23rd, 2015."

Chapter 54

The commissioner was the first to speak. "Rubbish!" She tugged her crisp work shirt firmly. Her gaze was withering. "Just because you say it, does not make it true. Where are the supporting facts? The evidence?"

Parth turned to Dr. Lorso. "Doctor, please share your findings from the autopsies of the bodies."

"Sure." Dr. Lorso beckoned someone inside the room. Two peons came inside carrying a white board.

"Another board!" Someone groaned in the room.

"I examined the bodies of five out of these seven girls. They all had ingested high doses of valium. The strangulation marks around their necks match in width and size. Same pair of hands asphyxiated them." Dr. Lorso saw that she had the room's attention. "The girls were raped in a similar manner. There was spermicide found in all of them, that means the killer wore a condom. And afterward, he cleaned them by pouring bleach over the girls' torso and genitals. There were no fingerprints or DNA of any kind on the bodies." Dr. Lorso paused. She swallowed as if in pain. "He did not respect the dead. Some injuries and sexual acts were posthumous." She became quiet.

"Why have you not shared all this information with us earlier, Dr. Lorso? Or do you only speak with the CBI?"

"Commissioner, I had mentioned the similarity when I got the second victim," Dr. Lorso looked pointedly at the cop who had insulted her earlier. "But he never listened to me."

Commissioner glared at the officer who was smart enough to avoid his superior's eyes.

"SSP Mangal found more victims and made the connection. We went back and exhumed the bodies of Nafeesa and Julie and did their autopsy again. The MO, the way their bodies were staged, and the presence of bleach confirmed it. These homicides are the work of the same killer."

"This has to be done by the tourists. That's why I hate tourists. They come with their money and peculiar tastes and kill innocent girls," a middle-aged cop sitting directly behind the commissioner shouted.

"Ah! Tourists!" Parth clicked his finger. He walked to the map pinned on the board. The map had seven red dots on it. "Komal was found at Lopez Point, Aditi at a place further from Ashwem Beach, Thoi near the out-of-town Bascillica." Parth touched the appropriate dots. "Julie at the tomb of St. Francis, Nafeesa in a remote area of Salim Ali Bird Sanctuary, Sandhya at Canaguinim Beach and finally Ann at Donna Paula Beach."

"So, all tourists spots, just like Arvind said." the commissioner pointed out.

Parth shook his head. "Yes, all the bodies were found at a tourist spot but that does not mean that they were killed there. Dr. Lorso, please."

Dr. Lorso moved to the front of the room. "Because of the lack of blood or bleach where the bodies were found, it is evident that the girls were killed somewhere else and then brought to those places." She glanced at Parth.

Parth walked next to her. "Yes, these are tourist spots. The tours that go to these spots are more expensive, so not too many people take these tours. But these spots are also known to the locals."

"Then he must be a guide," another cop shouted.

The commissioner had fallen into a sullen silence, like a coach of the losing team.

"Good deduction, and that is what I thought at first, but then Jacob and I did an experiment of sorts." Parth sat on a desk, his one foot resting on the floor and another swung lightly, bent at the knee. "Tell them, Jacob."

"Uh . . . what, Sir?" Jacob clearly was not prepared for the spotlight.

"Jacob, what happened when we went to Beber?" Parth reminded.

"Oh yes, yes! Sir tried to get friendly with the girls but they all said no." Jacob blurted out.

Some laughed openly, and others snickered at Jacob's flustered confession.

Parth gave a wry smile. "Sad, but true!"

"But he got one finally. Very beautiful." Jacob wiped his forehead, his expression clearly saying that he would rather be anywhere but here.

"And that girl is a CBI officer, DSP Sangeeta Malhotra." Parth shared a look with Jacob. "So, you were right earlier Jacob. I got no girl."

"So, has CBI been running an undercover operation in my city without informing me?" The Commissioner frowned heavily.

Parth stood up. "There was no undercover operation, Commissioner. DSP Sangeeta is a computer tech from our Cyber department. She helped me in research. But we can talk about it in your office." He turned to Jacob. "So, the girls we sought out, we told them that we were police, right?"

Jacob nodded heartily.

"Is there a point to this here or are we supposed to sympathize with your dismal impressions on women?" the Commission snapped.

"There is a point. All these girls," Parth glanced at the board, "are beautiful. And not simply pretty but drop-dead gorgeous, confident girls. These girls are feisty, somewhat snobbish and the kind who are not intimidated easily, not even by a police officer. DSP Sangeeta studied their backgrounds. They were educated from good schools and colleges, lived in big cities, and belonged to affluent families. They would never go anywhere with a mere guide. They are the kind that are not scared of the law even if they break it. And that was the experiment Jacob and I did that night at Beber. Not a single girl came with us, even though we flashed our badges. The nice ones laughed at my face and a few told me to do something with myself that I would rather not. So, my question is that, how did this killer convince these beautiful, confident and educated women to come with him?"

Chapter 55

Parth became quiet and let his question sink in the room. All the expressions were thoughtful.

"What else are you not sharing with us, Parth?" The Commissioner asked.

"Today I'm sharing everything, Commissioner." Parth again sat back on the desk. "For all these dead girls, I went to the places they were seen last. There were CCTV cameras at the places Komal, Julie, and Nafeesa were last seen. Sangeeta procured and studied that footage. The victims were behaving normally. They didn't appear threatened or scared for their lives in any way. However, in all the footages, the person they were talking to is always off-camera. He kept himself hidden from the CCTV. That again points in the direction of this killer not being a tourist. He is someone who has scoured the location before and knows exactly where to stand so his face stays hidden."

"But what about Donna Paula? That is not a far-off spot. It is a popular beach and right in the heart of the city." A policeman said, scratching the back of his head.

Parth gave a 'thumbs up' sign. "Absolutely right! Ann was not a premeditated kill. Out of all these murders, she was the only one who was the spur-of-the-moment, an opportunistic kill!" Parth turned to Dr. Lorso.

Dr. Lorso stood up. "There was no bleach on Ann. He never got a chance to clean the body, either because he was disturbed or because he was in a hurry. Ann's body suffered the most damage than all the other girls. So, when he killed her, he was possibly in a frenzied state. Unfortunately, he threw her in the sea, so the fishes and water damaged a lot of evidence," she shook her head regretfully.

"Why would somebody who has been killing so methodically, suddenly indulge in a spur-of-the-moment killing?" The question came from the commissioner.

"Going by Ann's body temperature and level of rigor mortis, Ann's time of death was any time between twenty-four to twenty-eight hours before her body was found." Dr. Lorso remarked.

Parth continued. "That very night, around a few hours earlier, a model was attacked in her sleep. Her attacker tried to strangle her, but he had to run because of the timely arrival of the girl's aunt and a few others, including myself."

"You were there?" Commissioner asked.

"Parth Sir has been hanging out on the beaches and the bars every night." Jacob offered the information.

"One more ritualistic thing about this killer: he kills at the same time every year. He is a creature of habit. He can't help himself; he has to kill. I was hoping to catch him before but. . ." Parth's eyes glimmered with anger.

"So now we wait till December?" Commissioner asked.

"No, we have to catch him before that. My gut tells me that if we find out how he is luring these girls, we will get him. That is the key! Also, we should reopen conversations with those who were with the girls when they disappeared. Friends, family etc. It is quite surprising what things people tend to remember after some time. What they think to be trivial or unimportant could be the thing that breaks this case open." Parth said. "I have shared everything that I know, Commissioner. Now you all know as much as I do."

The Commissioner got to her feet and faced her team. She appeared far from happy. "These murders happened here under our noses. We will find this man. Inspector Arvind, get a team of our best people. I want you and SSP Mangal leading this investigation and I want results fast. Every single lead, big or small, must be investigated. Am I clear?"

"Yes, Ma'am!" Everyone saluted the commissioner sharply.

The Commissioner turned to Parth. "Get the job done. You will get all the resources that you need."

Parth saluted her. "Thank you, Commissioner."

The commissioner extended her hand toward the doctor. "Thank you, Dr. Lorso, for all your help. Welcome to the team."

"Thank you Commissioner. We will find him."

The Commissioner left the room.

"Parth Sir!"

Parth turned. "Jacob?"

"Sir, I want to be a part of your team too." Jacob's look was humbled.

"To spy on me for the Commissioner?"

"No, Sir, to learn from you. I thought you were eccentric." Jacob swallowed. "But you are also brilliant. Please let me be a part of the team. Sir, I feel useful for the first time. I feel like police."

"You are right, I'm a hardcore eccentric. You have nothing to worry, Jacob. You *are* a part of my team." Parth nodded. "Do me a favor, get all the information you can on Aisha Khatri."

"SSP Parth," Dr. Lorso joined him. "There is something else I did not say to the room. Something that came to me today morning . . ."

"Go on."

"These murders are too well-planned to be done by one person."

"There could be more than one killer?" Parth lowered his voice. "Like a team?"

The doctor nodded.

"Are you sure? Any evidence?"

The doctor shook her head. "Not yet, but I'm looking. But my gut very strongly says so. The killer just seems very organized to be an individual working by himself."

Parth nodded, his expression thoughtful. "Then, let us keep this to ourselves till we find conclusive evidence."

"I will keep looking . . . examining the bodies," she grimaced. "And, I thought I had seen it all!"

"Call me if you think of anything else. I'm going to deep storage."

"Why deep storage?"

"Because all the victim's things are stored there. The killer might have taken a souvenir." Parth shared. "This too stays between us."

"Sure." Dr. Lorso said. "I hope you find what you are looking for."

"Actually, I'm hoping *not* to find it." Parth was thinking of the text Aisha had send him earlier asking to check each victim's footwear.

Chapter 56

Next Day

Parth was in the room he was sharing with Inspector Arvind and Jacob when Aisha called him.

"Yes?" Parth's voice was brisk.

"I have profile, Parth . . . Sir." Aisha fumbled on the last word.

"Parth is fine." He said, placing his cell on his new desk. "Hold on. I'm putting you on speaker." He gestured at Inspector Arvind and Jacob to come over.

"So, Ms. Aisha, I have Inspector Arvind and head constable Jacob with me. Gentleman, this is Ms. Aisha Khatri, our consulting behavioral analyst."

"Behavioral analyst! Who will we be calling next? A tarot card reader or the Voodoo lady?" were Inspector Arvind's opening words.

Aisha grew quiet.

"I would not make such acerbic comments, Inspector, given your team's unsuccessful attempts at catching this guy." Parth took charge of the conversation. "Also, you are free to leave this room. The commissioner will be informed of your reluctance to work with me."

The inspector grunted and mumbled a quick apology.

"Aisha, please continue." Parth slapped on some extra courtesy in his words.

Aisha took a deep breath and began. "Okay, so here goes. This killer is rare. Usually, serials killers are either Psychopaths or Sociopaths. But this one is a mix of both."

"Explain the difference between psychopath and sociopath?" Parth asked, understanding Arvind and Jacob's expressions.

"Sociopaths are unstable, nervous, and easily agitated. They are prone to violence. They can never hold a job down or function properly in a society. Sociopaths can form attachments. They commit violence haphazardly. They are unorganized and prone to spontaneous violence rather than organized acts."

"Should I be taking notes?" Inspector Arvind interrupted.

Parth waved a dismissive hand. "Keep going."

"Psychopaths, on the other hand, are unable to form any attachments. They feel no remorse for their crimes and are very dangerous for they can mimic a normal life to the T."

"What does that mean? Mimic?" Parth asked.

"A psychopath can easily hide in the society because he can lead the life of a regular person. He will have a steady job, be married, and get along well with others. Also, Psychopaths know how to manipulate others. Their crimes are always planned meticulously over some time. Psychopaths are hardest to catch because they hardly make mistake or leave any clues." Aisha paused.

"You make them sound like superheroes, madam." Jacob voiced.

"Sorry, don't mean to. Just letting everyone on the table know that Psychopaths are hard to catch. Like Raman Raghavan, Ted Bundy, John Wayne Garcia to name some." Aisha answered.

"You said this killer is a mix? Why?" Parth asked.

Chapter 57

"Good question." Aisha said. "All the first six victims were the act of a psychopath. Cool and calculated and without any clues. But Ann Jacob was different. His frustration was high, and adrenaline was pushing him to rape and kill. So, he did."

"So, for Ann it was wrong place, wrong time." Arvind remarked.

"Yes. But if he were a true psychopath, he would never have gone after Ann. He would not commit a random act of crime." Aisha finished.

Everyone in the room lapsed into thoughtful silence.

"Parth said earlier that the night this madman had attacked Ann, he had also made a similar attempt on a model. Do you know about that?" Arvind asked.

"Yes." Aisha did not mention that Kiara was the model or how she was related to her. Parth had already asked her not to share any personal information with anyone on the team.

"So, unlike all the other victims, this model was assaulted in a rather public surrounding—a house full of people. Why?"

"Arvind is right. That attack on the model was different. The risk was too high. So, except for the month being March, the month he always kills, there is nothing similar to his attack on the model. Then, he goes and kills Ann in a random frenzied manner. Why did he do that?" Parth said.

Arvind and Jacob gave Parth blank looks. Even Aisha kept her silence.

"Okay, anything else, Ms. Aisha?"

"Yes, some personal stats. He is a male between twenty-five to forty years of age. He is single and has a steady job. He is either a local or he has lived here and knows this town well."

The door opened, and DSP Sangeeta Malhotra walked in. "Morning!" She took a seat. "Sorry Parth, I was finishing another call."

Parth introduced Sangeeta to everybody and gave her a quick update. "Anything else, Aisha?"

"One very important thing." Aisha cleared her throat. "He hates beauty."

"No, he doesn't! He only kills beautiful women!" Arvind argued.

"When was the last time any of you hurt something you liked?" Aisha said, stoically.

"We are talking about the insane, obsessive kind of hatred for beautiful women and beautiful things. He kills beautiful women and puts their bodies in beautiful places to defile the beauty of these spots. My guess is, someone very beautiful did something awful to him."

"Mummy issues?" Parth quipped.

"Or wife or teacher, but a very beautiful woman damaged him or that is what he thinks." Aisha answered. "And these girls remind him of that woman. In his mind, he is simply killing that woman over and over."

"Wow. That narrows the field down." Sangeeta mocked. That earned her a smile from Arvind.

"The murders go back three years. Anything before that?" Aisha asked.

"Not yet. We are looking." Parth stretched his arms over his head.

"You should be looking for attacks on beautiful women, specifically in the month of March and December." Aisha corrected.

Those in the room glanced at each other. "Now that does narrow the field." Parth quipped.

"Also, one more thing, Parth. Do you have map of the city handy? Essentially his killing zone?" Aisha asked.

"Yes, we do," Sangeeta said.

"Hold on!" Parth got to his feet and pulled out a map from his laptop bag. He unrolled the map and spread it on a table. Arvind, Sangeeta, and Jacob gathered around the table. "We have the map out!"

"Okay, grab a marker and join the dots of the location where these bodies were found." Aisha said.

Jacob handed Parth a marker and Parth followed Aisha's suggestion.

"Holy cow!" Sangeeta murmured.

"It's almost a circle." Parth remarked.

"Yes, patterns within a pattern." Aisha said.

"As in?" Arvind asked.

Parth rubbed his chin thoughtfully. "As in, he will complete the circle. The next place to leave the body will be a tourist spot that falls somewhere between Salim Ali Bird Sanctuary and Canaguinim Beach. That would complete a circle. Right, Ms. Aisha?"

"Yes, that's right." Aisha replied.

Arvind slapped the table. "That is very good. There are only a few tourist spots between these two points. We can have surveillance there. We will get this bastard."

"No point, right now. Closer to the end of October or November. He will stick to his pattern. He is done for right now." Aisha said. "Also, two more things about the circle."

"Go on!" Parth said.

"The circle, if you put on a body, resembles a mole. A beauty spot. Could you check if these girls have a beauty mark, a prominently visible one, somewhere on their bodies?" Aisha spoke quietly.

"Hold on." Parth nodded at Sangeeta.

"Sure," Sangeeta opened her laptop and started scrolling through her files.

Everyone waited impatiently as Sangeeta checked the laptop.

"Aisha's right, Sir! All the girls had moles on their faces. Prominent ones either above the upper lip or under the left eye." Sangeeta confirmed.

"Yeah!" Jacob made a fist.

"This is super, Ms. Aisha." Arvind said, his face wreathed in a smile.

"Thank you." Aisha responded.

"Aisha you said there are two things about the circle. What is the other?" Parth asked.

Aisha sighed. "Circles have infinite number of sides. So, once this circle is complete, another circle will be started somewhere else."

"What does that mean?" Arvind asked.

"That means that this killer will never stop killing. When this pattern is complete, He will simply start a new one."

Chapter 58

Khatri Apartment, Mumbai.

Next Evening.

The sound of the doorbell made Aisha drop what she was holding. The wooden spoon clattered to the floor.

Putting it in the sink, she emerged from the kitchen, smoothening her hands over her printed red and black A-line knee-length dress. Her hair was shampoo-ed, blow-dried, and clipped at the back of her head, half up and half down. Her make-up was simple and light. All this preparation was for a special guest—Kabir Rana. Kiara had done the honors of inviting her boss over for dinner without consulting Aisha and on the night Aisha was cooking.

Aisha's feelings about meeting Kabir were ambivalent. A big part of her could not wait to meet him and was missing him terribly since they had parted in Goa, and yet, a part of her wanted more time away from Kabir so she could make her mind up about him.

Being close to Kabir distracted Aisha from any other thought, except how much she craved and enjoyed his company. His brooding looks, chiseled face, and dry wit coupled with a sharp mind eclipsed everything and everyone else from Aisha's mind.

Play it cool! Aisha took a breath and opened the door. Her eyes immediately went past Kiara and snagged with Kabir's dark ones. He gave her a warm smile that made her want to curl her toes.

"I'm here too, Boo."

Aisha felt her cheeks grow warm, especially when Kabir's grin only became wider.

"Come in guys." Aisha stepped back.

"You look hot! You should dress up more often." Kiara walked in airily, leaving Kabir and Aisha at the door.

Kabir moved closer. "You look beautiful, Aisha. I missed you." His voice was husky as his lips tilted in a tender smile.

Aisha stared up at him. Her whole body warmed to his presence. There must be some other explanation for his being on the beach the night I found the shoe.

"Ah, there you are." Aisha's father came out of his room. He and Kabir shook hands. "Welcome, Kabir. Shall we sit on the terrace? It is a very pleasant evening."

"That's a good idea, Papa." Aisha said.

"Sure, Sir!" Kabir added. Aisha's father walked toward the terrace and began switching on the lights.

"These are for you. Kiara said you like orchids."

Aisha took the violet flowers. "I do! Thank you, they are beautiful." She hid her face behind the flowers, trying to gather her composure that was running away faster than a dog without a leash.

"It smells good in here. Is it you or the food?" Kabir murmured. He seemed reluctant to move away from her.

"Are you saying I smell like garlic?" Aisha tried to sound less awkward by laughing some.

"I like whatever you smell of," Kabir said, his hand grazing hers.

A thrill shot through her. Her fingers curled in her palms. Aisha felt warmer than the food in the oven. "Please!" She entreated, not sure what she was asking for.

Kabir stepped away. "I'm sorry. I always end up making you uncomfortable when that is the last thing I want to do." He turned sharply away from Aisha and went in the direction of her father, a bottle of wine in his hand.

Shucks, he misunderstood me!

Aisha went to the kitchen where she helped Pinky arrange the appetizers and placed the orchids in a vase. Holding the appetizers, Aisha joined her father and Kabir on the terrace.

"I was telling Kabir about how you landscaped this Zen garden." Retired Judge Khatri shared. "We all love spending time here."

Aisha smiled and nodded, walking to the wooden dining table with long cushioned benches on either side. Her eyes sought Kabir's. He smiled, and Aisha felt herself relax.

Kabir deftly helped Aisha lay out the table. He saw the retired Judge observe him. "I studied and lived abroad. I'm used to doing things around the house."

"I also do house work." Aisha's father volunteered.

"Dada, carrying your cup to the kitchen is not house work." Kiara teased, joining them. She had changed into a casual and comfortable dress.

"Well, neither is carrying your plate to the kitchen." Retired Judge parried.

"Ignore these two." Aisha said to Kabir as they all sat down. "Sometimes, I feel there are two kids in the house."

"You heard that, Dadu? Boo called you a child." Kiara said, picking up the bruschetta and offering it to Kabir.

"A man is known by the company he keeps," the retired Judge quipped.

Much to Aisha's delight, the conversation flowed freely for the rest of the evening and the food tasted good. Kabir was a suave courteous guest, with funny tales to share and compliments to give.

"Some coffee?" Aisha's father asked.

"Sure. And some tiramisu." Aisha got to her feet.

"No Aisha, you sit. My granddaughter and I will take care of the coffee and dessert. C'mon, Kiara."

Kiara groaned mockingly. However, she got to her feet. "Never be the youngest in a household."

"Let me come and help you guys." Aisha stirred.

"Don't be silly. You can't leave our guest alone! Stay with Kabir and that's an order." Her father waved her down and walked back in the house with Kiara trailing him.

Chapter 59

Suppressed nerves began singing again. "Hope you enjoyed the food." Aisha glanced at Kabir sitting across from her.

"Aisha, I have to confess something." Kabir's tone was urgent. He leaned forward and took her hand. Aisha braced herself for the worst even as she enjoyed the feel of her hand in his. "That afternoon when you were in my room, the reason I stopped when I did was because I did not want to take advantage of you. You were vulnerable and emotional and so was I. I didn't feel it was right to . . ." His hold on her tightened possessively. "You know I—"

"Are you hiding something from me, from everyone?" Aisha blurted out.

"Are you scared of me?" Kabir's smile was wry. He gently let go of Aisha's hand and placed it back on the table, fleetingly caressing her fingers. Aisha felt cold at the loss of his touch.

Kabir sat back and a familiar aloofness came into his eyes. "I'm not an easy person to be with Aisha."

Every time he takes my name, I feel like somebody just poured liquid chocolate on me.

"Stop looking at me like that." Kabir cleared his throat.

Aisha averted her face and inhaled sharply. Every instinct of hers screamed at her to kill the physical distance between Kabir and her.

"So, which nights of the week do you cook?" Kabir attempted to lighten the intense moment between them.

"Which nights are you free?"

Kabir chuckled and then sobered. "I just wanted to tell you—"

"Kiara, take out the cups with those golden things." Her father's voice fell on their ears.

Kiara's dry response followed. "Those golden things are flowers, Dada. You don't know flowers?"

Aisha and Kabir shared a smile. "Those two are funny. They should have a show of their own."

"They probably will. Papa is bringing out the best chinaware. After all, we don't have royalty over every day." Aisha teased, rolling her tongue against her cheek.

Kabir's smile fell off his face faster than a coin in a slot machine.

"What? What did I say wrong?"

"That title never brought me happiness. It is where all my problems began. I have left that part of my life behind even though it refuses to leave me." Kabir's mouth twisted bitterly.

"Hold on," Aisha acted as if she were getting up. "I'll ask Papa to take out the steel or the disposable glasses." She tried to inject some levity. *I'm already missing his smile!* Kabir's austere expression lightened. "So how is the villa in Goa? Was there a lot of damage due to the storm?"

"Nothing that can't be repaired. You really helped me that day. You know how thankful I am, right?"

"All in a day's work." Aisha rested her chin on her hands and gazed at him. Kabir fell quiet, returning her gaze unblinking.

Desire and longing seeped the silence and their eyes.

A sudden breeze blew some loose hair on Aisha's face. Kabir caught the strands and tucked them behind her ear, letting his fingers trail over her cheeks. Aisha turned her cheek against his fingers. Kabir inhaled sharply. "Aisha . . ." His voice was husky.

"Coffee is here." Kiara's emergence made Kabir drop his hand from Aisha's face. Aisha too moved back on the bench.

"Kiara has awful timing." Kabir mumbled, his gaze still heated.

Aisha grinned. "I know." Her cheek still held the warmth of his touch. "Where's Papa, Kia?"

"Right here with tiramisu." Her father followed Kia.

Content and relaxed, Aisha let the conversation flow above her head as she ate her tiramisu.

"When do we get to see the calendar pictures, Kabir?" Kiara asked.

"They are nearly done." Kabir replied, even as his gaze kept wandering to Aisha's bent head and the soft smile on her delectable and distracting mouth

"So, you are based in Goa?" The retired judge asked.

"No, Sir. Mostly Mumbai and wherever else my shoot takes me. I usually go to Goa around March and again around New Year." Kabir remarked, sipping coffee.

Aisha looked up. "So, around March and December?"

"Actually, end of February and December for sure." Kabir said. "This tiramisu is very good." He complimented.

"Thank you," Aisha forced herself to smile. She felt the warmth of the past hour slip away. She simply waited for Kabir to finish his coffee and dessert. She faked a yawn and acted as if she were trying to cover it.

"The Chef is tired." Kabir teased.

"Sorry, I just . . . please ignore that." Aisha said, knowing very well Kabir wouldn't overstay his welcome.

Kabir rose to his feet. "It's almost eleven. I should go. I really enjoyed the evening." He included the retired judge and Kiara in his glance, but his eyes kept straying back to Aisha.

Aisha bit her lips, guilt gnawing at her.

"Thank you for a lovely meal, Aisha!"

Aisha kept her smile causal. "You are welcome. It was our pleasure."

Kabir stared at her until Kiara coughed rather loudly.

"Spare the rod and spoil the child." Aisha muttered under her breath.

Kabir left soon after.

Aisha went to the kitchen and helped Pinky clear and put everything away even as Kiara and her father discussed the dinner and their guest.

Fifteen minutes later, Aisha snuck in her room and locked the door behind her. She went to the bathroom and locked that door too. She was quick to dial a number.

After a few rings someone answered.

Chapter 60

"Okay, so you saw the news?" Parth said.

"No, what happened?" Aisha frowned. "Did you find another . .
."

"No, not another body. A prominent local newspaper ran the story with some inside leaks."

"That's not good. Not good at all." Aisha shook her head. "The fact that he leaves the bodies on display clearly reeks of attention-seeking personality. This kind of news coverage will only make him want more attention."

"I know. *And* the copycats." Parth said.

"Yikes. Did the article give away a lot of confidential information?"

"Enough to know that the leak is an inside job." Parth barked. "I'm glad you and I withheld the shoe element from the rest of the team."

"That the killer takes the shoe from each victim as a souvenir?" Aisha nodded, lowering herself on the bathroom floor. "Why did you ask me not to mention it to the others?"

"Because CBI and local police are never the best of friends. I learned it the hard way. And today's article just confirms that it was the right thing to do." Parth added. "Why does he take a shoe? Not some jewelry or a piece of clothing?"

"The shoe probably means something to him. It must be connected to what happened to him, what made him who he is. If we catch him, we will have an answer to that."

"When we catch him, not if!" Parth corrected. "Do you think he could be a shoe salesman?"

Aisha's smile was wry. "He's too smart to be that obvious. He will be anything but a shoe salesman."

"Hmm! So why did you call?"

"Um!" Aisha hesitated. She remembered Kabir's face as he had brushed her hair from her face. "Um!"

"Miss Aisha?"

"Uh" Aisha exhaled. "Yeah! So, Kiara, she went to work today. And she is going tomorrow."

"Okay?" Parth waited.

"That's it!" Aisha grimaced. "So, should I let her go to work?"

"Don't worry. I told you your niece is protected. Just keeping her shadows invisible."

"Shadows?"

"The cops who are protecting her are staying out of sight."

"Okay. Thank you."

"One more thing, Aisha. I'm not your buddy, so don't just pick up the phone and call me randomly. *Only* call when you have something important. Good night."

Parth hung up.

"Jerk!" Aisha glared at the phone. *Why did I not tell Parth about Kabir's travel plans?* She rested her chin on her knees. *I will investigate Kabir but on my own.* Resting her head back on the tiled wall, Aisha touched her cheek where Kabir had touched her. It felt cold.

#

Several Hours Later.

Kabir again turned on his side. He saw the faint light of dawn behind the dark silk curtains of his bedroom. "Dammit!" He got up from his comfortable bed. Adjusting his pajamas and thin tee, he used the remote on his bedside table to draw the curtains. Sliding the balcony doors open, he stepped out.

His second-floor apartment overlooked The Marine Drive and the brownish gray ocean beyond it. He rubbed the overnight stubble.

I thought I was too old to spend a sleepless night over a girl.

The whole night he had reminisced over Aisha—her face, her varied expressions, her gestures, her sweet lilting voice, and her body. He had seen her curves on the day they had gone running—all tight and voluptuous in those skin-hugging tights. And the dress she wore at dinner last night? He was already imagining taking it off her. Kabir ran a hand over his eyes. "Horny bastard!"

I know her for merely a week and here I am, lusting after her. What the fuck is wrong with me? Why can't I resist her?

"Dammit!"

Kabir went back inside. Aisha was nothing like the models he dated on and off, or even his late wife. Aisha was simple, grounded, and funny. *Last night, I saw another side of her,* Kabir thought while brushing his teeth. *The binding force of her family. Can so much goodness heal someone? Even someone like me?*

Kabir's onyx eyes held hope and anguish. He hurriedly washed his mouth and went into his room.

"I should call Shreya. She will set my head straight and put an end to all this bullshit!"

Sitting down on the bed, he dialed a number and put the phone to his ear. Shreya did not answer. Kabir smacked the phone against his thigh. "Dammit, Shreya, talk to me. I don't want to hurt Aisha. You have to stop me before I do!"

Chapter 61

Next Day

"**So, are** you seriously going to pick me up from work?" Kiara asked, getting off the car.

"Yes, Ma'am!" Aisha pushed the food basket toward Kiara's recently hired spot boy sitting at the back. "Raju, take care of madam, okay?"

Only Aisha knew that Raju was a martial arts expert and a perfect marksman, security for hire.

Nodding, Raju took the basket and got off the car.

"What are your plans for today, Boo?"

"I need to run a few errands," Aisha lied. "SMS me when you know what time the shoot will get over."

"Aren't you overdressed just for errands?" Kiara gave her a sly smile.

"Bye!" Aisha hurriedly turned the car around and drove some distance and pulled to the side of the road.

Grabbing her cell, she dialed a number. It did not go unanswered. "Hi Vikas, this is Aisha Khatri, Kiara's aunt. Kia gave me your number." Aisha bit her lip at the lie. She had scrolled

Kiara's contact list hoping to find Kabir's number. Not finding Kabir's number, she had settled for the second best—Vikas, his PA.

"Yes, it is very important that I speak with Kabir. It is about Kiara, yes. Do you know where I can find him?"

Vikas promptly gave her the address to Kabir's studio.

"Thank you. I appreciate this. You take care. Bye!"

Ignoring the palpitations, Aisha drove to the address Vikas had given and lied about an appointment with Kabir to get inside the complex.

Aisha walked to the second-floor apartment. *This seems like a residential complex.* Taking a deep breath, her fingers wrapped in tissue, Aisha pressed the doorbell.

A man wearing a crisp white uniform opened the door. "Yes?"

"Hi! I'm here to meet Kabir Rana. Is he here?"

"Do you have an appointment, Madam?" The man asked, stifly.

"Here, give him this please!" Aisha handed him her card, which he took rather dubiously like she was handing him something covered in mold. "He had dinner at our place yesterday." That thawed the man's expression—somewhat.

"Please wait here!" The door closed on her face.

Aisha adjusted the butterfly pendant around her neck. Today, her skirt was white with colorful embroidered flowers and pale blue brocade *kurti* with light silver thread work on the cuffs and collar. She had blow-dried her hair and her make-up was just right to highlight her eyes and cheekbones.

Aisha didn't have to wait for long. The door opened within minutes. Kabir stood there—a surprised expression riding his handsome face. "Hello Aisha!"

Aisha felt her insides melt just looking at him.

Kabir stood back and opened the door wider. "Please come in. What, no leftovers from last night?"

Confused, Aisha hesitated at the threshold. "Was I supposed to? Did you ask—"

Catching her wrist, Kabir pulled her in. "I was kidding," he teased.

"Oh!" Aisha tried to keep her expression casual but Kabir was warming her simply by the way he looked. His tall lean body was clad in a navy blue T-shirt that clung perfectly to his ripped chest and he wore snug blue jeans while his feet were bare. His hair was damp from the shower and was curling over his forehead. *I want to sink my fingers in his hair.*

Taking quick steps, Aisha walked past him and stopped. "Wow!"

Kabir's spacious apartment was decorated in black and white with stunning pictures of people and nature dominating the walls, adding color and 'oomph' to the minimalistic and masculine décor. "I just hired a good interior designer."

"But you did take all these pictures."

"It's my hidden talent," Kabir joked. "Have a seat please," he gestured at the sofas.

"Thanks!" Aisha took a seat facing the windows that overlooked Marine Drive and the sea. "Do you live here?"

Kabir took a seat across from her. "Yes, were you expecting someone else?" he looked amused.

Aisha shook her head. "No, no! What I meant was that I had asked your assistant where I could find you and he said that you would be in your studio. And then he gave me this address."

"This apartment is a duplex. The upper portion is the studio and my bedroom."

"Oh!" Aisha nodded and sat quietly, chewing on her lips, and tapping her heel. There was silence for a few seconds.

"The way you are fidgeting, I'm guessing this is more than just a social call?" Kabir murmured.

Aisha smoothed her skirt over her knees.

Kabir kept the conversation neutral. "What will you have, coffee or tea or something else?"

"Coffee mixed with Red Bull!"

"Serious?"

"No." Aisha shook her head. "Just coffee, thanks."

"Sure." Kabir got to his feet and disappeared in a room to the side of the hall. He was back within seconds.

"Hi!" Aisha swallowed.

"Hi . . . again." Kabir watched her, his eyes bent at the ends, his look tender. "What's going on, Aisha?" He reached out and lightly took her hand in his.

Okay, screw everything, I'm just saying it. Aisha inhaled sharply. "Do you like me?"

Kabir jerked his head, his eyes narrowed even as his grip tightened on her hands. "Like you? What do you . . . mean?"

Aisha gripped his hand back. "You know exactly what I mean."

"Aisha, it's not that simple." Kabir's eyes held pain as he let go of her hands and got up. He walked up to the glass and leaned against it. Aisha watched him, her eyes huge. "I'm not right for you." His eyes were dull. "You deserve better!"

"That's not what I asked." Aisha cleared her throat. "Do you like me? Because you give mixed signals." She adjusted her cuffs, her voice sounding as troubled as she felt. "Blow hot, blow cold all the time. It confuses the hell out of me . . ." She trailed off while watching him.

Kabir come back and sat down next to her. "I'm sorry, I'm such as asshole!"

"You are. But I seem to like it." Aisha blurted then closed her eyes. "I'm sorry, I think I'm losing it," she opened her eyes as Kabir cupped her cheek.

"I do like you." Kabir stared deep into her eyes. "Probably more than I should."

Aisha returned Kabir's tender gaze with everything good she felt for him.

"Please don't. My self-control isn't the strongest around you." His voice was thick.

"What am I doing?" Aisha asked, her face still against his hand.

Kabir rubbed the soft skin of her cheeks with his thumb. "Just being yourself, sweet Aisha. Honest, open, loving. And so darn sexy!'" His thumb slipped near to her lips.

Kabir's eyes followed his fingers. The hunger in his eyes was unmistakable. He brushed the edges of her mouth and Aisha's breath hitched in her throat. She forgot all about the investigation, her suspicions of the man in front of her. Everything except how Kabir was making her feel simply by the passionate look in his eyes and his tender touch on her skin. Aisha's lips parted, and her eyes darkened.

"You are driving me mad!" Kabir growled.

Unknowingly, she leaned toward him.

Chapter 62

A sudden cough interrupted Aisha and Kabir. They jumped apart.

"Dammit!" Kabir moved his feet to make way for his help wheeling in the coffee.

Aisha shifted back, trying to calm her uneven breathing down. The man placed the coffee cups and a tray of mini pastries and crackers and cheese on the table.

Kabir waited till they were alone again. "Aisha, you should leave before I hurt you." He said, his head hung down.

"I want to know you."

That earned her a confused glance. "What?"

"I want to know you, know things about you . . ." Aisha did not hide her vulnerability. She patted the seat next to her, the one he had just vacated. Kabir took his spot back. Their legs were close enough to touch.

"I have already shared my worst with you!" Kabir's eyes held torment.

"I want to know the best too." Aisha pleaded.

"What if there is no best, sweet Aisha?"

Aisha shifted closer to him. "You survived the worst all by yourself and stayed strong and creative." She gestured at the pictures on the wall. "There has to be good inside you."

"You don't know me!" Kabir rubbed his knuckles under her chin.

"I want to. That's what this whole conversation is about." Aisha caught his hand and brought it on her lap.

Kabir studied their hands. "You are sure about this? What if I hurt you or you find out things that you don't like about me?" He turned to her. "I don't think I could bear you hating me."

Aisha wanted to cry but she pasted a smile. "I promise never to hate you, but I might get irritated."

Kabir gave a wry smile. "I might too."

Aisha rolled her tongue against the soft lining of her cheek. "More than what you usually are?"

Kabir dipped his head and brought his mouth close to Aisha's heart-shaped lips. His hot breath grazed the soft pinks of her mouth. "I'm not irritated all the time."

Aisha's eyes flickered to his lips and then back to his eyes. Kabir waited as if asking her permission for the kiss.

Aisha inhaled a sad sigh. "Can we hold off . . . on this? For a bit?" She saw her disappointment reflected in Kabir's eyes.

Kabir pulled back and got to his feet. "Drink your coffee. It's getting cold." He grabbed his cup and moved to another sofa.

"Thanks!" Aisha wrapped her hand around the blue cup with the white patterns. She cleared her throat. "Becoming a mother to Kia when I was fifteen never left me any time for any romanticism—in life or in thought." Aisha sipped her beverage and met Kabir's eyes. He was listening. "And no guys wanted to be with me, knowing very well that they would come second to my niece."

"It must have been hard." Kabir responded quietly.

"On some days, yes. I stopped attending weddings in my late twenties. There were people asking questions and my answers had not changed."

"I'm sure there were several men who would have shown interest in you. In the past week alone, you had three men chasing you," Kabir teased.

"Three?"

"The Doc, the cop, and me!" Kabir smiled at her over the rim of his coffee cup.

"Yeah, but I'm only chasing one . . ." Aisha stumbled, and her cheeks grew heated seeing Kabir's wolfish smile. "Did I take a name?" She laughed at the sour look Kabir tossed at her.

"You are such a buzzkill. So, how do you get to know me better? Do you have a plan in mind?" Kabir sat back. There was nothing casual about how he looked at Aisha.

"The usual way. We spend time together." Aisha could not meet his eyes. *Gosh, when I jump, I really jump in the deep end and that too without a harness!*

"So, when do we start?"

"Whenever!" Aisha licked her lips.

"Hold on." Kabir gave her a calculating look. "You aren't doing all this to keep me away from Kiara, are you?"

"Are you interested in Kia?" Aisha spoke slowly, wondering why she dreaded his answer so much.

Kabir grinned. "I never was."

Aisha pulled her neck back. "Yes, you were!"

"Shreya, a dear friend, suggested it. But I spent a few minutes with Kiara and knew she was too young. Then *you* came along."

"But you did ask Kiara out on a date!" Aisha's expression was confused.

"To get you mad." Kabir kept his cup down. "You are stunning when angry."

Aisha, who was glaring at the floor, gritted her teeth.

"Are you angry now?"

"No, not at all!" Aisha gave him a tight smile. "Do you like me angry?"

"Maybe!" Kabir teased. "But I definitely love your voice. It is very attractive. You remember the night on the pier? Your voice was what caught my attention first."

"What? You like my voice more than my photography skills?"

Kabir got up, a broad grin on his face. "So, do you want to hang around my pad for some time? I just need to finish up a few things."

"I don't want to intrude."

"Don't be silly. Give me twenty minutes." Kabir grabbed a TV remote and brought it over to Aisha. "And my butler's name is Prakash. Ring nine on the phone and he will answer it."

Aisha nodded and smiled at Kabir. Impulsively, he raised Aisha's hand and planted an open-mouthed kiss on her knuckles. Aisha could only stare at him.

Reluctantly, Kabir dropped her hand. "I will never get any work done around you." He said as he went up, taking the stairs two at a time.

Chapter 63

Aisha immediately put the TV on and left it on a news channel. Casting furtive glances around, she got up hoping to snoop around the house. Her phone rang.

Parth!

"Morning, Parth."

"You are fired!"

"Excuse me?" Aisha stuttered. "What . . . happened?"

"You lied to me. You are no certified behavioral analyst." Parth spat out the words. "Your license and degree are as big a lie as you are, Aisha Khatri. That bloody university was shut down six years ago for giving out fake degrees."

Aisha kept quiet while chewing her bottom lip. *Shit! How did he find out?*

"Do you know what damage you have done?" Parth sounded furious. "These past few days, the CBI, the entire Panaji police, has been focusing on the profile you gave to me."

"My brief is accurate." Aisha protested.

"Bullshit! The only reason I'm not arresting you and throwing you in jail is because going after you would waste my time. But I promise, after the case is over I'm coming after you, Aisha Khatri. With all the power of the CBI."

Aisha grimaced. "Please hear me out—"

"You are a liar and a fraud. I'm coming after you. Ask your father to take his robes out. His retirement is over."

"How dare—" Aisha realized Parth had hung up already. "Bloody hell!"

Aisha felt her stomach roll and her mouth tasted sour. She clasped her knees. *How the hell did he find out? Damn. This is not good.* She took hurried steps toward the front door. The tissue in her hand lay forgotten on the sofa.

"Going somewhere?"

Aisha glanced up. Kabir was smiling down at her. "I just thought I would . . ." She felt dazed. "Are . . . are you done?"

"Yes, come on up. Let me introduce you to my family." Kabir misunderstood the nervousness in Aisha's face. "I will behave myself. You are safe with me." He cocked a smile.

Maybe safe from you but not from a crazy cop.

Aisha climbed the stairs, trying to shake the melancholy and panic Parth's threat had pushed her in.

"You look upset?" Kabir asked, watching from the top of the stairs.

"I'm fine!" Aisha pushed a smile on her face.

They entered a bedroom done in gray and blue shades with white accents. The furniture was contemporary and minimalist. Her eyes were fixated on a king-size bed that dominated the bedroom with silk sheets and patterned cushions.

"Like the bed?" Kabir teased.

Aisha tossed him an irked glance.

Kabir stopped next to rectangular dark wood table with several framed pictures. "My family."

Chapter 64

Aisha reacted to the vulnerability on his face. She realized that Kabir did not share this side of him with many.

Just like me!

She quickly walked over to Kabir, trying to forget Parth's threat. "So, who's who?"

Kabir pointed at a picture of him and a young woman. Kabir looked much younger in it. The woman's smile was strained and Kabir sported his usual cagey expression. "That is Lavina and I. This was a week or two before she . . ."

"She was very beautiful."

"On the outside, anyway." Kabir pointed at a picture of a family with four grown-ups and two kids. "My paternal grandparents, my parents and that," He pointed to a beautiful teenager, "is, was, Kriti and that's me."

"May I?" Aisha asked. Kabir nodded. Aisha picked up the frame and studied the picture. "Your sister and you resemble your Dad and Dadi a lot." She put the frame back. "You have a beautiful family."

"*Had* a beautiful family," Kabir straightened the picture. "Dad passed away a few years after Kriti. Now everyone lives in London."

"Do you visit them?"

"No, but we do talk on Diwali and on Kriti and Dad's birthday."

The coldness in Kabir's face seared her. Aisha chose to distract him. "So, who is this girl? She is in a lot of pictures with you."

Kabir's mouth softened as he gazed at those pictures. "That is my childhood friend, savior, shrink, and family all rolled into one—Shreya Kulhar."

"Your savior?" Aisha ignored the stab of jealousy that pierced her.

Kabir sighed. "After Kriti and then Lavina, each time I went to a very dark place and each time, Shreya was the one who pulled me out. She saved me every time. Even though I always told her that I wasn't worth saving. I—"

Whatever Kabir was about to say was interrupted as Aisha clasped his hand, her expression earnest. "You are worth saving. Every life is worth saving."

Kabir tugged her close. His gaze roved over Aisha's face with a deep hunger.

"Thanks to social media, the world will always need good photographers." Aisha tried retracting her hand from his.

Why do I get so carried away around him? I must keep this light.

"I want to see the other pictures."

"Sure, you do!" Kabir held her hand for a second longer but then let go.

Aisha picked up a picture placed in the back. "Hey, I know this guy!"

"He's Shreya's ex-husband. How do you know him?"

"Isn't he the channel head of Vision TV?"

"Yes, the same. Cheated on her after marriage. They divorced around two years ago."

Aisha nodded. "Poor Shreya. He's known in the industry as a creep. Hits on anything female that moves."

"Let me know if he ever bothers you."

"Okay!" Aisha quashed her pleasure at the possessive note in Kabir's voice. "Why do you have a picture of him though?"

"We all had gone to Maldives for a vacation. Look at the sky in the picture, how stunning it is." Kabir said.

"Unbelievable!" Aisha rolled her eyes at Kabir's unrepentant smile.

She leaned toward the wall focusing on a large picture on it. "What is this? The population of a city?"

"Nope, that is the entire royal family. Aunts, uncles, nephews, nieces. . . everyone."

"Hmm! You know I visited your palace a couple of years ago."

"The hotel?"

"Yes, we stayed in the hotel. We wanted permission to shoot in the residence, but we were denied."

"No visitors are allowed in the residential side. I don't go there much. It's quite neglected, I have been told. And I want to keep it that way." Kabir's expression was grim as he rubbed a hand over his eyes as if he was trying to forget something painful. "After Kriti's death, that place was tainted for us."

"Understandable! But it is a beautiful palace." Aisha sighed. "So, no one lives in the residence?"

"A few caretakers and their families."

"Where is Shreya based?"

"She lives a few kilometers away. But right now, she is attending a conference in the US. She will be back soon. You'll like her." Kabir reached out and again took Aisha's hand. "You are so open, so easy to get along with, sweet Aisha."

No, I'm not! Aisha felt her heart dip, yet she tried to smile.

Chapter 65

Kabir took a step closer to her. Aisha moved back, her glance surprised. She couldn't help but inhale his spicy musk. Kabir rubbed her cheek with his callused thumb.

Aisha closed her eyes, letting the delicious sensation wash over her. It felt like hot suede against her skin. She felt drenched with desire.

"Open your eyes, Aisha," Kabir's voice was husky.

Aisha opened her eyes, her gaze heavy. Kabir rubbed her lower lip, back and forth, back and forth, like the penetrating strokes of a brush on a canvas. His eyes became hooded.

Aisha felt her flesh throb under his fingers with a yearning that mirrored the desire in Kabir's dark eyes. It made her feel oddly powerful.

"Whenever you are ready to take this, take us . . . to the next level, you let me know." Kabir's voice was hoarse.

Aisha felt her body tighten in response and a soft mewl escaped her lips.

Kabir crowded Aisha against the wall. He put his arms on the wall next to her, trapping her between them. Aisha's eyes became large. "I'm so already there," he said, dipping his head to nudge the base of her neck with his nose. His warm breath fanned her fast heating skin.

"Where?" Aisha lashes fluttered against her cheek. Unknowingly, she tilted her head to the side giving his lips more access to move over her.

"A very hopeful place!" Kabir spoke every word slowly against her skin. It was like every word became a kiss.

Aisha felt her breasts ache as her nipples tightened, her body pining for his touch. She wanted to wrap every inch of herself around him.

"Where it's just you and me," Kabir's lips kept pressing on her skin, growing more demanding.

Moaning, Aisha slowly rubbed her cheek against his soft thick hair. Her body arched against the wall.

Kabir's lips traveled from her neck to her chin. His head nudged Aisha's face back as he pressed urgent kisses on her soft chin. Restlessly, Aisha clenched her fingers in his shirt and pulled him close. She thought she would go mad if she did not touch his hard body.

With a groan, Kabir fell into Aisha and wrapped his arms around her. He pulled her in a possessive embrace. Slowly, his hot lingering kisses moved from Aisha's chin to the side of her mouth. "I want you so much, sweet Aisha."

"Umm!" Aisha moaned restlessly, moving her face, eager to taste Kabir and to be tasted by him. Her breasts strained against his chest. It felt so good that she rubbed her hard nipples against his chest.

Kabir groaned and pushed his pelvis into her soft stomach. His hard arousal thrust against her. "You were made for me, Aisha," he whispered hotly against her lips.

"Kiss me already." Aisha turned her mouth into his. She was done waiting. Her hand slipped from Kabir's back and fell on the table with the framed pictures. Her fingers touched something circular, something metallic.

A pendant.

The light around her changed suddenly.

Aisha felt herself pushed into a heavy and dark storm. Rain and winds howled around her. She felt herself plummeting back from a height. As she fell, her crazed gaze fell on her legs. They were not hers; neither were the thin, bony arms. Suddenly, her body broke in two. The pain was excruciating!

Aisha saw herself rise above her still body and then she turned down to look at herself. The face that stared back at her wasn't hers. Nor was it alive.

Aisha screamed.

Princess Kritika's lifeless eyes stared back at her.

#

Kabir rubbed Aisha's hands anxiously.

"Wake up, Aisha. Wake up, sweetheart." He sprinkled water on Aisha's face.

Aisha winced and moved her head.

"Prakash, why isn't the doctor here?" Kabir addressed his butler, standing behind him.

Aisha clutched her head and got up slowly. She was lying on Kabir's bed.

"I'm fine," her voice was hoarse.

Kabir wiped her forehead with a cool cloth. It was sticky. "We were about to . . ." he paused because of Prakash's presence. "When your body turned ice-cold and you fainted in my arms."

Aisha shifted back on the bed and reclined against the pillows. She was shivering. "I haven't eaten anything since last night and I went for a run today morning." She inhaled deeply. "I think it was low blood sugar."

Kabir covered her with a thick soft quilt and tucked it under her chin. "You scared the life out of me."

Aisha felt some color return to her face.

Kabir's knuckles skimmed her cheek. "Prakash, let's make a tray of food for Aisha madam." He got up. "I'll be right back with some juice."

Aisha's eyes wandered to the table with the family pictures. "Oh, something dropped on the floor."

Kabir walked over and picked it up. It was a gold necklace, the kind that opened.

"Whose necklace is it?"

Aisha wasn't asking, just confirming.

"Kriti's. She always wore it. It has pictures of mom, Dad, and me. I kept it. This is the only thing I have of her." Kabir gazed at it.

Aisha nodded understandingly. Keeping the pendant back, Kabir left the room followed by Prakash.

Aisha stared at the pendant.

That is not the only thing left of Kriti here. There is a whole lot more. Like a whole freaking ghost.

Chapter 66

By the time Aisha and Kiara reached home, it was close to eleven p.m. They let themselves in quietly. The living room was dark because the ex-judge retired to his room every night at 10:00 pm. Not 9:59 pm, not 10:01 pm, but exactly at 10:00 pm!

"Are you going to sleep?" Kiara whispered.

"Uh, yes, genius!" Aisha kept her voice low. They made their way quietly with hands outstretched.

"Why was Kabir giving you such hot intense looks and why were you blushing so much around him, Boo?"

Aisha frowned and muttered. "Next time you are not coming with us."

"Oh, there is going to be a next time?"

"Shit! Ow!"

"You okay?"

"I stubbed my darn toe."

Kiara switched on a lamp and helped Aisha sit in the retired Judge's chair.

"Let me get some ice."

"Can you get some coffee too along with the ice, Kia, please!"

"Fine," Kiara flounced away toward the kitchen.

Aisha shook her head and sat back, resting her foot on the table. Parth's ugly words still loomed over her head.

"Stupid CBI!" Aisha rubbed her head. Bending down, she took out a notepad from her bag. Mostly, she used it to jot down story plots or ideas that came to her. This time it was more specific. Aisha flipped to a new page and started writing.

KABIR

No painkillers or antidepressants or drugs in the medicine cabinet, bathroom. Only a big fat ghost. Why is she still here?

No suspicious looking things or documents in his bedroom. Need to search more in there? How? HECK, YES!

Find out more about Lavina's death. How were husband-wife relations? Where was Kabir then?

Why he is so damn irresistible? I am falling for him Help!

Any other suspects?

Make a trip to Sirsa. Soon!

Parth is an ASSHOLE.

"Damn!" Aisha shut the notebook and slipped it back in her bag. As she rubbed her head, Aisha's gaze fell on the folded newspaper her father had left on the coffee table. She read the headline. **Demolition of fraudulent ACT University building to cost the Government crores.**

"Aha! That's how Parth found out."

Carefully keeping her father's reading glasses on the side, Aisha picked up the newspaper. She scanned the article. It talked about ACT University and its practice of falsifying credentials and handing out fake degrees. How a body of students had sued the university and the Court had shut it down, causing much embarrassment to the sitting Government as a few of the high-ranking politicians or their relatives sat on the University's Board of Directors. There had been a flurry of arrests and resignations. The university campus built on a prime five-acre state-owned land within the Capital was to be demolished, costing the Government crores in labor and hardware.

"I was a freaking victim too, Parth!"

An article below caught Aisha's attention. She was about to read it, but Kiara came back with a tray.

"Coffee and ice, dear Boo!"

"One more favor and I will will everything to you." Aisha pleaded.

"You will will everything to me willingly?" Kiara narrowed her eyes.

"Very willingly, I will will everything to you. If you will put the tray on my bedside table." Aisha's said with a face straighter than a foot ruler.

Kiara snorted. "I will willingly if you will will—"

"Oh, for goodness' sake, just put the damn tray in my room." Aisha giggled, and Kiara joined in.

"Keep it down, girls!" Her father called out in a heavy sleep-laden voice from his room.

"Sorry, Papa!" Limping, Aisha trailed Kiara.

"Thank you, kiddo, you are the best. Good night, darling."

"Don't forget the will." Kiara gave an exaggerated bow and exited the room.

Chapter 67

Aisha locked the door and hobbled to the bed. Sitting down on the bed, she read the article under the one about the university. Something in it had pricked her mind. The article spoke about rising prices of chemicals, but one chemical caught her eye. High test calcium hypochlorite.

"Where have I read this term before? Where? Where?" Pursing her mouth, Aisha shifted on the bed restlessly. She closed her eyes thinking, centering her thoughts. A few seconds later Aisha opened eyes that positively shone.

Hastily, Aisha turned and opened the drawer where she kept the victim's files.

Going on her knees, she spread them out on the bed. Next, she limped to the desk and brought her laptop to the bed. She was working in a frenzied state.

Logging in, Aisha kept the laptop aside. She scanned the files on the bed for the term in the article that had caught her eye. Aisha did not have to look for long. She tilted her head and read the sentence that was common to all the victims. High test calcium hypochlorite residue found inside and around the vagina, on thighs, under the buttocks and on the breasts.

Narrowing her eyes, Aisha pulled her laptop closer. In the search box she quickly typed, 'What is high test calcium hypochlorite' and pressed enter.

The search engine opened links to several pages. Aisha clicked the first one and perused it carefully. She hit the back key and went to the search page. She opened the second article and read it. She closed it and went back to the third article. She did it multiple times until she had nearly scrutinized fifteen pages within twenty-five minutes.

Aisha sat back and straightened her foot. "Ow!" Her toe stung. She turned to the tray on her bedside and lifted the ice pack that had left a sizable puddle on the tray.

The ice is warm and the coffee's cold. Ironic!

Aisha slapped the pack on her toe and sipped the coffee, resting her back comfortably against the pillows.

So, hypochlorite is most commonly found in industrial bleach. Aisha chewed her lips. He was removing all evidence. She shuddered. Must have been so painful for the girls. Monster. She blinked her eyes rapidly and rubbed her head.

Bleach, bleach. What am I forgetting?

Aisha's laptop went into sleep mode and began running a preset slideshow. She had recently uploaded Goa pictures from her phone and camera to her laptop. Aisha saw the pictures of dolphins framed against the sunset. She jerked up and the ice pack slid to the side.

"Holy cow!" her eyes glimmered with excitement. "Where is it? Where is it?"

Aisha picked up Dr. Lorso's notes she had clicked pictures of. She skimmed to a line and read it aloud. "Lack of blood on the scene where the body was found points to the fact that the victim was killed somewhere else and her body was transported to the site where she was discovered."

Aisha brought her laptop out of sleep mode and opened the recycle bin. She scrolled through all the images she had deleted. "Yes!" Aisha squealed, double clicking on an image.

The image was that of the green van, the one Aisha had chanced upon on her hike to Lopez Point, the one that strongly smelled of bleach.

"Shit! This where he kills them. It is only after I touched the van that the names of these girls came to my mind. Oh God! Were they trying to reach me?"

Aisha, for first time, felt scared for herself. She remembered the faces with black holes for eyes, mouths with sharp teeth open in agonized screams. She was used to a ghost or two connecting with her and moving on. But this was an entire crowd of angry spirits in pain.

What did I get myself into? This might damage me beyond repair!

Aisha broke in cold sweat.

Chapter 68

For the next few days, Aisha immersed herself in what she knew—writing for television.

"Good night, Veena. See you tomorrow." Aisha tidied her desk, smiling at her assistant dialog writer.

After connecting the van to Dr. Lorso's deductions, Aisha had sent a text off to Parth, asking him to investigate it, along with the pictures of the van.

Parth had never responded to her text. Even though the suspense was killing her, Aisha did not reach out to him again.

"Night, Boss! We have a late shift tomorrow. Twelve-to-nine. Will you be here?" Veena asked, following Aisha's example, and logging out of her machine.

"For the first half definitely!" Aisha reached the office and opened it. She stopped short on seeing who waited at the door. "Oh! Hi!"

"Hey!" Kabir waved.

"What are you doing here?" Aisha asked, trying to act casual even though she felt happy enough to sing upon seeing Kabir.

"I was looking for a ride." Kabir replied casually. "Can you drop me home?" His face creased in a boyish grin that lit up his eyes like he was upon a secret.

Aisha nodded slightly dazed. "Sure. But how did you get here?"

"By my car," Kabir tapped his foot against the soft soil, drawing out the suspense, his face full of mischief.

Aisha sighed resigned. "And where is your car now?"

Kabir shrugged. "I don't know. Maybe the driver took it back?"

"Really?"

"You haven't called or made any efforts to meet for the last few days, so I dropped by." Kabir crossed his arms and looked down.

"Wow, you are a needy bo—" Aisha swallowed. "Friend."

Kabir leaned down, causing Aisha to take a step back self-consciously. "I can be whatever you want me to be."

"Stop it!" Aisha laughed nervously. "Let me introduce you to my team member, Veena." She pivoted and stopped. "Veena this is—"

"Whatever you want him to be." Veena rolled her tongue against her cheek, her expression coy as it winged between Aisha and Kabir.

"Very funny. Let's go." Aisha beat hasty retreat from the room. "I'll drop you to your place."

Kabir put an arm on her elbow, stopping Aisha. "Technically, you are dropping me at your home. Kiara called. Your dad wants to play chess with me and treat me to whatever has been cooked tonight."

"Oh!" Aisha stopped. Kiara and her dad were not the kind to have impromptu dinner guests over.

They are playing matchmakers for me.

"Oh *good* or oh *bad*?" Kabir teased.

"Oh, very good!" Aisha blurted. Her cell beeped. "Excuse me!" She rummaged in her purse and checked her cell. It was a text from Parth. "Google Panaji news."

"Everything okay?" Kabir asked upon seeing Aisha's puzzled expression.

"Parth just texted me." Aisha replied absentmindedly.

"Why is he texting you?"

"Something related to Kiara's attack."

"Did they catch the guy?"

"We are working on it." Aisha replied, putting her cell back in her bag.

Kabir halted mid-step. "We?"

"As in them, we all, the police . . . whatever . . . we can do to catch the creep." Aisha stuttered.

Kabir simply grunted.

Aisha gazed at his profile; it appeared unyielding.

Does he not want the man caught?

"Do you want to drive?"

Kabir glanced at her, his expression distant, all trace of humor and mischief gone. "Sure, if you want me to."

"I wouldn't ask if I didn't!" Aisha handed him the car keys.

#

Kabir drove Aisha's car out of the studios. Except for the constant noises from the road, there wasn't much conversation between them.

Why did she smile in that happy and excited manner when the cop texted her? Is there something going on between them? Is she like Lavina, stringing men?

He honked with more force than required on the vehicles in front of them. Kabir felt Aisha turn and cast him a look but he kept his eyes on the road.

I was so excited at the prospect of seeing Aisha. I was missing her more than I would miss anyone I had met merely ten days ago. She is not anyone.

Kabir sighed. "Sorry!" He admitted gruffly. "All this is new to me."

"More than it is to me?" Aisha asked in an amused voice.

"Touché!" Kabir replied, his expression wry. He reached out and took Aisha's hand that lay in her lap. "I missed this."

Aisha's fingers curled around his. "Me too," She confessed softly.

Kabir turned and watched a face that he had started obsessing over. "You are beautiful, sweet Aisha," he said, his voice husky.

Kabir felt himself get hard as he saw the color rise in Aisha's cheeks. *The things that I could do to her would make her feel hot enough to explode.* He gave her a hand a last squeeze and let go.

"Aisha, you remember that clause about taking us to the next level, right? Maybe I did not make myself clear, but you can do that anytime." He watched the mischief bring a sparkle to her eyes.

"Even at 2:00 am?"

"Yes."

"What about 3:00 in the afternoon?"

"Yes."

"What about 6:00 in the morning?" Aisha continued to tease.

"Oh God, yes!" Kabir groaned.

Aisha was boggled at Kabir's response.

"I'm imagining you and me having sex at all those times."

"Oh!" Aisha's voice was a squeak and he saw the answering desire in her eyes.

Why is she holding back if she wants me too?

Kabir observed Aisha swallow. "I promise to be gentle and very, very thorough," he said, his voice low and silky.

"Just shut up and drive!" Aisha muttered, crossing her arms and legs tightly.

Kabir could not help the laugh that rumbled out of him.

Chapter 69

Next day, Aisha woke up feeling like she ruled a country. She went into the bathroom and hummed right through the morning ablutions, breakfast, Pinky and Kiara's everyday argument about the taste of food and her father's grumbling about the neighbor's teenage son who played rather loud music late into the night.

Kabir is a big part of how I'm feeling today, no denying that. Parth's text also has me thrilled. I'm such a tart!

Once Kabir and Aisha had arrived home, Aisha had disappeared in her room on the pretext of taking a shower. In her room, she had opened her laptop and done as Parth asked. She had typed Panaji and then hit search.

Aisha's eyes glowed like embers when she opened the first page the search engine threw back. The article showed the picture of the green van surrounded by a few constables. The headline was: ***How the Killer Moves? The killing machine found.***

It then went on to report that Panaji police, assisted by the CBI, had received a tip from a credible source that had led them to a hidden van at Lopez Point. An anonymous but official source had told them that it was too early to say anything conclusive but inside the van they had found industrial strength bleach and stains on the floor that could be old blood. The article also mentioned that the van was missing number plates, so it would be hard for the police to track the owner of the van.

"Boo, are you listening to any of us?"

Aisha shook her head, coming back to the present. "Sorry, what were you saying?"

"Kiara was asking what your plans are for today." Her father replied, half-hidden by the newspaper he was reading.

"I have an appointment at the Vision TV corporate office."

"You looking to move to another channel?" Her father put down the newspaper.

"Nope. Just networking." Aisha demurred. She had taken an appointment with Shreya's ex-husband for today morning. Aisha was known in the industry well enough to get meetings with other channel heads.

She left her house a few minutes later and drove herself to the Vision TV's corporate office, which was a glass building comprising of several floors. She did not have to wait long and was shown to the room of Mr. Sudhir Vyast, Shreya's ex.

Gosh, he is such a sleaze ball.

Aisha diplomatically pulled her hand out of Sudhir's clammy palm. They chitchatted about a few common acquaintances. Aisha let him think that she was planning to jump ship. After ten minutes or so, she put a bag in between them.

She was tired of Sudhir staring at her breasts. *They don't squirt rainbows, lecher!*

"We have another connection."

Sudhir's face lit up.

"Kabir Rana, the Ad maker."

Sudhir's mouth twisted like he had tasted something bitter. "How well do you know him?"

Aisha shrugged. "Bumped into him last week."

"Stay away from that man."

"What do you mean?" Aisha's expression was nonchalant.

"He is a fucking psycho! He broke my marriage."

Aisha's fingers gripped the arms of her chair. She struggled to keep her expression neutral. "Really?"

"Yes, absolutely! All the time hovering around my wife umm .. . ex-wife. We all have friends but who takes such liberties? Buying Shreya expensive gifts for no reason. My wife's birthday and he throws a big surprise party for her. And guess who that asshole forgets to invite? Me, the husband. Convenient, right? All the time, he would drop by our house unannounced." Some spit pooled at the side of Sudhir's mouth for he was speaking forcefully.

Aisha could not help but remember how Kabir had showed up at her work without informing her.

"Shreya and he would talk for hours late into the night. And my wife would be always, Kabir this, Kabir that. Those two are a match made in hell." Sudhir sat back, his expression far from pleased.

"I'm sorry, I was told that you cheated on her."

Sudhir grunted but did not deny it. "It happened much after. I was fed up, man!"

Aisha nodded somberly. In her ethics book, cheating was a big no-no, but Sudhir was showing a very troubled side to his marriage. And even if it were fifty percent true, Kabir did seem to be at fault.

Sudhir leaned forward. He wasn't finished. "And when Shreya asked for divorce, this Kabir hired the best lawyer money can buy and wiped the floor with me. Shreya got everything! If that asshole had his way, I would have probably been left with only my underwear." Sudhir smacked the table. "Thankfully, Shreya stepped in, so I have at least one apartment and one car. But the other two houses, my three-acre farmhouse, my four cars . . . everything went to her."

Aisha genuinely felt contrite. "I'm sorry. That must have been awful."

"And if that wasn't enough, he got a restraining order against me. I can't go anywhere near Shreya or him. As if I would want to go anywhere near those two."

Aisha processed the information. Her heart dove straight to her feet. After another fifteen minutes, during which Aisha had no recollection of what they had discussed, she finally got to her feet. "Thank you for meeting me."

"Of course, the pleasure is all mine." Sudhir got the door for Aisha. "Maybe we can meet for dinner sometime this week. I can tell you more about the opportunities here." He placed a hand on Aisha's back and stroked her through the blouse.

"Get your fucking hands off me!" Aisha hissed at him.

Sudhir reacted as if she had slapped him across the face. "Now listen—"

Aisha opened the door and walked out of the room. Sitting in the car, she rested her hands on the steering wheel. Her mind was churning faster than juice in a blender. She cupped her head.

What the hell is going on?

Her cell rang, and Aisha glanced at it. It was Kabir. Ignoring the call, she started the car.

I'm not sure about you anymore.

Chapter 70

Parking the car, Aisha walked to the set. Her head was still muddled from the meeting with Sudhir Vyast. Her cell rang again. An unknown number. She answered it. "Aisha here!"

"Aisha, this Dr. Lorso from Panaji."

"Hi, Dr. Lorso, how are you?"

"Good. And you?"

"I have been better! How can I help you?"

"Have you heard from Parth?" Dr. Lorso asked. "I have been trying his cell but it's coming unreachable or switched off."

"Oh! He is not in Goa?"

"He went to Mumbai today morning and he said he would be getting in touch with you."

"I haven't heard from him." Aisha glanced around and lowered her voice. "With finding the van and all, I thought he'd have a lot to do there."

"It was because of the van that he has gone to Mumbai. He called me up from the airport. He was excited; he said he was close to catching the killer."

"That's huge!" Aisha's hand fisted at her side. "Did he say anything else? Anything at all?"'

"No, that is all he said. Your number was on our team contact sheet, so I called."

"My number is in the team contact sheet?" Aisha felt her dismal day brighten.

"Yes, and Parth sort of scratched it out after he found out about the fake accreditation."

"Oh!" Aisha cleared her throat.

"If you hear from Parth, let him know I was calling just to make sure he reached. Bye!"

"Bye!" Aisha hung up. Her phone rang immediately. Aisha glanced at it. She let Kabir's call go to voicemail. Then she texted him. *Super busy at work. Will call you tomorrow.*

Close to seven that night one of the assistant directors tapped on Aisha's shoulder. "Ma'am you have visitor."

"We are about to shoot a scene here." Aisha said.

"I know, Ma'am, but your guest is very . . . impatient." The young AD kept flicking her eyes nervously over her shoulder.

"Excuse me. I'll be right back." Aisha lobbed an apologetic glance at Sarita, the serial director, sitting next to her. Ignoring the director's frown, Aisha walked out of the set and yanked the large door that led outside.

She saw her visitor. "I got this." Aisha assured the AD.

At the sound of her voice, Kabir stopped his frantic pacing and turned. His expression was harsh. "We need to talk!"

Chapter 71

Aisha shut the door behind her. "I was working!"

Kabir caught her elbow. "It's important. It's about Shreya."

Aisha let him take her to the side. She could see people from the production team and some spot boys loitering nearby watch them with avid interest. Kabir led her to a post behind the set.

Aisha leaned back against the wall and crossed her arms. Her face mutinous, she stared ahead of her.

"Did you go to meet Sudhir Vyast? Shreya's ex-husband?"

News travels fast. That rat.

"I was exploring new opportunities." Aisha fibbed. "Work opportunities."

"Go on!"

"Then your name came up and Shreya's name came up and he just wouldn't shut up. He wanted to tell his side of the story."

"And you wanted to hear it?" Kabir said, his face etched out of stone. He reminded Aisha of the Kabir she had first met.

"Ugh!" Aisha snorted. She knew she was making a hash of things with him. But there were too many doubts about Kabir for her to come to any conclusion about him. "I just didn't interrupt him. I was being polite."

Abruptly, Kabir grabbed Aisha's shoulder.

"Hey!" Aisha protested, her expression wary as she glanced at him.

"What's got into you? Why are you being such . . . such a tight ass?"

Aisha pulled his hand off her shoulder. "Tight ass? Really?" She shook her head. "Watch your tone."

"My tone!" Kabir's eyes widened incredulous. "Because of you that jerk, Sudhir, called Shreya and threatened to sue her, insisting that she was harassing him through her people. Shreya called me; she was so upset."

"Got it." Aisha smacked her forehead mockingly. "So, you are super upset because Shreya is upset? And now you want me to be super upset about a person who I haven't even met?"

"Aisha, you of all people should understand why I'm angry about this. Shreya is family. You have sacrificed your whole life for your family."

Aisha made an impatient click of her tongue. "Sacrificed? I haven't sacrificed anything. They are my family. My blood relations."

I'm such a jealous shrew!

Kabir took a step back. His voice rose above Aisha's. "Oh, so just because Shreya and I are not related, that means she and I can't have a strong bond? I can't feel for her? Is that what you are saying?"

Aisha could no longer hold back her accusations and doubts. "I don't know of friends who cause trouble in their friend's marriages. Who calls newly-married friends in the middle of the night or throw surprise parties for their married friend and not invite the husband," she lashed out.

Kabir's expression was part incredulous and part furious. "Are you saying I broke Shreya's marriage? Are you?" He pulled her close, glaring down at her.

Aisha smacked his hands away, her mouth a tight thin line. "Don't touch me! And yes I am. Prove me wrong."

Kabir studied Aisha's mutinous face and he ground out. "Not that it is any of your business, but it was Shreya who used to call me because of that asshole of a husband cheated on her from day one. He neglected her, humiliated her, and did not miss a single opportunity to belittle her. She needed a friend, someone to support her and that is what I did. Frankly speaking, I don't care what you think or what anyone else thinks about her and my relationship. Whenever and wherever Shreya needs me, I am going to be there for her. No questions asked."

"Good for you and good for her!" Aisha whipped her hair.

Kabir grabbed her elbow, his eyes glittering wildly. "And what about *your* morals, Aisha? You are stringing along the cop, me and God knows how many others? What does that make you? A tease, a cheat or something even worse?"

Aisha felt slashed by Kabir's insinuations. "For your kind information, I'm actually helping the cop solve these horrific murders and also saving *your* ass!"

Kabir flinched like she had struck him. "Saving me from what?"

Oops! Aisha remained quiet.

"I'm asking you something, Saving me from what? Answer me. What or who the hell are you saving me from?" Kabir loomed over her.

"The police. All the murders happened in March and December, the two months you are always there in Goa." Aisha raised an accusing finger at Kabir's angry face. "Seven girls were killed in those months. The killer dislikes beauty and what did you say to me the other day? "Beauty can be ugly too!" Also, the police found the van, the one in which the bastard kills these girls at Lopez Point—the place where you shoot your ad every year," she paused, unable to meet his eyes.

"You are a hack. So are the police, if that is the basis of accusing someone of killing . . ." Kabir swallowed. "Killing innocent women . . ."

The hurt on his face made Aisha defensive and guilty "The killer takes a shoe of the girl he kills as a souvenir. The first night at the beach, I found a shoe. It belonged to one of the murdered women. And there was no one else there on the beach but you and I," she paused, her chest heaving. "No one else." Aisha heaved with the burden of her revelation.

Kabir stared at her with the deathly stillness of a statue. His finally spoke, his voice flat and his eyes anguished. "So, tell me Aisha, how long have you been investigating me?"

Aisha felt like crying at the pain in his expression. "I'm not investigating you. I was just trying to get to the bottom of all this."

She tucked her hands behind her back and leaned against the wall.

"And why are the police taking your help?"

Aisha scuffed her sandal against the loose gravel. "Because of my degree."

"Speak up, Aisha!"

"Dammit! Because of my fake degree!" Aisha cringed, closing her eyes. "Sorry, that came out all wrong." She opened her eyes. "What . . ." She trailed off seeing Kabir walk away.

"Hey!" she called out.

Kabir stopped, dropped his head down and then straightened up. "Stay the hell away from me!"

He looked at Aisha. His gaze was steadfast. "Whatever this was—genuine on my part, fake on yours—ends right here, right now."

Aisha straightened and spoke, her tone weary. "I'm going to keep digging!" Her eyes were overtly bright.

This is not supposed to hurt so much.

"Just stay away from me!" Kabir spun around and walked away in the darkness, becoming an indiscernible part of it.

Aisha inhaled deeply and twisted her mouth to control her tears. She sniffed.

It wasn't supposed to end this way. It wasn't supposed to end!

Chapter 72

Aisha wasn't sure how long she stood there after Kabir left but when she moved away from the wall, the tears had dried on her cheeks. She went back inside the set, her movements robotic as she hid in the corner behind the camera team. Pack up was declared around an hour later.

Aisha picked up her bag and walked to her car, dragging her feet.

"You okay, Boss? There is something on your face." Rustom came up to her, a clipboard in his hand.

"I'm good, Rusty, probably some dust." Aisha wiped her face. "So, tomorrow's scenes?" she pointed at the clipboard.

"Yup!" Rustom held out the clipboard.

Just then, Aisha's cell beeped. She had received a text. She was quick to grab her cell, her expression wishful.

"Not the text you were expecting, Boss?"

"What?" Aisha gazed at her assistant vacantly.

"Your expression!" Rustom gestured. "Never mind. I will be in the production room." He walked away.

Aisha re-read the message again. It was from Parth.

Meet me at 29/A2 Gandhi Kunj, Mahim. It is the building behind Mahim Park.

Aisha stared at the text for a few seconds and glanced at her wrist watch. It was nearly 8:00 pm.

At this time? Why? She messaged back.

Close to catching the bastard. You should be here.

"Oh!" Aisha exhaled.

Parth sent another text. We are meeting at Vikas's apartment. He has been instrumental in getting all the evidence against the killer. Someone you both know.

Aisha clutched her stomach. Shit! Kabir! She typed with shaky fingers. He was just here. You all could be wrong. Kabir is not our killer!

It's not Kabir. Parth's text read.

Aisha read the message repeatedly till she could absorb the words. She felt lightheaded with happiness. Aisha started laughing hysterically. "It's not him! It's not him!" She felt as if a crushing boulder had rolled off her chest. She could breathe again, and she would finally be a part of something she had yearned for since she was eleven—the police.

Bending her head, she was quick to text Parth. It will take me around one and half hours to get there. Would that be okay?

Fine. Don't share this with anyone!

Of course. Dr. Lorso had called me, wondering about your whereabouts.

Don't tell him anything. Once we catch the guy, we will share it with everyone. Right now, it's just my team, you, and Vikas. Hurry!

On my way! Aisha did not bother correcting Parth's typo on Dr. Lorso's gender. Happy that Kabir was innocent, she pressed her eyes and took a few deep breaths. Aisha walked back to the set wanting to use the restroom for it was going to be a long drive.

She rounded the corner. The first people she saw were Rustom and Sarita Tanwar.

"Where were you, Aisha?" Sarita looked displeased.

"What happened?" Aisha asked, observing Rustom's worried glance.

"There were continuity issues with the dialog and we were looking for you. Can I talk to you?" Sarita asked.

"I have it right here?" Rustom held up the papers in his hand.

"It's okay," Aisha followed Sarita to her makeshift office.

Sarita closed the door behind them.

"What's going on, Sarita?"

The older woman sat down in her chair. "You tell me. Obviously, there is something going on in your life. You are here."

"Sarita, I had so much vacation time. I just took two weeks."

"I know, but you took it suddenly. You said one week and then you came back and took another. You know how a daily soap works. We only have a bank of one week's episodes. But because of your absence and the chaos that happened, now we have no bank. We are shooting next day's telecast literally a day before. If the management found out they will fire me, Aisha."

"What are you saying?"

"Take a sabbatical for a month or ten months or whatever time you need. When you have resolved everything on your end, come back. You have long relations with the company; they will always have something for you." Sarita smiled reassuringly.

"Are you firing me?" Aisha felt her stomach churn.

Sarita avoided her eyes. "I'm just saving my job, Aisha. This is a show that runs many households. I can't screw all that for one person's inefficiency. I'm sorry!"

Ten minutes later, Aisha walked off the set carrying two years' worth of her work-life in a 24*12 box.

"I can't believe she did that!" Rustom said for the umpteenth time.

The news of Aisha's firing had spread fast on the set. Aisha was on good terms with nearly everyone. Rustom, Veena and other people from the set, including some actors, walked Aisha to the car.

"It's okay, Rusty and Veena! Make me proud." Aisha hugged everyone. She kept the goodbyes short and drove off. She had somewhere very important to be.

"Heartbroken and jobless all in an hour!" Aisha muttered, squeezing her eyes to clear them of tears.

Somehow, losing the job hurt less.

Chapter 73

After stopping once to ask directions, Aisha pulled up in the parking spot of the building Parth had asked her to come to. She bent under the windshield and stared at the four-story decrepit building that appeared even bleaker in the poor street lighting.

"Gosh, what the heck is this place?"

Aisha took tentative steps in the direction of the entrance, avoiding the moths that buzzed under the broken lamp nearby. There was no security at the gate or inside. Hesitantly, Aisha went past a few brown and wilted pots that lined the grounds.

Someone had painted "out of order" in red on the rusting elevator door.

Wouldn't take it anyway!

Aisha went up the stairs that smelled of dust and some other not-so-pleasant things. The walls around her were peeling and patched. A naked bulb hanging above the stairs washed the place in a sickly yellow light.

Aisha clutched the bouquet in her hands a little tighter, worried that the toxic surroundings would spoil the freshness of the flowers she had picked up on the way for Vikas's ailing mother.

Aisha heard footsteps coming down. She paused. An older man came down the stairs. His white hair was long straggling and dirty like the creased kurta and checked lungi he wore. He paused, his watery eyes widening in surprise as he saw Aisha.

Aisha paused, uncertain. He was too old to be any real threat, yet the man did not seem harmless. He resumed walking and Aisha lowered her eyes, giving him room to pass. He stopped in front of Aisha and stared in her face.

"Ugh!" Aisha averted her face for his breath smelled fouler than rotten eggs.

"Do you have some money?" He whispered.

"No."

Aisha skirted around and rushed up the remaining distance. She paused at the second floor. The corridor she faced was dark and narrow. A dim bulb at the end of the corridor was the only light.

"Shit!" Aisha took small steps stepping over some questionable spill.

A radio played old Hindi movie songs behind a scratched door. A stray dog sat curled in front of another. It raised weary eyes to see Aisha and went back to snoozing, its ribs clearly visible under its skin.

What the heck, Vikas? Why do you live in this dump?

Aisha paused in front of the pale weathered door with A2 painted on it. Seeing no doorbell, Aisha knocked twice, sharply, and quickly.

"Who is it?" Vikas's response was muffled and instantaneous.

"It's me, Aisha," She kept her voice low.

The door opened immediately.

"Come in," Vikas smiled, ushering her in.

"Thanks!" Aisha entered the flat, expecting to find a few policemen inside. She was wrong. It was empty.

Closing the door, Vikas turned to her.

"For your mother!" Aisha handed him the flowers. "How is she?"

Vikas appeared surprised and then gave her a slow shy smile. "She is sleeping right now. But she loves flowers. Yellow roses are her favorite. Thank you!"

"Welcome!"

"Have a seat," Vikas ushered her to a chair. Aisha sat down and looked around. All furniture in the room, including the sofa she sat in, was covered with a transparent plastic cover.

"After chemo session, mummy has become susceptible to infections, so I take precautions to keep everything germ-free.

"Oh, of course!" Aisha nodded understandingly.

How about moving out of the septic tank?

"I got Parth's text. So, where is everyone else?"

"They are in the other room," Vikas pointed at a closed door across from them. "They will out be in a few minutes. A top-secret conference call is going on. I was kicked out too!"

Aisha's smile was wry. "And to think it is your house!"

"I will put these in a vase. I'll be right back."

"Sure. By the way, your apartment smells so much better than the outside."

Smiling, Vikas disappeared in the hallway that faced the living room.

Aisha stared at the door where Parth and his team were working. Her cell buzzed. It was Kiara.

"Hi Kia!" Aisha whispered.

"Where have you been, Boo? I must have called you like twenty times! Rustom called up. He told us you were fired. Are you okay?"

"Sorry, Kia, my phone was on silent. Listen, don't worry, I'm fine. We'll talk when I get home."

"Why are you whispering? Where are you?"

Aisha could hear the concern in Kiara's voice. "I'm okay, don't worry."

"Where are you, Boo? Why aren't you telling me where you are?"

"Oh gosh, Kia!" Aisha shook her head exasperated. "I'm at Vikas's apartment."

"What the hell! What are you doing there? And, again, why are you whispering?"

Aisha winced. Her niece's voice was loud in her ear. "It's a long story. I will tell you everything when I get back home. And I'm whispering because his cancer-ridden mom is sleeping, Kiara!"

"What bull cock! His mother died three and a half years ago. Around the time I joined the agency. It was December 2013, I think."

Chapter 74

"Not funny, Kia." Aisha said.

"I'm not kidding, Boo. December 2013, I'm positive. I and the other models were on a shoot and he was with us when he got the news. Vikas was very distraught!"

"Kiara, I gotta go." Aisha ended the call abruptly. She felt her mouth go dry.

Why would he lie about his mother being dead?

And then something registered.

"Oh, good Lord!"

Aisha realized why Vikas's flat smelled different from the outside.

Bleach. I'm smelling the same bleach I had smelled near the green van.

Aisha rushed to her feet. Her eyes fell on the front door. She saw the many bolts on it and the large gray lock that sat tight on the door.

He's locked me in.

Aisha's hands fisted at her sides and her stomach clenched painfully.

That's why he made the typo and called Dr. Lorso a "he" in his text. Vikas did not know Dr. Lorso is a woman. Oh gosh, why did I not call Parth before blindly showing up? Where the heck is Parth? Aisha wiped the sweat off her upper lip. Don't panic. Think, Aisha think.

Aisha tried to calm down her heart that was hammering between her ribs. Her ears were alert trying to listen to the teeniest of the sounds in the apartment. Some tinkering sounds came from the kitchen.

Vikas is busy!

Aisha glanced at the cell phone still in her hand. She dialed Parth's number and waited. Muffled sounds of his ringtone came from behind the door Vikas had pointed at. Aisha ended the call after one ring.

Keeping her eyes on the hallway Vikas had gone in, Aisha took quick soft steps toward the closed door. She put her hand and pushed it. The door swung open with a low creaking noise.

Aisha's saw the sprawled body that lay on the floor. It was Parth!

He had a head wound that was bleeding, turning a side of his face bright red even as the other half of his face was pale as chalk. Aisha covered her mouth, trying not to gag at the sight of considerable blood.

A strong push on Aisha's back had her hurtling inside the room. As she fell forward, her head hit the edge of a table. Her eyes rolled back in their sockets as she passed out.

Chapter 75

"Ugh!" Aisha felt her head. It hurt enough to feel as if someone had run a car over it. The shooting pain would not let her slip into comforting unconsciousness. Aisha groaned because of the effort it took to open her eyes.

Something hard nudged her head. Groggily, she raised her head and felt the object with unsteady hands for her vision was hazy.

A shoe?

Raising herself on her elbows, Aisha blinked, trying to see beyond the shoe. A body and a face took form. "Parth! Parth!"

The CBI officer lay prone on the ground. Aisha held his ankles and dragged herself closer.

"Tsk! Poor Aisha!"

Aisha froze at the voice. She swung her head. Vikas sat cross-legged a few feet away from them, swinging a gun in his hand.

Aisha's eyes fixed on the gun.

"Not my favorite weapon to kill." Vikas mimicked a sad expression. "I prefer my hands. It is more personal. Choking the life bit by bit from bodies that are beautiful from the outside but as ugly as the pus-filled spores on a leper's body on the inside." He smiled slowly.

Her head continued to pound, yet Aisha managed to sit up partially and face him. "You killed all those girls? Why?"

Vikas continued to hold the gun lightly. "Because I have seen the ugly side of beauty. My own mother, she was very beautiful. She had a mole right here. A beauty spot." He pressed the gun on his jaw.

Hope the damn thing goes off! Aisha watched him. *Didn't I have my cell phone in my hand when I passed out?*

"Tell me about your mother!" She pleaded. She felt around her, under her skirt.

"Why? So, you can find a way to stop me from killing? Are you that good a shrink?" Vikas chortled in glee like a small child.

"I'm not a shrink."

Vikas moved the gun from his face and aimed it back at her casually. "Are you honest?"

"There is no point in lying." Aisha's smile was glum. "I don't think I'm getting out of this alive."

"You are smarter than you look."

Sarcastic and armed! Some people have everything.

Aisha changed tactics. "The police were sure they would catch you."

Vikas' nostril's flared. "Police are a bunch of baboons. They will never catch me. You saw the van and this cop indulged in too much digging. You two are the only ones who know about me and look where it brought you both." He pointed the gun at Aisha. "Right in front of me."

He wants to talk, otherwise I would be dead by now.

Aisha steered her eyes from the chilling barrel of the gun staring at her, straight between the eyes. "Why do you think Parth hasn't told anyone else about you?"

"Do you see anyone else here besides him?" Vikas's smile was coy.

"But how did you figure out I was involved? Nobody knew that. Not even my family!" Aisha made sure to sound amazed.

Vikas gave a smug smile and flipped his hair. "From this idiot's cell. You sent him a picture of the van."

He slithered forward. Aisha had no time to react. He pushed the barrel on her forehead.

"Oww!" Aisha shrieked as the cold metal pressed down on an already throbbing bruise. "Understood! Understood." She gritted her teeth, clamping her jaw tight and fighting the pain.

Vikas removed the barrel and moved back to his prior position.

Aisha again changed her tack. "So, your mother . . ." She stuttered. "Do you think she would be happy with what you are doing?"

"Stop talking about her!" Vikas screamed. Aisha jerked. "She would not care. I was a mistake!"

"A mistake? No mother can think like that?" Aisha made her face sympathetic.

"My mother, the hooker, can and did! She thought she could be a heroine. But she could not resist men. One man after another! Her body was like a revolving door. Men just went in and out, in and out, in and out." He made a crude gesture with his hands. "She had no idea who my father was. She tried to abort me. But she went to someone cheap. They messed up, so I survived."

Aisha stared at him. "That's awful! I'm sorry! Where were you when all those . . . all those men?"

"She would stick me in the shoe closet. A smelly dark tiny closet! I would sit there for hours like this!" Vikas pulled his knees into his chest and wrapped his arms around them. "And if I made the smallest sound then she would hit me with the closest shoe." He relaxed his pose. "I call smell a shoe from a distance."

That explains the shoe fetish!

"Sorry you had no one who cared for you, but—?"

Vikas punched his knee with his free hand. "Yes, there was. She came around and saw me. Truly saw me."

Aisha blinked, confused. "Your mother?"

"Not my mother. My darling mummy even threw her own son at the men, just to have them stay!"

That explains the rapes. He too was a victim.

"I'm very sorry for what happened to you. No child should have to go through that."

"Your niece is also very beautiful! She reminds me of my mother. I will cut her uterus out."

Chapter 76

"**Kiara is** nothing like your mother." Aisha strove to control her fear.

"Oh, she is. I have seen it in her eyes. Kabir follows her like a puppy. I almost killed her that night, but you got in the way. That night I went outside and then sneaked right back in the house through the front door. Right under all your noses! See how clever I am?" Vikas chuckled.

Aisha could not hide her panic. "Kiara is nothing like your mother, I promise. You can do what you want with me. But please, promise me you won't hurt Kiara."

"I'm not going to kill your slut niece for me. I'm going to kill her for my love. My true love who sees me for who I am. She connects with me here." Vikas touched his forehead. "And here!" He touched his chest.

He hears voices.

"Vikas, please listen to me, your mother is dead. The cancer killed her three and a half years ago. She can't hurt you anymore."

Vikas scratched his chin. "Only her body is gone. Karma is a bitch or in her case, cervical cancer. That's what she had." He smiled manically. "You know I made her suffer. I begged the doctors to give her the strongest chemo dosage. The loving son who can't do without his mother! And I took away her pain killers. She would yell and scream in agony, but I never gave her the prescription painkillers. She would scream, scream all the time, rotting in her own filth. That's why I moved her in here. Everyone here is deaf!" He waved the gun all around him.

Aisha watched the gun warily. She glanced at Parth who still lay inert. The blood from his wound had stopped flowing. She hurriedly moved her gaze away from it. "So, she is gone then, right? Dead."

Vikas leaned close as if sharing a secret. "No! She is not dead. She keeps coming back. Every time I kill her, but she keeps coming back. She loved Goa. That is where I go to find her. But don't tell her. Otherwise she will run away to some faraway place and I don't have a passport."

Aisha watched Vikas's child-like demeanor.

A groaning sound interrupted them.

Parth was coming around.

Vikas scooted back and pointed the gun at him.

"Please don't!" Aisha slid protectively over Parth's legs.

"You want to die first?" Vikas questioned, his smile mocking.

"Aisha . . . move!" Parth weakly pushed at Aisha's shoulder.

Vikas got to his feet and pointed the gun down at Aisha and Parth.

"Vikas, I'm so amazed at all that you have done."

"Move, Aisha!" Aisha felt Parth's legs under her outstretched arms.

"Parth, stop. Vikas was telling me about—"

A sudden click Vikas fired the gun.

Chapter 77

Aisha screamed. The gun shot was deafening; it felt like a bomb had gone off in her head. Her ears rang with the noise.

Parth's yelp cut through the buzzing noise. Aisha glanced down and saw the front of his shirt turn a brazenly crimson. "How could you?" Aisha screamed at Vikas who watched the writhing form of Parth with fascination.

Parth twisted in pain yet he tried to say something to Aisha.

"Aisha!"

Someone was pounding on the front door.

Kabir!

Adrenaline shot through Aisha's body.

"Open the door!"

Thudding sounds came from the living room. Kabir was throwing himself at the door.

For a second, Vikas appeared confused. He turned sideways, toward the front door.

It was all the time Aisha needed. She yanked Parth's right trouser leg up and smoothly pulled out the compact Glock 26.

Aisha grabbed it with her right hand, firmly inserting the grip of the gun in the cup of her hand. She placed her left hand to steady the gun. She knew she had mere seconds.

She aligned the tip of the barrel to the back of the cylinder and aimed it at Vikas's head.

The killer spun to face her.

"Like the view?" Aisha said through gritted teeth.

Vikas's eyes widened.

"Cops often carry concealed weapons. I should know! My brother was a cop."

"Don't you dare touch her!" Kabir kept throwing himself against the door. The thudding was loud. The door was beginning to creak.

Vikas's little-boy expression altered to a menacing rage. His lips pulled back to show his clenched teeth. "I was feeling sorry that I had to kill you, bitch." He raised his lowered hand. The hand with the gun!

"Please put the gun down. Please!" Aisha pleaded. It was one thing to hold a loaded gun and another to fire it to kill. She also knew Parth was slowly dying right next to her.

Vikas flashed a familiar coy smile. "You won't kill me. You can't kill me. You buy flowers for strangers, you mother a child who is not your own." He chuckled. He jerked the gun up.

Vikas aimed the gun at Aisha's face.

Aisha did not waste a fraction of a second.

She fired.

Chapter 78

The beauty killer collapsed to his knees. A red wound appeared on his tanned forehead. He fell forward and hit the ground. And stayed there.

Aisha dropped the gun and turned. "Parth! Parth," she shook him. Parth did not react, he stayed still. Blood had seeped through most of his shirt.

A pair of masculine hands touched the base of Parth's neck. "I can feel a light pulse." It was Kabir. He had got through.

"Have to save him! He can't die." Aisha's face was ashen. Her voice shook.

"Get me a towel! Anything to keep the pressure on the wound to slow the bleeding. The police are on the way."

"What?" Aisha could only gape. She could feel her mind shutting down.

"Aisha," Kabir hollered in her face. "You have to move now to save your boyfriend." He reached out, squeezing her arm. Kabir's touch got through the numbness that was covering her mind. "Go!"

Aisha went out, her movements erratic. She noticed the front door swinging loose. Ironically, the old door had broken from the hinges. The locks and bolts still held it upright.

She rushed into the first room that she came upon. It was a room with a mattress, a closet, a table, and pictures—several pictures lined up on the wall. Under them, a line of women's shoes were displayed—a single shoe instead of a pair. Aisha cupped her mouth as bile rose in her.

His shrine!

As Aisha rummaged through the drawers of the closet, she kept glancing at the pictures of Komal Das, Aditi Kavuri, Thoi Elviz, Julie Fernando, Nafeesa Khan, Sandhya Arora and some more girls.

Their pictures were plastered all over the wall. Some taken as Vikas held them captive and others taken after their death. Aisha averted her eyes just as her hand settled around a rough terrycloth-like fabric.

I shot him. I avenged all their deaths!

Aisha grabbed the towels and ran out of the room.

A second later, Aisha came back inside.

What the hell!

She stared at a girl's picture on the extreme left corner of the wall. Shivers broke out on Aisha's body. She was staring straight at a face she had seen recently.

Lavina. Kabir's late wife.

Chapter 79

"**Here, sip** some coffee. This should warm you up," Kabir sat down next to Aisha and picked her hands from her lap. He gently wrapped them around a thin plastic white coffee cup.

"Thanks!" Her hands weren't the steadiest and she spilled some hot liquid on them. Aisha flinched.

"Here, let me," Kabir took the cup from her hand and held it to her mouth. "Have a sip."

Aisha saw deep concern for her in Kabir's eyes. Bending her head, she took a sip. The sweet coffee went down her throat.

"Thank you," she sat back, pulling the blanket provided by the hospital tightly around her. The hospital chairs weren't the most comfortable.

"He'll pull through," Kabir reassured her, alluding to Parth who was in surgery.

Parth had weak pulse but he was still breathing when he was rushed to the hospital. He had been in the surgery for over two hours.

Two police men were standing nearby and several others were in the waiting room down the hall. A CBI officer was one of their own.

"Why don't you try sleeping for a while?" Kabir suggested as Aisha took another sip.

"I can't sleep. Not now." Aisha sighed.

"Why were the policemen questioning you?" Kabir was referring to the meeting Aisha had returned from twenty minutes earlier with a DSP and his team.

"Because till Parth doesn't wake up and gives them a statement, I'm a suspect. I'm the only one walking out of the three in that apartment." Aisha sighed, resting her head against the wall.

Kabir had not left her side for more than a few minutes since he had broken into Vikas's apartment.

"Maybe I should call a lawyer for you, just in case." Kabir began to pull out his cell from his pocket.

Aisha shook her head. "Please don't. You have done enough. You are the reason I'm alive."

Kabir grimaced. "I did nothing—"

"Yes, you did. Knocking on that door was the best thing you could have done. It distracted Vikas, giving me enough time to pull out Parth's gun."

"So, you can shoot too?"

"Practicing for last so many years at firing range paid off." Aisha closed her eyes only to open again.

"Hush," Kabir raised a finger and wiped a tear that had slipped from the corner of her eye.

Aisha did not realize she had been crying. She pulled in a fractured breath. "How did you happen to come to Vikas's apartment? Did he call you too?"

"No. Once I cooled down after our argument earlier, I realized a few things. All the times I was in Goa, Vikas always accompanied me. All those scenic points where I shot the calendar were his haunts. Vikas had introduced them to me. He was from Goa. And lastly, that night when we met for the first time, minutes before you had appeared on the beach, I had spotted Vikas there. That was the reason I had been walking in that direction. But he had disappeared by the time I got there. And then you captured all my attention. I just forgot all about him."

"Oh!"

"I tried calling you to tell you about Vikas, but you didn't answer. So, I called up Kiara to inquire about you and she told me that you were at Vikas's apartment. I just rushed there."

"I'm glad you did!" Aisha managed a smile. "You didn't mention anything to Kiara, did you?"

"I had to, just now. While you were with the police. She has been calling repeatedly. I could distract her only so much." Kabir replied, tossing her empty coffee cup in a bin.

"Damn, she will be worried now. She has probably told Papa too."

Their eyes met and Kabir broke the gaze. "Why don't you talk to her now." He handed Aisha his phone. "Do you know where your phone is?"

"Vikas probably took it when I passed out."

Kabir stared straight ahead, his mouth clamped in a tight line. "I can't believe he was capable of what he did. How could I not see it? He worked with me for so many years. Fuck!"

"He was good at duping." Aisha took the phone from Kabir. Her hands brushed his.

Kabir nodded and withdrew his hand. "I'll be right back."

Aisha took a deep breath and called her niece. She answered in one ring.

"Boo, are you okay? We are coming to get you." Kiara's voice was urgent.

For the next ten minutes, Aisha pacified her niece and shared with her all that had unfolded in the last few hours.

"I am coming to the hospital right now!" Kiara repeated.

"No, you are not. It's close to 3:00 am. I'm fine. I will come when the surgery is over."

"Let me talk to her." Kabir was back.

Aisha handed him the phone. Closing her weary eyes, Aisha had no recollection of falling asleep.

Sometime later, a gentle hand tapped on Aisha's shoulder. Wincing, she raised a groggy head. Her eyes were burning as she rubbed them.

"Did I fall asleep?" Aisha raised her head from Kabir's shoulder.

"For ten minutes or so. The doctor is here," Kabir pointed, getting to his feet.

Aisha turned. It was the doctor who was operating on Parth. He was a thin wiry man with oval glasses, a small face, and a pronounced nose. He was still in his blue scrubs. Aisha too rose slowly.

"The operation was successful. SSP Parth will recover fully. The bullet missed his heart or any other arteries by inches and embedded in the soft tissue around the shoulder. We were able to extract the bullet with no damage to the surrounding area."

"Thank you so much." Aisha shook the doctor's hand. "Can I see him?"

"Sorry, the first person Parth asked was for the case in-charge. Your boyfriend is very committed."

Aisha nodded and sat down.

Kabir sat down next to her after thanking the doctor. They sat in silence for the next few minutes.

"Excuse me, Aisha Ma'am!" A policeman approached them. "Parth Sir wants to see you."

Chapter 80

"Hi!" **Aisha** walked in a room that smelled strongly of bleach. Parth lay on a bed, his shoulder bandaged. His face was the color of the pale walls.

"Do you smell the bleach?" she asked.

Parth wheezed. "Don't make me laugh!"

Two inspectors were also present in the room.

Aisha and Kabir stopped at the foot of his bed.

"Where did you learn how to shoot?" Parth asked.

"At the firing range. I told you I was serious about wanting to be in the police."

Parth nodded and glanced at a stoic Kabir. "Thanks."

"You don't have to thank me. I was there for Aisha."

Parth nodded. "You should go home now, Ms. Aisha."

"I just wanted to know how you found out about Vikas? If one of you could tell me, I will sleep better." Aisha glanced at the other two cops in the room.

Parth smiled weakly. "You are persistent."

One of the policeman spoke up. "The van at Lopez Point, the one you discovered Ms. Aisha, had been frequently sold and resold. The last owner was a late zamindar of Priol—a small village seventy-five kilometers away from Panaji. It was here that Parth Sir got some sketchy details about the zamindar's mistress, a drunkard Nellie Varghese and her weird son, Tony Varghese."

Parth took over, his speech strained. "Vikas Mishra was actually Tony Varghese from Priol. His mother, Nellie Varghese, was a small-time starlet in Konkani film industry and an alcoholic. She was asked to leave the village around 1985 when she became an unwed mother. When he was fifteen, Nellie and Tony moved to Mumbai." Parth paused and asked for some water. The inspector who had spoken earlier came forward and helped him sip from a paper cup. "You continue," Parth said, falling back against the pillows.

The Inspector put the cup down and extracted a clipboard tucked under his arm. He scanned the document, probably Parth's statement.

"In Mumbai, the mother and son started living near Kamatipura area. When Tony was sixteen, he was sent to a juvenile home for attempted murder. After serving his time, Tony worked there for nearly a decade. Around the time Tony worked there, a fourteen-year old boy Vikas Mishra was sent to the juvie house. A few months later, Vikas disappeared under mysterious circumstances. The officials assumed Vikas had run away. As he was an orphan, no one really bothered about him."

"You think Tony killed Vikas?" Aisha asked.

Parth nodded.

"So, Nellie and the late zamindar stayed in touch even after she moved to Mumbai?" Aisha asked.

Parth nodded. "The zamindar continued his relationship with Nellie on and off. And when the zamindar was not able to come to Mumbai, Nellie would visit him, accompanied by her son Tony. The zamindar, in his later years it seems, had also developed a taste for young boys." Parth's mouth twisted in disgust. His speech got slurred.

Everyone became quiet in the room. "Tony had a horrible childhood," Aisha heard pity in her voice even though she had no guilt over the fatal shot she had fired.

Parth spoke after taking another sip of water. His lids were getting heavy. "I got ambushed. I went to the apartment looking for Nellie Varghese because officially, she had never died. The hospital records simply stated that she had stopped coming for her chemo sessions. The doctors had anyway told her son that there was nothing more they could do. The cancer had corroded her body from the inside. She was past the point of recovery."

"All the pictures of Tony Varghese and Vikas Mishra were removed from their juvie home records, so Parth Sir had no idea what he looked like."

"He was thorough?" Aisha murmured.

"Yes!" Parth nodded. He was having trouble keeping his eyes open.

"I'm guessing you will never find Nellie's body?" Kabir said.

"Hmm," Parth nodded.

Everyone was silent for a few seconds.

"I think I would like to go home now." Aisha said, sounding as tired as she felt.

"I'll take you home," Kabir asserted. Aisha did not argue.

"You get some rest, Parth!" Aisha turned away.

"Aisha," Parth called out.

She paused.

"I could not have cracked this case without you. You would have made a great cop." Parth's eyes were gentle as they closed and he drifted off.

Kabir helped Aisha into his car and with her seatbelt. She was bushed.

"This is probably not the best time," Kabir hesitated, yet his voice was low and burning. "Aisha, please tell me, is Parth your boyfriend?" He paused and swallowed. "Are you seeing anyone?"

Aisha sighed and closed her eyes. She was too weary to be tactful. "I thought I was seeing you, Doofus!"

Chapter 81

A loud crack resounded near her ear. A bullet! Her eyes flew open and Aisha sat up with a jerk.

Kiara was sitting next to her on the bed, a book in her hand, which she immediately placed aside. "Boo, it's okay. You are in your room." she hugged Aisha.

"Sorry," Hiding her face in Kiara's shoulder, Aisha took a few calming breaths. Sitting back, Aisha pulled the thin sheet off her body as she was sweating heavily.

"Here," Kiara held a glass of water toward her and she wiped Aisha's brow with her other hand. "Gosh, you scared the crap out of me when you sat up like that."

"How did I get home?" Aisha felt muddled. Her last memory was getting into Kabir's car.

"Kabir dropped you, no, carried you home. You were fast asleep. You did not move a muscle." Kiara put the glass down. "Let me get Dada; he has asked to be informed the moment you woke up. Oh yeah, Kabir came over in morning and dropped your cell phone off. It was in that sicko's apartment."

Aisha drank the fresh cool water. "What time is it?"

"Close to 2:00 in the afternoon," Kiara said, leaving the room.

Aisha scooted back. Her body felt rested, but her mind felt like the ground had been scraped with it.

Ragged and raw!

Aisha grabbed her phone and switched it on. Several messages downloaded on it. Most of them were from Kabir and he signed off as 'Doofus.'

A tiny smile came on Aisha's face as she read them. Most of them showed his concern and were repeat requests to call him if she needed anything, or just call him.

"Aisha!"

She looked up. It was her father. His eyes held worry and he seemed to have aged overnight.

"Papa," Aisha raised her head. "Sorry, I didn't tell you about all this."

"Tell me now," He pulled a chair close to her and took Aisha's hand.

He has been crying.

Aisha swallowed heavily and shared everything with him even as Kiara sat on her other side. Aisha severely downplayed her role in it. It was unsettling to see her father, who faced stone-cold criminals and weathered death threats all his career, so terrified at the thought of something happening to her.

Close to five, Aisha emerged from her room, fresh from a shower. She pulled Kiara to a side. "Kia, I'm going out for a while."

"What? Where?"

Aisha cleared her throat. Her blush gave her away

"Oh!" Kiara smiled. "Well go. I will cover for you. Tell Dada you are going to see that CBI chap in the hospital and tying up some loose ends with the police."

Aisha hugged her. "Thanks, Kia."

Kiara hugged her tight. "Sorry for being such a pain in the ass, Boo. I love you so much. If something had happened to you . . ."

Aisha hugged her back tightly. "I'm okay, kiddo. I'm not going anywhere until I play with your babies."

"Oh, stop!" Kiara moved away and turned around. Aisha knew Kiara never let anyone see her crying. She had always been like this.

Aisha hugged her from behind. "I'll be back before dinner."

"We will see." Kiara rubbed Aisha's arms. "Just don't get shot, please."

Chapter 82

Kabir sat on the sofa, leaning forward. He tapped his soles on the ground and kept playing with the cell in his hands. *Why hasn't Aisha texted back? She should be up by now. Should I call her?*

The nervous energy that flowed in him would not let him focus on anything even if he tried. He had to take a few calming breaths.

The pealing doorbell shattered the silence in the apartment.

Kabir jumped to his feet and went to the door, waving his butler off. When he opened the door, he could only stare.

"Hi, Doofus!" Aisha smiled at him.

Kabir's smile was quick and inviting, his voice deep. "Come inside. Should you even be walking?"

"I'm fine," Aisha replied, walking past him. She sat at the edge of the white suede sofa, her fingers repeatedly drumming the top of her knees.

Kabir stopped right next to her. "Can I get you something? Water or coffee? Or coffee and Red Bull?"

"Have a seat . . . please!" Aisha mumbled, trying to speak over the throbbing blood between her ears.

"Okay," Kabir sat down close to her.

Keeping her eyes lowered, Aisha fiddled with her silk and gold skirt. She had teamed that up with a simple sleeveless white lace blouse. Her hair was loose, and she had applied some make-up in the car.

Turning to her, Kabir placed an arm on the sofa behind her. His spicy musk smell swarmed her. "You have nothing to be nervous about."

Aisha ran her eyes over his lean torso in a black tee, the strong column of his neck, his face that had seen the sun, a mouth that was relaxed but not smiling, his straight nose and his dark eyes filled with concern for her.

Just effing say it!

Taking a deep breath, Aisha stared in Kabir's eyes and whispered throatily, "I want to take it to the next level."

She saw his dark eyes glimmer and then his mouth widened in a broad smile. Kabir took her hands in his. His grasp was warm and enveloping. "Are you sure, Aisha? I want this," He shook their clasped hands. "God, I want you more than any woman I have ever wanted in my life. But you have just experienced a big trauma. I don't want to take advantage of a situation—"

Aisha leaned in. "Shut up and kiss me!"

Kabir studied her face for a few seconds and then got to his feet. Aisha's gaze was one of surprise.

"Come on! I don't want us to be disturbed."

Licking her lips with the tip of her tongue, Aisha felt excitement unwind in her. She felt her knees knock against each other.

Wordlessly, Kabir led Aisha up the stairs to his bedroom.

Chapter 83

Once inside, Kabir shut the door and turned Aisha to him. Wrapping a muscular arm around Aisha's waist, he pulled her in. "Are you sure about this?" Kabir asked, twisting a loose tendril of her hair around his finger, watching her all the while longingly.

"Kabir, please!" Aisha's voice was raw with yearning as she arched against him.

Kabir needed no more assurances. He bent his dark head down, tipping her chin up simultaneously. Aisha sighed as all her senses tingled.

Kabir rubbed his lips back and forth over her soft mouth. Aisha moved her body closer and Kabir wrapped his arms around her plaint form, meshing them together. Aisha curved her arms around his neck even as her eyes fluttered close. Heat built in her body and moisture pooled between her legs.

Aisha's fingers stroked the base of his nape. Kabir groaned and possessed Aisha's mouth. His tongue delved into her hot wet cavern, dueling with and stroking her tongue. Their first kiss was everything Aisha had imagined—passionate, long, and arousing. Their lips clung to each other just like their bodies.

Aisha mimicked his movements, chasing his tongue with hers. Groaning, Kabir thrust his fingers into Aisha's hair and clasped her head as he feasted on her mouth. He sucked her tongue as if he was thirsting for it.

Aisha felt her nipples harden, her limbs felt weightless as she sank more into him. He was relentless. Aisha felt like an exposed mass of nerves. Every inch of her skin, where he touched and caressed, sparked. Kabir's hands ran down her back, molding her to him. Then his hands moved between their bodies and cupped her soft breasts. He rolled her nipples between his fingers.

Aisha bit off her moan and arched her back, pushing her breast deeper into his hand. She moved restlessly against Kabir.

Kabir broke apart to get some air. "You are so damn sexy, Aisha," he spoke thickly. "I could love you all day!"

Aisha stared at him, her eyes laden with desire, her cheeks suffused with color and her lips swollen from his kisses. "Did I stop you," she murmured throatily.

Kabir's answering smile was wolfish. Picking Aisha up effortlessly, he carried her to the large bed and placed her gently on the silk sheets.

"I . . ." Aisha sat up and trailed off, unsure of what she wanted to say.

Kabir sat next to her and nuzzled her neck, pressing urgent kisses into the soft skin of her neck. "We will stop anytime you want. Promise," He straightened and smiled even as one of his hand lowered the zip on her top.

Aisha leaned away from him, smiling mysteriously. In one fluid move, she took her top off but chickened out at the last minute and covered herself with it.

Kabir's eyes roamed over her fair, petite shoulders. A slight smile creased his face, contrasting with the heat in his eyes. "This is the only thing *you* remove," he cupped her face.

Aisha laughed and hid her face in his shoulder. "As you say, Doofus."

He slid the strap of her camisole and bra down one shoulder even as he placed wet kisses on the skin he was exposing bit by bit. He gently nipped Aisha's shoulder and then laved the spot with his hot tongue. She jerked with pleasure.

Kabir pressed Aisha down on the bed. His hot mouth laid a damp trail of kisses down to every piece of clothing he removed off her. By the time the last piece was removed, Aisha was clutching his broad shoulders, pleading with Kabir to take her. When he first thrust in her, Aisha was slick with desire.

Kabir kissed her deeply as Aisha shuddered and climaxed, with him embedded deep in her love pool. Sheathed inside her tight walls, her bare legs wrapped around him, Kabir could not hold back any longer. His orgasm was powerful. His body jerked as he continued to thrust in Aisha, the pleasure deep and soul searing. Kabir felt like he had permanently fused himself with sweet and brave woman in his arms. His possessive touch, heated gaze and seeking hands and mouth left no room for any doubt. Aisha was all that he wanted and more.

Amidst heated, plundering kisses, roving hands and sweetly spoken words, Aisha learned how an experienced lover's touch and heated coupling bodies can evoke an earth shattering experience. Twice.

#

"Ummm!" Waking up, Aisha stretched her arms above her head. She was alone in Kabir's bed. Her body felt deliciously worn, her breasts raw from the attention they had received from Kabir's mouth and hands, the place between her legs still tingling from his long, stroking thrusts.

Aisha's heart felt overloaded with love for Kabir. She affectionately stroked the pillow next to her, the one on which he had lain after he had made love to her, his expression awed, his mouth creased in a smile. "Thank you!" he had said with such reverence.

I love you would have been good too!

Aisha turned and saw that all her clothes were folded neatly on the ottoman at the foot of the bed. Sometime later, she went looking for her newly-minted lover. She found him sitting with his back to her on the sofa downstairs.

Chapter 84

Kabir heard her come down. Swiveling his head, he put his hand out to Aisha, his glance hot and possessive. "Hey!"

"Hey!" Shyly taking his hand, Aisha came around the sofa and settled next to him. Aisha rested her head against his bare chest for his shirt was unbuttoned. Her eyes fell on the laptop open on his lap. A woman with delicate bird-like features stared back at her. "Holy cow!" Aisha jerked up.

Next to her Kabir dissolved in chuckles.

"Hi!" The woman greeted Aisha, her expression bemused.

"Hi!" Aisha said, even as she dug her elbow into Kabir who was still laughing. "You are horrible."

"Sorry, sweetheart." Kabir sobered. "Shreya, this is—"

"Kiara, I'm guessing?" The woman on the video call spoke dryly.

Aisha and Kabir exchanged a puzzled glance. "No Shreya, this is Kiara's aunt. Aisha."

Shreya's look was bug-eyed. "She is the aunt? But you said she was a pain in the ass." She covered her mouth. "Oops!"

"Shreya!" Kabir murmured. He took Aisha's hand. "That was much earlier. When we . . . met."

Aisha patted his hand. "It's okay. I have said worse about you."

Shreya was quick to make amends. "It's lovely to meet you, Aisha. May I be the first to offer congratulations on the impending nuptials?"

"Umm!" Aisha looked at Kabir, her expression like what-do-I-say-to-that?

"Shreya, you are on a roll." Kabir shook his head.

Shreya looked sheepish. "Sorry, Aisha, I'm just exhausted. The conference is long and tiring. I'm super happy for you guys."

"It's okay." Aisha smiled. "Don't worry about it."

"So, when do you get back?" Kabir changed the topic.

"Actually, sooner than I had planned. A problem with one of my patients." Shreya's rolled her eyes. "Anyhow, I look forward to meeting you in person, Aisha. I haven't seen Kabir happier. And I think it's all because of you."

Feeling awkward, Aisha could only nod.

"Bye, Shreya. Call me when you land here." Kabir ended the call. He raised Aisha's hand and dropped lingering kisses on her fingers.

Aisha closed her eyes. His lips on her skin set off familiar tingles in her body. She was melting again. "She isn't mad with me because I spoke to her ex-husband?"

Carelessly pushing his laptop to the side, Kabir crowded against Aisha and turned her face to his. His lips were centimeters away, but not for long. He kissed Aisha for several minutes and then pulled apart. "She is very nice, just like you. How are you feeling now, sweetheart?"

"Haven't felt better." Aisha snuggled against him.

"Hungry?"

"Hmmm!"

"How does dinner in bed sound?" Kabir pulled her up against him.

"You, Sir, are a mind reader."

Kabir's hand purposely brushed her breast. "But I'm hungry for dessert first."

Chapter 85

A week later

"**Have you** decided what to wear tonight?" Kiara asked as she and Aisha walked through a Mall, looking for a gift.

"I don't know. Maybe the pink skirt or the one you got for me from Cottons." Aisha scrunched her nose up. "I hope Shreya likes me."

"Of course, she will! What is—"

Just then Aisha's cell rang. It was Parth. "Hold on to that thought!" Aisha answered her cell.

"Hello?"

"Aisha, can I meet you today? The sooner the better." Parth sounded serious.

"Sure. Everything okay?"

"I will tell you when we meet." Parth replied.

"I can meet you in an hour." Aisha said. "Can you tell me what it is about?"

"It's about Kabir."

#

In less than an hour, Aisha walked into a coffee shop. Parth stood up and waved her down. He had taken the last booth in the cafe.

Aisha made her way past the other occupied tables. The smell of baked products and coffee left a pleasant aroma inside.

"How's the arm?" she said, pointing at Parth's arm in the sling.

"A pain in the ass!" Parth said rubbing the gray strap around his neck. "Now I know how a collar feels around a dog's neck. Have a seat, please."

"So, what is it about Kabir?" Aisha came straight to the point, placing her purse on the plastic padded bench with a small rip in it.

Parth lowered himself across from her. "You want something? Coffee?"

"Regular, no sugar or milk." Aisha waited as Parth placed their orders. She watched quietly as Parth tipped half the sugar jar in his cappuccino.

"I like it sweet," He offered, stirring his coffee.

"No kidding," Aisha murmured.

"Stay away from Kabir," Parth too was a straight shooter.

Aisha jerked her head back. "Excuse me?"

Parth opened a folder kept on his side and placed two pictures on the table. "Do you know these women?"

Aisha glared at him. "His sister and his wife."

"His dead sister and his dead wife." Parth placed the pictures back in the file. "Both died when Kabir was the only one with them."

"No, he wasn't!" Aisha contested, her insides curdling at Parth's insinuation.

Parth raised an eyebrow. "Did he tell you that?"

Aisha frowned as she tried recollecting that particular conversation.

"And is it a coincidence that a prolific and active serial killer works with him for so many years and Kabir has no idea what his assistant is doing?"

Aisha opened her mouth to defend Kabir but Parth cut her off.

"You must have had an assistant. What do you know about him or her?"

Aisha sat back, her expression sullen. "Everyone has different personalities. I know more about my assistants because we both like to share things. I don't think Vikas, sorry, Tony was good at sharing and we all know why. And Kabir doesn't talk much about himself until he is very close to someone."

"Like he is to you, nowadays?" Parth sipped his coffee.

"Excuse me?"

"We are watching him. That is how I know you and he meet every day for prolonged hours at his apartment."

Aisha turned a deep shade of red. "You are watching him? Seriously?" She placed her elbows on the table and narrowed her eyes. "Are you watching everyone who worked with Tony?"

Parth placed a transparent plastic bag with a smaller picture in it. Aisha sucked her cheeks in and retreated into the leather sofa.

"So, you saw this too? I'm guessing we both saw it at same place, a peeling wall."

Aisha nodded, turning her gaze away from Lavina's photograph—the one Tony had put up on his shrine.

"Any idea why a serial killer, who decorated a wall with pictures of all his victims, had Kabir's late wife's picture there?"

"Well, the only one who could shed any light on this is dead." Aisha mumbled.

"Or maybe he is alive." Parth replied quietly.

It took Aisha a few seconds to comprehend Parth's insinuation. "Are the doctors sure only your arm was damaged?"

"Just because you are involved with Kabir, you are not seeing all these connections. Princess Kritika, Lavina Salve and the serial killer who killed numerous women. They all have one common thread—Kabir Rana."

Aisha grabbed her purse. "I think I'm done here!"

"A good cop never shies away from evidence."

Aisha paused. "Neither does a good cop fabricate evidence."

"Do me a favor, ask Kabir where he was the night Lavina allegedly killed herself."

"Don't waste my time, Parth. If you have something to say, then say it. Obviously, holding back is not you forte."

"So, his wife stumbles around in a drunken stupor, crashing and upturning furniture in her bedroom and living room, somehow manages to pull open a heavy balcony door of their high-rise apartment on a particularly windy night and jumps to her death. And Kabir who is asleep in the guest room, a few feet away from the living room, claims to have heard nothing. Absolutely nothing!"

Aisha hated herself for asking that question. "There were no servants in the apartment?"

"Coincidentally, it was their monthly night-off. So, no witnesses. Convenient, don't you think?"

Aisha slid out from behind the table. "I think we are done here."

Parth too got to his feet. "I wasn't kidding when I said you would have made a good cop."

Aisha chewed her lower lip. "If I ask you to back off, will you, Parth?"

"You know I can't!" Parth's expression was stony.

"Because a good cop does not shy from evidence?" Aisha repeated his words.

"Something like that." Parth finished his coffee in one sip. "Then I guess our lines are drawn."

"You follow your evidence and I'll follow my instincts." Aisha turned to go.

"Evidence relies on facts not feelings."

Aisha paused. "Exactly. Kabir was found innocent because there was no evidence that he had anything to do with his wife's unfortunate death. Factual proof!"

Exasperation flashed in Parth's eyes as he put his dark shades on. "Just be careful, will you? Kabir is not what he looks."

"Another feeling?" Aisha scoffed, walking away.

Chapter 86

Later That Night

"Right on time!" Kiara said as the doorbell rang and she went to open it.

Aisha got up from the sofa and smiled in anticipation.

Kabir stood at the door, looking handsome in sharply fitted black trousers and a crisp pale lavender formal shirt. "Hey, Kiara!"

"What, no black Kabir?"

"Just ..." Kabir self-consciously tugged at his collar.

"Ignore her," Aisha walked up to them.

Kabir took Aisha's hand. "Kind of hard to. She is my top model."

"See?" Kiara poked her tongue at Aisha. "Okay, I will get Dada."

"And the gift."

Kiara left them alone. Kabir dropped a swift hard kiss on Aisha's lips. "You look beautiful."

Aisha took a second or two to recover. Kabir's kisses always left her weak-kneed. "Thank you. You look very handsome too." She stroked his cheek.

"Can we go to my place after dinner?" Kabir pulled her suggestively against him.

"Behave! Papa might come out any time." Aisha put some distance between them. "We'll see. I can make excuses in the day but at the night, what will I say when I leave?"

"Then I guess you shouldn't have to make excuses. Maybe it's time—"

Aisha stopped him. "Let's just take it one day at a time. I hope Shreya likes me."

Kabir pulled Aisha close again. "Hey, Shreya will love you just like—" he paused.

Aisha glanced at him. Is he going to finally say the three words?

Kabir and Aisha spent as much time as they could with each other, made love every time with crazy intensity, talked for hours, enjoyed finding out and doing what the other liked, yet Kabir never said those three words. *Call me old-fashioned, but I want him to say it first.*

"You have nothing to be nervous about." Kabir finished.

"Yup!" Aisha nodded, hiding her disappointment as she moved away just as her Dad and Kiara joined them.

Thanks to Mumbai traffic, by the time reached Shreya's flat it was close to 9:00 in the night.

"You should have eaten a snack, Papa." Aisha admonished, getting in the elevator.

"Aisha, stop fussing." Her father returned, pursing his mouth.

Aisha heard Kiara whisper to Kabir. "She's a nag. You can have her for good."

"Kiara!" Aisha used her warning tone. Kabir chuckled behind them.

Dinner went well. The food was great and Shreya a pleasant person and a very good host. Except, Aisha had to fake her enthusiasm.

So, what if he is taking his time saying those three words to me? They are just words. His actions are what matter. Is Kabir unsure of us? And that idiot Parth. He and his silly insinuations. Should I ask Kabir where he was both those nights when his sister and wife died?

Throughout the evening, Aisha caught Kabir glance at her questioningly and each time Aisha replied in a smile more blinding than the sun itself.

Post dinner, Shreya led Aisha into the kitchen when Aisha offered to help with the coffee.

"You have a lovely family." Shreya said, filling the percolator.

"Thank you." Aisha stopped inside the modular kitchen in the shades of cream and gold marble, complete with deep brown cabinets. "Your flat is so beautiful."

"Thank you. Interior decoration is my hobby." Shreya took out two small cappuccino cups. "Let's have a cup each first."

"But the others are outside." Aisha murmured.

"Kabir will take care of them." Shreya remarked, pouring some sugar in a porcelain dish.

"You and Kabir are tight," Aisha said.

Shreya paused and gave Aisha a clear-eyed glance.

"I'm not jealous. I'm just saying. It is good that he has you." Aisha was quick to assure her. "Everyone needs a family."

Shreya smiled and nodded. "And Kabir needs a woman like you. One who can overlook his past and accept him for who he is."

"What do you mean?" Aisha asked, a part of her dreading the answer.

Please don't be the second person today to ding my boyfriend.

Shreya gazed at her, her expression guilty. "Umm . . . nothing. Nothing at all. So Kabir said you write for television. Any current shows?"

Aisha immediately warmed to Shreya at the evasion. "It's okay, Shreya, I know about his late sister and wife."

Shreya smiled relieved. "You do? I thought I had let the cat out of the bag."

Aisha shook her head. A sudden thought pierced her mind. *Shreya can help me. She would know for sure.* Aisha scratched her temple as she cleared her throat, "So do you know where Kabir was when Lavina jumped from the balcony?"

Shreya's eyes hardened; she went back to arranging the tray with more cups. "You should ask him, Aisha."

Crap, she took offense.

"It's kind of a delicate topic to broach with Kabir. You know . . ." Aisha trailed off uncomfortably.

Shreya kept her back to Aisha. "Then check the Internet. Enough sleaze was posted about Kabir and his family at the time of Lavina's death," her voice was curt.

Grimacing, Aisha persisted. "Kabir mentioned that he met Lavina at your place."

"More of social acquaintances; she lived in the same building as I." Shreya removed the boiling percolator and set it on the tray. Her movements were brisk. She pivoted with the tray in her hand. "Maybe we should just have coffee with everyone else."

Aisha nodded, her eyes downcast.

So much for becoming BFFs.

Shreya walked past Aisha and then paused. "FYI Kabir will be his moodiest in the next few days. Kriti's death anniversary is coming up."

Aisha felt a shiver go through her as Shreya mentioned Kriti. Aisha immediately started counting the number of things in the kitchen.

"And so is Kabir's birthday. Those two dates are mere days apart. He doesn't commemorate either. Please be kind to him." Having said that, she sailed past Aisha.

Aisha hunched as she followed Shreya.

Kabir's face lit up as Shreya and Aisha rejoined them. Gazing at Aisha he patted the seat next to him on the sofa.

Gosh, now I feel like scum. Stupid Parth!

Aisha sat down next to him and nodded sedately to his questioning gaze.

For the rest of the evening, Shreya was distant, not even glancing Aisha's way, focusing all the while on Kiara and the retired Judge. Aisha stayed quiet for the rest of the evening.

Something tugged at Aisha's mind, but she ignored it because of the self-reproach going at her heart with a sledgehammer.

Chapter 87

"**All evening**, I have been dying to do this." Kabir leaned across from his seat grinning wolfishly.

Aisha put her hand on his chest. "Wait!"

Kabir glanced over his shoulder. "Your Dad and Kiara have gone up."

Aisha shifted in her car seat, her expression uneasy. After dinner at Shreya's place, Kabir had driven them all back. Her father and Kiara had gone upstairs, giving Aisha and Kabir some time to say their goodbyes in private.

"Dammit, come here, woman!" Kabir growled possessively as he unbuckled her seat belt.

"Kabir, please stop." Aisha's tense expression finally got through to him.

Kabir stayed close. His eyes narrowed in concern. "What happened, sweetheart?"

"I don't think Shreya likes me."

Laughing softly, Kabir rubbed his lips on hers and pulled back. His gaze was soft as his caress. "She adores you."

Aisha focused on her words with effort. "She doesn't. I asked her about Lavina."

Kabir stiffened. He sat back in his seat. "What did you ask?"

A wave of apprehension swept over Aisha. "I asked where you were when Lavina died." Aisha's voice was low and troubled.

"Still investigating me?" Kabir's voice grew chilly.

Aisha swallowed nervously. "Why didn't you tell me that you were in the flat when Lavina had jumped off the balcony?" She could hear the bitterness in her tone.

Kabir's expression told her that Parth had spoken the truth.

"You did not ask. If you had, I would not have lied." Kabir replied curtly.

Aisha hung her head for it felt weighed down by a sudden load. I'm keeping secrets too—Kritika's spirit, Tony's wall and Lavina's picture on it, my own freakishness!

Resigned, Aisha reached out for the car door. "I'll see you—"

Kabir grabbed her wrist, his grip tight. "Shreya holds herself responsible for bringing Lavina in my life. She has enough guilt about that already and then you ask her about Lavina the very first time you meet her? Fuck!" His face was bunched up in anger. "Why the hell didn't you ask me first?"

Aisha was taken aback by his tone. "I don't need your permission to talk to people or for anything else."

Kabir's nostrils flared and his mouth clamped in a tight line. Dropping her hand, he moved away from her and spoke in a clipped voice. "Goodnight!"

Aisha got off the car and closed the door, resisting the urge to slam it. Her words, 'talk to you later' were drowned by the roar of the engine as Kabir immediately sped away.

He always escorts me to the flat.

Aisha watched the glowing tail lights of his car until they disappeared. Angry tears filled her eyes. "Why does it have to be so hard?" Years of being remarkably sensible presented her with another thought.

When has it ever been easy?

Thankfully, Kiara and her father had already retired by the time Aisha came up. She sat on her bed in the company of her muddled thoughts and laptop.

Her cell beeped. She had received a text message.

"Shit!" Aisha felt her heart race as she read Suvabrata's text.

Accept who you are. Open yourself to them. The spirits will guide you.

Aisha switched off her cell and tossed it aside. "Sorry Suva, I can't handle you right now." *I might have just messed up one of the best things going on for me.*

Absentmindedly, Aisha removed her jewelry. Why did Kabir get so mad? So, what if I asked a question? Just because it's uncomfortable doesn't mean it's wrong. I'm not a school kid who is blindly going to trust a guy.

"That's it!" Changing into her nightclothes, Aisha pulled out her laptop and sat with it on her bed. She researched Kabir Rana—the love of her life! After nearly four hours of reading and re-reading articles on the net, and making notes, Aisha shut her laptop. Her eyes stung, and she saw two of everything.

Grabbing her cell off her nightstand, she typed the dreaded three words. "You were right!"

And she sent the message to Parth.

Carelessly, Aisha pushed her laptop to the side making room on her bed.

In the darkness, Aisha wiped the scalding tears that overran her cheeks.

Chapter 88

A week and a half later

Aisha walked on the lush green grass. The smell of citrus trees hung thick in the air and the afternoon sun, further dimmed by overcast clouds, held no sting. The breeze was strong enough to bend the weeds and scatter some dried brown leaves. A flowering myrtle tree laden with lavender colored flowers framed the sky overhead.

Brushing some flowers off her head and flicking a grasshopper off her shoulder, Aisha cast yet another glance over her shoulder to make sure that no one had followed her.

Placing her hand against a nearly ten-feet high wall covered completely by thick vines and foliage, Aisha made her way parallel to it. She did her best not to stumble on the clumped and stunted brushes on the ground. Finally, her hand fell upon it—a metal latch.

Excitement riding her face, Aisha put both her hands on the spot and felt around it. "Yup, definitely a gate." In less than a few minutes, she found what she was looking for.

Holding up the lock that had aged and rusted in the passing years, Aisha retrieved a key from her pocket. Pursing her lips, she fitted the key and twisted it. "A thousand-rupee note can truly open locks!"

After a few tugs and pushes, Aisha was able to open the wooden gate. She stepped through the gate.

Studying the statuesque but isolated and severely neglected structure, Aisha took a seat on the dusty marble bench overlooking a large oval-shaped deep pond with a tall, rusty waterspout in the middle.

The water was a dark, unhealthy green. Flotsam—thick short branches, yellow brown leaves, two severely chipped barrels that were once blue—floated on the surface. The pond stank of moss, rot, and putrid things. Aisha shivered as she caught a thick, speckled yellow and green tail of a water snake disappear behind the barrel.

Aisha pulled out her cell from the back pocket of her jeans and dialed a number. After a few rings, a woman answered it.

#

"Hi Shreya, Aisha here."

Shreya was quiet for a few seconds. "How are you and where are you?"

"I'm good. And where I am is a bit tricky," Aisha's laugh was nervous.

"Kabir is very upset. He told me that you have asked for some time away from him."

"Yes, I have."

Shreya sighed. "Aisha, if you are angry with him because of me or anything that I might have said, then please forgive me. So many years of looking out for him has made me over-protective about Kabir."

"It is a bit more complicated than that. Kabir and I barely knew each other, and we jumped headlong into a relationship. He is too intense." Aisha sighed. "Very quick to react. He tires me, Shreya."

"Please don't be quick to judge him. Kabir is complicated but he is not bad at heart. Give him another chance, please." Shreya pleaded.

Aisha exhaled heavily. "I will have to. Unfortunately, I no longer have a choice in the matter." She hesitated and then spoke bluntly. "I'm pregnant."

Chapter 89

Aisha heard Shreya inhale sharply. Shreya went quiet, long enough for Aisha to speak. "Are you there, Shreya?"

"Yes, I'm here. You are sure it is Kabir's?"

Aisha's eyes widened and then she laughed wryly. "I was not expecting this. But I can assure you, it is his. Kabir was and is my first," her voice wavered.

"I'm so sorry!" Shreya hurried. "I was surprised . . . Sorry . . ."

The silence of a few moments between them weighed heavy.

"You know, Aisha, there are options."

A gasp escaped Aisha.

"I was talking about couples' therapy!" Shreya clarified.

"Oh!" Aisha's laugh sounded relieved. "For a second I thought . . . never mind."

"I'm guessing Kabir doesn't know?" Shreya deduced.

Aisha tapped her fingers on the bench. "I don't know how he is going to react to this. I'm requesting your help in breaking the news to him. You are his best friend and family. Please help me, Shreya. Bring him where I am." Her words were rushed.

Shreya sighed. "So, that's why you called. You know, Aisha, I don't mean to sound rude, but I do have a life of my own. I was hoping that with you around, I can stop being Kabir's emotional crutch. I have news of my own. I met someone when I was in USA—a businessman from Delhi."

"Wow!" Aisha breathed. "Congratulations and I'm sorry I offloaded my crap on you. Has Kabir met him?"

"No. With all that is going on between you two, how could I tell him about my happy news, especially when he is either moping or mad all the time?"

"Sorry," Aisha repeated, scuffing the ground with the tip of her sneaker.

"It's okay," Shreya sounded resigned. "So, where do I have to bring him?"

"Tomorrow is Kriti's death anniversary, right?"

"Is it?" Shreya paused checking the calendar on her desk. "You are right, it is."

"I think Kabir needs to overcome that tragedy. So, could you bring him to me tomorrow?"

"I can't make promises, but I will try my best." Shreya answered honestly. "Where are you? Hold on. Let me get the notepad to take the address down."

"You don't need to write it down. I'm in Sirsa. Looking at the palace right now, the royal family's residence."

Aisha's eyes traced the arches and columns of the magnificent sandstone creation—Kabir's home!

"Oh my God, you are seriously mad, Aisha. Kabir is going to be so angry that you went there. That's his private space; no one is allowed there. Also, do you know that severe storms come in that area at this time of the year? It is not safe for you to be there."

"I know about the storms. They are expecting one tomorrow or the day after." Aisha replied causally, her eyes hooked on the swarm of inky dark clouds visible at considerable distance.

Clouds, like bad news, can travel fast.

"Please come back, Aisha. Are you traveling alone or is there anyone else with you?"

"Alone. And I would appreciate it if you and Kabir would not mention this to Kiara or my father. Please!"

The two women again fell quiet.

Shreya was the first to speak. "I will tell Kabir, but I can't promise that it will be a happy reaction. Gosh, I'm scared for you, Aisha."

Aisha chuckled nervously. "That is exactly why I'm glad you are going to be there."

Shreya paused. "I'm not going to be there, I'm sorry."

"What? Why? You are the pillar to my plan."

"I'm so sorry, my boyfriend and I are going for a mini vacation to Lonavla."

"But . . ."

"Sorry, Aisha, maybe next week?" Shreya suggested.

"No, no it has to happen tomorrow. Will you call and text me after you speak with Kabir?"

"Why don't you call him?"

"I'm too nervous. I'll probably botch it up and we will end up fighting. Please, Shreya. Consider this a last favor. Please."

"I will try. Aisha, this might end everything between you two." Shreya warned.

Aisha chewed her lower lip. "I'll wait to hear from you. Thank you so much," she ended the call.

Getting to her feet, Aisha walked to the palace and stopped under an arched grand entrance. Her nervous glance snagged on the extended terrace above the porch.

The terrace that took a life.

Glancing down, Aisha retrieved a thin bunch of keys from her other pocket.

A shadow fell over Aisha. Her startled gaze flew to the terrace.

No one was there.

Inadvertently, Aisha shivered and then stilled. A familiar, yet unpleasant, cold sensation brushed her nape.

"I'm bringing him here for you," Aisha whispered in the slight breeze and then went to sit on the front steps, waiting for the cleaning crew she had called.

#

Shreya toyed with things on her desk. She knew she was buying time to organize her thoughts that were more scrambled than eggs in a skillet.

After few minutes, Shreya finally picked up her cell phone, her hand unsteady. "Gosh Kabir, this is the last time I am doing things for you!"

Chapter 90

The night was wet and black. The gusting winds howled like a pack of hyenas. Thick treetops bent down skimming their roots like old arthritic men tying shoelaces. The rain pelted the grounds like a rockslide. Electric wires swung as though trapeze artists were pulling at them.

It was a deathly storm—one that could kill, one that *would*.

The black figure that seemed a part of the night emerged from behind the front pillars and went up the stairs. The footfalls were quick and soft as the killer made their way around the cane furniture littered on the patio.

The thunder gave fair warning to the dark form who ducked behind the walls every time lightning struck, illuminating the porch. Taking small steps, the masked intruder looked through the glass door.

The light inside was faint with only one or two bulbs switched on. Aisha was clearly visible sitting in a chair, her head bent, reading something on her lap. She was alone.

Loathing arose in the killer. The gloved hands clenched and unclenched at the sides. Hissing breath escaped the mouth, clouding the pane.

Aisha glanced up.

The dark form was quick to duck and slide down to the floor. The form crawled on the floor, moving toward the side glass door—the one that opened closest to where Aisha sat.

Stupid girl! She will die because of her meddling.

Under the balaclava mask, the smile on the killer's face was grisly. Murder was simply a means to an end!

Quietly going on the knees, the dark shadow inserted a tiny silver key in the keyhole and turned it lightly. The lock opened with a soft click. The noisy storm outside masked the sound. The intruder opened the door; just a crack and peered in.

Aisha was focused on the tablet on her lap. The door did not make much noise as the intruder smoothly opened it and slipped in, locking it from the inside all the while staying on the knees.

When the killer turned, Aisha was on her feet staring right at the killer.

Aisha did not appear stumped, only surprisingly sad as she said, "Hi, I thought you were going to Lonavla?"

Chapter 91

The killer stopped and glanced around. Aisha was alone in the room. Slowly, the mask came off.

"Don't try anything stupid."

Shreya revealed the gun in her hand. It glinted in the light.

A sudden thunderclap outside startled Aisha.

"I told you, this is the time of crazy storms." Shreya clucked her tongue and pointed at a chair with her gun. "Sit!"

Aisha did as told. "In less than a month, this is the second time I'm staring at a gun." She shook her head.

Shreya closed in on her. Her teeth gnashed as she spoke, "That stupid Vikas should have killed you when he had a chance. But he could never do anything right," she spat. Shreya towered over Aisha. "But how did you know it was me? Tell me, what mistake did I make?"

"Not you," Aisha paused. "Your puppet. Tony left a clue."

"So, you know his real name? Keep talking!" Shreya ordered with the gun. Gone was the sweet and kind woman Aisha had met over dinner. The woman standing in front of her was cold and aggression poured out of her. Aisha knew that Shreya would feel no remorse or hesitate in killing her.

"He had Lavina's pictures on the wall where he proudly displayed images of the girls he had killed."

"That bloody twerp." Shreya frowned. "That by itself isn't enough. That fool said something, didn't he?"

Aisha fidgeted. "He spoke about you cryptically. I had no idea at that time. He hinted that he was trying to kill Kiara for his true love, the one who connected with him in the head and heart. The one who saw the real him." Aisha took a breath remembering the moment she was trapped in Tony aka Vikas's flat.

Nothing has changed much. I'm back with another killer. This is a sequel that should never have happened!

"I thought he heard voices of his dead mother in his head."

Shreya brought the gun dangerously close to Aisha's face. "The fool imagined himself in love with me. But if he did not give you my name, how did you know it was me?"

Aisha stared at the hollow end of the barrel facing her. "From your resume."

Chapter 92

Shreya's expression was one of confusion. "My resume?"

"Yes," Aisha nodded. "After dinner at your place, I researched Kabir and everyone else related to him. And, that made me look you up. Your resume is the first thing that popped up. Usually, people skip the boring details, but *I* was seeking the boring details, all the boring details."

Shreya still wasn't following her.

"On your resume, your work experience was listed—all the places where you had worked, including the organization where you did pro bono work. One of the juvenile homes listed there was the one where Tony aka Vikas worked and lived. On a hunch, I requested a cop friend to check the pharmacy shops near Vikas's house. He found a small pharmacy shop that had a standing prescription in Vikas's name for Valium with regular refills. The Valium that Vikas used to drug the women he raped and killed. And the doctor who wrote the prescription was you."

"You are sharp!" Shreya playfully touched Aisha's head with the gun's handle.

Aisha jerked her head back. "How could you? He used the Valium to dupe innocent young women. Torture and kill them!"

"He was useful to me so I was useful to him." Shreya shrugged. "Those women were dumb. All Vikas had to do was dangle Kabir's business card in front of them and they went rather willingly with him. Vain, dumb women seeking quick fame! There are enough of pretty young things in this world. If a few are gone, who cares?"

Aisha gulped. "There is one more thing."

What the heck? Am I trying to impress a psycho?

"Go on," Shreya kept the gun firmly pointed on Aisha.

"Vikas had probably been to your house?"

Shreya shrugged. "Yes."

"Well, I went to his apartment and he had me wait in his living room, so I kind of remember the layout and the furniture, but of course, everything was covered in plastic!" Aisha shared. "That night when you invited us over for dinner? Your furniture and layout were the same, except his stuff was way cheaper. Very tacky actually!"

Shreya's expression bordered on incredulous. "That asshole did his flat up like mine?"

Obviously, we are not showing any respect to the dead. Aisha nodded.

Shreya, abruptly, leaned forward and Aisha sank back. "You knew about me since then?"

"A friend—a cop—showed me pictures of Princess Kritika, Lavina and Tony and said that all of them had one thing in common—Kabir. And that I was defending Kabir because of my feelings for him and not facts. He was right; my gut screamed at me that Kabir wasn't capable of taking a life. So, to back my gut I started matching facts. And, wherever there was Kabir, there was Shreya. So, I started looking at you and things started falling in place."

Shreya raised an eyebrow. "You are so stupid. You came here alone?"

"I was hoping to be wrong." Aisha flicked a worried glance at the gun.

The storm was dying down. The wind was no more the roar of a beast but the yowl of a whipped dog. The rain had tapered to a steady pitter-patter.

"Why did you kill Lavina?"

"So that Kabir would come to me. First his sister dies, his family breaks apart, and then his wife dies. He was supposed to come to me." Shreya said, her jaw clenched.

"He was always with you." Aisha reminded.

"As a friend; never as a lover like he is with you." Shreya sneered.

"So, you took a woman's life? She was his wife—"

"Who made that alcoholic his wife?" Shreya twisted her mouth. "She lived in my building; I bumped into her regularly. I saw the signs—the trembling hands, bloodshot eyes, her breath always smelled of booze." Shreya tossed her head to the side. "The watchman told me of the several men who went in and out of her flat. She was expendable."

Aisha gasped.

"Don't look so shocked. It wasn't like she was going to find a cure for AIDS. She was a bloody drunk. I took her in, helped her get sober and then coached her to become the girl Kabir would definitely fall for." Shreya sighed. Her eyes glazed as she recalled a fond memory. "I did a commendable job with that useless drunk. Kabir fell for her hook, line and sinker. He felt they had a connection. Within weeks, he proposed to her. Lavina said yes and they got married, never to live happily ever after," she jeered.

"What did you do?" Aisha asked, her voice a quiet whisper.

"Reminded Lavina of her first love, the bottle." Shreya chuckled. Her laugh was brittle. "And the fool resisted. She had genuinely started loving Kabir. The effect he has on us poor women?" Shreya's expression was coy. "But I'm very persistent. Lavina succumbed to one sip that became a bottle in an hour. Kabir saw the real Lavina and their fights started."

"So, you sent Vikas to kill Lavina?"

"Yes! I sent him to kill that useless drunk!"

"Kabir was in that same apartment. If you cared," Aisha couldn't bring herself to call it love, "If you cared for him then why? Did you not realize that Kabir might be blamed for it?"

Shreya's smile was saucy.

Aisha understood. "You wanted him to be blamed? You were hoping that he would break so that you could build him back up? And he then he would fall in love with you. A warped version of Pygmalion."

"Hmph! Everything was planned. I went to their place for dinner. Lavina was drunk in her room. I coerced Kabir to take some sleeping pills. Fights with that useless tart were taking a toll on him. Vikas was supposed to kill Lavina quietly, but that drunk did not drink enough so she woke up and fought back, but Vikas was stronger."

Aisha sat back, her head hung low. *She is sick!*

"Why did you marry that sleaze ball, Sudhir Vyast?"

"Oh please!" Shreya rolled her eyes. "Another useless person I had to invest my time in. I knew that lecher's character perfectly before our wedding. There was no way he would not go back to his cheating ways after the marriage."

Aisha rubbed her forehead to stay focused in face of such deviousness. "Another ploy to get Kabir's sympathy?"

Shreya's grin was self-depreciating. "You think I'm pathetic?" Her expression changed, and her eyes glinted cruelly. "But I'm not. I'm strong and persistent. Someone who does not let anyone, or anything get in the way of her goals."

"Goal," Aisha corrected, "Kabir!"

"Enough talking. I'm eager to call Kabir and give him the news of your death. Let me show you the terrace." Shreya dug the gun in Aisha's stomach. "The place where I committed my first murder. Twenty-one years ago, on this day."

Aisha could only stare at her, stumped. Her tongue was stuck to the roof of her mouth. Finally, she said hoarsely. "Princess Kritika!"

Straightening, Shreya giggled. "Bingo."

"Shreya!"

A roar came from the darkened corner of the living room. A man thundered toward them. Another man grappled with him, trying to stop him.

Shreya turned as pale as a ghost. Startled, she took jerky steps back. "Kabir!" Her lips trembled.

Chapter 93

"Let me go!" Kabir raged, pushing Parth to the side, his fury focused on Shreya.

Aisha jumped to her feet. "Kabir, please."

It happened in seconds. Shreya was quick to come up behind Aisha and hooked her arm around Aisha's neck. She pulled Aisha.

Not expecting the pull, Aisha fell back. Shreya pressed the gun on Aisha's temple.

"Stop right there! I will not hesitate to shoot her. You know I can kill."

Kabir froze even as his eyes glittered with rage. "Let Aisha go!"

"Why, you love this one too?" Shreya yelled, digging the gun into Aisha's soft skin.

"Ms. Shreya, I'm a CBI officer." Parth interceded. "End this peacefully. Let Aisha go. We can work out a deal for you."

Shreya clucked her tongue impatiently. "Would that deal make Kabir mine forever?"

"Shreya!" Kabir growled warningly.

"How did you get here? You were in Goa. I dropped you at the airport myself," Shreya shouted.

Kabir stayed quiet; his nostrils flared as he stared at Shreya with deep-seated hatred.

"I arrested and brought him here," Parth butted in. "Kabir thought I was taking him to Mumbai. Then Aisha convinced him to be a silent spectator."

"Can't you see all that I did for you, Kabir?" Shreya cried out as if in pain. "You don't see my pain, my sacrifices? Nothing! You don't see how much I love you?"

Aisha felt Shreya tremble against her in anger. Kabir's gaze dipped to Aisha. "Nothing will happen to you, I promise!"

"Stop talking to her!" Shreya shouted.

"Why? Why did you kill Kritika? Wasn't she your best friend?" Aisha spoke hoarsely, struggling to breathe with Shreya's arm choking her, the gun pinching her temple.

"What a curious one you are!" Shreya dug the gun some more. Aisha resisted the pain.

Parth stood alert, ready to jump into action like a coiled spring.

"I killed Kritika because of you, Kabir. It was all your fault."

Kabir's mouth opened but no words came out. He swallowed a few times.

Aisha saw his tortured look.

"I fell in love with you, Kabir, the first time I saw you when my father and I visited this palace. I made friends with Kritika just to get close to you, Kabir. But you never noticed me. Why didn't you?" Shreya cried out.

"I noticed you." Kabir said, even as his eyes misted.

"You are lying. Just like your precious sister. I kept begging her to arrange a date with you. For I knew, you would not say no to her. I begged her so many times that entire two weeks I stayed here. She just kept putting me off." Shreya raged. "And then the day before I was leaving, Kritika finally told me to my face that she was never going to set me up with you, Kabir. I wasn't good enough for her brother. She called me a 'crazy psycho!'

"So, you killed her just for that?" Parth asked.

"Yes! I followed Kriti to the terrace when she went to get her Walkman. She begged me to let her go. But I was mad. I pushed her off the terrace. Satisfied? Is everyone bloody satisfied now?" Shreya screamed.

Chapter 94

Keeping Aisha close to her, Shreya glanced at the door she had just come through.

"The place is surrounded by the police. You can't get away." Path warned.

"Bullshit! I did not see them coming in," Shreya shot back.

"Then go ahead and step outside," Parth encouraged, taking a few steps toward them.

Shreya pointed the gun at him. "Do they know of the side entrance from the courtyard?"

She increased the pressure on Aisha's throat. Aisha gagged. Parth blinked.

"See, you don't know this place like I do."

Shreya dragged Aisha and went behind the stairs. Aisha tried to keep pace with the deranged woman tugging painfully at her neck.

"SHREYA, DON'T!" Kabir roared, moving closer.

"If any of you try to stop me, I will shoot her," Shreya called out. She hit Aisha on the head.

Aisha winced, trying to choke her scream.

Kabir made a strangled noise in his throat.

Parth put a restraining hand on his arm. "Don't be the reason she shoots Aisha."

Kabir gave him a tortured look but stayed where he was.

Aisha felt Shreya tremble in rage. "Still feeling for another woman? Why can't you love me, Kabir? Why?" She again hit Aisha on the head.

Aisha whimpered in pain and saw momentary blackness.

"Please, let Aisha go. Take me instead," Kabir voiced, unsteadily. His gaze locked with Aisha's.

Shreya pulled something out from her pocket. It was a zip tie. "Put this on." She put it in Aisha's hand. "Don't try anything smart. I have nothing to lose."

Aisha put the bind around her wrists. Shreya reached over and yanked hard.

"Ouch!" Aisha could not help a startled yelp as the ridged plastic bit into her skin. Her head felt raw and throbbed from Shreya's blows.

"Does he know, sweet Aisha?" Shreya mimicked the term Kabir often called her by.

Aisha's eyes flew open.

What is she talking about?

"Hey, Kabir!" Shreya pushed Aisha.

Aisha faltered and fell on her knees in front of Shreya.

"Did your precious girlfriend tell you that she is pregnant?" Shreya's laugh was cruel.

Kabir face turned white, he swayed unsteadily. Parth caught him and held him up.

Chapter 95

"**No! No!**" Aisha yelled out to him. "I'm not, Kabir. I lied to push her over—"

Shreya grabbed her hair and yanked Aisha back up. "You little bitch! Stay there, you both," she pointed the gun at Kabir and Parth, "don't follow me. I will not hesitate even for a second in killing her!" Shreya roughly turned Aisha around and hit her on the back. Aisha struggled to stand straight as her back stung.

"Did I make my point boys?" Shreya cooed.

Aisha had to wipe her eyes for her temple was bleeding.

"Move, c'mon! Go in that corridor!"

Shreya pushed the gun on Aisha's back. Wincing, Aisha put her hands on the wall and limped to the dark corridor. The pain in her head was sapping her energy, weakening her.

"Turn left."

"Ouch!" Aisha's foot hit something hard. A chest of drawers.

Shreya grabbed Aisha's neck. "Don't slow me down or I will shoot you."

Aisha croaked, "If it makes any difference, Kabir did not believe me for a second. He was sure you would never show up because you weren't capable of . . ."

"Shut up! Keep moving!" Shreya led Aisha through the corridor and stopped suddenly. She knew her way around the palace.

"Open that door to your right," Shreya pushed Aisha toward a metal door. "Unlock it, hurry!"

Shreya shone some light through a pen torch. She looked over her shoulder, so did Aisha. Kabir and Parth had followed them but were keeping their distance.

Aisha felt around the door and found the latch. She worked on it, trying to slide it out even as the latch creaked in protest.

"Oh, for goodness' sake!"

Shreya reached out and shoved the latch all the way back. Aisha cried as the skin of her forefinger got caught in it and broke away. Shreya pushed Aisha outside and quickly turned around, locking the door on the other side.

Rain fell on Aisha as she somehow managed to get to her feet, holding her bleeding hand close to her chest. She was muddy all over. The ground was slippery.

"Keep walking. You will get me out of here," Shreya yelled over the pounding Parth and Kabir were doing on the other side of the gate.

"Back off or I will shoot her," Shreya shouted. They immediately ceased.

She pressed the gun into Aisha's back. Biting her lower lip, Aisha took small steps on the wet floor. Rusted furniture lay upturned around her. Pots that had long ago lost their plants and broken lamp posts lined their ways like mourners of a funeral.

The wind slammed Aisha's body, making her break into shivers. The night was dark. The swaying trees cut off any light filtering in from the hotel nearby.

"Please don't do this!" Aisha's teeth chattered as a sob, the first of many, escaped her clamped mouth. She kept seeing the faces of Kiara and her father.

"Cut the drama. Keep walking." Shreya shouted to be heard over the din the storm was making.

Rain crashed into Aisha's face. She shaded her eyes to look ahead. A familiar smell assailed her.

The pond! We are near the pond!

Shreya put the gun to the back of Aisha's head. Her laugh was low and humorless. "I can't be second best for Kabir! Never!" Her words held an air of finality.

"Please Shreya, think of my family," Aisha sobbed.

"No one thought of me," Shreya whispered. "I will kill you. If Kabir can't be happy with me, then he can't be with anyone."

Bleakly, Aisha closed her eyes, "That's pathetic!"

Shreya smacked her hard.

"Argh!" Aisha fell against a metal chair. An iron leg slammed into her face. Aisha felt her eyes blacken momentarily. She struggled to stay conscious. A sharp metallic taste filled her mouth. Blood! Her blood!

"You, stupid tart," Shreya roared, staring down at her. She aimed the gun at Aisha's face. Aisha slithered back. Shreya followed.

The lightning behind Shreya lit her, making her appear demonic.

Aisha smiled a broken smile, even as her cracked lip stung. "I will not go in fear, I will go in love! Love for Kabir, love for Kiara," Aisha's voice broke, "love for my father! I will go in love! And you can never take that away from me."

"Fine, then die in love!" Shreya shouted.

"I will die for love!" Aisha spat some blood out of her mouth. "Like Kriti died protecting her brother. I will die to free Kabir from your lies, free him from your hold, once and for all."

Aisha's smile was peaceful.

"YOU BLOODY SLUT!" Shreya pulled back the safety of the gun, aiming it between Aisha's eyes.

"Kabir!" Aisha howled.

Shreya clucked her tongue and fired.

Chapter 96

The bullet whizzed past Aisha's ear. Her heart thundered and her ears rang.

Someone screamed.

Aisha realized it was her own voice.

Shreya aimed the gun squarely at Aisha's forehead and pulled the trigger again. Something was off. The gun jammed.

Hit her with something! Run!

The rain was pelting hard and the darkness didn't help. Aisha managed to get up, only to slip back to her knees.

Kabir! Scream out to him!

Aisha opened her mouth to scream just as a bolt of lightning lit up the dark grounds. She froze.

They were not alone.

Ghostly pale, eerily blue, dry as a bone, stood Princess Kritika. The rain seemed to fall right through her.

The gardens went dark again.

Chapter 97

Aisha's mouth opened and closed, making no sound.

Shreya fiddled with the gun, rattling it, and tugging at it.

Aisha got to her feet, her hands still tied in front of her. The pelting rain made everything harder. Even escape.

Another bolt of lightning!

Princess Kritika was closer. Merely a few feet behind Shreya.

A click sound confirmed that the gun was back in play.

Shreya put the pen torch between her teeth and pointed the gun straight at Aisha's head. "You are dead now! No more misses!" she hissed.

Aisha had no idea what a bullet traveling at 1,100 feet per second would feel like, ripping her brain apart. She heard the ominous rumble of the thunder over the wind and rain. Another bolt of lightning was on its way.

"Turn around!" Aisha's voice was guttural.

Shreya's look went from murderous to puzzled, "What?"

"Turn around!" Aisha cried, as the lightning struck.

Shreya turned.

Princess Kritika stared right into her face. A flash of lighting hit the ground behind them. Kritika smiled—a frightening black hollow visible between her lips.

"Can't you see her?" Aisha sobbed out.

"What the fuck are you talking about?" Shreya snapped, boring down on Aisha. "Who can't I see?"

Aisha backed away. "Princess Kritika. Can't you see her? She is right there."

Shreya's hand, holding the gun, shook violently like her body. "Shut up! Kriti is dead."

Aisha tried to stand upright.

Shreya bent down and swiftly picked up a piece of rusting chain from the ground. She wrapped it around Aisha's neck.

"Stop! What are you—" Aisha struggled with the sudden weight around her neck. "Please don't!" she whimpered, trying to fight Shreya off but her tied hands made the attempts pitiful.

"You will die one way or another. I will make sure of it," Shreya pressed the gun on Aisha's wound and pulled the safety.

Not again! Aisha cowered. "Please!"

A flash of lightning and Aisha saw Kritika right behind Shreya.

About fucking time!

Princess Kritika raised her finger to her lips; and then, with a familiar hollow smile, she raised her bony hands and pushed. At the same time, one of the lamp posts came unhinged and slammed on Shreya's back.

Startled and off balance Shreya fell on Aisha.

Aisha wrapped her arms around Shreya. The gun got wedged between the two.

Shreya fought back.

Aisha felt herself tip over, right into the murky depths of the pond!

"NOOOO!"

The soiled water rushed into her mouth cutting off Aisha's scream.

Strange electric tingles broke over Aisha's skin as she went deeper in the shadowy darkness. The pen torch was somewhere near throwing pale light in the olive-green water.

Shreya was on top of Aisha, struggling and kicking.

Aisha struggled to close her mouth. The water tasted foul. There was so much of it. The chain around her neck was crushing her throat.

Shreya landed a hard kick in the soft flesh of Aisha's stomach. Aisha screamed. More water rushed in, choking, and crushing Aisha's lungs. Terror paralyzed her.

I can't breathe!

Shreya pushed Aisha's head down, her teeth gnashed even as her eyes widened manically, showing the white of her irises. She grabbed the zip tie, holding Aisha close. They both sunk lower.

Transfixed by the deranged woman's gaze, Aisha's mouth opened wider. All the fight left her. Her eyes rolled back as consciousness began to desert her. Aisha gurgled as a slew of bubbles escaped her mouth.

I'm dying!

Chapter 98

Open yourself to them. The spirits will guide you.

Aisha saw the words float in front of her. Suvabrata's last text.

"Let me in," the water seemed to whisper in her ear.

A distant form swirled above them.

Floating between life and death, Aisha saw Princess Kritika swim down to them, the black hollow smile intact. Her bony hands reached out to Aisha . . .

Somehow, Aisha dredged up the strength to lift and slip her hands in Kritika's icy ones.

#

Kabir's head broke the surface of the dirty green water. He wasn't alone.

Parth and a couple of other police officers helped him and Aisha out of the pond.

"She is barely breathing!"

They rolled Aisha over on the cement. Kabir bent over and performed a quick CPR.

"Argh!"

With a jolt, Aisha turned to her side and threw up the water blocking her trachea. Gagging, she fell down on her back. Her throat felt like it was burning, and her chest hurt with every breath she took.

"Aisha, sweetheart, you are going to be okay!" Kabir feverishly rubbed her hands and feet. Gently raising Aisha, he hugged her like he would never let her go.

"I'm fine," Aisha's voice was weak. Her eyelids fluttered shut and she shivered uncontrollably.

I survived!

"Thank God for that light. I would never have known where you were had it not been for the pen torch floating near you," Kabir sobbed in her hair, apologizing repeatedly. Aisha surrendered to the comfort of his arms and his thundering heartbeat that reverberated in her chest.

"Excuse me, Aisha!" Parth broke in.

"Not right now," Kabir curtly shot back.

"We should have a doctor examine her," Parth retorted.

"Is the doctor here?"

"Inside."

Kabir helped Aisha up and carried her back into the house.

"Just rest," he murmured in her ear.

Aisha cast a furtive glance at her hands and then closed her eyes with sheer exhaustion. She wondered if she would ever be able to tell anyone what had happened in the water . . . The moment she had opened herself to Kritika's ghost.

The pain and cold had suffused her body as Kritika had taken over. The horror on Shreya's face made Aisha wonder whose face Shreya had seen at that moment.

Was it me or Kriti?

With the newfound strength in Aisha's arms, she had snapped the zip tie apart, unwrapped the chain around her neck and then turned on Shreya, grasping her throat.

I did try to stop Kriti.

Aisha had struggled to gain control of her body as she had seen her own hands choke the life out of Shreya and push her down to the depths of the pond.

I know exactly where her body lies at the bottom, broken and twisted.

A sob escaped Aisha's throat.

"Hush," Kabir kissed her forehead, his breathing labored.

The moment Shreya had breathed her last, a giant heave had brought Aisha close to the surface, near the torch.

Where Kabir found me!

"Excuse me, Aisha," Parth spoke. "I have your phone. You just got a text from someone—a Suvabrata?"

"What does it say?" It hurt to speak.

"Thank you for accepting. It's over!"

"Now, who's Suvabrata?" Kabir asked.

"My late grandmother's best friend," Aisha replied weakly. It still hurt to speak. Her shoulders slumped.

Kabir nodded and placed a kiss on her forehead.

Aisha understood what Suva was referring to. In her fight to live, Aisha had welcomed the dead, opened her mind to their energy. She was now on a tricky slope.

Now, the radio is on 24x7! What challenges will this bring for me? Aisha sighed and tucked her face in Kabir's chest.

Rain continued to come down on the uneven grass, mangled trees, overturned furniture, broken lampposts, and pots.

It was a deathly storm—a storm that could kill, a storm that *did.*

Epilogue

A month and a half later

Aisha sat on the soft bed engrossed in the book she was reading, "Introduction to Forensic Science."

A soft knock sounded on the door. Setting it down, Aisha smiled softly. Her body tingled in anticipation. She straightened her hair and out of habit, touched the small and faint scar near her left temple. Momento from the night she nearly died. The soft knocks now came in urgent succession.

Impatient, are we?

Aisha slid off the bed and straightened the straps of her slinky nightdress as she unlocked the door.

She did not have a chance to say anything. The man pushed himself inside her room and was quick to lock the door behind him.

"Excuse me!" Aisha attempted indignation.

"Excuse me, my ass!" Kabir hauled Aisha back in his arms and pressed her into the wall. "I haven't kissed you for weeks." he growled, as he took Aisha's mouth in sheer domination.

Aisha was more than a willing captive. She opened her mouth under his and they kissed each other longingly. Kabir grabbed her butt and lifted her up against him. Aisha wrapped her legs around his hips and her arms around his neck as their tongues dueled and mated.

They only broke apart to breathe. Aisha tongued his ear lobe, moaning against his skin as she deeply inhaled the spicy cologne of the man who now mattered to her more than herself.

"I have missed you so much!" Kabir pressed open-mouthed kisses against the column of her neck and the curve of her shoulder, grinding himself against her, leaving Aisha in no doubt about which part of his was thirsting for her. He unzipped himself hastily.

Aisha yanked his shirt out of his jeans and hurriedly unbuttoned it, revealing his muscled and supple skin to her roving hands. Digging her fingers in Kabir's shoulders, Aisha felt herself melt against his arousal.

"Against the wall?" Aisha rubbed her center against his arousal.

Kabir groaned, moving his tongue across the slope of her breast. "Yes, sweet Aisha, yes."

Aisha and Kabir did not talk much after that, putting their hands and mouth to better use—on each other.

Aisha was the first to come and Kabir cut of her orgasmic mewl by meshing his mouth with hers even as he continued thrusting in her. Arching her body, Aisha tightened herself around Kabir and he too found his release.

Sweaty and spent, Kabir gently dropped Aisha's legs to the floor.

"Oh, they feel like rubber!" Aisha sighed, straightening her clothes with unsteady hands. Her heartbeat was still racing, the color on her face ran high. He body shook with the feelings of explosive connection she always felt with Kabir after a bout of sex.

"Can you carry me to the bed?" Kabir smiled, staring in her eyes even as he wiped the sweat off her brow.

"Sure, if you carry me first!" Aisha nuzzled his hand.

Somehow, they made it to the bed and collapsed side by side. Kabir reached out and gently tugged her hair. "I love you, sweet Aisha!"

Aisha turned to her side facing him. "I love you too, baby."

Kabir caressed her lips and her cheek, his touch like his look, tender. "I don't say it often enough, but thank you for coming in my life, sweetheart. Thank you for hanging in, despite everything and everyone in it."

Aisha smiled. "Stop saying that. It is my pleasure! Like literally, *my* pleasure." She winked at him.

Kabir settled back comfortably on the pillows and dragged Aisha on top of his chest.

"Your mother is very nice!" Aisha snuggled against him. Kabir had been in London for the last two weeks. His mother had accompanied him back.

"I can't believe that bitch got to her also."

"Shreya created distances between you two. And a lot of misunderstandings."

"I should have reached out to mum." Kabir stroked Aisha's bare back.

"I'm just happy that you are reconnecting with her and your grandparents."

"Do you like the newly renovated interiors of the palace?" Kabir dropped a kiss on her head.

"I love it!" Aisha moved and rested her face on her elbows. "Kiara and Papa are coming here the day after. What if our families don't like each other?"

"Then you and I just run away." Kabir trailed his fingers on her forearms. "I love touching you. I missed you so much."

"Me too!" Aisha beamed at him.

"So, you are okay with the long-distance relationship? You in Mumbai and me here in Sirsa?" Kabir asked, playing with the strap of her nightdress.

"Stop!" Aisha playfully smacked his hand away. "This place is not too far. We will travel back and forth to each other. You like it here, don't you?" Aisha and Kabir clasped and unclasped their hands.

"I do like it here! I don't know if it makes sense, but I feel closer to Kritika here." Kabir rubbed his chin. "You can call me crazy, but I feel like a part of her is still here. She is not all gone."

Nope, she isn't! Aisha nodded.

"I'm selling the Panaji house." Kabir sighed. He planted a swift and deep kiss on Aisha's soft lips.

"Good call. The house and the kiss!" Aisha ran her tongue over her lips. She could still taste Kabir on her lips. "I'm hungry. I'm going to the kitchen. You want something?"

"You. Preferably naked."

Kabir grinned, dropping years from his face. He was a changed man now. He rarely frowned and was taking a keen interest in the royal residence renovation and the palace hotel's management.

"Hold on, stud! I'm here for a week." Aisha rolled away from his reach. "The plane food sucked." She walked to the door and put a robe on.

"I wish you could stay here forever with me!"

Aisha paused at his words and turned slowly. Kabir sat against the pillow, his buffed chest at display. His face was somber, but his eyes positively dazzled with emotions.

Say yes, dimwit!

Aisha hesitated and then she opened her mouth, her heart in her eyes. Kabir leaned forward hopeful.

Angry bird sounds filled the room.

"What the hell?" Kabir looked around.

"Kia recently changed my text tone." Aisha picked up her cell and read the text. "Parth wants to know if it's okay to call."

"No! Tell him you are taken. Actually, give me the cell and I will tell him very clearly in my way." Kabir griped.

Aisha blew Kabir a kiss. "Coming right back for round two. On the floor, me on top!" She knew Kabir loved it when she was on top.

Kabir groaned. "Come back right here, you tease!"

Aisha left the room and closed the door behind her. She quietly went down the curved marble staircase.

Kabir had done wonders to the royal residence. New paint on the wall, silk curtains, rich wood furniture, soft plush floor rugs, family pictures and some of Kabir's work hung up on the walls. A few pictures of hers had also found their way on the wall.

Aisha paused in front of her favorite picture. Kabir's family portrait. "Are you there?" Aisha said softly, looking at Princess Kritika's smiling face.

She waited and felt it. A soft sensation passed through her; it was cold. A pair of legs settled on top of the picture frame.

Aisha glanced up at Kritika's spirit sitting atop the portrait of her family.

"Never got a chance to say this before, but, thank you for saving my life. If you hadn't come when you did. . ."

Kritika's pale figure smiled, an onyx cavern for a mouth. She simply shrugged.

Aisha, still struggling with the fact that not only she could sense sprits, but could even see one, asked, "Umm, did you see your mother and brother?"

The Princess nodded again but her smile faltered.

"You don't have to be here, you know. You have had your revenge. Be at peace now."

"No! I'm staying." Kritika shook her head and frowned. Her voice came as if speaking from far. Getting on her feet, she leaped from the picture to the banister and ran up on it and disappeared into the wall.

I must talk to Suva about her! Aisha made a mental note.

Her cell phone beeped. Another text from Parth.

Aisha made her way down to the dimly lit living room. She could hear some staff milling in the kitchen. Aisha ignored her rumbling stomach and called Parth.

Parth answered on one ring. "Hi, Aisha."

"Hi, Parth. Got your texts. What's up?"

"Are you alone? Can we talk?" Parth's voice was wary.

"Yeah, sure!" Aisha drawled, sinking in a sofa.

"The last time we met, you said that if I ever found an interesting case I should call you."

"Yes!" Aisha felt her pulse race as she sat straighter.

"A body of a taxi driver who had been missing for a while was found last week in Raxaul. It's a busy small town in the East Champaran district of Bihar."

"Okay?"

"The driver had been shot execution style." Parth paused. "The bullet did fragment a bit, but it was mostly intact and was recovered from his brain. It matched the bullets recovered from a previous crime scene."

This time his pause was longer.

"I'm listening!" Aisha prompted.

"The bullet was fired from the same gun that killed your brother. It was a hundred percent match."

Aisha felt her world pop off its axis.

**

Thank You Note

Thank you for reading 'Killer Moves.' I hope you enjoyed reading it as much as I enjoyed writing it. While you were reading 'Killer Movies,' I was probably busy writing the next Aisha, Kabir and Parth story.

I hope you will spare a minute to two of your time to leave a spoiler free star rating review of this book on Amazon. It would mean a lot to me as an author as well as help readers like you find 'Killer Moves.'

Thank you once again for being a part of Aisha and Kabir's story.

Other books by Varsha Dixit

~ <u>Right Fit Wrong Shoe</u>

~ <u>Wrong Means Right End</u>

~ <u>Rightfully Wrong Wrongfully Right</u>

~ <u>Only Wheat Not White</u>

~ <u>Xcess Baggage</u>

~ <u>The Wallflowers</u>

~ <u>A Hasty Hookup</u>

~ <u>Miss Matched</u>

Acknowledgements

"When we give cheerfully and accept gratefully, everyone is blessed." Maya Angelou

A big thank you to my parents—my kind and fun-loving mom and my source of eternal joy and love, my late father. I wouldn't be a quarter of the person I am without all that they have done for me and continue to do. I feel immense love for my husband and daughter for their binding affection and for always having my back. I may be busier because of these two but I am definitely stronger and happier as well. To my in-laws for their love and encouragement. Thank you to my brother and his beautiful family, my sister-in-law, for all the love that one can never have enough of.

A shout out to my BFF and beta reader Richa Sharma—the first person to hear the rough plot and read my 'crappy' drafts. Thank you for your never-ending patience. A very big thank you to Rubina Ramesh for being a mentor in the confusing field of self-publishing, and more than that for being such a good friend.

A heartfelt thank you to Dola Basu Singh for her immense and invaluable contribution as my editor. Thank you for bringing out the best in my work.

A big shout out to all the members of TBC (The Book Club) for their immense support and helpful suggestions.

Thank you to Germancreative for the beautiful cover design. Thank you to Eark Tec for formatting the ebook.

Thank you to each and every one of you who has helped me in this journey. Your contributions are priceless to me.

And the biggest thank you to all my readers. You enrich and empower the writer in me. Thank you for making me the author I am.

Meet the Author

Varsha Dixit is the author of the bestselling novels, *Right Fit Wrong Shoe* (2009), Xcess Baggage (2010), Wrong Means Right End (2012), Only Wheat Not White (2014), and Rightfully Wrong Wrongfully Right (2016). She worked in the Indian television industry before moving to the US with her family. She feels enriched and blessed to be an author and a woman.

Varsha actively interacts with readers through:

Website: www.varshadixit.com

Facebook   Author   Page:
https://www.facebook.com/varshadixitauthor/

Twitter: https://twitter.com/Varsha20

Instagram: https://www.instagram.com/amrain20/

Drop Varsha an email at varsha@varshadixit.com